BY KAREN TRAVISS

STAR WARS: REPUBLIC COMMANDO
Hard Contact
Triple Zero
True Colors
Order 66
Imperial Commando: 501st

STAR WARS: LEGACY OF THE FORCE
Bloodlines
Sacrifice
Revelation

STAR WARS: THE CLONE WARS

STAR WARS: NO PRISONERS

GEARS OF WAR
Aspho Fields
Jacinto's Remnant
Anvil Gate

WESS'HAR WARS
City of Pearl
Crossing the Line
The World Before
Matriarch
Ally
Judge

GEARS OF WAR.
ANVIL GATE

GEARS
OF
WAR®

ANVIL GATE

KAREN TRAVISS

BALLANTINE BOOKS

NEW YORK

A Del Rey Trade Paperback Original

Copyright © 2010 by Epic Games, Inc.

All Rights Reserved. Used Under Authorization.

Published in the United States by Del Rey, an imprint of The Random House Publishing Group, a division of Random House, Inc., New York.

DEL REY is a registered trademark and the Del Rey colophon is a trademark of Random House, Inc.

Gears of War® copyright 2006 Epic Games, Inc. Gears of War®, Marcus Fenix®, and the Crimson Omen® are trademarks of Epic Games, Inc. All Rights Reserved.

ISBN 978-0-345-49945-5

Printed in the United States of America

www.epicgames.com
www.delreybooks.com

4   6   8   9   7   5   3

Book design by Christopher M. Zucker

For Marcus Bevan

ACKNOWLEDGMENTS

My sincere thanks go to Mike Capps, Rod Fergusson, and Cliff Bleszinski at Epic Games, Allfathers of the best damn universe ever; Epic's artists, directors, and animators—the new Old Masters—for inspirational art; Dawn Woodring, protection dog trainer, for advice; and "Raven Maven" Wade Scrogham, USAF historian, for rotary aviation support.

GEARS OF WAR®
ANVIL GATE

PROLOGUE

Main mess bar, Vectes Naval Base, New Jacinto—capital of the Coalition of Ordered Governments. Date: last week of Brume, 14 a.e.

I'm not a people person. But you probably guessed that already. And no, I don't want you to buy me a beer.

If you think there's some nice guy inside me trying to get out if only someone would give me a chance—forget it. But then you're dumb, like 99 percent of human beings. You can't help it.

"Come on, Baird. Don't be an antisocial dick all your life. Take a day off." Her name's Sam Byrne; all mouth, leather, and tattoos, and about my age—so she's old enough to know better. She slams a brimming shot glass on the bar and shoves it at me. "Muller's teaching us to play navy chess."

"Oh, that's so exciting. I think I just wet my pants."

Sam waits a beat and then snatches the glass away. If it's Dizzy's moonshine, she's doing me a favor. "Fuck you, then," she says, and stalks off.

I need to cultivate that Marcus Fenix thing. He can sit at a bar on his own all night and no asshole goes near him. But then he's Fenix. It's not just the Embry Star war-hero vibe. It's something

else. It's like the guy's got warning buoys around him, even
though nobody's ever seen him really lose his shit with anything
except grubs.

Even morons still have some survival instincts, I suppose.

Shit, I wish someone would turn off that frigging TV behind
the bar. Listen to that asshole yakking on about the future and the
chance to build something better. *What* fucking future? We
haven't got homes or running water for most of the refugees yet,
but whoopee, we got a TV channel on air. Actually, it's just radio
with still shots. Everyone's got a radio. There's a few TVs in the
communal areas, and the civvies here think that's terrific. A boon.
An improvement. Well, hoo-fucking-rah.

Dumb people are lucky. I envy them.

I mean it. Ignorance really is bliss. The problem with being in
the top 1 percent—yeah, I am, does it make you squirm because
I say it?—is that you understand just how badly fucked the world
is. And it's not getting any better. It's just *changing*. But any shit
looks better to most folk as long as it's *different*.

Nice new media channel for the people. You think? Well,
Chairman Prescott needs a way to feed all the dumb bastards his
propaganda. And keep the frigging journos busy so they don't actually do any real reporting, of course. And you think we should
celebrate because the grubs are gone and we can start over?
No, we just replaced the Locust with a new kind of two-legged
vermin—Stranded crime gangs. We've bombed the world back to
the last century and sunk our own damn city, so now we've got no
manufacturing, no infrastructure, and no way to rebuild the rest
of Sera.

But Prescott says it's all going to be fine because we've got shitloads of fuel thanks to Gorasnaya. Flip that coin, though, and the
other side is taking in four thousand ungrateful Indie bastards
who were still technically at war with us until a couple of months
ago.

Look, I could go on forever. But even a dumbass like you
gets the idea by now. Right?

A big, heavy hand slaps me on the shoulder and grips it like a vise. It's Cole. Most people would be more use as pet food, but Cole's not one of them. I just don't get why such a smart guy is so happy all the time.

"Baby, you want a Cole Train charm lesson?" He leans over and whispers loudly in my ear. "You're *never* gonna get any action if you treat the ladies like that. Not even *sheep* ladies."

"That was *Sam*." The bitch always wants to arm-wrestle, out-drink you, or out-swear the boys. "Not *ladies*."

"Come on. You know Bernie wants you to spawn plenty of blond surly know-all grandkids for her."

Cole can get away with that. For some reason, he never pisses me off. "Yeah? She better place her bets on Dom, then."

He sighs under his breath, for real, not his Cole Train act. "I think she's gonna have a long wait."

Dom's a mess. I don't expect a guy to shrug off having to blow his wife's brains out, but he started mourning and making her into a saint ten years ago when she first went missing. If he didn't move on then, what's going to shift him now? Look, he's not stupid. I stick with Delta Squad because they've all got opposable thumbs and IQs in the three-figure range. But that doesn't mean they're all *sane*.

So me and Cole sit at the bar and drink in silence. Sam's enjoying her navy chess at full volume. I don't want to spend too long looking in case they think I give a shit, but if I just turn a little I can see full shot glasses on the board instead of chessmen— moonshine for the white pieces, rum for the black ones. Oh, I get it. There—Muller's taken one of Sam's pieces, so he downs the shot in one. So how do they know what kind of piece it is?

See, this is what I mean about dumb people. That's not chess. It's checkers. But they'll be too shit-faced to care by the time they've finished.

The mess doors open. Someone cheers. The barracking starts. "It's a dog!"

Another smart-ass chimes in. "Don't talk about Sergeant Mataki like that. The word's *bitch*."

That's as far as the jeering goes. Bernie Mataki just gives

them that look, like she thinks they're cute little boys of no real importance, which always works better than Sam's shot-slamming. Don't think I've changed my views on letting women serve frontline—bad idea, bad, *bad* idea—but Bernie can shut the guys up. Maybe it's because she's old and eats cats. Maybe it's her service record. And it just might be because everyone knows she cut off some guy's balls. But she really does have a dog on a leash, a big, wild-looking thing with a wiry gray coat, thirty kilos at least.

"Isn't he a beaut?" She rubs his ears and he looks up at her with big brown puppy eyes, just like frigging Hoffman. The whole bar stops to *ooh* and *ahh* like they've never seen a dog before. "Meet Mac. He hunts Stranded. I've borrowed him for a while."

"Does he do tricks?" Cole asks.

Bernie walks the mutt over to me. This thing's head is level with her hip. It looks like a wolf that's had a bad hair day. "Mac, this is Blondie. No humping his leg, okay? No, I'm talking to *you*, Baird."

If I react I'll only encourage her. "Does your pedigree asshole-hound know you eat pets, Granny?"

"Just cats. He's fine with that. Aren't you, fella?"

"Nice doggie," Cole says. "You're gonna save us a lot of time."

"Come on. Let's go walkies." Bernie could put a saddle on that damn dog and ride it. I hope it's okay around helicopters. "If *we* can't flush out those Stranded bastards, let's see what dogs can do. Time we found out where these tossers are holed up."

"Can we call 'em *gangs* or somethin', Boomer Lady?" Cole asks. "On account of most Stranded bein' like Dizzy. Harmless. Nice, even."

Navy chess doesn't do a thing for me. But hunting assholes . . . now that's a sport a guy can take some pride in. Yeah, Cole's got a point. This is a whole new species of Stranded. Not the parasitic bum variety—this is organized crime, piracy, rape, murder. Don't give me any of that bleeding-heart crap about how we've all got to stick together now that we're trying to rebuild human civilization. There's never been a better time than this to put out the trash.

"Okay, call 'em vermin," I say. "And I vote that Mac gets to keep the chewy bits."

Anyone outside the curfew zones with no business being there is fair game. Right?

Don't look at me like that. You don't know what it's been like for the last fifteen years. I don't regret a damn thing, except not doing some of it sooner. What are you—my frigging mother?

CHAPTER 1

COALITION OF ORDERED GOVERNMENTS
NAVAL BASE VECTES

NONCITIZEN INCIDENT LOG SUMMARY
THAW 1 TO BRUME 35, 14 A.E., INCLUSIVE.

Attacks on property: 35
Attacks on civilians: 20
Casualties, civilian: 15 injured, 6 dead.
Casualties, COG personnel: 18 injured, no fatalities.
Casualties, insurgents: 30 dead.
(Injury data unavailable. No wounded detained.)

VECTES NAVAL BASE, NAVY OF THE COALITION
OF ORDERED GOVERNMENTS, NEW JACINTO:
FIRST WEEK OF STORM, 15 A.E.

"Welcome to New Jacinto," said Chairman Prescott. "And welcome to the protection of the Coalition of Ordered Governments. May this new year be a new start for us all."

Hoffman had to hand it to Prescott; he could always manage to look as if whatever lie he was telling at the time was the holy truth. The two men stood on the jetty as the Gorasni container ship *Paryk* disembarked its human cargo, five hundred civilians from an independent republic that had still been officially at war with the Coalition until last month. They were part of the COG now, whether they liked it or not. Hoffman guessed that they didn't.

"They don't look in a party mood, Chairman," Hoffman said.

A statesmanlike half-smile was nailed to Prescott's face, probably more for the benefit of his local audience—a detachment of Gears, a medical team, some civilian representatives—than for the new arrivals.

"I hope it's disorientation and seasickness rather than a lack of gratitude," he said.

Hoffman eyed the procession, looking for potential troublemakers and wondering if any of the refugees spoke the language well enough to see the irony in the COG's title. *Governments?* There was only one government left, a city-sized administration on a remote island a week's sailing time from Tyrus. That was all that was left of a global civilization of billions after fifteen years of fighting the Locust.

But on a sunny day like this, not a typical Storm day at all, Vectes must have looked pretty good compared with the mainland. No grub had ever set foot here, and it showed. The Gorasni bastards should have been grateful. Safe haven and food in exchange for all that extra fuel they didn't need? It was a good deal.

"Maybe they just hate our guts." Hoffman tried to imagine the mind-set of a pipsqueak nation that ignored the Pendulum Wars cease-fire. That was some serious grudge-nursing. "It was their leader's idea to join us. I'm betting he didn't take a vote on it."

"Let's hope they think of it as a bring-a-bottle party."

The Gorasni certainly weren't arriving empty-handed to drain the COG's limited resources. They were surrendering their imulsion supplies—an operational offshore drilling platform—in exchange for a refuge. In a world burned to a wasteland, fuel and food were the two assets that meant there'd be a tomorrow. Hoffman wasn't crazy about the Indies and he was damned sure they weren't crazy about him, but these were desperate times.

Can't be too choosy about our neighbors. At least they're not Stranded. They're not killing us—yet.

A security detail of Gears lined the jetty, channeling the

refugees to the reception team at an old storehouse that was built into the fortresslike walls. Hoffman glanced at the faces around him and wondered if any war could ever make you forget the one that preceded it. But the Vectes locals had never even seen a Locust. Their monsters were still the Indies, the old human enemy from an eighty-year war—the people landing on this jetty.

"Bastards." An elderly man from the Pelruan town council wore a chestful of Pendulum War medals on his threadbare jacket, including the Allfathers' Medal. No, he wasn't about to forget. "Can't forgive any of them. Least of all those who still aren't sorry for what they did."

Hoffman noted the campaign ribbons and chose his words carefully. It was hard to navigate that dividing line between mortal enemies one day and new allies the next. The name that made his bile rise wasn't Gorasnaya, though, so he could look at these Indies with a certain distance.

Should I? I know what they did. I know what the old guy means. But they weren't the only ones. We all did things we weren't proud of.

"They're Indies with plenty of fuel," Hoffman said at last, conscious of Prescott eavesdropping. The man could look engrossed in something but that slight tilt of the head said he was taking in everything within earshot. "Nobody's asking you to forgive. Just take their imulsion as war reparation."

The old man stared at Hoffman as if he was an ignorant kid rather than a fellow vet.

"My comrades died in a Gorasni forced labor camp." He tugged at his lapel so Hoffman could see a timeworn regimental pin with the trident badge of the Duke of Tollen's Regiment. "The Indies can shove their fuel up their ass."

"Mind my asking why you've come today?"

"Just wanted to see how they looked without a rifle in their hands," said the old man. He was probably in his seventies, maybe only ten or fifteen years older than Hoffman, but the border with old age always moved a few years ahead with each birthday. "Everyone needs to look their monsters in the eye. Right?"

And all monsters needed to acknowledge their guilt before forgiveness could begin. Gorasnaya hadn't even come close. Maybe that would never have been enough anyway.

"Right," said Hoffman.

The veteran turned his back on the stream of newcomers filing along the quay and hobbled away. The Gorasni weren't going to get a welcome parade from the townsfolk in the north of the island, that was for sure.

Prescott took one step back and bent his knees slightly to whisper to Hoffman. "Doesn't bode well, Victor."

"What did you expect?"

"It was a whole war ago. It's history now."

"Not here." While most of the world fried, Vectes had waited without much to distract it. The island had been cut off from the rest of the COG when the Hammer of Dawn was deployed, although whether it thought itself lucky now was another matter. "It's still yesterday for some of them."

"And you?"

"I never served on the eastern front," Hoffman said. He had his bad memories like any other Gear, but they had nothing to do with Gorasnaya. "I don't imagine some Indies have fond recollections of us, either."

Prescott inhaled slowly, eyes still on the procession of Gorasni. "I won't allow human society to rebuild ghettos, but let's be prudent. Keep the refugees apart from the rest of the civilians until we're absolutely sure that everyone's used to the idea. Like the rehabilitated."

"Is that what we're calling them now?" Hoffman had now had a bellyful of euphemisms. "Let me strike the word *Stranded* from my operational vocabulary, then. I thought we were keeping the *rehabilitated* ones separate for opsec reasons so they didn't tip off their *unrehabilitated* buddies about our patrols."

If Hoffman's irritable lack of deference irked Prescott, the man didn't let it show. In fact, the slimeball smirked. "Who says a certain caution about the Gorasni refugees isn't for operational security too?"

Refugees was an ironic term. Everyone on Vectes—except the native islanders—had fled from Old Jacinto only months earlier. Lines were drawn fast in this new post-Locust world. Hoffman glanced up the jetty to watch three Pelruan councilmen talking in a tight knot, one of them far too young to have served in the Pendulum Wars anyway. So were a lot of the Gorasni. That didn't mean they hadn't inherited opinions from those who weren't.

Nobody's ever seen more than a few months of peace. Any of us. How long does it take people to forget? Or do we never manage to?

"Trescu's going to keep his people in line, and so will we," Hoffman said at last. He didn't like the look of a couple of the men disembarking, in particular the way their jackets hung as if draped over something bulky underneath. Gorasnaya might have been relaxed about arming civvies, but the COG wasn't. They'd have to deal with that, diplomatically or not. "It's all about keeping folks fed and busy."

"The voice of experience."

And you know where I acquired it, don't you, asshole? "Nothing's more trouble than hungry, bored people."

"Where *is* Trescu?"

"With Michaelson, working out tanker rosters."

"Good." Prescott lost interest in the refugees right on cue. He checked his watch and took a couple of steps up the jetty in the direction of his office. "I want a permanent detachment of Gears on that rig. Can't be too careful."

"Already in hand, Chairman. I'm putting Fenix and Santiago on it. They're heading out shortly to do a security assessment."

"Wouldn't they be better tasked rooting out the Stranded? We can destroy a Locust army, but suddenly we can't eradicate a few hundred half-starved vagrants."

"I know who my best problem-solvers are, Chairman." *And I'm the frigging chief of staff here. I decide how I deploy my men.* Hoffman ignored the sly criticism. "That imulsion platform is going to be a bigger problem than pest control."

Prescott gave him a brief frown but didn't ask for an explanation. It didn't take a genius to work it out anyway. Gorasnaya couldn't protect that damn rig—or maintain it—without having to crawl to the COG for help. It was going to tie up COG resources. But the COG needed the imulsion to keep the fleet running, build a city, and drag this damn place out of the last century.

Prescott gave Hoffman his best statesman's public relations smile—no display of teeth, just a curl of the lips. "I have absolute faith in you, Colonel. We would never have survived this far without your leadership. I look forward to the report."

Prescott had a way of saying things that Hoffman knew were anything from bullshit to barefaced lies, but that were somehow true as well. Not a single word ever escaped Prescott's mouth by accident or without being cross-checked first. The bastard probably thought Hoffman was an overpromoted grunt who couldn't grasp the real meaning. He had that slightly amused you-don't-get-it look.

Hoffman threw up a perfunctory salute and took a shortcut to CIC on the way to see Michaelson. He was halfway along the next quay before he fully unpicked the words. Prescott was lining up someone to blame if the shit hit the fan. *Leadership* was Prescott-speak for responsibility. *As in—not his. Mine. Crafty asshole.* Even though Prescott had absolute power, his politician's reflex to duck and dive was as strong as ever.

Not entirely true. His power comes from my Gears. Always has. And now—even more so.

Ah. I get it. He's testing the water with me. Is he starting to worry what the army will do if things don't turn out as he's promised? Is he scared of a coup?

Hoffman paused to look up at the anchor and cog naval crest that towered above the base, a striking stone column against a glass-clear turquoise sky that made the season look more like Bloom than Storm. Optimism wasn't his style; but just being in a place where the walls weren't bullet-pocked, the pavement wasn't shattered by grub emergence holes, and the horizon wasn't permanently shrouded in dark smoke made him dare to believe things might be on the upturn.

He'd never admit to that, of course. Everyone would think he'd finally gone senile. He walked into the ops room, and the duty watch sat bolt upright in their seats.

"All quiet, Lieutenant?" he asked, leaning over the comms desk to check the incident log for Stranded raids. There were a couple a week, a lot of damage but relatively few serious civilian casualties yet. Any dead civvie was bad news for morale, though. "Are those vermin breeding in the sewers or something? I'm catching hell from the Chairman."

"One more enemy contact an hour ago, sir." Donneld Mathieson edged his wheelchair away from the console. "Two confirmed dead by Sigma Squad."

"And where's Lieutenant Stroud?"

"Out on patrol. Testing canine units with Sergeant Mataki. Remember?"

Yes, he did. He'd promised Anya more frontline tasks and now he had to honor that. "I'm all in favor of low-tech solutions."

"And I need to task that woman who used to be in Major Reid's EOD team."

Reid. Two-faced asshole. "Which woman?"

"Private Byrne." Mathieson paused. He had a habit of punctuating with silences, and the longer the silence, the more negative adjectives he seemed to leave unsaid. "Sam Byrne. The one who does everyone's tattoos."

"Ah. Her. Yes, it's a Kashkuri thing."

"You knew her father, didn't you? She mentioned it."

Knew him? One of my own. Twenty-sixth Royal Tyran Infantry. Anvil Gate just isn't going to let me forget it today.

"I did," Hoffman said. "Team her up with Mataki and Stroud. I pity the Stranded asshole who runs into that gang of harpies."

Hoffman never openly expressed concern for a female Gear's safety, but Mathieson probably knew him well enough to decode the comment. There was no allowance for gender. Either women could do the job as well as a man or they couldn't, and if they couldn't—then they didn't serve on the front line. But Anya Stroud lacked experience, and Sam Byrne always had to prove she could take more risks than a man even when she didn't have to. Bernie would have her hands full keeping an eye on two liabilities at once.

Bernie knows what she's doing. She'll be a steadying influence. Stick Byrne with the men, and she'll be too busy picking fights with them.

"Indeed, sir," Mathieson said. "I've always thought that women are a lot worse than us when they get going."

Maybe it was a general comment. Maybe it was about Bernie, because her line in rough justice had evolved from common knowledge into regimental mythology now.

Either way, Hoffman didn't take the bait. "Wise to steer clear of the ladies. How many patrols have we still got out?"

"Eight, sir. One more thing—probably nothing, but I took the precaution of monitoring the Indie ship-to-ship channels. One of their frigates is in trouble."

"They've only *got* one. What kind of trouble?"

"It struck something submerged, radioed for assistance, and then lost contact."

"Ran aground? What kind of goddamn weekend sailors are they?" *Quentin's going to be pissed off. He really wanted that frigate for NCOG.* "Have you told Captain Michaelson?"

"Not while he's with Commander Trescu. I don't think the Indies know we can eavesdrop on that frequency. And I don't know how Trescu keeps in touch when he's ashore, because he doesn't route calls through here."

"You'll make a politician one day, Donneld."

"No need to be insulting, sir . . ."

Hoffman would have taken that entirely as a joke if he hadn't known how badly Mathieson wanted to return to a combat role. With the limited prosthetics available now, that wasn't going to be anytime soon. The COG had sunk most of its technology along with Jacinto. Everything that could have helped Mathieson walk again was under a hundred meters of seawater.

There was a hell of a lot of rebuilding to do, and it wasn't all bricks and mortar.

"Keep me posted," Hoffman said. "I better go see how our gallant captain is getting on."

CNV *Sovereign* was the navy's flagship, but that wasn't saying much these days. She was overdue at least five major refits. The daily struggle to keep the carrier running showed, from the rust streaks on her superstructure to the broken jackstaff at her stern. She was an equally sad picture below decks.

As Hoffman made his way through the passages to Michaelson's day cabin, he had to duck to avoid jury-rigged cable conduits sagging from the deckheads. The wiring was exposed in some places and even routed through vent hoses in others. Even in the cabin itself, cables snaked across the deck and vanished under the bunk. The captain sat in one of the timeworn blue leather chairs, chatting to Miran Trescu just like the two of them had been buddies at naval college. It all looked a bit too cozy for Hoffman.

"Don't let me interrupt, Quentin," Hoffman growled. "I can come back when you two are done discussing barnacles. Commander, do I hear you've got a ship in trouble?"

Trescu didn't turn a hair. "A missile frigate, Colonel. *Nezark*. We have patrol vessels out looking for her."

"Do try to keep me up to speed with these things." Hoffman parked his backside on the edge of Michaelson's desk and gave him a meaningful look. "We're all COG now. Your military secrets are our military secrets."

"Force of habit, Colonel—my apologies." Trescu's mouth smiled but his eyes didn't. "Probably a major electronics failure. No radio and no radar."

"That would explain the collision, then." Michaelson twitched an eyebrow. So Trescu hadn't told him *that*. Hoffman didn't elaborate, because he knew he'd learn more by comparing what he already knew with what Trescu told Michaelson when he was gone. "And I take it you're happy now for Delta Squad to land at Emerald Spar for a security assessment."

Trescu smiled. "We can trust one another. We have kept our bargains, yes?"

"We have."

"Then they may board the platform. I advise caution."

"Why? Your guys a little trigger-happy?"

"Rigs are dangerous places. For anyone."

"I'll be sure to pass that on."

Hoffman headed back to his office. Maybe Prescott had started him off on the wrong foot today, but he found himself picking over Trescu's comments for hidden meaning. There were probably none to find. He always assumed the worst, so the only surprises he ever got were that the situation wasn't quite as badly screwed as he first thought.

When Hoffman reached his office, the door was ajar. It was only a midsize storeroom but it had a wonderful view, and that was all he needed, chief of staff or not. When he sat down at the desk, its varnish polished thin by decades of someone else's elbows resting on it, he found a gray-furred lump sitting on a sheet of old paper. There was a note scribbled on it: THE REST OF THE RABBIT IS IN A STEW. IT'S WAITING FOR YOU IN THE MESS.

So it was a rabbit's foot. Yes, he could see the claws now. He thought these things had to be cured and preserved longer than a day or two, but maybe Bernie decided he needed some urgent luck. At least the borrowed dog was earning its keep.

He had to smile. "Crazy woman," he said to himself. The severed foot would stink the place out in a few days. "You South Islanders. *Feral*, the lot of you."

KING RAVEN KR-80, INBOUND FOR GORASNI
IMULSION DRILLING PLATFORM EMERALD SPAR,
350 KILOMETERS NORTHWEST OF VECTES.

It was a lonely thing marooned in the middle of a vast ocean—the tallest man-made structure left in the world. If Dom Santiago needed reminding how little remained of the old Sera, the pre-Locust Sera, this rig did the job just fine.

White cascades of bird shit and rust coated its upperworks. Dom scanned it through his binoculars, one hand gripping the Raven's safety rail. A group of platform workers huddled on the edge of the landing pad. Gray gulls were lined up on one of the crane jibs like an honor guard. Beneath their roost, something equally gray turned and twisted in the wind, but the Raven banked too sharply for Dom to work out what it was. It might have been a weather-shredded flag.

He couldn't even recall what Gorasnaya's flag looked like. Stripes? An eagle? The geography lesson was long forgotten. Gorasnaya had never been all that important until now.

"Man, that's a long way from home," Cole said, staring out the crew bay. "Imagine being stuck there and runnin' out of coffee."

Baird seemed riveted by it. "Awesome engineering. You know how deep that water is? Three thousand meters. Our submarines can't go much below three *hundred*. Those tethers had to be sunk via a remote."

"Aww, Baird's in love with another hunk of metal," Cole teased. "Baby, you gonna end up marryin' a bot. Maybe we better ask Jack if he got a sister."

"Come on. It's clever shit. Admit it."

Cole laughed. Dom didn't find the rig awesome at all, however impressive it was. He didn't like the idea of somewhere he couldn't walk or swim away from if things went to rat shit. He wasn't even sure where the nearest land was. "You certain that thing isn't going to fall over? Looks top-heavy to me."

"They all look like that," Marcus said, unmoved.

Gill Gettner's voice cut into the radio circuit. "Those things are built to withstand hurricanes. It's exploding in a fireball that you ought to worry about."

"I meant the shitty state of repair, Major," said Dom.

"Good point. Jump out and test the helipad for stability." Gettner never sounded as if she was joking. She probably wasn't. Her crew chief, Nat Barber, peered out of the hatch as if he wasn't too sure either. "I'll just hover."

Dom wondered how the hell the battered platform had lasted this long. How did Gorasnaya maintain it, let alone defend it? They had even fewer resources than the COG. When the Raven settled on the pad—Dom never trusted that crazy bitch Gettner not to be literal—he half-expected to hear the creak of buckling metal. But it held. He jumped down after Marcus, and the squad went to meet the Gorasni welcome wagon.

They were a grim-looking bunch, and Dom couldn't help but notice all four of them were cradling huge wrenches. Maybe they had a lot of servicing to do today. He didn't plan to turn his back on them and find out the hard way.

"So you've come for our dowry." The biggest guy held out his hand to Marcus, but Dom noted he still had a firm grip on that wrench. Marcus shook the man's hand without a blink. "Remember that looks aren't everything. I'm Stefan Gradin. This platform is my personal kingdom, so nobody fucks with it, okay?"

"That'd be why your boss wants us to help you out—when you're busy," Baird said, but Cole nudged him in the back.

Marcus grunted and peered over the side of the helipad. "What's your capacity?"

"One hundred and fifty thousand barrels a day at full production." Gradin had a heavy Gorasni accent but he was perfectly fluent. "In practice, twenty thousand. We don't need to process more and we haven't got the bulk tankers anyway."

"What else haven't you got?"

"I thought you were here to look at our security."

"Yeah. So I am." Marcus glanced at the wrench but didn't wait to be shown around. He slid down the ladder onto the deck below and paced around, checking out the platform from various angles. Dom could see that he was working out how he'd launch an assault on the rig, noting the vulnerabilities and blind spots. "How many times have you been attacked?"

Gradin followed him like close personal protection. "Six, maybe seven times this last year. But only the tankers in transit. Never the platform."

"Lose any men?"

"Yes." Gradin nodded. "And so did they."

Dom, Cole, and Baird trailed down the ladder after Marcus. Dom kept the three other wrench-wielders in his peripheral vision. It was a tough job to hijack a structure like this, but that wouldn't deter the seagoing Stranded. He'd seen them take lethal risks even against the COG.

But Stranded wouldn't want to wreck the rig, of course—the

imulsion was too precious. And they'd need the crew alive to run the drilling and processing, and that would eat up manpower. Yeah, it made sense to try to hijack the tankers instead. That way they got to keep the fuel *and* a ship.

Marcus pointed down at the deck. "What's below here?"

"Crew quarters." Gradin paused like he was debating whether to risk giving Marcus more information. They really had taken this no-surrender shit seriously, then. After a few seconds, he seemed to give up and pointed at various structures like a tour guide. "The section in the center is the drilling module. The other side of that is for treatment and condensate handling. That's where gas is flared off when it builds up. The big flame. You know?"

"I get it," Marcus said. "And the only way to board is to fly in or climb the legs."

"Then it's like hijacking a big ship. Same problems, except it doesn't go anywhere."

Marcus just nodded. Gradin seemed to have thawed enough to slip the wrench into a pocket on his pants leg. Now the squad got the rest of the tour. The crew accommodation looked ragged after years of neglect, but still pretty comfortable and well equipped, like a run-down business hotel that had seen better days. The deck vibrated under Dom's boots in two distinct rhythms—the steady throb of machinery and the slower, more ragged pulse of pounding waves. It felt like ships he'd been in. When he got outside again and the spray peppered his face, he had a sense that the rig should have been heading somewhere.

It was only when Dom reached the end of the drill module gantry and studied the cranes that the reality of life on Emerald Spar really hit home.

A gull swooped in and took a peck at the tattered flag, making it swing around. Now that Dom was close enough, he could see that the ragged shape wasn't a flag at all.

It was the top half of a badly decomposed human body dangling from a rope.

Marcus seemed to notice at the same time. Gradin nodded as if he'd been waiting for them to catch on.

"They want to play pirates?" he said. "Good. We play pirates too. Amuse the gulls."

Baird perked up. "Does that deter them?"

"We don't care," Gradin said.

"Okay, so you can take care of yourselves." Marcus made no comment about the half-pirate dangling from the crane. "But we'll put a squad here. And I didn't see any close-in defenses."

"We don't have any." Gradin tapped his wrench. "Just these — and plenty of rifles."

"Your navy can afford to lose a few deck-mounted guns. How many of your security cameras are working?"

"About half."

Marcus looked at Baird, who just nodded. He was gagging to play with this rig and now he had his chance.

"We'll fix that," Marcus said. "And you'll need a detachment of Gears on every tanker run."

While Baird and Marcus went off to draw up a parts list, Dom explored the platform with Cole. One of Gradin's wrench party trailed them at a constant five paces. A name was embroidered on his orange overalls—EUGEN—but there was no guarantee that it was his. He spoke for the first time when Cole swung ahead of Dom and went to climb a ladder for a better look at the drilling deck.

"No, you stay *here*," he said. He pushed in front of Cole and barred the way. "Too rusty. And you—too heavy."

Cole was a big guy even by Gears' standards, still built like the pro thrashball player he'd once been. He gave Eugen a broad grin. "Thanks for lookin' out for my safety."

He might have meant it, of course. Cole was like that.

Eugen, stony faced, beckoned them to follow and walked away toward the crew accommodation section. These Indies really were paranoid. As Dom picked his way down metal stairs wet with salt spray—not easy in bulky boots—he passed a roaring air-con vent and heard female voices drifting up from somewhere, but the words meant nothing. The vented air smelled temptingly of fried onions. It was one of the most delicious scents Dom could imagine. It smelled of home—the home he grew up in.

Eugen shook his head. "My wife," he said, suddenly and unexpectedly frank with them. "*Still* damn angry with me."

So one of the voices was hers, then. The Gorasni guys had their families with them. Or maybe they'd just paired up with coworkers because this was a lonely and scary place. Dom was finding it less sharply painful now to think about other folks' families; Maria was gone, and at least now he knew she was gone for good, not just missing and suffering in ways he could only imagine. He hated himself for sometimes feeling relieved by that.

These days, it was his kids he felt worst about. He felt he hadn't mourned them enough.

"Okay, we're done here." Marcus hauled himself over the edge of the deck by a grab rail and stood up. "We'll ship out as much equipment as we can on the next inbound tanker."

"And when will you send Gears to bravely defend us poor ignorant Gorasni?" Gradin asked, straight-faced.

"Soon as I radio back to Vectes," Marcus said, equally expressionless. "And they'll bring their own supplies."

Dom couldn't work out if Gradin had finally decided the COG wasn't the worst that could happen to him or if his war still wasn't over yet. The whine of the Raven's engine starting up cut through all the sea and machinery noises like someone calling Dom's name in a crowded room, and he found his legs making for the helipad a few seconds before his brain engaged.

Gettner was in more of a hurry than usual to get airborne. She lifted clear before everyone had strapped in. Barber had his head down, hand pressed to his right ear as he listened to voice traffic.

"Never mind us," Baird said. "We're just ballast. Dump us overboard anytime, Major."

The cockpit door was dogged open. Gettner seemed preoccupied, because she didn't tell Baird to go fuck himself like she usually did.

"Going back via the scenic route," she said. "Just to check what's getting our new friends so excited. I don't suppose you asked them about their missing frigate."

Marcus grunted. "They weren't in a chatty mood."

"Well, their CIC's crapping themselves about that ship. What are you getting now, Barber?"

Barber didn't answer for a few seconds. He was staring straight ahead with his palm resting against his right ear, listening intently to his radio.

"Wreckage," he said at last. He must have been listening on a Gorasni ship-to-ship channel. Dom wondered what language they were speaking if Barber could follow the chatter. "They've found a couple of buoys and some polyprop line. Nothing else. They're discussing how fast she went down. I'm missing a lot, but that's the gist of it."

"Shit."

Marcus did a slow head-shake. "It was broad daylight. Even without radar—you can navigate by sight and charts. You sure they said *grounded*?"

"That's another weird thing," Barber said. "The ship was nowhere near any hazard. Sandbanks can shift over a few years and catch you out if you don't keep charting them, but rocks can't. And we have to be talking about a big, rigid obstruction here."

Dom could guess what everyone was really thinking. The Stranded pirate fleet could have raised its game. He couldn't imagine how patrol boats could take out a frigate, though, not even with a belt-fed grenade gun, but he said it anyway.

"Shit, you think the Stranded got lucky with a missile system?" No, that was dumb. He tried to think of the ways he'd been trained to sabotage a warship as a commando. They were all beyond the scope of the average Stranded. "Or was the frigate a wreck waiting to sink?"

"Last radio message said they'd struck something beneath the hull," Gettner said. "They must have based that on instruments, ship handling, noise, whatever. They'd know if they'd been hit by anything explosive . . . Wait one, I'll try offering assistance again. Because those paranoid assholes aren't going to volunteer anything."

Gettner switched to the shared emergency channel. Dom had

to retune to eavesdrop. He caught Marcus's eye, then Baird's, but neither was offering theories.

"COG KR-Eight-Zero calling Branascu Control, do you require search assistance?" Gettner asked. "We're two hours from *Nezark*'s last position."

Branascu Control—which was probably now on board a warship heading for Vectes—took a few moments to respond.

"We are grateful, KR-Eight-Zero," said a female voice. "But we have ships in the area already. We are . . . revising our charts to take account of seismic activity."

"Say again, Branascu?"

Baird perked up. "Whoa, shit . . ."

"Seismic activity," Branascu Control repeated. "Sonar is detecting uncharted solid formations just beneath the surface. Perhaps this is connected to the geological disturbances when you sank Jacinto."

Even Gettner didn't snap back an answer to that.

"We'll warn off our vessels, then," she said at last. "Flash us if we can assist. KR-Eight-Zero out."

Baird curled his lip, evidently not impressed by the cover story. "I call bullshit," he said. "Collapsing the bedrock under Jacinto couldn't cause seabed shifts like that more than a thousand klicks away."

"Yeah, and if we told them we did it by blowing up a lambent Brumak, they'd call bullshit too," Marcus said. "I bet Prescott left out that detail."

So Gorasnaya wasn't leveling with the COG, and the COG wasn't sharing everything with Gorasnaya. It was a shitty start to a relationship. Dom focused on the view of the ocean from the Raven's open door and reminded himself how much cleaner and better this was than dying, besieged Jacinto.

"Fuck it, we'll find out soon enough," Gettner muttered. "Worst-case scenario—piracy. Most likely—floating death traps crewed by morons."

Ships went down all the time, Dom told himself. The ocean was a dangerous place, as unknowable and deadly as anything the grubs had cooked up underground. That meant he didn't have to worry about pirates armed with antiship missiles—just the natural hazards of a world that was always trying to kill you.

That, at least, was something to be grateful for. As far as the sea was concerned, death was nothing personal.

CHAPTER 2

*Power is about perception. The COG thinks it's still got it. It
hasn't—it's just a town with a few ships and a fraction of its
old army. But it can't think small when it needs to. That's our
advantage. You want to go back to the status quo, where the
COG runs Sera? Where it can wipe out the rest of the world
just to save its own ass? Now's the best time for the whole dis-
enfranchised community to unite and deal with the COG—
the seagoing trading communities, the enclaves ashore, and
our associates on Vectes. They call us pirates. But our time
has come.*

(LYLE OLLIVAR, HEAD OF THE LESSER ISLANDS FREE TRADE
ASSOCIATION, SUCCESSOR TO THE LATE DARREL JACQUES,
PREPARING FOR A NEW WORLD ORDER)

TWO KILOMETERS NORTH OF NEW JACINTO,
VECTES: EXCLUSION ZONE PATROL, TWO DAYS
LATER.

The Gorasni refugee camp had sprung out of nowhere like some
kids' pop-up book, orderly rows of identical but threadbare tents
hugging the outer wall of the naval base. Bernie had to give the
Indies full marks for rolling up their sleeves and getting on with it.

"They've posted their own guards," Anya said, elbow resting on

the vehicle's open window. "Look. Do you think that's to keep
something out, or something in?"

Bernie drove around the perimeter more to show the Gorasni
that the COG was on the case than in any expectation of trouble.
The security fence—erected by the refugees, no help requested
and none given—was a mix of razor-wire and chain-link fencing.
In a world of shortages and make-do, it was a weird thing to bring
along for the trip.

But then fences were a fact of life now. They kept things out—
and they kept things in.

A couple of men wandered along the other side of the Gorasni
wire with rifles over their shoulders, passing a smoke back and
forth. Bernie gave them a perfunctory wave and drove on. Everyone was used to patrolling to keep an eye out for grubs, so it wasn't
a habit anyone was going to abandon overnight—with or without
Stranded gangs around.

"It might be for us, ma'am," she said. "Maybe they think we
had something to do with sinking their frigate."

"That was weird. I hate mysteries."

"*Did* we?"

"What, sink it? No, Michaelson wants every hull he can grab."
Anya made a little puffing noise as if something had occurred to
her. "Prescott wouldn't tell me anyway."

"You wouldn't think he still gave a damn about secrets, would
you?"

"Do you think people change? The Gorasni, I mean."

Or Prescott. Or Marcus. "No. We haven't, have we?"

"Good point."

Bernie wasn't too worried about the Gorasni. If they'd been Indies from Pelles or Ostri, that would have been another matter.
That had been *her* war, *her* mates killed, *her* knee-jerk hatred. But
it was the Stranded who were uppermost in her mind now. Somehow the bastards just melted into the countryside.

*We've forgotten how to fight our own kind. Gone soft. Out of
practice.*

A wet nose caught her ear from behind and smeared dog snot

on her face. Mac, confined to the back seat, wanted to see what was going on. He thrust his head forward, tongue lolling. Anya leaned away a little.

"He won't bite, ma'am." Bernie revved the Packhorse to climb out of a shallow ditch and rejoin the paved road. "Not unless you ask him to. Mac? You want a nice juicy bad guy? *Seek!*"

Mac barked once. He didn't bark much, and in the small cab it was loud enough to make Anya flinch. Bernie translated it as *What the fuck?* Here he was, being told to *seek* when he was stuck in this tin box with nothing to scent or see. She could see the disdain on his face. He thought humans were wasting his time.

Anya rubbed Mac's head warily. He yawned, displaying an impressive set of teeth. "It just feels too much like sport."

"Vermin control," Bernie said. "Someone's got to do it."

People could be squeamish about strange things, Bernie decided. Anya slipped into a combat role pretty easily for an officer who'd spent her entire career in Ops, but using dogs to chase down other humans seemed a step too far for her. Hosing them with heavy-caliber rounds from an Armadillo's gun turret obviously wasn't. Anya had done that without blinking. She had a lot of her mother in her.

"I'm not criticizing," Anya said at last. "They had the same offer of amnesty as their families."

"Another brilliant Prescott idea. Every Stranded male we kill—one more woman inside our walls with a death to avenge. We can't trust them."

"Not really an amnesty, then, is it?"

"No, ma'am. It's politics. Although it's not like he needs their votes, is it?"

"So what would *you* do?"

Bernie tried to keep her mind on the route ahead. These Stranded bastards had already booby-trapped a construction site up by the reservoir, and raids were a constant threat. Either they had a huge arms cache or they were getting resupplied somehow. Either way they didn't seem to be running out of ordnance.

"Ma'am," Bernie said, "are you asking what I *want* to do, what

I know I *ought* to do, or what the rules of engagement say we *can* do?"

"I'm just asking a friend who also happened to be my mom's friend what she thinks is right."

Bernie had never thought of herself as Helena Stroud's friend. The major had been her commander. There'd been mutual respect and equally mutual loyalty, but friendship was for equals.

"There's no right answer," Bernie said.

"Any answer would do."

Gears had this kind of conversation about grubs without batting an eye. In fact, it rarely even warranted discussion; every grub had to die. It was a fact of life. There was no truce to be had, no peace to negotiate. But there'd probably be no cease-fire with these gangs, either. The solution was inevitable, even though that didn't make it any easier to say.

"You really want to put an end to it?" Bernie said. "Then wipe them all out. Leave nobody to bear a grudge. It only takes a few survivors to keep a blood feud going." She realized how bad that sounded, but she meant it. "Give it a century or two, and we'll evolve into two separate factions at war again. It's our national sport."

"But would *you* do it?"

Bernie didn't know. She was sure she'd do it in the heat of the moment, provoked or under fire, because she'd already done a lot worse. Cold policy was another matter, though. She still wasn't sure why. Maybe Anya was just testing to see how close she was to whipping out her knife again and settling scores the personal way.

"I'd probably need an excuse," Bernie said. The countryside changed from scattered building sites to newly plowed fields awaiting sowing, furrows so straight and even that they looked like a landscape of brown corduroy. "Or a reason. Same thing."

Anya didn't sound shocked. "Prescott says pragmatic politics means accepting that the right outcome often comes from the wrong methods."

"Yeah, he'd slot every last one of them if he thought he'd get away with it." Bernie cut Prescott some slack for being willing to get his hands dirty. "At least he's not some fancy academic moralist."

Maybe we'd all do it. Maybe even the best of us would do one shitty thing if we thought it would do some good. Nobody knows for sure until they have to make the choice.

"Okay," Anya said, "At least I'm not missing an easy answer."

Bernie changed gear as the Packhorse groaned its way up the hill. She made sure the subject was closed by giving Anya something more immediate to worry about. "Keep your eyes open, ma'am. Remember how different things look from ground level."

Anya was used to seeing the battlefield through an airborne bot's camera. But bots like Jack were in short supply now, and that meant keeping them in reserve for critical jobs. Patrolling the thousands of square kilometers between the naval base and New Jacinto in the south and Pelruan on the north coast had to be done by Gears. Anyone who didn't have authority to be off-camp—everyone except farmers, work parties, and their protection squads—was a legitimate target. The exclusion zone meant what it said.

We didn't protect Jonty, though, did we? Poor bastard.

She still didn't know which of the Stranded had murdered the old farmer. That was a pretty good reason for slotting all of them as far as she was concerned, just to make sure.

The dash-mounted radio crackled. "Byrne to P-Twelve, over."

Anya took the mike one-handed, still cradling her Lancer. "Stroud here. Go ahead, Sam."

"I'm ten klicks south of the hydro plant. Recent enemy activity—I'm looking at a lot of disturbed soil on the main road. Grid six-echo, five-nine-zero by two-eight-eight."

"Explosives?"

"A remote device," Sam said. "I can't see if there's a wire. But it's too far off the track to drive over it, so it's not a mine. Someone's got to be watching the road with a trigger in their hand."

Anya hesitated for a moment. Bernie didn't see her reaction because Mac shoved his head forward again.

Come on. You could do it in Ops. You can do it now.

Bernie waited agonizingly long seconds, giving Anya a chance to make the decision before she intervened. She had to learn to make the call herself.

"You can't deal with this on your own," Anya said. "Stand by for backup."

That probably sounded like fighting talk to Sam. "Look, I can work out where they are, okay?" Her accent made her sound even more aggressive than she was. "They need line of sight. They need to bury the det wire. So the only vantage point is a wood five hundred meters from the road. The rest of this place is open fields."

Bernie checked the terrain on the map. It was open country, the road overlooked by a tree-covered hill, the kind of location you could slip into at night but couldn't approach unseen by day. If there was a Stranded unit there, the best option was an air strike, but they'd hear the Raven coming half an island away.

And here I am, calling them units like they're real troops . . .

Anya flicked the mute button on the mike. "You think we could ambush *them* instead, Sergeant?"

"Overland?" Bernie visualized the location as best she could and began estimating where they'd have to leave the Packhorse to make an approach on foot. "It'll take an hour or so to get in position, if we're the closest unit."

"Okay." Anya frowned to herself, then opened the mike again. "Sam? Sit tight . . . Control, this is P-Twelve. Contact in grid six-echo, five-nine-zero by two-eight-eight—Byrne's located a roadside device and thinks enemy personnel are still in the area. We're going in. Any other units nearby?"

"Control to P-Twelve," said Mathieson. "Are you asking for air support?"

"Negative."

"Wait one."

Bernie kept a wary eye on the countryside as the Packhorse idled in the middle of the road. Eventually Mathieson came back on the radio.

"P-Twelve, Rossi's unit is ten klicks north of Byrne's position," he said. "He's moving in. Control out."

Sergeant Rossi was an old hand; he'd expect a lot from Anya as the senior officer, and it looked like she was all too aware of that. She slapped her palm on the dashboard.

"Let's do it."

Bernie refolded the map with the six-echo grid uppermost and handed it to Anya. "Okay, we'll go off-road at the stream and come around the back of that incline. It's on foot from there. Where are you going to put Rossi?"

Anya pored over the map. "Here . . ."

"How about a little further over *here*?" Bernie pointed. "Then he can cut them off to the north *or* the east."

"Good call, Sergeant." Anya nodded. "Thanks."

It was a sergeant's job to nursemaid the junior officers until they were safe to be let loose on their own. Bernie was all too aware that this would be Anya's first real firefight. She wouldn't have the armored protection of a 'Dill and a bloody big gun this time. Mac could probably smell the sudden tension, because he started making little whining noises in the back of his throat and squeezed his head past Bernie's shoulder to poke his nose out of the open window.

"Good boy," Bernie said. "Quiet, now. Okay?"

Mac was only thirty kilos of vulnerable, unarmed meat, but somehow having a dog alongside made Bernie feel a lot safer. It was primal. A dog said *weapon* to any human.

"Byrne, Rossi—Stroud here," Anya said. "Anything moving?"

"Byrne here. Nothing, ma'am."

"Rossi here. Where do you want us?"

"Five-eight-zero by three-eight-zero, close to the stream."

"Roger that."

He didn't sound worried. Bernie glanced at Anya as she released the switch on the mike. She'd definitely honed that reassuring voice to perfection over the years, but she kept licking her lips in a way that said she was scared shitless. Bernie was, too—sensibly afraid, the way any sane soldier should have been—and almost hoping the Stranded would make a run for it before they showed. But they were scumbags, and they had to be put down. She felt ashamed of herself.

I really am getting too old for this shit. Baird's right.

"Where's Sam from?" Anya asked. "I can't place her accent."

"Tyran father, Kashkuri mother. She's from Anvegad—Anvil Gate."

Anya seemed genuinely distracted for a moment. "I didn't realize."

"I like to know what I'm taking on. It's a habit to cultivate." Bernie watched Anya doing the mental calculations. Everyone did, wondering if Sam was old enough to remember the siege. "No, ma'am, she was born a few months after it all ended."

"Sergeant's telepathy." Anya looked embarrassed, too diplomatic to ask the obvious questions. Any mention of Anvegad and its COG garrison—its romantic Kashkuri name reduced to the prosaic Anvil Gate—inevitably led to Hoffman's involvement there. "Handy."

"Sam's had a lot to live up to." Bernie hesitated, because she'd never said aloud to Anya what everyone thought—that her war-hero mother was a tough act to follow. "Like you."

But Anya didn't say anything. She kept her eyes on the road. They were ten klicks from Sam's position now, and Bernie started looking out for a break in the fields where she could drive across uncultivated land rather than churn up crops.

But she still had her personal radar tuned to anything that didn't look *right*.

Gears didn't see roads the same way civilians did. Civvies looked for oncoming traffic and hazards from side roads. Gears looked for choke points, kill zones, and ambushes. They were always on the alert for combat indicators. Bernie found herself checking for blind spots and cover to either side.

"Five hundred meters is a damn long wire," Anya said. "Must have taken them some time to bury it."

"They're not in any hurry." As she drove, Bernie was starting to get that *feeling*. The instinct was born of years moving through hostile places, rational clues that could be analyzed later—a weird stillness, things that should have been there and weren't, a thousand subliminal details—but now it simply told her to get ready to fight. "It's a war of attrition. We're not used to that."

"Why are you slowing down?"

"That bend ahead." The angle was so tight that the road seemed to vanish into an isolated stand of trees. For once, she couldn't see any birds around. "If I was going to jump someone—look, humor me, there's something not quite right."

Anya picked up the mike again. "P-Twelve to Byrne, P-Twelve to Rossi, stand by. Possible contact, grid six-delta . . . zero-one-three, two-five-four."

But there was bugger all that the others could do for them if the worst happened. Anya checked her Lancer. Bernie prepared to pull off the road down a shallow slope fifty meters ahead. The road was in poor repair here, a mass of potholes and cracked concrete patches, and suddenly that surface became the only thing she could focus on.

Yeah, something's wrong.

The Packhorse bounced as the nearside front tire hit a hole. The next thing she knew—something smashed down hard on her head, the Packhorse was going *up* and not *along*, and the road vanished. The dog fell on her, yelping. She had no idea how, but she was sure she was falling too. And then she hit bottom.

For a few moments, she couldn't work out where the hell she was. Then she realized she was lying with her head under the steering column and the Packhorse was upside down, maps and water bottles and windshield fragments everywhere. The driver's door was gone. She could taste smoke, cordite, and blood.

"Shit." That was all she could manage. She fumbled for her Lancer—it had to be close by—but caught a handful of fur instead. Mac whimpered. At least he was still alive. "Anya? Hey, *Anya!*"

"Get clear. Come on." There was a metallic sound and a loud grunt. Anya's voice seemed to be coming from a distance. "Can you hear me, Bernie? Can you move?"

"Yeah. Yeah, I can. I can." Bernie grabbed her Lancer automatically, struggling out of the crushed gap where the door had been, expecting to come under attack. *It's an ambush. What happened? Grenade round, bomb, or what?* She went into the drill without thinking. *Assess, cover, evacuate.* Just because you were still alive, it didn't mean the incident was over. "You hurt?"

Anya crouched beside her against the underside of the stricken Packhorse, Lancer raised. The vehicle had come to rest in a shallow roadside gully, stopped from settling completely on its roof by the slope. "Can't tell," she said, scanning 180 degrees. "You sure you're okay?"

"I'll wet my pants and cry later." Bernie suspected she might well do at least one of those, but the operative word was *later.* Right now she took a strange comfort from the fact that she could still handle it. She was scared shitless and in shock, but the hardwiring created by years of drill pushed that aside and went straight into a defensive routine. "Let's call a cab. If we start walking, we'll get picked off or hit another mine."

She had to assume that. The words were out of her mouth before she remembered that she had to leave more decisions to Anya. *Never mind. Either way, she learns.* Anya pressed her finger to her earpiece, her voice just a little shaky.

"Control, this is P-Twelve. Control, come in. This is P-Twelve. We've been hit, position grid six-delta, main road—"

"P-Twelve, we've got you," Mathieson said. "We're scrambling a bird."

"No hostiles spotted, but we might be bait."

"Understood. Injuries?"

"We're both T-three." Not in immediate danger—and if either of them was bleeding internally, they were too pumped on adrenaline and shock to feel it. "The Packhorse is wrecked."

"P-Twelve, I'm diverting another squad to Byrne's position. Wait one."

Bernie edged around the rear of the vehicle, head level with the burst nearside tire. There was a ragged crater about thirty meters behind them. One side of the road had been ripped up, and lumps of concrete were scattered around. It was a smaller hole than she expected.

Shit, we drove over it. Or we hit it and it threw us forward. A few seconds—that's all that saved us.

That reality would sink in later. The tailgate of the Packhorse looked like someone had hosed it with random caliber rounds. The front end was just mangled by the hard landing, still hissing hot, rusty water from the broken radiator. The vehicle's tail had taken the blast. Whatever the device had been, it had detonated late. And it had been planted since yesterday's patrol. It was hard to spot disturbed soil out here because of the thick vegetation that flanked the roads.

Astonishingly, Mac was wandering about, sniffing the churned soil around the vehicle and looking none the worse for his experience.

A fresh trail for the dog. Shit, now would be the best time to track these bastards.

"You don't look too good, Bernie," Anya said. "You sure nothing's broken?"

"I hit my head. I can use that as an excuse for being cranky for days." Bernie had had more than a few close calls with ordnance over the years. Doc Hayman said an explosion didn't have to kill you or even knock you out to do brain damage. "I really should get the dog on the trail. It's less than a day old."

"You're going straight to triage," Anya said firmly. "And that's an order."

Bernie suddenly felt that tracking these bastards was more important than anything. Mac seemed okay. And if she had any brain damage, there wasn't much Doc Hayman could do about it. They had no state-of-the-art neurology unit. The COG had just lost a century in technology terms.

She could hear the clicking of cooling metal, so at least the blast hadn't deafened her. Eventually it gave way to a distant droning sound overlaid with the chatter of rotor blades. The Raven was coming.

"Two explosive devices today," Anya said, still scanning trees a couple of hundred meters away. "You think they've got a new strategy?"

"If they have," Bernie said, "I'd love to know how they're being resupplied."

"P-Twelve, this is Byrne." Sam's voice buzzed in Bernie's ear-piece. "Rossi's in position. You're going to miss the party."

Bernie supposed that was Sam's way of checking they were still okay. "Sorry for the no-show. I'm sure we'll get another chance to have a girls' day out with extreme violence."

Mac paused in his investigation of the soil and stared out across the grassland into the trees, trauma apparently forgotten. It might have been rabbits that got his attention.

Bernie found herself hoping it was bigger quarry.

KING RAVEN KR-239, TWENTY KILOMETERS NORTH OF VECTES NAVAL BASE.

The Packhorse lay belly-up like a dead animal. The dog was sniff-ing around in the grass at the side of the road, but Baird couldn't see Bernie or Anya yet.

They were here, though. They were still in radio contact, but that didn't seem to make Marcus any less agitated. The warning signs were no more than a fixed stare and a twitch of jaw muscles, but Baird knew him well enough by now to see when the guy was wound up. He really didn't like Anya doing any hairy-assed stuff. Baird wondered if they argued about it in private.

They occasionally disappeared at the same time. Baird noted things like that.

"Well, at least I know where to set down safely," Sorotki said. "Seeing as Mataki's been kind enough to do the route-proving and trigger the device . . . I'll land on the road." The Raven banked in a loop, coming up on the other side of the overturned vehicle. Bernie and Anya were crouched in its cover with their rifles ready. Bernie shielded her eyes from the grit whipped up by the chopper's downdraft. "Stick to the paved surface, boys and girls. No telling what those bastards have planted either side."

Bernie's voice came on the radio. "You can set off mines with downdraft, you know."

"Stand by, kitten-killer . . ."

Baird leaned back into the crew bay to talk to the crew chief. Mitchell was huddled over the Raven's door gun like he was trying to hatch it. "Hey, the Pack's in one piece," Baird said. "We can lift it underslung."

Mitchell didn't take his eyes off the ground below. "Has anyone ever told you that you're just too caring?"

"I never leave a wounded machine behind."

"Dizzy can swing by with the salvage rig later and haul it back. Casevac first."

"It'll be picked clean the minute we leave. You think these assholes don't stake out their devices or know when they catch something?"

"Too bad." Marcus did his slow head turn, the one that said he was seriously pissed off, and fixed Baird with a cold blue stare. "We'll just have to reclaim the shit when we catch up with them."

Baird wasn't scared of Marcus, but he knew when to back off. The man wasn't *knowable*. Although Baird knew what Marcus would do in a given situation, he didn't know how his mind worked, and that bothered him. Any mechanism—human, animal, machine—could be analyzed, its component parts evaluated, and its workings and functions understood. Not understanding Marcus was the most unsettling thing about him.

Yeah, but you're not immune to all this shit, are you, Marcus? Look at you sweating over Anya. Caring screws you up, man. Just switch it off. Life gets a lot easier then.

Sorotki set the Raven down on the road. Bernie and Anya emerged from behind the Packhorse, tottering under the weight of an ammo box and two fuel cans.

"Can't leave it here," Bernie said. She had maps stuffed under one arm. "Got to clear the vehicle."

Baird blocked Bernie's path and tried to take the crate from her. "Women drivers. You must have inherited extra lives from all those cats you ate, Granny."

She hung on to the crate, but he could see she was struggling. "Thanks, I can manage this."

"Sure you can." He wrestled the box from her arms. He wasn't sure if he was embarrassed for her, or just trying to avoid looking as if he gave a shit. "And then you'll have a stroke, and I'll have Hoffman on my back for letting you."

Marcus relieved Anya of the fuel cans and steered her toward the Raven. Bernie shrugged wearily. "We're going to need some mine-clearance kit, Blondie. Invent something."

"Already got a plan for putting a mine flail on a grindlift rig. Now get your ass in that bird before you break anything else."

"*Arse.*" She ignored him and snapped her fingers at the dog. Mac trotted to her side and sat to attention like he was waiting for orders. "Mac? Want to find bad guys? *Seek.*"

"You got perforated eardrums, or just going senile? Time to go."

"It wasn't much of a bomb. I'm fine." Mac was already rooting around and making a line for the trees. "The trail's less than a day old, though. Best time to follow it."

"Head injuries. Subdural hematomas." Baird wondered if he was going to have to haul her on board. He found himself worrying inexplicably about how to grab her. "Delayed onset of cerebral swelling. Coma."

"Thanks. You're such a cheery little bastard."

But she gave him a motherly pat on the back, just like she did with Cole, and went after the dog. Marcus was still examining the crater. He looked up.

"Where the hell's she going?" he asked.

"Asshole hunting. It's an Islander thing."

"And you let her."

"Hey, I'm not a geriatrics nurse."

Marcus sighed and pressed his earpiece. "Mataki? Get back here."

There was a pause before she came back on the radio. She must have been in a dip, because Baird could only see gray hair and the top of her backpack bobbing above the grass as she walked.

"Mac's picked up a trail," she said. "You want to pass this up?"

"How hard did you hit your head, Mataki?"

"Not hard enough to forget I owe these tossers a really bad time."

Marcus didn't bother to argue. He gestured at Baird to follow her and pressed his earpiece again. "Sorotki? We're going after them. Get Lieutenant Stroud back to base."

"Roger that," Sorotki said. "Call us when you need us."

Anya's voice interrupted. "Look, I'm fine. I should be out there with—"

But she was cut short by the whine of the engines as the Raven lifted clear. Baird didn't approve of women in combat roles, but it was asking for trouble to override her like that—and not just because she outranked Marcus. She wouldn't take that dismissal lightly, whatever the motive.

"Wow, harsh," Baird said. "You won't be getting any for a *long* time."

"Shut it, Baird," Marcus muttered.

Baird never had much control over his mouth, and he knew it. Something smart-ass always emerged unbidden; he couldn't even blame it on stupidity. Sometimes it was fear, sometimes frustration, but mostly it was habit, and he wished he could just keep it zipped. He realized that all the people closest to him—this squad—were those who seemed to understand that and knew when to ignore him.

It was kind of comforting. For once in his life, he felt easy with a group of people.

His earpiece radio clicked. "They'll hang around, won't they?" Bernie said. "They'll be somewhere relatively close."

"They'll want to know if they hit their target," Baird said. "They'd have to be deaf not to hear the explosion."

"Are we checking the farms for missing chemicals? They make their own sodium chlorate and nitrate fertilizer here."

"Oh, great."

"You can kill someone with most anything if you want to. Farms need agricultural chemicals, Blondie."

"Spoken like a farmer, Granny."

She had a point, though. The Stranded would use whatever they could find to make explosives, whether that was weed-killer, fertilizer, or even old and unstable TNT. And when they ran out of the chemical stuff, and then ran out of bullets, it would be pit traps with shit-smeared wooden stakes at the bottom. Whatever they used, however low-tech the guerilla war became, people would still end up dead or injured.

We'll end up chasing them forever. Too many places to hide. Not so many places for them to target, though. They've got to come to the settlements or ambush vehicles in transit. Time we lured these assholes into our own ambushes.

Marcus grunted, finger pressed to his ear. He was listening to the comms between Rossi and Control. "They've lost them," he said. "Sam's gone back to dismantle the device. She says she needs the materials."

"Crazy bitch. Good luck civilizing her, Granny."

"Waste not, want not, Blondie."

"We beat *grubs*, man. We should have done the same with these assholes and bombed the shit out of them when they were all still in one place."

"Amen," Bernie murmured.

Marcus cut in. "I think we should all shut the fuck up."

The dog led them along a zigzag path toward a patch of woodland. Baird caught up with Bernie as she came to a halt at the edge of a steep bank. A couple of meters below them, a stream glittered through a mesh of thin tree trunks jutting out from the slope, and Mac trotted back and forth along the edge, sniffing the air.

Bernie snapped her fingers to get his attention. "Seek, Mac. Did they cross here? Did they? Go on. Find 'em."

The dog picked his way down the bank and paddled a few meters along the shallow bed, looking lost. Baird didn't trust all this wilderness shit.

"You sure that mutt can hunt?" he said. "If all it takes to throw him off the scent is some water, he's not a lot of use."

"Blondie, who's the survival expert around here?"

"Here we go again. The wild woman of the frigging woods."

Marcus squatted on his heels to watch Mac casting around but said nothing. After a few moments, the dog paused, showed a lot of interest in a mud scrape on the opposite bank, and went charging up the slope.

"Game on," Bernie said.

She set off after the dog, probably still buoyed up on the adrenaline of the explosion. Baird wondered how long she'd last.

"If he finds a Stranded camp, does he have the sense not to go charging in?"

"Probably not. Better keep up with him."

It was hard going over ground knotted with tree roots and blocked by undergrowth, but the dog seemed to know where he was heading, and Bernie looked like she believed him. She kept pausing to check broken branches and other signs of recent foot traffic. Baird, radio tuned to the squad frequency, overtook her.

"Wait up," Marcus said suddenly. "Listen."

Baird stopped and Bernie passed him again. Someone had to keep an eye on the dog. Marcus gestured to Baird to listen in, and that meant switching to Control. Marcus was rarely without that damn earpiece, even off duty. Baird was pretty sure he slept with it in place most nights.

"Well, *shit*." Marcus stared into the trees with that defocused look that said he was listening rather than looking. "It's showtime."

Baird switched channels. His ear was filled instantly with a welter of voice traffic straight out of the nightmare they thought they'd finally left behind on the mainland. Squads out on the roads were calling in explosions and ambushes. It was hard to pick out the detail. He found himself listening intently for Cole's name in case he'd decided to help someone out and been caught up in this shit.

Mathieson's voice was deceptively calm. "Say again, Ten-Kilo. How many down? Is Andresen T-one? How bad is he?" Then a more familiar voice cut in—Anya. She was back in Ops by the sound of it. "Ten-Kilo, KR unit Three-Three is inbound for casevac, estimate ten minutes. Stand by."

Andresen. Baird didn't hear what had warranted his T1 triage rating—serious abdominal wound, traumatic limb amputation, whatever—but he knew the sergeant well, and that somehow shocked him more than the whole Locust war. Baird had lost comrades every day to grub attacks and dealt with it. But this wasn't the war, and they weren't up against grubs who didn't know how to be anything else but murdering assholes, and that made Baird spitting mad. They hadn't survived years of grub attacks to get picked off by human vermin. He'd never felt this angry in his life. The urge to hit back almost choked him. But he was stuck in the middle of nowhere with nothing to kill.

Marcus just looked through him, unblinking. "Fenix to Control. Checking in. Need us to do anything?"

That gave CIC a breathing space to respond in their own time. Anya came on the link. "Marcus, we've got ten incidents ongoing, including one involving Gorasni troops. It looks like a coordinated campaign. If you need air support, you might have a wait on your hands."

"No problem, Control. No contact here so far."

"Hoffman says to remember to bring back some live prisoners."

Marcus suddenly focused on Baird. "I'll make sure we don't forget that." He paused. "Keep us posted on Andresen. Fenix out."

Marcus liked Andresen. Bernie did, too. They both drank with him in the sergeants' mess. Baird suddenly didn't feel he was wasting time tracking a few assholes through the mud.

"Shit, I heard." Bernie walked back toward them. She had Mac on a leash now, straining to hold him. "And that's how a handful of arse-wipes can screw up a trained army. Come on. Mac's busting to kill something."

"I bet the Gorasni are just ecstatic to find their new home's a battlefield," Baird said. "That'll take their mind off their missing frigate."

"Cheapest form of warfare." Marcus shook his head, that slow side-to-side gesture that was more disgust than anything. "Not a battlefield yet."

"Yeah, tell that to Rory," Bernie said, leaning back on the leash to slow the dog down. "If he survives."

They resumed the trail in silence. Baird's pulse was still thudding in his neck. It didn't slow down to normal until Mac came to a sudden halt and stood with his ears pricked, staring intently past the trees at the slope of a rocky hillside. He never made a sound.

Baird was expecting him to bark like a guard dog, but he just stared, and not even movement around him broke his concentration. The mutt was definitely trained to hunt with a handler.

Bernie crouched next to him. "What is it, fella? You got something?"

Marcus gave the dog a wide berth and stood on the other side of Baird with his binoculars in one hand. He didn't seem comfortable around the animal. Baird squinted at the hillside and tried to imagine what the dog would see from here. Maybe he could smell something, or even hear it. The dog's senses were much more acute than his own.

Then he saw it. It was just a fleeting moment, but he was certain; a wisp of smoke or a fragment of ash from the rocks, gone in a couple of seconds on the breeze. Mac's nostrils twitched.

"Camp, maybe," said Baird. He directed Marcus, trying not to blink and lose the point he'd focused on. "Elevation forty degrees, left of the bushes. See the deep shadow?"

Marcus panned with his field glasses. Bernie cradled her Lancer, catching her breath, and Baird had an unwanted thought about whether he'd have softened toward his mother if she'd lived to be old and gray.

No, she'd still be a bitch. And this isn't guilt.

"Shit." Marcus lowered his binoculars. "Caves. Just like old times."

Caves were meant for entering. Baird wasn't afraid of what he'd find inside. He'd already found real monsters under his bed way too many times to fear his own kind.

"Hey, flea-bag," he said to Mac, looking for the best route up the hill. "That better not be rabbits in there."

VECTES NAVAL BASE, NEW JACINTO.

Dom had always wondered if Cole had what it took to shoot another human being, but the last few months on Vectes had cleared up that question pretty fast.

Yeah, he could pull that trigger, all right.

They were officially off duty, but that didn't mean a thing now. Medics moved in as KR-33 touched down on the parade ground, and all they carried out of the crew bay was an occupied body bag. Two of Rory Andresen's squad walked to the infirmary under their own steam, faces covered with blast wounds. It had been an everyday scene in Jacinto, but it sure as shit shouldn't have been one here, not now. They'd left all that behind.

Cole walked up and stood beside him, a half-cleaned section of Lancer chain in one hand and a time-frayed wire brush in the other. Dom didn't meet his eyes.

"It's Andresen," Dom said. Just saying his name made it real. Up to that point, it had somehow been optional whether to believe the guy was really dead. "I just heard from Anya."

"Aww, shit, man." Cole shut his eyes tight for a moment. "Where's his old lady?"

"Reid's gone to find her. They come through fifteen years of grubs and he dies *here*. He dies *now*. I tell you, there's no frigging sense in it."

Sense. Yeah, that was it. There really had been some sense to fighting grubs, even though nobody knew what the hell the assholes had really wanted to achieve other than wipe out every human on Sera. Now Dom was back to the gray areas of the Pendulum Wars, where his enemy was someone whose motives he knew and shared. Humans should have known better. It was harder to take.

He checked his Lancer. "Should have gone with Marcus . . ."

"Yeah, maybe, but—"

Whoomp.

Cole's voice was drowned out by a blast that made Dom drop instinctively. There was a split second of silence before the ball of smoke and flame shot up above the level of the naval base walls, and he found himself running toward the explosion. Everyone who didn't have their hands full right then did the same thing. He couldn't pick out the exact location, but it looked like the Gorasni camp beyond the perimeter walls.

If it was *inside* the walls, then the COG's problems were a lot worse than anyone thought.

But it wasn't. Cole and Dom reached the northwest gate in time to see a couple of open trucks heading up the main access path into the mass of Gorasni tents beyond the perimeter. The smoke was spiraling up from the far side of the camp. Even CIC seemed to be having trouble working out what had happened and who'd been hit. The Gorasni were chattering away in whatever they spoke, and CIC was trying to get sense out of them in Tyran. It wasn't working out too well.

Dom's instinct was the same as every Gear's in that base—to deal with the situation, whether by helping the injured or securing the site. They strode into the camp, but two Gorasni guards moved in on them right away.

"We have everything under control," one of them said in Tyran. He sounded as if he'd been trained to repeat the phrase but didn't actually understand it. "Thank you."

"That's a *bomb*, baby." Cole always wanted to help. He really did. "That don't look like *under control* to me."

"You want to do something?" the guard said. He understood Tyran just fine, then. "You do your job, Gear. Keep the roads free of bombs. You don't know how? We show you. But *later.*"

"You're not in Gorasnaya anymore," Dom snapped. "There's no goddamn border here."

"We have people trained. Too many of you run around here—you just get in their way." The guy's tone wasn't aggressive now. But he didn't move, either. "Thank you."

Cole caught Dom's shoulders and turned him around to steer him back to the base. "Other things we can do. You heard the man."

"Ungrateful assholes." The guy was right in a way, but Dom wasn't used to being told to run along. The frustration—shit, he wasn't sure what it was, whether it was a reaction to Andresen or Maria or any one of a hundred other shitty things. He just knew he didn't want to stand around and think. He pressed his earpiece. "Santiago to Control, you need me and Cole to do anything?"

Control was going to be overwhelmed right now and the last

thing they'd need would be Gears asking for work to do. But there was a plan for emergencies, and bypassing that made more work for Ops. There was a long pause before Mathieson responded.

"You could give us a hand up here, Dom. Drive a radio for me."

"On our way," Dom said.

The main naval base building was part of a terrace of red-brick barracks four or five stories high, all winding stairs, varnished floorboards, and dark green paint. Dom and Cole struggled against a tide of Gears and emergency volunteers coming out of the main doors. Dom took the stairs to CIC two at a time, tidying his fatigues as he went, although nobody had given a shit about uniform standards for a damn long time. As soon as he walked into the room, the wall of sound hit him—radio chatter on the loudspeakers, Ops staff with phones to one ear and radio headsets held to the other. A group of the Vectes locals was maintaining a tote board on the wall to keep track of the various incidents and plotting them on a hand-drawn map. Mathieson swiveled in his chair and pointed Dom and Cole at a comms desk near Anya without breaking his conversation.

"Just as well Marcus kicked me off the hunting party," she said, not making any sense. "It's gone crazy out there. Dom—get on the radio and find Sigma Two. They haven't called in. Cole— keep a line open to Pelruan. They haven't had any incidents yet, but I need a rolling sitrep from them."

Anya had a few scratches on her chin. She'd rolled up her sleeves, and when she reached out to pick up the phone, Dom could see a big bruise ripening just above her elbow.

"You okay?" he said.

"Yes, it went off some distance behind us." She glanced past him at the tote board. "Only one of fifteen so far, though. Two Gorasni dead, four Gears, and some nasty injuries. I'm lucky."

Ops was a lot harder than Dom expected. It was the waiting, the inability to grab a rifle and use all that spare adrenaline the way that nature intended. He found himself following a dozen one-sided conversations while he cycled through the frequencies trying to raise Sigma. The transport squadron was trying to rig a mine-clearance vehicle, construction workers up at the new housing site had found a suspicious patch of freshly dug soil, and the operating theater needed an electrician to fix some lights. The words *serious abdominal wound* leapt out at him and he made a conscious effort to ignore it.

Carlos.

Sometimes Dom didn't think about his brother for days at a time, and then he'd be all he *could* think about, even seventeen years later. Time definitely didn't heal. It just left longer gaps between the hurt. All you could do was fill your mind with the here and now, and not give the past a space to squeeze into until you felt up to dealing with it again.

Hoffman strode into CIC with Michaelson. Dom had his back to the door and was trying to read what one of the civvies was chalking on the tote board, but Hoffman's voice, even at a whisper, always got his attention. The colonel was his old CO. Part of Dom's brain was still tuned to him even now.

"Until we know what they're using for explosives, we can't break the supply chain." That was Michaelson. "Are they *stealing* agricultural chemicals? Are they making them? Damn, Vic, they might even be shipping them in. Even with radar pickets, I can't make the coast watertight."

Hoffman grunted irritably. "Well, if Trescu's so sure he can instruct us in the finer points of sucking goddamn eggs, let *him* run the patrols."

"Well, if we're talking about resupply from the sea—I'll be damned if I'm going to waste time and fuel on rummage crews," Michaelson said. "I'm not doing customs interdiction for contraband. Any vessel that isn't one of ours—we sink it. They'll get the message fast."

"Here he comes," Hoffman said. "Put on your grateful face, Quentin."

Prescott walked in with Trescu. Dom watched discreetly. Trescu was used to being a head of state and being treated like one, even if that state was a few thousand people. He had that

I-make-the-decisions-around-here air about him. Prescott seemed
to find that funny. If Dom could see that, then Trescu sure as shit
could too. The two men were having one of those icy arguments
that were all clenched teeth and no raised voices, but that didn't
mean they cared about the grunts listening in. Dom felt like a kid,
or the hired help, expected not to notice what his elders and bet-
ters were saying. Prescott parked his ass on a vacant desk and sat
gazing intently at the Gorasni leader with a concerned frown.

"My decision was *not* popular," Trescu said. "Many of my people wanted to stay on the mainland and take their chances.
I promised them they would be safer in your shadow, and now
you make a liar of me. A hundred or so starving vermin, and you
can't get rid of them? So much for the mighty Coalition that
brought the Independent Republics to their knees."

"Because this isn't a damn war," Hoffman growled. "It's terror-
ism in our front yard. We can't burn them out or bomb them out
because this is the only place we've got left. So we pick them off.
You got a better idea? Last time I looked, you'd lost a whole frigate
and didn't know how it happened."

Trescu—late thirties maybe, a real hard case with buzz-cut
dark hair and a neat beard streaked with early gray—leaned close
to Hoffman, not buddy-buddy but right in his face. Dom waited
for the colonel to lose his shit with the guy. But all Hoffman did
was clench his jaw as if Prescott had told him to keep it zipped no
matter what happened.

"Colonel, you COG are *soft*. You are *tolerant*. You give
amnesties." Trescu somehow made it all sound like some kind of
perversion. "And so you have a Stranded problem, despite holding several hundred potential hostages and informers within your
very walls. But we are *not* soft. We *solved* our Stranded problem."
He paused a beat. "And our frigate—I *shall* find out what happened."

Prescott joined in. "They aren't hostages, Commander," he
said. "They accepted an amnesty. Mostly women, children, and
older men."

"Like I said. *Soft*."

Hoffman was almost shaking. The old bastard had a temper, and Dom always expected him to have a stroke when he blew a gasket. Trescu pulled back slowly.

"Feel free to teach us how it's done *anytime*," Hoffman said. "Pull out a few fingernails. We're not good at that."

Trescu was talking a tough game for a man who had just a few ships and an imulsion rig. "Bring me some Stranded and I will," he said. "You need intelligence from them—I'll get it."

For a moment, Dom thought Trescu was asking them to round up the Stranded who'd been given amnesty and beat some information out of them. He could see some logic in that—the folks in New Jacinto couldn't have forgotten everything about their buddies on the other side of the fence—but it made him uneasy.

"We have a squad in pursuit right now, Commander," Prescott said, glancing at Mathieson. "They'll detain live prisoners."

"Then I want them." Trescu picked up a folded map from the table. "And you can wash your hands of it all to keep up your pretense of being civilized. Now, I have to go and calm my people down."

Trescu stalked out. Prescott looked at Hoffman and raised his eyebrows.

"Excitable fellow, isn't he?" Michaelson studied the chart on the wall, arms folded. "But with only three or four thousand people, the scale of the threat looks very different to him."

"We lost good men today too, Quentin," Hoffman said. "I feel pretty threatened myself."

Prescott was obviously back in his own world of power games again. "We need to wean him off the idea of *his* people and *his* territory. Let's watch our semantics in front of him, shall we? Us, us, *us*."

"So I can't call him a pissant who'd be scrubbing latrines if he didn't have a lot of imulsion." Hoffman ran both hands over his bald scalp, eyes on the tote board. "But we can't shit ourselves and hide every time a bomb goes off. We can't let this turn into a siege."

"Bring a few of these animals back alive for Trescu, then,"

Prescott said. "Give him a sense of ownership of the problems. If we don't, he'll take prisoners himself and sit on the intel. He has to accept he's part of the COG now."

"I've never been squeamish about civilians, Chairman," Hoffman said. "But if you're going to play really rough with the Stranded *outside* the walls, you better start worrying what the ones *inside* will do about that. Regardless of whether Trescu's the one wiring them up to the power supply, or us."

Dom must have forgotten to maintain his I'm-not-listening look. Hoffman turned suddenly and stared right at him. "Santiago, you taken up knitting or something?"

"Helping out, sir. Off duty."

"I can find a non-com to do that. You and Cole go back up Fenix. Sorotki's standing by. Don't come back until you find me a live one."

Dom had his orders. He also had a pretty good idea what was going to happen to any asshole he caught and handed over to Trescu. For a moment, he struggled with the idea and wondered how different that was from his urge to take a few of them down for Andresen. Maybe it was no different at all. But the fact that he stopped to think about it told him that—for him, at least—it was.

"You got it, sir," Dom said.

CHAPTER 3

FROM: NCOG COMMAND
TO: ALL SHIPS AND SHORE BATTERIES
SUBJECT: ROE AMENDMENT, MARITIME EXCLUSION ZONE

WITH IMMEDIATE EFFECT, ANY VESSEL IN THE MEZ THAT CAN-
NOT BE POSITIVELY IDENTIFIED AS AN AUTHORIZED FISHING
BOAT, FREIGHTER, OR NCOG ASSET IS TO BE ENGAGED AND DE-
STROYED, WHETHER IT PRESENTS AN IMMEDIATE THREAT OR
NOT. A WARNING WILL BE BROADCAST ON ALL CHANNELS
KNOWN TO BE USED BY STRANDED. MESSAGE ENDS.

OBSERVATION POINT, TWENTY-FIVE KILOMETERS
NORTH OF NEW JACINTO.

Bernie's radio crackled. "Andresen didn't make it," Anya said.
"I'm sorry."

Everyone paused halfway up the slope, even the dog. Bernie
found her head level with Marcus's boots. He took one hand off
the rock above him to press his earpiece.

"Okay, Anya. Thanks."

"KR-Two-Three-Nine is inbound with Dom and Cole. Orders
are to take live prisoners. Do you have an RV point?"

"Negative, Control. We're at grid seven-echo, approximately

nine-four-zero-nine-eight-zero. Tell Sorotki to stand by while we check this cave. Fenix out."

Baird prodded Bernie in the back of the leg. The slope was about forty degrees here, a real hands-and-knees job, and he was right beneath her foothold.

"Consider me extra-motivated," he said. "Get moving, Granny. You feeling okay? I'm only asking because I don't want you collapsing on top of me."

"'Course you are," she said. *Poor bloody Rory.* Even after so many years, so many deaths, it still punched her in the gut. But she was halfway up a precarious hill with the palms of her gloves punctured by thorns, and about to run into the enemy. She swallowed it for later. "Yeah, let's make them pay for Andresen."

Bernie wasn't expecting to find anyone home in the cave. If it didn't have a rear exit they hadn't spotted, then it was a place where you could only get trapped, because even the most direct path to it was a long, steep slog. On the other hand, it was a good place to lay up undetected.

And the Stranded had to stash their explosives somewhere close. Fertilizer bombs were bulky. If you had to move around on foot, you needed caches close to your targets.

Marcus scrambled onto the shelf of rocky soil where the hill leveled off. They'd come up at the side of the cave entrance. Bernie caught Mac by the scruff and put the leash back on him before he ventured in.

He'd definitely scented something. He stared unblinking into the shadows, back legs shifting impatiently like a sprinter on his blocks. Bernie gave Marcus a thumbs-up.

Marcus jerked his head toward the entrance. *Send the dog in.*

Bernie's first thought was to hang on to Mac until they knew what they were dealing with. She crouched to follow him into a low space, leash wrapped around her left hand. She could let him loose and grab the rifle two-handed if they ran into trouble.

Ricochets. Shit. Can't fire in a small space like this.

But that was what the chainsaw bayonet was for. Combined with a dog, it made her feel invulnerable. The explosion that had nearly killed her felt like it had happened to someone else—for the moment. Adrenaline was a wonderful thing.

Baird squeezed past her. She tried to elbow him out of the way before it occurred to her that he was moving forward to cover a right-hand fork in the passage. She patted his shoulder in silent apology. This wasn't the public kiss-my-arse Baird.

And, somehow, it wasn't pitch-black in here, either. As her eyes adjusted, she could see Baird's scrubby blond hair lit up like a faint halo by dim light. It wasn't from their armor indicator lights. There had to be other vents in the rock here.

A hand grabbed her shoulder and she almost shat herself before she realized it was Marcus.

"*Smell*," he whispered.

The faint odor she inhaled was a cross between a greasy diner and a cow shed—old fat, burned meat, and a hint of animal shit. There was a metallic rasp as Baird pulled something out of his belt.

"Go," Marcus said.

Now it was down to the dog. As soon as Bernie snapped the leash from his collar, he shot into the tunnel and vanished. Marcus went after him. The passage was too narrow and uneven for running, and Bernie stumbled a couple of times. Baird grabbed her webbing and hauled her upright. The diffuse light was getting brighter; she expected to hear barking and firing any second, and glanced down to check that her chainsaw indicator light was on, but she could now see what looked like a bright chamber at the end of the tunnel. Marcus stood silhouetted in the light.

"Nobody cough," he said.

Baird edged past Bernie again and looked over Marcus's shoulder. "Hey, talk about overkill. Look out for a trip wire. Bernie? Careful where you put your boots . . ."

The chamber looked so regular that at first she thought it had been built that way, but it was natural, a void left by lava. There was an opening at the top like a chimney. And most of the space was filled with old fuel drums and other rusty containers. It took her a few seconds to add it all up and realize the Stranded were making nitrate bombs, or at least storing the stuff here.

"They can't have gone far." Marcus poked around the floor with slow care. "Warm ashes."

"Where's Mac?" Bernie asked.

Marcus pointed down the continuation of the natural tunnel. Baird started examining the haul, crawling around the stacked drums as if the risk didn't apply to him.

"I don't see wires on most of these," Baird said. "But that doesn't mean we're not five seconds away from being ground beef."

The element of surprise was gone now, and locating this stuff at least meant that it wouldn't be used against the COG. But Mac was still on the trail. Bernie set off after the dog, suddenly aware of bruises and pulled muscles every time she stooped to negotiate the twists in the rock. Marcus followed her.

"Great, you're leaving me babysitting the explosives?" Baird called.

"Come on," Marcus said. "When we get a radio signal again, call it in to Control."

"Can you hear a Raven?"

Bernie couldn't hear anything over her own ragged breathing now. Sorotki had their position. Shit, if he was hovering overhead now, and those bastards were making a run for it—or maybe they were already an hour away, already in some other hideout. It looked like there was another way out of the honeycomb of passages under the hill. Mac hadn't come back.

Now she was relying completely on the faint light from three sets of armor. For a stomach-churning moment, she wondered how the hell they'd find their way out again if they hit a dead end. Somehow she'd never worried about that while going after grubs. Fear didn't bother with logic.

And Andresen's gone.

She kept forgetting the news, and then remembering it again every time her attention wandered from the task at hand.

Bastards.

Suddenly the ground reared up in front of her and became a

rocky slope. And yes, there was light ahead, getting brighter with every step she took.

"It'll be a frigging sheer drop," Baird muttered. His voice didn't even echo. "Anyone consider whether those assholes had *another* route out to the front door?"

"Trust the dog," Bernie panted. She could definitely hear the chattering rotors of a helicopter now. God, she was running out of steam fast. "Most recent traces—probably the strongest scent."

Marcus grunted. "Hey, we got comms again. Sorotki, can you hear me?"

Mitchell answered. "Loud and clear. No visual on you, but we can see the dog."

"We're still in a tunnel. Call the engineers to clear a cache of explosives in there. Can you set down anywhere?"

"Small patch of grass at the base of the hill. I'll aim for the pooch. Two-Three-Nine out."

Bernie scrambled out into bright daylight, and a dense mass of waist-high thornbushes that snagged the exposed fabric of her pants. The Stranded gang didn't have armor, so they must have been shredded to hell escaping through here—and that meant blood, skin, and sweat traces for Mac to follow. No wonder he was excited.

"Sorotki? The dog's still tracking." Marcus waded through the bushes, finger pressed to his earpiece. The Raven dropped onto long grass at the foot of the slope. "We'll continue on foot and narrow down the search area for an aerial recon." He looked at Bernie for a second as if he was weighing up her reaction. "Stand by to extract Mataki if necessary. She should have been casevacked hours ago."

Bernie grabbed Mac as he raced back to her. *If I stop now, I won't get up again.* "What've you got, fella?" She put the leash on him. "*Seek!* Good boy."

The dog nearly wrenched her arm from its socket in his frenzy to resume the chase. It was like water-skiing on rubble. Her spine jolted with every stride. Mac followed the line of the trees, head-

ing deeper into the woods, where the Raven couldn't see what
was happening on the ground.

"Can't expect the assholes to make it easy for us." Baird jogged
alongside her without so much as panting, reminding her what it
was to be young and fit. "Might be leading us into an ambush."
Maybe he was chatting to keep her going. But the more stressed
he was, the yappier he tended to get. "Except they'd have made it
easier to follow."

The Stranded had to be on foot. They couldn't run their
junkers through woodland like this. And vehicles were too noisy
for covert action here—four-wheelers, at least.

The radio clicked. "Byrne to KR-Two-Three-Nine, I'm in your
grid. Want an assist, Lieutenant?"

"Two-Three-Nine to Byrne, you got the bike?"

"Yeah. Just direct me. I can get pretty well anywhere on this.
Byrne out."

Rat bikes could handle dense woodland. And if Sam wanted to
teach Baird a lesson, this was as good a time as any to do it. Mac
dragged Bernie for another hard kilometer. She knew exactly how
far it was because Marcus was keeping up a running sitrep on
their position for Sorotki.

"They're heading for the river," Marcus said. "I don't think
that's going to fool the dog."

"Delta, I've lost visual on you again," Mitchell said.

"Two-Three-Nine, go ahead of us—north—and come back
down the course of the river. If the dog's on the right track, then
they might be moving along it—*in* it."

"Two-Three-Nine to Byrne," Mitchell said. "Sam, are you getting this?"

"I'm about five klicks north of you. Moving in."

Bernie caught a glimpse of the Raven's strobing rotors through
the tree canopy as it crossed from right to left, then the engine
noise faded into the distance. Marcus kept pace with Bernie, but
that pace was getting slower by the minute. He held out his hand.

"Give me the damn leash," he said.

"Leave the dog to me."

"You're going to drop."

"I'm not bloody Anya," Bernie snapped. "Stop nursemaiding me."

In the heat of the moment, Gears said all kinds of shit to each other. It was just adrenaline. Bernie regretted it the instant she said it, but she'd have to save her apologies for later. Baird was to her right, jogging about ten meters parallel to her. There'd come a point where she had to let Mac loose, but she needed to be much closer to his quarry first, and nobody knew just how fresh this trail was—except Mac. He was acting as if he could see something she couldn't. Maybe he could hear it. By the time they reached the river, he was practically walking on his hind legs, and she struggled to hold him. The leash was wound so tight around her hand that her fingers were numb.

"Sorotki's on his strafing run," Baird said. The Raven was getting louder again, heading back toward them. "Listen."

"Better not be," Marcus said. "*Alive*, remember?"

Then Mac stopped and cast around, throwing his head up from time to time. He edged down to the water—shallow, fast-moving over a pebble bed—and stood with his nose pointing upstream for a moment before lunging forward on the leash. He'd been trained to hunt silently but his excitement was forcing little squeals out of him. Marcus turned his head slowly as if he was scanning the trees, but Bernie got the feeling he was just keeping a cautious eye on Mac. He'd even been wary of the sheepdogs at Jonty's farm. She found herself filling in gaps again as she caught her breath, wondering where Marcus might have run into a dog that made him mistrust them all that much.

"Your asshole-hound's telling us they went in the river *there*," Baird said, wading across to the other bank. The water was knee high. "Or else we've been chasing a frigging aquatic *rabbit*."

Marcus gestured to Baird to cross to the other bank and move forward. Bernie was sure she could hear the sporadic revving of a bike. Sound carried for a long way out here. There was a moment of absolute quiet broken only by everyone's breathing, and then Sorotki's voice came on the radio.

"Got a visual," he said. "Yeah, in the river. Actually *in* the river. Whoa, there they go. Three adult males, moving up the south bank—your *left*, Delta—and armed. I'm coming around again to drop Cole and Dom."

Byrne cut in. "I'm on it, Two-Three-Nine."

"I see you, Byrne. Head green thirty."

The Raven looped and came straight back down the line of the river at full throttle. There was a loud crack, and Mitchell reacted: "Hey, did that bastard fire at us?"

"Confirmed, they've got rifles. Lost them now. They've gone under some trees. Okay, stand by—turning again. Then I'm dropping off."

Bernie's focus was cut to an instant, narrow intensity. She'd never done anything like this with the cattle dogs on the farm back home. Whatever they chased didn't pack a rifle. As Baird splashed across the stream to follow Marcus, Mac scrabbled up the bank and almost pulled her off her feet.

"Okay, dog *loose*," she said. "Delta, Two-Three-Nine, Byrne— I'm letting him go, so watch for him." She fumbled for the clip on his collar, rehearsing the commands Will Berenz had given her. "Fix 'em, Mac. Go on. *Fix.*"

The dog was gone in a second. He was a big animal with a long stride, and he went off like a rocket. There was no way anything on two legs—not even Cole—was going to keep up with him. She simply jogged along, exhausted, trying to keep Marcus and Baird in sight, and knew she should have stuck to being a sniper. Her adrenaline was already ebbing, replaced by a shaky tearfulness that she'd never finish that card game with Andresen now, and a few mental flash-frames of her husband griping about her never being home on leave when he really needed her help on the farm. She hadn't thought about the bastard in a long time.

"I'm bettin' on that puppy." Cole's voice boomed in her earpiece. "He's a natural born racin' hound."

Cole always managed to snap her out of it, whether he planned to or not. "Where are you, Cole Train?"

"On your right, Boomer Lady, comin' through the trees."

Bernie was a long way behind now. The Raven was circling high over the open ground between the patches of woodland, with Mitchell calling directions.

"They've split," he said. "One's heading back to the river and two are making for the woods."

The rest of the noise in Bernie's earpiece was ragged breathing and disjointed words. "Cole, Dom—take north." That was Marcus. "Baird—you take the guy in the brown coat."

Now the ground dipped away a little, and Bernie caught sight of the dog pelting through knee-high grass on an intercept line with the other two Stranded. Then they parted in opposite directions. If they thought splitting up would confuse Mac, it didn't work. The dog was set on his prey—the guy in brown—and he jinked left like he was closing in on a rabbit. Baird was about fifty meters behind him. Then Mac put on a sudden spurt. Bernie found her second wind and started running again.

It was almost impossible for Bernie to take in the sequence, and not just because she felt her eyes were being shaken out of their sockets with every stride. The Stranded guy slowed, turned, and tried to level his rifle to aim. But the dog was racing at fifty kilometers an hour and simply launched himself into the air about four meters out. It was like watching a missile hit a ship broadside. Mac smashed into the man at chest height and knocked him flat. The rifle didn't matter a damn to a dog.

Bernie couldn't tell where Mac had sunk his teeth, but now that he'd pinned his prey down he was getting stuck in. The man was screaming, curled up in a ball. This wasn't a police dog carefully trained to seize a specific limb and hang on. Mac didn't know what an arrest meant.

The other Stranded guy stopped, took a few paces backward— he had a handgun—and seemed to realize he couldn't get a clear shot at the dog. Was he going to abandon his buddy? He lost crucial seconds. He hesitated, then aimed as Marcus ran at him yelling at him to drop the weapon. Marcus really was going to try to take the guy alive, the crazy bastard. He was going to get killed. No Stranded was worth that.

"Drop him!" Bernie yelled. "For fuck's sake—"

She stopped to aim her Lancer but in the second it took, she saw a blur of blackened metal shoot out of the trees behind the guy and cannon into him so hard that he lifted bodily into the air. The thud was sickening. The noise of the bike seemed to follow later. Sam Byrne skidded out of control, tearing up grass and soil, but righted herself and circled the bike to a halt by the man's body. She was on him in a second with her chainsaw to his throat.

"*Shit,*" Marcus said. "Did you have to?"

"Yes, I *did.* He had a clear shot at you, and you were going to *tackle* him like some thrashball game." Sam felt for a pulse, then looked up, indignant. "See? He's not dead."

Marcus checked for himself. "Let's get him on the Raven."

But the screaming went on. For a moment Bernie thought it was the man Sam had run down. But it was the one Mac was still busy savaging. Baird hovered uncertainly, trying to break it up.

"Shit, Bernie, how do I call off this thing?" Baird panted. It surprised her that he wasn't just standing there applauding the dog's technique. "He's *killing* this asshole."

"Say *out.*" She tried to yell a command that Mac would hear, but her lungs could only handle so much at once. "*Out. It's out.*"

This is how I'm going to die. Trying to keep up with men half my frigging age. And a bloody dog.

By the time she reached Mac, she could see the blood. Baird was yelling "Out!" and the dog had stopped shaking and tearing, but his jaws were now clamped tight on the man's shoulder. *That was nearly me. Wasn't it?* She'd once been exactly where this man was. Only armor and fellow Gears with chainsaw bayonets had saved her.

"Mac, *out*! Leave! Drop him!" Bernie went through every command she'd used with her cattle dogs in the hope that something would trigger him to stand down. "Leave it! Down! *Off!*"

Mac lifted his head and backed away, clearly reluctant. But he did it. He even came to heel. The Stranded bomber was moaning and trying to curl up in a ball.

Marcus moved in to check him over. He let out a long breath. "Sorotki? Mitchell? We've got *two* casevacs now."

"That's . . . the . . . idea." Bernie gasped for breath, bent over with her hands braced on her hips. Her legs were shaking with the effort. "Deterrent."

Mac looked as if he was deciding between going back in to finish the job and waiting for praise. He even wagged his tail and looked up into her face: *Am I a good boy? This is what you wanted, right?* It was sobering to see that wonderful, adoring, anything-to-please-you expression with blood around the muzzle.

"Yeah, good boy." She managed to suck in some more air. Tomorrow was going to hurt. "You got him."

Sporadic fire rattled in the near distance. Dom and Cole must have pinned down the third man. Mitchell jogged toward Marcus clutching a small red plastic case and knelt down to examine the Stranded. The guy who'd been run down was unconscious. The one Mac had caught was awake and making that thin, animal wailing sound of someone in shock.

"Shit. What's your name, buddy? Can you hear me?" Mitchell didn't get an answer. "That thing nearly ripped his scalp off."

"You bastards," the man said suddenly. "You *bastards*. You're worse than the fucking grubs."

That seemed to hit a nerve with Marcus. Bernie could feel his distaste again—the gradual turn of the head like a slow-motion shake, the long blink as he shut his eyes for a moment. It never felt like it was aimed directly at her. It seemed more like his general disgust at human excess seeped out of him some days.

"Our doctor's going to treat you right alongside the Gears you blew up," Marcus said. "So shut it."

He turned his back and stood with his eyes closed, talking quietly to Control. He didn't seem happy with the answers he was getting, and looked over his shoulder at Bernie.

"What?" she said.

"These guys are a special delivery for Trescu. I don't think he's planning to bake them a cake."

"Ah." Bernie had a pretty good idea of Gorasnaya's old reputation. "Whose idea was that?"

"Not Hoffman's, if that's what's worrying you."

"Come on, Sam." Mitchell straightened up, first aid finished. "Give me a hand. Let's get this chew toy back to Doc Hayman and make her day."

Dom and Cole reappeared, dragging the third man between them. Actually, he wasn't a man. Up close, he looked about fifteen, if that. Bernie had stopped seeing kids as noncombatants a long time ago, but it still brought her up short.

"Get your fucking hands off me," he spat, all terrified bravado. "Where's my dad? I want my dad. What have you done to him?"

Everyone has a dad. Even monsters. It doesn't change a thing. His dad is blowing up my mates. And so is he.

It still wasn't easy to ignore. But seeing the enemy's point of view didn't end a war any faster than reducing them to monsters. It just made it harder for her to get the job done.

Bernie hung back with Marcus while the others loaded to the Raven. Only the dog would hear what she said to him now. And Mac was too busy licking himself.

"Look," she said. "A dog tearing you apart isn't any more immoral than a land mine shredding you. It's all dirty either way. They didn't stop to worry if Andresen had a family."

Marcus was expressionless. "You think it's okay to hand them over to Trescu?"

"These bastards have moral choices too." Bernie didn't know. She didn't even want to think about it right then. "It's not our sole responsibility."

"But you'd feel better if it was an honest firefight."

"I feel better if I'm not frigging *dead*," Bernie said. "And so would Jonty, if they hadn't cut his throat. One-sided rules of engagement are for lawyers."

Marcus gave her that here-we-go-again look. Yes, they'd had this argument before, about what actually survived if you were prepared to do anything to stay alive. It had to be a constant and painful dilemma for a man whose father helped incinerate most of Sera to save it.

"Got to envy that dog," Marcus said, walking away.

Mac trotted after them, a nice friendly dog again. Bernie tapped her leg to bring him to heel. "Yes. He lives in the moment."

"I meant that he sees everything in black and white," Marcus said, and jogged off.

CHAPTER 4

You're going to be an officer, Hoffman. No fraternization with the ranks. It's time to stop seeing that Islander woman.

(MAJOR ROSS HOLLEND OF EAST BARRICADE ACADEMY, TO STAFF
SERGEANT VICTOR HOFFMAN, ON HIS ACCEPTANCE FOR LATE-
ENTRY OFFICER TRAINING)

FORMER UIR PATROL VESSEL *AMIRALE ENKA*,
VECTES NAVAL BASE, NEW JACINTO: 0600
HOURS, THREE DAYS LATER.

Sam looked up at the heavily patched Gorasni patrol boat from the jetty. "You a good swimmer, Baird? 'Cos I'm not."

"Hey, they've only lost *one* warship under completely inexplicable conditions," Baird said. "It's just a day trip. Enjoy the bracing air. Learn the strange ways of the sea from these colorful old salts."

The old salts—a bunch of Gorasni seamen—were leaning on the ship's gunwale, staring down, surly and silent. One of them was munching something with slow deliberation like a cow chewing the cud. He paused and spat over the side into the water.

Byrne strode up the brow. "What's the Gorasni for *up yours?*"

"Just smile. These guys haven't seen a woman in years. They'll never know the difference."

"I just want you to know that Bernie gave me orders to punch you out if you asked me to go find the golden rivet."

Baird wondered if Sam just mouthed off out of embarrassment. It bothered him more than it should have, because sometimes he caught himself doing the same thing.

"Just maternal affection," he said. "I'm the wayward, maladjusted son she always wanted to nag to death."

Baird followed Sam up the brow. He had to admit the bike stunt was a pretty good move, and he didn't blame her for using the first weapon that came to hand, even if it did have two wheels. But if he told her so, he'd never hear the end of it. And it sounded a bit too close to approving of female Gears. He kept his praise to himself.

Dom came up behind him. "Don't start any fights you can't finish," he said. "Cole Train's not here to rescue you."

Baird did feel lost without Cole, and he didn't need to admit it. But he felt more disoriented by being teamed with Dom. Things worked certain unspoken ways in four-man squads, and it was always Marcus and Dom, or Cole and Baird, or even Cole and Marcus, but rarely Baird and Dom. Baird couldn't make small talk with Dom even before all the shit with his wife, so he had no idea how the hell he was going to manage now.

Dom wouldn't expect him to, of course. Baird could retreat into the socially inept smart-ass role he'd built for himself. It solved a lot of problems.

"Dom, just tell me why we get all the job-shadow kids," he said.

"Because we're the number-one pirate-slaying team." Dom was all weary patience. He seemed to have withered into middle age in a matter of months. Life had finally kicked all that perky optimism out of him. "Look, Sam's been a Gear as long as you have. You went through all this crap with Bernie, too, and now you kiss her ass. Just grow out of it before Sam does some special Kashkuri needlework on you."

"She's not going to put any of her frigging tattoos on *me*."

"Not talking about ink, Baird . . ."

"What?"

"Ask Hoffman. A chat we had once, about some of the things he saw in Kashkur during the war. Nasty."

Baird was instantly consumed by morbid curiosity. "You're just trying to freak me."

Dom shrugged and said nothing. One of the Gorasni crewmen diverted the conversation by greeting them with an outstretched grimy hand. Baird hesitated before taking it, then jerked his thumb over his shoulder at Sam.

"And this is Private Byrne," he said. "She's here to cook and swab the decks."

Sam clenched her jaw. It wasn't for effect; it was too brief. Baird could see that she didn't want him to know he could get to her, but it was too late for that. Now he knew the trigger. He'd use it when he had to.

It was just self-defense, nothing more. He wasn't bullying her.

"Corporal Baird likes hospital food," she said. The Gorasni looked her over and didn't make it to eye level. "And *you'll* learn to like it if you check me out one more time, Indie boy."

The guy bowed with a flourish and indicated the foredeck. "Our humble ship is yours, *duchashka*. I shall keep my unworthy eyes to myself."

Baird reminded himself to stop assuming the Indies didn't understand what was being said to them just because they gabbled away in their own language most of the time. Despite himself, he almost liked their attitude. And the trawlers weren't going to spend weeks away like factory ships. Baird decided it wouldn't be so bad being stuck in this tub for a couple of days if the Gorasni provided some amusement. It was a run-down boat. There'd be plenty of interesting new Indie stuff to dismantle and fix, and he could lose himself in that for hours. CPO Muller was in charge. He'd let Baird nose around even if the Gorasni crewmen didn't like it.

Yeah, a bit of diversion. But I'd rather be capping assholes back on the island.

The boat vibrated as it picked up speed and made its way out of the basin into open water. The sun was coming up, the overnight rain had stopped, and the thinning clouds showed all the makings of a nice day. In a couple of hours, they'd be on station in the fishing grounds to keep a watch on the small trawler fleet in case of another pirate attack. All in all, it was a routine day.

Baird leaned on the control panel in the wheelhouse and scanned the horizon through binoculars. The Gorasni helmsman just looked at him, nodded silently, and went back to staring dead ahead at the bow with one hand on the wheel. Sam had taken up position on the gun mounted on the foredeck without being asked. Dom wandered up to chat with her for a while and then came back inside to check the radar.

He leaned on the console next to Baird. "Don't you think it's kind of sick that we're taking care of those Stranded guys until they're fit enough for Trescu to beat the shit out of them? Because that's what's going to happen."

Baird shrugged. "Yeah. Total waste of medical resources. And are those assholes in the same ward as our guys? Now that *is* sick."

"I meant—ah, forget it."

"What? What did I say?"

The Gorasni helmsman grunted. "Waste, all right. Better to ask them questions while they still *hurt*."

If Dom wanted a discussion on rules of engagement, he'd picked the wrong time. "Okay, I'll leave you and your new buddy to discuss morality," he said. "I just think it's *wrong*."

"Don't mind him," Baird said to the helmsman. "He's the nice guy. I'm the realist."

Some things had been a lot easier when the grubs were around. Baird hadn't had the time—or the option—to think about anything beyond making it through the day alive. He'd been scared shitless. Now he was finding he missed that clarity. What else did he expect? Fighting Locust had taken up nearly half his life. Things were still pretty rough even though the grubs were gone, but in a different, less urgent way.

All I wanted to do was engineering. Join the army or kiss your inheritance good-bye, Dad said. So I gave in. And what did I get? A shitload of grubs while the family fortune went up in smoke.

And now Baird had come full circle. He got what he'd wished for—everyone thought he was God's gift to engineering. And what did he feel was missing? Pissing himself with fear. He didn't *want* to go through all that again. He was just conscious of its absence in a way that made him feel restless. His father would have given him that I-told-you-so smile. His mother would have told him he was congenitally ungrateful.

So what the fuck do I want? And why?

Frank Muller came into the wheelhouse. "Oilfish," he said flatly. "The trawlers have found shitloads of oilfish. All this fuss for a sandwich filling." Muller's buzz-cut hair revealed an old white scar running from his left ear to the crown of his head. "Come on, do the magic shit with the radar, will you? Every time we use the comms, it scrambles. Can't isolate the fault."

"Shielding, crappy wiring, corrosion." This was simple stuff for Baird. He loved it when the dim kids watched him slack-jawed like he was performing a miracle. He took a screwdriver from his belt and began removing the inspection panel. "Okay, switch it off. Might need to cannibalize something else when we get back to replace bits, though."

The helmsman squatted down to stare Baird in the eye. "*Blondie,*" he said. "They call you Blondie because you are blond, yes? Well, I am Yanik, Blondie, and they call me that because I will *yanik* your intestines if you mess with my ship."

Baird thought an unblinking response would get on Yanik's best side. "Thanks for the language lesson." He carried on unscrewing the plate. "I'm *improving* this wreck. And only Mataki gets to call me *Blondie.*"

They really didn't like anyone poking around in their stuff. Muller leaned over and pointed at Baird. "Give him a paper clip and a ball of string and he can turn this wreck into a fucking racing yacht. Let him do his stuff."

Yeah. Right. That's me. I can do anything.

Baird was satisfied by that. And it was always good to know who was smart enough to understand what he could do. He poked his way into the tangle of cables and began tracing the wiring harness, working out which cables he could swap over to test where the interference was happening. It wasn't cutting-edge tech. The hardest part was getting into spaces and rummaging through tool lockers to find parts he could adapt to make new connections. He had to take off his upper body armor to squeeze into gaps, and he realized how naked that made him feel.

When he ran the diagnostics, the radar fired up exactly as he expected. He watched the display as Muller made a test transmission.

"Steady as a *rock*." Yanik peered over his shoulder. "So, Blondie-Baird, we let you live. For now." He winked conspiratorially. "Maybe we even let you mess with our ship again."

Muller watched the screen for a few moments. "Keep an eye on this while I go below to see if the engineer's strangled anyone yet. If you see anything that wasn't there before—give me a shout."

Muller didn't give Baird any instructions. Even with the radar controls labeled in another language, Baird could work it out from basics. Any idiot could do that. He could see the five points of yellow light flaring and fading every time the radar swept around, showing returns from the trawlers. He could see the clutter generated by waves. A radar was a radar was a radar.

Dom wandered back in. "Glad we got one of our own Marlins stowed. I wouldn't send Mataki's dog out in one of their inflatables."

"I would," Baird said. The more he saw of Gorasnaya's remaining fleet—a tanker, a submarine, six patrol boats—the more he realized that the snazzy submarine had been window dressing. All the Indie bastards really had to offer was that imulsion rig. Maybe the frigate had been the jewel of the fleet before the thing sank, but he doubted it. "That animal's psychotic. They do say dogs take after their handlers."

The put-down just slipped out, like it always did. It also reopened the topic of the captured Stranded bombers, and where nice civilized people drew the line in how roughly they treated assholes who deserved everything they got.

"I bet Marcus had something to say about it," Baird said, not needing to specify what *it* was.

"You know Marcus." Dom shut his eyes for a second as if he'd remembered something he should have done, frowning slightly. "He likes to do the right thing."

Yanik the entrail-remover eased the wheel fifteen degrees to starboard. "This Marcus . . . enemies do not respect you for doing *right*. They think you a weak fool, and then they *kill you*."

Yanik could certainly kill a conversation. It turned into a long morning. Sam stayed on the gun, leaning on it with one arm resting on the guard like she wouldn't give it up to a mere man without a fight. *Amirale Enka* was now in the middle of the fishing grounds, and Baird could see a couple of the fifteen-meter trawlers even without binoculars—little toy-like white hulls with bright red and blue wheelhouses. They seemed to be on a winning streak, judging by the radio chatter with Muller.

One of the boats—*Trilliant*—radioed in. "Jackpot, *Enka*. We'll be full to capacity in six hours."

Muller picked up the mike. "Copy that, *Trilliant*. How much catch is that?"

"Close to a hundred tonnes."

"Everyone better like oilfish, then."

Baird checked through the binoculars. The nearest trawler was drawing her net, a huge writhing ball of silver. Both the radar and the lookout confirmed a complete absence of pirates. Baird wasn't heartened by that. If it wasn't about lack of fuel—and they never seemed to be short of it—then they were just biding their time and waiting for a better opportunity to attack.

"Sam's going to be disappointed." He put the binoculars down and checked the radar again. "We'll have to find her some land-based scum to shoot up."

Muller took the remains of a cigar from behind his ear and lit it. "See, girls fight dirty. My mother warned me." The radio circuit buzzed with the voices of trawlermen sorting their catch for the freezer, discussing shale eels and commenting on some fish that had to be from the abyssal trench. "I can't stand oilfish. Have they caught any lobsters?"

"Imagine having this conversation a year ago," Dom said. "We'd have eaten the net and been grateful."

"I still don't get why they shot up *Harvest*. They need the hulls as much as we do."

"Do we know how many of the locals have firearms? I know they don't have—"

Dom was interrupted by a muffled boom like a distant roll of thunder. They all looked around at the same time to see a column of black smoke rising from the sea about five klicks away to the port side. Sam swung the gun around and lined up on it.

"That was more than just a fuel tank," she yelled. "Trust me on that."

Muller didn't give a helm order, but *Amirale Enka*'s motors roared to life as the Gorasni guy simply pushed the throttle hard forward and aimed for the smoke. The collision alarm sounded. The radio net went crazy as the trawlers tried to raise one another. "It's *Levanto*," a voice kept saying. "Look, she's gone, it's *Levanto*, I saw her damn well go."

"*Shit*," Muller said. Crew appeared on the deck from nowhere. "What the fuck's happening? Who's out there?"

"Nothing on radar, nothing on sonar," said the helmsman. "*Nothing*."

"What if it's bloody *mines*?" Baird said.

Muller must have thought of that even if the helmsman hadn't. And here they were, making full speed into what might be a mined area.

"*Enka* to all trawlers, hold your positions," he said. "Don't move until we know what we're dealing with. We're on our way." He turned to Baird and flicked the radio to receive-only. "It's too deep for bottom mines, and I can't see a bunch of pirates being able to lay tethered ones."

"What if it's a drift mine?" Baird asked. "Some shit left over from the Pendulum Wars? Contact mines. A plastic hull wouldn't save you from that."

Muller leaned out of the port-side door. "Hey, Lookout—keep an eye open for surface mines. Nothing on sonar, but that doesn't mean shit in this tub."

"So we're heading into it at fifty knots," Baird said. "Great." But there wasn't a lot of choice. He switched on his radio earpiece and went onto the deck.

Sam gestured imperiously at the wheelhouse. "Dom? Dom, take the gun. I want to go and see this."

"Leave it to me," Baird said.

"Hey, I'm the ordnance expert, genius. I've done mines. You just drive the rubber boat and leave the explosives stuff to me."

"Y'know, I prefer Mataki. She eats cats and she's *still* classier than you."

"Tough shit. You got me."

Dom came out on deck and took up the gun position. *Amirale Enka* was almost on top of the trawler fleet now. The boats had taken no notice of the order to stay put. One was chugging steadily toward *Levanto*'s last position, now marked only by smoke hanging in the air, but Baird could see nothing left to burn. There was something bobbing on the surface. It looked more like a fuel slick.

Muller's voice came over his earpiece. "All stop . . . Okay, everything's clear, Baird. No mines that we can detect—nothing. Not for thirty klicks. You can launch the Marlin now."

Baird swung the inflatable into the water and held it on the line while Sam climbed in.

"Can't be a sub, can it?" she said. "Wouldn't be the first to pop up and surprise us."

Baird was about to remind her that the sonar had drawn a blank, but seeing how the Indie submarine *Zephyr* had gone undetected until she was almost up the COG's ass, he wasn't so sure.

I'm shit-scared again. Got my wish. Great.

They moved into a thin mat of drifting debris made up of pieces so small that it was hard to identify them as a boat. Sam propped her Lancer on the gunwale one-handed to reach into the water. She scooped up some pieces in her palm and peered at them.

Baird was looking for bodies. He was also watching out for drifting mines, keeping one of the Marlin's oars within easy reach.

"We should be seeing chunks," Sam said. "Even if you swallow a grenade, you still get chunks. Not confetti."

"Shit, maybe they hauled up a mine with the catch."

"Well, you better tell 'em to ditch their catch and get the hell out," Sam said. "But I still don't think this is an old mine."

Sam was still staring at the contents of her palm. Baird looked around to see *Trilliant* bearing down on the Marlin, close enough now for him to read the name on the bow.

Sam looked around at the surface of a vast ocean with no enemy in sight. Then she looked over the side, and Baird knew what she was thinking—that whatever lurked down there could be as deadly as grubs that erupted from solid ground.

"If this is the Stranded," she said, "we're in deep shit."

ISOLATION WING, VECTES NAVAL BASE INFIRMARY.

Doctor Hayman shut the ward door behind her and stared into Hoffman's face.

"Unless your Gorasni chum has a bunch of flowers and some grapes, I don't want him in my hospital," she said. "Those men are *patients*. Assholes or not."

Hoffman factored Hayman-wrangling time into his day. The old girl knew her stuff, but she was hard work.

"Those men gave you a ward full of blast injuries," he said. "I think that entitles us to ask a few questions."

"If you expect me to put these men back together again when you've mangled them, then you'll damn well abide by my medical decisions."

"And the next time your emergency room fills up with my Gears, and they end up like Mathieson, you'll be fine with that, will you?" It was a cheap shot. He knew how much amputations distressed her. He also knew it would work. "Let me do my job, and maybe you won't have to do so much of *yours*."

"You're a bastard, Hoffman. You really are."

Hayman was in her seventies, but age hadn't mellowed her into a sweet old lady. Hoffman had to think hard to remember her first name; she was just Doc Hayman, and if he hadn't seen her records, he would never have known she was called Isabel. She definitely didn't look like an Isabel.

"And I'm a bastard who wants an end to this," he said. "So are they well enough to talk to Trescu?"

"Depends how he's going to question them." Hayman fumbled in the pocket of her lab coat and pulled out a half-smoked cheroot. "You've got any number of people capable of interrogating them. Why Trescu?"

"Prescott's orders."

"Hand-washing, more like. My job still has some ethical demands. I don't patch people up for others to damage them all over again."

"That's all military medicine is, Doc."

"You know damn well what I mean. I expect you to make sure these patients aren't tortured. You're not a brute, Hoffman, for all your bluster."

Hoffman wasn't sure if he was a brute or not. He'd done things he regretted, terrible things, some entirely of his own volition. If he made some principled stand and refused to be party to this session, then Trescu would do it anyway, with Prescott's blessing.

I went through this over the Hammer of Dawn. Same argument. Same excuse. If I didn't do it, someone else would. Better to be a man and front up.

So the two Stranded would get a good hiding. They'd probably get the same from any of Andresen's buddies, too. If it meant he never lost another man like Andresen, Hoffman could live with it.

"Fine, wait until they recover," he said. "You get a clear conscience. But they get the same end result. Except in the meantime, you might see more patients with their goddamn legs blown off or worse."

Hayman stuck the cheroot in her mouth unlit. It didn't go with the white coat. However bad things got, she always managed to keep that coat bleached to a pristine whiteness. It was shiny with wear in places, and frayed at the cuffs, but by God it was *white*, and Hoffman never knew if it was just an act of professional reassurance for the patient in a grubby, primitive world, or some kind of manifestation of her need to erase something. But he didn't have time to analyze all that shit. He had enough invisible stains of his own to worry about.

"Okay, I'm as bad as Prescott. Salving my conscience. Self-delusion." Hayman patted her pockets for a light and started walking down the corridor toward the exit. Then she turned. "Oh, and your lady friend—retire the poor bitch or give her a desk job before she gets herself killed. I know these South Islanders are tough native stock, but they die just like the rest of us."

"Don't sugarcoat it, Doc," Hoffman muttered. "Say what you mean."

Hoffman didn't like the idea of Bernie risking her neck, but forcing her off the front line would break her heart. Worse, in fact; the idea terrified her, like it was the beginning of the end, and he knew it. He asked himself if he'd have retired a man of her age, or even a woman he wasn't emotionally attached to, and the answer was—shit, he didn't know. All he knew was that he couldn't do it to Bernie and that she deserved better from him.

He waited outside the ward door, reading through the note that one of the medics had left for him. The Stranded bomb makers were Edwin Loris—the one Sam Byrne had given a fractured pelvis, two cracked ribs, and concussion—and Mikail Enador, who was doing pretty well for a man who'd been half-eaten by that rabid mutt. Enador's son, Nial, was unhurt but terrified. All the medic had been able to get out of the three of them was their names. But Hoffman had already asked Dizzy Wallin to keep an eye on the Stranded community inside the wire to see who their friends or family members might be. It made sense to know who the grudge-bearers were.

I ought to leave you to clear up your own shit, Prescott.

But Hoffman didn't. He couldn't walk away from anything. Then his radio crackled in his ear. It was Anya.

"Sir, we've lost another fishing vessel. There's been an explosion—all hands lost. Baird's reporting no visible signs of attack, but he doesn't think it's a stray mine."

"Does Pelruan know yet?" Hoffman asked. The civvies in the

small town—the island's *only* town—wouldn't take the news well. It was the second trawler lost from a tiny fleet in a few months, more trouble brought to their door by the arrival of the COG. "I'm going to have some explaining to do to Lewis Gavriel."

"Oh, they know," Anya said. "The trawler fleet always stays in radio contact with Pelruan."

Shit. "Get hold of Gavriel and tell him I'll come and see him as soon as I'm done here. Have you told the Chairman?"

"You needed to know first, sir. I'll get a briefing note together for you."

What a loyal kid. "Thanks, Anya."

How the hell are they doing this? What have they got that we don't know about?

Hoffman's first thought was another submarine. Nobody who'd been caught with their pants around their ankles when Trescu's *Zephyr* popped up would ever rule that out. But boats like that took a lot of maintenance, and if the Stranded gangs could manage to run one, then they were a much bigger problem than he'd imagined.

He paced slowly down the echoing corridor and back again while waiting for Trescu to show, inhaling an institutional smell of carbolic soap, decay, and misery. He could shut out the smells. But the nagging voice getting louder in his head was a tougher irritant to ignore.

Trescu's testing Prescott, and Prescott knows it. A pissant tribe just a fraction of the size of the COG. If Prescott wanted that imulsion, he could just take it.

But maybe the Chairman knew that nobody had the stomach for another war, however much peace still seemed like a strange and purposeless new country.

Boots suddenly echoed along the tiled corridor. Hoffman was surprised to see Trescu emerge around the corner on his own. He radiated the confidence of a man used to power, much more power than just control of a village-sized population.

A village with control of an imulsion rig. And we're a town that's got the Hammer of Dawn. Funny how the world scales down.

Trescu strolled up to Hoffman and nodded politely, then indicated the closed door with the slightest jerk of the head. "Our friends," he said. "Are they well enough to receive visitors?"

Hoffman pressed the handle and swung the door open. "I'll leave you to decide. Prescott's orders—your show."

"You have a problem with this? Then think of your dead sergeant and his comrades." Trescu put one boot across the threshold and paused. "Because I shall certainly think of mine."

Hoffman caught a first glimpse of Enador and Loris propped up in their beds, looking confused rather than defiant. Hoffman wondered how much painkiller the doctor had pumped into them. They watched him warily as he pulled up a rickety wooden chair and sat down in the corner, probably expecting him to be running the interrogation because he was wearing a colonel's insignia.

"You don't look like a medical man, and neither does your bagman," Enador said, glancing at Trescu. No, he didn't sound drugged at all. In fact, he seemed pretty chipper for a man whose head was swathed in field dressings. "Where's my son?"

"Under guard." Hoffman wasn't sure what Trescu was going to do. Prescott seemed more keen to make sure the jumped-up little shit felt he'd won rather than get any useful intelligence. "He's not been harmed."

"No, you're the good guys, aren't you? You don't beat up kids." Enador indicated Loris with his thumb. "You've got rules about how you treat enemy wounded, right?"

Hoffman wanted to punch the crap out of him. "You're a waste of medical supplies," he said. "I'll leave you to our guest."

Loris turned his head with difficulty. It was hard to tell that he was in worse shape than his buddy. There wasn't so much as a scratch on his face. "Ah, nice to see we've brought you two together at last."

Trescu walked across the small room and lifted a tubular metal chair by its frame, then set it down by the side of Loris's bed. If it hadn't been for the faded black uniform, he might have passed for a concerned relative.

"Gentlemen," he said. "I am Commander Miran Trescu. I am Gorasnayan, which should mean something to you. There are very few of us left, so every citizen I lose grieves me very deeply. I thought I would mention that so you understand why I must be *insistent* in asking you questions."

Enador watched him with mild interest. "Yeah, we know what Gorasni are like."

"Good." Trescu folded his arms and leaned on the edge of the bed. "So this would be a sensible time to tell me where you get your arms and ordnance, and where your camps are."

"I'll bet," Loris said. "Ram it up your ass, Commander."

"And how are your friends sinking our ships?"

Enador paused for a beat, as if he really didn't understand the question. "We haven't touched a boat since the last imulsion shipment. We don't sink them, Indie. We *commandeer* them."

"Two trawlers and a frigate."

"I told you—we'd keep them, not sink them."

Trescu didn't bat an eyelid. "I *had* hoped we could work together."

"Now what? You going to beat the crap out of me? Break a few teeth?" Loris strained to look past Trescu at Hoffman. He probably hadn't worked out who was in charge here. Maybe he thought they were pulling some nice-and-nasty double act. "Does he do your dirty work for you, Colonel? We thought you liked to do your own."

The asshole couldn't have known how near the mark that comment was.

"Very well." Trescu glanced at his watch. "My father gave me this. It still keeps good time. *Very* fine workmanship. I shall count five minutes on it, by which time I would like an answer to my question."

Hoffman wasn't sure what effect this was having on the two Stranded, but it was certainly unsettling him. The longer Trescu sat there doing nothing, the less Hoffman knew what was coming next. And that was the idea, of course. Uncertainty—fear— softened up a prisoner more than actual pain. He got the feeling that Trescu would suddenly punch Loris in the guts to make the most of that shattered pelvis.

Is that what I'd do? Why did it even cross my mind?

The fact that he could even imagine it shamed him. He wanted to walk out and not have to watch this, but he stood there, complicit and conflicted. The worst thing was that he believed Enador about the ships. He really did. It wasn't the gangs' style not to brag about their kills.

Trescu's fine gold watch ticked away audibly in the silence. He studied it, distracted, then ran his thumb across the glass as if to clean it.

"I am waiting," he said.

Hoffman waited, too, expecting that blow to land at any moment. Eventually, Trescu sat back in the chair and sighed theatrically.

"Very well. You had your five minutes." He took a radio earpiece much like the old COG issue from his breast pocket and pressed it into place. "Burkan? Please come to the isolation ward now."

Hoffman hadn't interrogated anyone for more than fifteen years. Nobody took grubs alive, so the COG had a serious case of skills-fade when it came to questioning prisoners. His stomach knotted as Trescu got up and walked over to the window to gaze out as if he didn't have a care in the world. Loris and Enador had obviously braced themselves for the worst. Enador's jaw was set in defiance, but one hand gripping the sheet betrayed his anxiety. Maybe Trescu had a point.

The door opened and a burly Gorasni sergeant walked in with Enador's teenage son in a restraining arm-hold. The kid was red in the face. Enador looked him over.

"Son, what have they done to you?"

"Nothing, Dad."

I get it, Hoffman thought. *This isn't going to be pretty.* Kids could—and would—kill you just as easily as an adult. This one made bombs. Hoffman reminded himself that kids younger than Nial Enador were considered grown men in other cultures.

Burkan said nothing. Hoffman waited for him to start roughing up the boy. Trescu just looked at his watch.

"One last time," he said. "And that is something I never usually concede. Mr. Loris, tell me where your camps and arms caches are."

So . . . he was going to lean on Loris, and the suspense would rattle Enador, who would do anything rather than see his kid harmed, and . . .

"You're finished, COG—and you, Indie." Loris struggled for breath as he sat up a little more. Hoffman preferred enemies who earned his contempt, but these bastards were as tough and committed as any Gear. "Your world order's gone up in smoke but you won't accept it. Believe me—you'll end up just like us Stranded, except we've had years of practice, and we've weeded out our weaklings. You'll just fall apart. Natural selection. It's a bitch, isn't it?"

"So it is," Trescu said.

Then he drew his sidearm and put it calmly to Loris's head. There was no threat, no pistol-whipping, no yelling, none of the plain old-fashioned brutality Hoffman had expected. Trescu just pulled the trigger.

The loud crack filled the room. Blood sprayed the scrubbed wall behind the bed and the yellowing starched sheets.

It was over instantly.

Hoffman was aware of Nial gaping—he *was* a kid, just a kid— but the next second went on forever, a ringing silence that turned into one thudding beat of Hoffman's heart.

The second of silence was many things; disbelief, shock, even that weird moment of horrified realization that a thing like that could never be undone, and how very short that terrible, irreversible moment was. Hoffman had seen many men die in far worse ways, men who were his friends, but he'd also pulled a trigger and felt less of a man for doing so. The past rushed after him and stood breathless at his side like someone he'd crossed the road to avoid. It would never leave him alone.

And then that second was gone. His heart hit that second beat, and another, and now it was hammering. Trescu took two unhurried steps to the other bed and put his pistol to Enador's temple. Nial was screaming abuse and struggling in Burkan's armlock.

"I will find it just as easy to kill your father." Trescu reached out and grabbed the kid one-handed by his collar, hauling him up so that they were almost nose to nose. "You'll come with me now, Nial, and we'll talk *sensibly*, yes?"

"Don't touch my dad!" The boy burst into tears. "Leave him alone! You lay a finger on him and I'll fucking kill you!"

But he wasn't going to kill anyone, and he wasn't going to hold out for long now. Trescu looked like he knew it. It was a neat mind-fuck. Hoffman hadn't seen it coming.

"Burkan, clear up this mess and see that Mr. Enador is comfortable," Trescu said. "There's no need for you to be present, Colonel." He indicated his earpiece. "Everything Nial and I discuss can be monitored by your splendidly efficient Control personnel."

Hoffman finally found his voice. But it didn't sound like the man inside, the man who'd seen one death too many, and sometimes walked the knife-edge between never being able to pull a trigger again and never being able to stop. Trescu probably thought he'd lose his nerve and let the boy go.

"Just remember to record every detail," Hoffman said. "And leave us to do the rest."

He had to go. He adjusted his cap, feeling for the metal badge and lining it up with his nose, and grabbed the handle. The clatter of boots at a run outside grew suddenly louder and the door burst open and hit him. Hayman stood in the doorway, white-faced and furious. The old girl must have seen some bad shit in her time, but Hoffman had never seen utter shock on her face before. It took her a few seconds to take in the room and speak.

"Get the fuck out of my hospital, you *animal*," she snarled. "And make sure you never end up in my ER. Because I'll let you bleed out on the goddamn floor."

She was talking to Trescu, but Hoffman had the feeling he was included. He didn't need prompting to get out anyway. He paused to look into Hayman's face just so she knew he didn't buy all that territorial shit.

"Take it up with the Chairman," he said. "I'm going to be too busy working out how they managed to blow up another trawler. All hands lost, in case you give a damn."

Hoffman seized the moment of silence to stalk out to the parade ground. *What next?* The upside of a continual stream of trouble was that he never had time to dwell on anything, and nobody expected him to. He had the Pelruan locals to worry about. And Michaelson—what the hell was the navy playing at? Couldn't they even manage to defend a few fishing vessels now?

I'm going to put my boot up your ass, Quentin. We have to do better than this.

Hoffman paused to call Anya on the radio. He could feel his hand shaking as he put it to his ear.

I hope that's just old age.

"You okay, sir?" One of the Gears on base security duty, Jace Stratton, jogged up to him with his rifle ready. The shot must have been heard halfway across the base. "Negligent discharge?"

"No." Hoffman needed to get a grip of himself before he walked into Ops. He'd take a few minutes in his quarters. "Just Indies showing us how to deal with prisoners. Stand down. Nothing we can do."

Stratton glanced past Hoffman as if he thought trouble might be coming through that door at any time. He didn't seem that much older than the kid who'd just seen his father's buddy shot through the head. But he'd been through a war on the front line, and he'd watched his family killed. That put some years on a man.

"You just say the word, sir," Stratton said. "They executing them now? Is that how it's going to be?"

Trescu's right, the asshole. Think about Andresen and the others.

"It's academic." Hoffman carried on walking. All the administrative offices—CIC, the infirmary, Prescott's office, even some of the barracks buildings—overlooked that space, making it impossible to cross unobserved. "We'd have shot the bastard anyway." He opened his radio link. "Anya? Tell Prescott that Trescu shot one of the prisoners. And get hold of Gavriel for me."

"He's called in, sir. He wants to come down and see you."

"Send a 'Dill to collect him. I don't want civvies splattered all over the road."

"Will do, sir."

Hoffman's quarters were a couple of small attic rooms in the roof of the HQ building, nothing fancy. He took the fire escape to avoid conversations he didn't want to have yet. As soon as he shut the door behind him, he ran cold water into the washbasin and rinsed his face. He wasn't even sure why. It just made him feel calmer.

They killed our guys. I should have done it myself. Shit, what's wrong with me?

Hoffman felt like a traitor to Andresen's memory for wasting even a scrap of conscience on those bastards. The nagging voice started up in his head again, the one that reminded him that he'd once been judge and jury too, dispensing justice with a single round, because it had to be done to save lives.

Okay, yes, I get it. Self-loathing. Transfer. Hypocrisy. All that shit. Trescu and me, cut from the same cloth. But knowing that doesn't stop it.

He ran his palms over his scalp and sat down on the edge of his bed to stare at the bare floorboards. For a moment, he could have been in his old quarters at Anvegad, right down to the small window with the endless view.

We do the same thing over every day until we die.

He wasn't sure how long he sat there. It was probably just minutes. Then the stairs creaked, and he lifted his head just enough to see a pair of boots planted firmly in the doorway.

"Vic?"

Hoffman sat upright, hands on his knees. Bernie leaned against the door frame.

"I just needed to compose myself before I see our glorious leader," he lied.

"Bullshit."

"You've heard."

"It's hard to miss a gunshot in here. Or Hayman in full rant demanding to see Prescott. It's all over the base now, Vic."

"Saves me explaining, then."

Bernie squatted on her heels to look into his face. Her bruises were already yellow and fading. "A few months ago you were ready to blow John Massy's brains out for what he did to me, and not a second thought about it. Why is this different? Those tossers killed Andresen and crippled half a dozen more Gears. I'll volunteer to slot the other two personally."

There was no lying to Bernie. However many years they'd been apart, she still knew him better than anyone alive. And she knew the old Hoffman, the *real* one, the confident NCO before he became something he should never have been.

"I think it's Anvil Gate," he said. "The last few days—every damn thing seems to remind me of it."

Maybe he'd done too good a job of not talking about the siege. Anyone old enough to remember it knew it had been desperate and didn't fit the COG's ideal of honorable combat. But they didn't know all the details. The only ones who did were dead, except Hoffman himself.

"We make a habit of not telling each other things, don't we, Vic?" Bernie said.

When Hoffman had told Bernie that they were the last two of their generation left of the 26th Royal Tyran Infantry, he hadn't been sure how true that was. Since then he'd worked through the battalion list as it appeared on the day before he'd taken up his commission, the NCOs and enlisted men and women, and he realized it was completely accurate. They *were* the last survivors.

"Where were you thirty-two years ago?" Hoffman asked. "The summer of Anvil Gate? Shit, I can't even work out the real year. The *old* calendar. Let's stick with the new one."

It was now recorded as 17 B.E., Before Emergence, seventeen years before the Locust erupted out of nowhere and brought mankind to the brink. Bernie shook her head.

"I was in Kashkur too," she said. "But I was at Shavad. And I hadn't seen you for some time."

That was what felt so strange. There were huge gaps in time, years when he hadn't even known where Bernie was or if she was even alive. Yet he'd first met her forty years ago, and it felt like continuous time, every void filled and closed in his mind.

"I better tell you, then," Hoffman said. "But let's clear up this pile of shit first."

It was time he told her what the official record didn't say about the siege of Anvil Gate. He was sick of secrets.

He vowed he was never going to keep one again.

CHAPTER 5

Anvegad's like a movie set. The buildings are straight out of a history book and there's even a street bazaar. But God, it's harsh up here, Margaret. I really miss you. Sometimes I wonder if I shouldn't have stayed an NCO—but then we'd never have met. And you probably wouldn't have noticed an enlisted Gear like Staff Sergeant Hoffman anyway.

(LIEUTENANT VICTOR HOFFMAN, COMMANDING OFFICER OF
CONNAUGHT PLATOON, 26TH ROYAL TYRAN INFANTRY, COG
OPERATING BASE ANVIL GATE, ANVEGAD, KASHKUR, IN A LETTER TO
HIS NEW BRIDE)

ANVEGAD, KASHKUR—FIRST WEEK OF RISE,
32 YEARS EARLIER, THE 62ND YEAR OF THE
PENDULUM WARS.

This was the ass-end of the world, Hoffman was certain.

No amount of fine Silver Era architecture or magnificent history was going to change the fact that Anvegad was a lonely rock of a place. He wouldn't miss it when he left. *Three months down, four to go.* He was counting down the days to the end of the deployment on a calendar pinned to the wall.

It was one hell of a view from this window, though.

He paused mid-shave and reached out to push the wooden

frame fully open, letting in cold air that made the foam on his face tingle. The plain spread out below him could have been from another world. There was nothing out there but stony yellow soil with occasional thornbushes and the pale line of a single lonely road running parallel with the imulsion pipeline into the refinery in the distance. Generations of goats had grazed the place to bare rock. On mornings like this, the refinery merged with a backdrop of mountains that looked like ragged purple clouds on the horizon.

It's only a few more months. I can handle that.

The briefing document had given him a description of Anvegad, but no sense of what it felt like to be here. It was a natural fortress on a rocky cliff overlooking the pass into Kashkur from the south. Armies had fought over it throughout history to control Kashkur's rich cities and silver mines. The silver had been mined out long ago, but Kashkur still had plenty to interest invaders— one fifth of Sera's imulsion reserves.

When Hoffman's COG transport rumbled down that road for the first time, and he saw the fort rising up out of nowhere from that crag, it looked like a mirage, a bizarre trick of nature. The air was so still and clear most mornings that every color, even the black shadows, seemed unnaturally vivid. Captain Sander, Hoffman's CO, painted pictures of it.

That was his hobby—watercolors. He said this place was *magical*, the poor deluded bastard. Hoffman was marooned here as second in command to a goddamn *artist*—and an artillery captain, at that. Maybe COG command was trying to civilize him, the same way that Staff College had instructed him on the right fork to use at dinner and how to press his best dress uniform. He was nearly thirty. He didn't need to be taught how to wipe his own ass, thanks. That still rankled.

Come on, you're an officer now. If you can't hack the internal politics . . . you should have stayed an NCO.

The spectacular landscape changed color as the sun rose. He'd have to take a picture for Margaret, or maybe she'd prefer one of Sander's watercolors. Married or not, Hoffman was still at the stage of worrying that he was just a bit of rough for her, a novelty she'd tire of and then wonder why the hell she hadn't married one of her own kind. She was a trial lawyer, for God's sake—college educated, having dinner with people who'd probably expect the likes of Hoffman to park their cars or mow their lawns. She was well traveled in the kind of way that didn't involve rolling into foreign towns with an armored division. She was out of his league. And yet—she'd married him.

Yes. A nice painting. She'll like that. Or maybe some of the local silver jewelry. Or is silver too cheap?

Hoffman went back to shaving. The mirror reminded him unkindly how fast his hair was thinning. He studied his scalp, moving a little so that the harsh light from the single bulb caught the worst reflection, and then made the decision he'd put off for some time. He wasn't going to turn into one of those insecure assholes who always fretted about their bald patch. *Fuck it.* It was just too much testosterone, that was all. He'd embrace it. He'd *flaunt* it.

His hair was buzz-cut anyway. There wasn't much to lose. He lathered the shaving soap over his head and took the razor to it.

It'll grow again if I change my mind. Or if Margaret doesn't like it.

When he rinsed off the soap in the shower—a trickle of tepid water, two minutes, nothing indulgent—there was still a haze of dark stubble under the skin. But he felt unburdened. He dressed and made his way down the steep stone staircase to the adjutant's office, not expecting anyone to be up and about yet except the duty sentry, whose task was more to keep out pilfering locals than the enemy.

Anvegad had one thing going for it, at least for anyone who wanted a quiet war, which Hoffman didn't. It wasn't on the front line. Vasgar—neutral, but not stupid when it came to keeping the COG placated—was a nice big buffer running the length of Kashkur's southern border. There were no Indies loitering in the front yard. Hoffman wasn't used to that.

"'Morning, Victor." Ranald Sander looked up from a pile of paper on the signals desk, phone pressed to his ear, and froze. "Is this the new barbarian look?"

Hoffman ran his palm over his scalp. "I didn't want to look too civilized."

"Good." Sander held up a finely pleated sheet of teleprinter paper soaked with black ink. He had three piles of paper in front of him on the desk, and he pushed one across to Hoffman. It was the stack of regular messages from the Gears' families. "Just going through the overnights and checking what's missing. This bloody thing's still jamming."

"At least the family-grams came through. Remember, if there's anything urgent from HQ, they'll call."

Sander seemed to need to be reminded of these things. He was very young, a brand-new captain at twenty-three. Hoffman felt like a sergeant nursemaiding a green lieutenant again but that wasn't a bad thing. He knew how to do that, even if he had never done it outside the infantry. It beat worrying about using the right fork at dinner.

Hoffman sorted through the messages, checking off the names with a stub of pencil. Some men didn't get messages at all. Some got the maximum allocation of three a month, two hundred words each. This far from home, morale hinged on a few basic things—letters from loved ones, a full stomach, and the weekly delivery of a single precious movie that everyone on Jacinto had seen a year ago. The full stomach had to be shipped in too. Anvegad relied mostly on food brought in by road from the north. A fortress city's strengths were also its drawbacks.

Sander put the phone back on its cradle a little too heavily. "Screw them. I can't wait all day." He took the vehicle keys off a hook on the wall and tossed them to Hoffman. "Come on, let's walk the course."

Sander grabbed his camera and a small wooden box with a brass catch. Hoffman humored him. Everyone was marking time here, and maybe one day Sander's paintings would be worth something. He drove slowly through narrow streets that were almost deserted at this time of the morning, catching scents of baking loaves, spice-laden coffee, and drains. There was one way in and out of Anvegad. The steep, winding track was just wide enough for a large truck, flanked by a sheer drop onto the rocks below. Even in the small all-terrain vehicle, Hoffman took things carefully.

"How's your wife, sir?" Hoffman asked.

"Complaining about swollen legs and indigestion," Sander said. "Five weeks to go. At least we've agreed on a name now— Terrance if it's a boy, Muriell if it's a girl."

Hoffman hadn't given much thought to families. They happened to other people, and he was still caught up in the adventure of being a couple. "You really should put in for compassionate leave."

"I'll do that. How's married life treating you? Your wife's a lawyer, isn't she?"

No need to sound amazed. "She is, sir."

"How did you meet?"

"She was working on an inquiry for the Defense Department." *It wasn't at a cocktail party after the opera, but you guessed that, didn't you?* "She asked me some questions and I gave her some frank answers."

That was what she told him later: *You're the most honest man I've ever met, Victor. And I don't meet many in this job.*

"Very cryptic," Sander said.

Hoffman let it drop. He breathed again when the track leveled out and all four wheels were on the flat. From the base of the cliff, he drove out on the usual route—the road south through the narrow V-shaped gorge that was the pass, seven kilometers down the pipeline to the Vasgar border, and then left to follow the invisible line that divided the Coalition of Ordered Governments from a nervous neutral world that hadn't made up its mind yet. There was nothing physical to mark it apart from a thick red strip painted around the girth of the overground pipeline, and the remains of a seasonal riverbed that had been dry for so long that even the maps didn't show it in blue.

Six more kilometers would have taken them to the refinery. Sander tapped the dashboard to bring Hoffman to a stop.

"I won't be long," he said. "Five minutes. Ten, tops."

It was the light. Hoffman had worked that out by now. Sander liked painting Anvil Gate when the sun was just above the horizon, because the shadows were dramatic, and this was the best vantage point to look back on the whole cliff.

Shame about the gun battery. And all the metal gantries. Spoils the Silver Era illusion.

Sander got out of the ATV and sat on the fender with the contents of his wooden box laid out on the vehicle's hood, roughing out a picture on a piece of card with a stick of charcoal. Hoffman jumped down from the driver's seat and wandered off for a smoke. He'd have to give that up before he next went home. Margaret didn't like it. It'd be the death of him, she said.

When he turned and ambled back toward the ATV, Sander was busy taking photographs.

"That's cheating," Hoffman said.

"It's that, or stay here for another hour or two." Sander frowned at the camera, fiddling with the lens. "Why's it cheating?"

"Aren't you supposed to depict what you notice with your own eyes?"

"And you keep telling me you're not a cultured man."

"I married a cultured woman. She knows all that stuff."

Sander chuckled to himself as if Hoffman was being witty. But Hoffman meant it. He didn't point that out. They climbed back into the ATV and carried on along the border for a while before looping back and returning to Anvegad. A truck was grinding its way up the narrow track, and Hoffman decided to wait until it made the gates at the top before he followed it. Trucks broke down on that gradient all too often. Turning or reversing all the way down wasn't something he fancied doing. By the time he saw its tailgate vanish between the huge carved pillars, his guts were rumbling in protest at being forced to endure goddamn amateur art while empty.

"I'll take the family-grams over to the barracks," Hoffman said. Anvil Gate was a small garrison, around a hundred men and women—a battery of Prince Ozore's Artillery, with two attached platoons from 26 RTI and the Ephyra Engineers. "I could use the exercise."

He'd grab breakfast with the men, too. There was no officers' mess to speak of, just a sitting room in the HQ building where his quarters were, and they often ate at one of the local bars that Sander had taken a shine to. But Hoffman missed the company of sergeants. Separation from the ranks left him feeling lost.

The Gears' quarters were spread across a number of buildings, some in regular barracks on the far side of the compound, some in the first cellar level of the huge gun emplacements. Anvil Gate was a vertical sort of place—more deep than wide, a small footprint with tunnels and cellars dug deep into bedrock that was already honeycombed with natural caves and fissures. There was even an underground river that branched off from the surface ten klicks away. Hoffman didn't like the underground world and its damp, fungal smells. When he wandered into the small mess in the main battery, the perfume of frying eggs and local sausage did a thorough job of disguising them.

"Safe as houses down here, sir," said Padrick Salton, pulling out a chair. "Fried egg sandwich?"

"It's a damn coffin," Hoffman muttered. He put the sheaf of printed messages in the center of the table. "Here's the mail. And yes, I *will* have one of your heathen delicacies, Private. Thank you."

Salton—"Pad" to everyone—was a South Islander who'd brought strange food habits with him, not that Hoffman was complaining. Pad didn't cook the exotic native dishes of fruits, strange roots, and goat meat. He was a descendant of northern colonizers. But he existed somewhere between the two cultures. His northern fried egg sandwich was laced with blisteringly hot Islander spices, and he had full-face blue tribal tattoos on freckled, pale skin. Hoffman was fascinated and always tried not to stare at him. What looked right on darker-skinned indigenous people looked disturbing when topped by red hair.

It wasn't just the stark contrast in color. It was a kind of warning that Pad had embraced everything about his particular island's culture, including the tendency to no-quarters-given warfare.

The sandwich was an experience. Hoffman's eyes watered as fierce chemical warfare was waged against his sinuses. The rest of

Pad's platoon showed up and helped themselves to the bread, fried eggs, and sauce, a ritual that seemed timed to the minute to coincide with the 0700 radio news.

"Ninety percent boredom, ten percent shit-yourself panic," said Sergeant Byrne.

"Make that ninety-nine percent here," Pad said. "Maybe a hundred."

Hoffman chewed in silence, wondering if having an officer there inhibited them, an officer who'd been one of them until recently. He also felt that nagging guilt that he was coasting here while most of 26 RTI—his comrades, his friends—were on the much tougher, much bloodier front line on the western border.

He wondered where Bernie Mataki was at that moment. She had tribal tattoos, too. None on her face, though. She said her tribe didn't do that.

The radio burbled away in the background. It was a weak signal this far from Ephyra, but nobody cared as long they heard voices in an accent and a language they could understand. The first morning bulletin with its international headlines was something they all knew their families would be listening to at that same moment. It gave them a sense of communion across thousands of kilometers.

Margaret listened to it, too. She'd promised she would. Hoffman closed his eyes and tried to imagine how she'd interpret the headlines. She always had something to say, and she didn't have a lot of respect for politicians. He liked that in a woman.

The crackling voice reading the bulletin this morning was a young man's. *"Vasgar's President Ilim is facing a vote of no confidence after his administration failed to agree to budget measures with the opposition Unity party. Meanwhile, on Vasgar's southern border, the dispute with the UIR over gas supplies to—"*

"I hope they can pay their imulsion bill," Pad said. "Or we'll have to go out there with a frigging big spanner and turn off the pipeline."

Everyone laughed and Hoffman got up to fry another egg for himself. Life went on. Bills got paid and letters got read. After more than sixty years of fighting, war had become the normal, the stable, the expected, and all of Sera—formally involved in hostilities or playing at being neutral observers—had rebuilt its reality around it. Hoffman wasn't sure if that was stoic resilience or plain damn stupidity.

He'd still rather have been on the western border at that moment. Sitting on his ass like this would drive him crazy. He took his seat again, and realized the only man not reading a message from home was Sam Byrne, his platoon sergeant.

Byrne's sense of home looked more centered on Anvegad every day. He'd acquired a local girlfriend, an interpreter who did the routine liaison for the army. She was a good-looking woman, typically Kashkuri with her dark eyes and olive skin. Soraya? Sheraya? Hoffman couldn't recall the name, but Byrne was a single man, and Hoffman wasn't about to warn him off. He was damned if he could think of any regulation barring a Gear from making friends with the local civilians.

There wasn't much else to do here except maintain the guns, after all.

"More eggs, anyone?" Pad asked.

THE FENIX FAMILY ESTATE, EAST BARRICADE ACADEMY, JACINTO.

Adam Fenix had always tried to do his packing in private to avoid upsetting Elain.

It wasn't as if she didn't understand his job; she just seemed to find the sight of him preparing to ship out a bit too much to bear. She wasn't a demonstrative woman, so there were no tears or histrionics. She'd just get that *look*, that way of turning her head very slowly as if she was imagining the worst that could happen to him and was dragging her eyes away from the awful scene.

And now he had to lock the bedroom door, because his son was old enough to understand where Daddy was going, and he'd get upset too. Marcus was nearly five. He'd learned to knock on the door and wait a few moments, but then he'd open it anyway.

It was time for Marcus to get used to partings. He had to start school in a few weeks, and that was going to be a bigger wrench than watching his father get ready to go back to the front. Adam folded his last pair of socks, forced them into the remaining gap in his kitbag, and secured the outer zip. There was a science to packing. He'd mastered it. He had everything he needed and nothing that he didn't, every item in that bag tested for necessity, and there were no bulges or edges straining against the canvas fabric to fray on hard surfaces.

Elain had a point. It did feel final. It always did.

He unlocked the door and went downstairs, one hand skimming the long, polished banister, conscious of the gaze of previous generations of Fenixes from the ancestral paintings that lined the walls. If anyone thought that long familiarity stopped him noticing them—it didn't. Too many of them had that implacable blue stare. Adam had been told he had it, too, but that didn't make it an easier gauntlet to run. The portraits had expectations of heroism.

I could donate them to the Tyran National Gallery, I suppose. Dad's not here to stop me now.

Adam walked from room to room, looking for Elain. Finding anyone in a house of this size always took some time. Calling for her always felt vulgar; he could almost hear his father's voice telling him that only the laboring classes and clerks yelled, and that the one fitting place for a man to raise his voice was on the battlefield.

It's my house now. But he's still here, dead or not.

He found Elain sitting at her desk, scribbling furiously. She didn't even look up. "Two minutes, darling . . ."

And there was I thinking my packing upset her . . .

Adam had never been sure if that cool distance was her coping mechanism or if she really did forget everything around her while she was working. She was a single-minded woman.

"Where's Marcus?" he asked.

"In the library."

"He's four. It's a lovely day. Whatever happened to playing in the gardens?"

Elain paused for a moment, looking as if she was checking the last line she'd written. "He's fine. The maintenance people are doing the lawns, anyway. Too dangerous with all that machinery about."

"I better go make my peace with him," Adam said. "By the time I finish this tour of duty, he'll be at school, and . . . well, everyone says kids change fast after that."

"Good idea." Elain swiveled her seat around and looked at him as if she'd noticed him for the first time. "Aren't you going to ask me what's so important?"

"Do you want me to?"

She indicated the computer screen, tracing her finger around the outline of an X-ray image. "Does this ring any bells, Doctor Fenix?"

Elain was a developmental biologist. Adam prided himself on a broad-based science education that went further than engineering, but she left him in the dust on morphology. He studied the ghostly outlines. It was a leg, that was all he could say. A hind leg. He could guess that from the way the joints articulated, because form and function spoke to the mechanical engineer in him.

"Not many, *Mrs.* Doctor Fenix." Elain had a doctorate too. Adam leaned over her and put his finger on the screen. "It's not human, and I think that bit *there* is the knee."

"Very good, dear. But didn't you read *Romily* as a child? The monster under her bed?"

"Oh, girls' stuff . . ."

"Don't mock, darling. How's the monster always shown? That story goes back centuries, and the monster always has the same features—long front fangs and six legs."

Tyran culture was rich in myth and fairy tales, but Adam was a scientist, a rational man, and even as a boy he'd recognized that monsters were invented to keep the curious and argumentative in line. If he'd been a psychologist, he might have gone as far as to identify the fairy-tale monsters as the darker urges of humankind, but he looked for the most obvious first and worked from there.

There were always monsters waiting in forbidden places to trap the disobedient and unwary.

He'd never believed in them.

He remembered crawling under his bed every night for a whole week with a flashlight and a camera, defying the monsters to appear so he could get a good look and prove or disprove their existence. But they never came, and he knew his father had been lying all along.

Monsters don't exist. But if they do—they're within all of us.

"Elain, are you telling me that's a sixth leg from a mammal?" he said at last.

"It is." She lit up. It troubled him that she only hit that visible peak when she was engrossed in her research. Sometimes he felt that neither marriage nor motherhood ever fulfilled her that much. "Adam, all monsters come from some reality. The six legs are a folk memory. Something like that once existed on Sera, and we reduced it to a fairy tale in the end, but now—I think I've found its nearest living relative."

"Just tell me you didn't find it under the bed."

"You want to see it?"

"You've got it, and you never told me?"

Elain laughed and pushed back her chair. "I shouldn't have given it such a buildup. You'll be disappointed. Just remember that things don't have to be on a planetary scale to change the world."

She went to the bookcase that filled the entire wall and moved a few volumes to pull out a glass jar hidden behind them. Adam hadn't realized that she kept specimens in the house; it seemed oddly old-fashioned, considering that she still had access to La Croix University's modern laboratories. But she'd insisted on being at home for Marcus until he was old enough to start school—no child-minders or nannies for her. She never trusted anyone else with the complicated jobs in life.

"There." She handed him the specimen jar. A tiny rodent floated in formaldehyde, perhaps seven centimeters long. "I kept it out of sight in case Marcus saw it. I think he finds that kind of thing upsetting."

Adam wasn't fond of things floating dead in jars of formaldehyde either. He felt slightly nauseous at the sight of the animal drifting like a drowned man. He imagined it alive, busy among leaves and grass, all twitching movement. Then he tried to imagine it as the subterranean monster from *Romily*, with six legs, claws, and fangs, and failed to make the phylogenetic connection.

"Now, I'm just a simple engineer," he said. "But I can count enough to see four legs. Not six."

"Okay, darling, I'll put you out of your misery. The legs are vestigial. You remember I did my master's thesis on rock shrew cell differentiation? Well, I found a dead one when I was out walking a couple of years ago, or at least I thought I had. But it wasn't a rock shrew. And I could feel these small symmetrical lumps along the pelvis."

"My wife spends her leisure time fondling decomposing vermin."

"*Examine*, darling. Not fondle. And *vermin* is an emotional classification, not a biological one." Elain gazed at the creature with a childlike expression of wonder. "Anyway, I found more of them over the last year, all with the same feature. When I dissected them, they all had the extra pair of vestigial legs."

"Good grief—are you telling me you discovered a new species? Are you sure it's not just a mutation?"

"Remember who's the embryologist here. Yes, that's entirely possible, but it seems widespread, and there are other variations that suggest they might be a different species. Genetic variations." She dropped her voice. "I think these shrews may be the remains of a genus that once included much larger tunnel-dwelling creatures."

Adam was genuinely taken aback, not because she'd made such an intriguing discovery but because she'd kept it from him until now. Years. *Years.* His hurt must have shown on his face, because she took the specimen from him and clasped both his hands in hers.

"Darling, you know what happens to scientists who speak too soon—they're made to look like fools," she said. "If I'd started talking about identifying a new species and then it was shown to be environmental mutation, my reputation would be ruined. And I *do* want to return to work. . . ."

But you could have mentioned it to me. I wouldn't have judged you. "So where did you find them?"

"Near the Hollow. I like walking up there. I used to take Marcus with me."

"That's a restricted area! What were you *thinking*?"

"Look, I *know* the ground's prone to subsidence. I don't go beyond the warning notices. It's not as if I go caving down there."

Marcus. Adam realized they'd been so caught up in this debate about morphology and new species that they'd forgotten him.

"Come on," he said. "The monster shrew from the pit of hell can wait—this is my last day at home for a few months. Let's spend it as a family."

"If you knew what aggressive, sex-crazed little beasts shrews were," Elain said, "you wouldn't think a two-meter one with six legs was a joke."

Adam found Marcus still sitting in the library, just as he'd been told to. He was perched on a chair that wasn't high enough for him, trying to read a book, with his chin about level with the surface of the table. Adam could see him swinging his legs, heels occasionally hitting the chair. He wasn't engrossed. He was just behaving, waiting as patiently as a small child could.

"How's my clever boy?" Adam said, standing behind him to see what he'd chosen. It was a book of maps. "Come on. Let's go for a walk. It's stuffy in here."

Marcus scrambled down from the chair and looked up at his father. He had a way of slowly turning his head to one side that made him look as if he never believed a word anyone said to him. Adam wondered if it was a gesture his son had picked up from him. No, it was very Elain. It was definitely Elain's look.

"You're going away."

"Not until tomorrow, Marcus."

"Why do you have to go?"

"It's my duty. I'm a soldier. A Gear. Soldiers have to go where they're sent, to protect everyone."

"But *why?*"

It was sobering to meet Marcus's fixed gaze. He definitely had the Fenix eyes, very pale blue just like Adam's own, and even in a child's face they looked more accusing than innocent. Adam was suddenly aware of Elain standing behind him. The answer was going to be as much for her as for his son.

"Because all the other Gears go when they're ordered to, and if I don't, I'm letting them down," Adam said. "They're my friends. They're the people who'll look out for me so I don't get hurt. We take care of one another."

Marcus blinked as if that had struck a chord in him, then looked away. "*I'll* be a Gear, too, then."

"Ah, not my clever boy." Adam went to pick him up—something he rarely did—but Marcus looked startled, and he thought better of it. "You'll be a scientist. You won't need to be a Gear. And the war will be over by the time you grow up, anyway."

Marcus frowned. That obviously wasn't what he wanted to hear. Adam had the feeling that whatever he said would do nothing to erase the impression that being a Gear was somehow so wonderful that he preferred to go to war rather than stay home with his son.

He could have stayed, of course. The post at the COG Defense Research Agency was still waiting for him. So was the standing offer to teach at the university. He could do both, in fact. He could have unpacked that bag right now, this very moment, and picked up the phone to accept the job, and the Kashkur border would have been another place he'd never visit.

But Adam Fenix couldn't live with himself if he did. The rest of the 26th Royal Tyran Infantry didn't have those choices, and neither did their families. It was best that Elain didn't know it was even possible.

Yes, maybe I've given Marcus the true picture after all. It's about loyalty. It's about comrades. But I still don't want him to follow me.

"Come on, Marcus," he said. "Let's have some fun. Did you know your mom's found a monster? It's got six legs."

Marcus still had that accusing ice-blue stare. "There aren't any monsters," he said gravely. "But if there are, you can shoot them. You can make them go away."

"Quite right," Adam said, laughing, but his heart broke to see Marcus's absolute faith in his ability to put the world right. He almost dreaded the day when Marcus was old enough to understand that the real world wasn't like that at all. "That's my clever boy."

Adam held out his hand. Marcus hesitated, then took it, and they walked around the gardens. Marcus could identify most of the tree species, and with their proper botanical names at that. It was pretty damn impressive for a little boy.

My son. What's he going to be like when he's my age? I don't recall ever being like him.

"Don't worry, he'll be fine when he starts school," Elain said. She could read Adam like a book. "He'll make friends. I feel guilty sometimes that we didn't give him a brother or sister."

"Never too late," Adam said.

Elain just swept past the comment as if she hadn't heard it. She didn't even blink. "Come on, Marcus," she called. "Time for lunch."

That evening, after Marcus was asleep and while Elain was taking a bath, Adam went to his study and settled down at his desk to listen to the radio. It was less distracting than the television. He could let the information wash over him in the background while he worked. The important details would leap out at him and demand his attention when necessary.

Vasgar did.

Adam put down the folder he was working on and sat back in his chair to concentrate.

"*. . . and President Ilim has resigned. We'll bring you more details when we get them, but Vasgar's official news agency, Corisku, is saying that he stood down before a vote of no confidence. He was widely expected to lose that vote, of course, so let's go over to our East Central correspondent to discuss where that leaves Vasgar and its neighbors. It's a nonaligned state, and that raises some interesting questions. . . .*"

Adam got up and walked across to the world map on the wall. It was covered with pins and notes—random comments, reminders, even scribbled diagrams—to mark places of concern to him. There was Vasgar, a long corridor sweeping along the borders of Kashkur, Emgazi, and the Independent Republic of Furlin. If Vasgar didn't hold its neutrality, the strategic map of the Eastern Central Massif would change drastically, and for the worse as far as the COG was concerned.

He took the packet of colored pins from his desk drawer and pushed them into the map at various points along the borders to mark the strategic cities and installations he suspected might be listening to the news of Vasgar just as carefully as he was. Almost as an afterthought, he searched for a speck on the map high in the mountains to use up his last pin.

It was a fortified city called Anvegad.

KANI PROVINCE, PESANG.

It had been a harsh winter. Now it was turning into a bad summer. Bai Tak wondered how long it would be before he had to give up on his herd and find work in the town.

He followed his last surviving cattle further up the hillside as they searched for grass. They grew more bony and wretched with every passing week, and it was getting harder to find decent grazing for them. His only option would be to slaughter some and dry whatever meat they were carrying for the winter. It wasn't much. But he could sell the hides, and the bones wouldn't be wasted either.

Maybe it'll rain. Maybe I should wait. But I'm not going to ask for help from the village—not yet.

His wife, Harua, was working further down the hillside, taking advantage of the tinder-dry vegetation to get ahead with collecting firewood for the winter. She was bent double under a wicker pannier full of branches, struggling to hack a dead tree into more manageable pieces. Bai let the cattle find their own way—they were in no hurry—and half-ran, half-skidded down the hillside to give her a hand.

"Come on," he said, drawing his machete. "Stand back and let me do it."

"It's only because I've got this stupid little girl's blade." She brandished her cutting tool, a smaller version of the one all the men carried. Women needed theirs for self-defense and kitchen duties. Only men needed the heavier blade for slaughtering animals or—occasionally—fighting marauding Shaoshi clans from across the Pesang border. "Why can't I have a proper one like yours? This isn't heavy enough."

"I'll buy you one when we have the money."

"That'll be never. As soon I've filled the fuel shed, I'm going to find some work in the town. Cleaning. Maybe even cooking."

Bai was appalled. It was the ultimate admission of failure to provide for his family. If he let his wife take a paid job, everyone would talk. Everyone would say he was a no-good, bone-idle bastard who made his wife do two jobs while he lazed around watching his herd die on their feet. He couldn't let that happen. It would bring shame on Harua, too, for choosing a useless idiot for a husband, and if anything ever happened to him, she'd find it hard to get anyone else to marry her. The responsibility for getting them out of this crisis was his alone.

"Can you manage to look after the cattle as well as everything else?" he asked. He shielded his eyes against the sun to check where the herd had gone. The cows were standing around listlessly, gazing back at him as if they were waiting for him to come up with a better idea than the parched scrub they'd found. "If anyone goes to town to find work, it's me."

Harua took off her bandana and wiped her face with it. "Every herder's suffering the same. You won't find men's work down there."

"I will if I look hard enough."

Harua grinned and cupped his face in both hands. She shook him a little, like he was a child she was teasing.

"You're always so determined," she said. "That's why I picked you and not your cocky brother."

But Seng—cocky or not—had done all right for himself. He'd served in the army, fighting for the Coalition of Ordered Governments, and what looked like modest pay to those city people in the west was a fortune back here. Seng had saved enough to set up a company exporting traditional Pesang clothing and build a really nice house with plumbed water. Bai would have followed him into the army if he'd been taller and he hadn't already married Harua.

And not just for the pay. For the honor.

Harua wanted him to stay home to run the farm. He couldn't really argue with that, especially as the land was hers. He was also a few centimeters below the COG regulation height, even for a Pesang. That had disappointed him more than anything.

"Okay, I'll go today," he said. "It'll only take me a few hours to walk into town. I'll stay a couple of days and see what work's going."

Harua looked more resigned than relieved. "If you end up working in town," she said, "I still want a baby. I can't manage the farm as well when the baby's small."

"If I get a job, you won't have to. I'll make enough to get help." He knew she didn't want to abandon the farm. The land had belonged to her family for generations. "It's only while we wait for the drought to end."

That was optimistic talk. But it beat looking at those starving cows and counting down the days to ending up just like them. At least he was doing something, taking action instead of hoping for some unseen force to bring the rains.

It took him three hours to pick his way down to the valley floor and join the rutted track that was the main road to Narakir. Trucks and oxcarts passed him in both directions, kicking up clouds of pale dust that hung in the air like a fog. The town wasn't as busy as usual. He made his way to the square, expecting to find at least a few traders there who might be looking to hire help, but there was just someone selling fabrics and an awful lot of scrawny goats and sheep in temporary pens waiting to be sold. Nothing for him there, then; he decided to trawl the inns and workshops. He'd need to find somewhere to stay the night anyway.

Bai wandered into an open shed where a strong smell of animal piss made it almost impossible to breathe, even for a man used to living alongside cattle. It was the local tannery. Preparing leather was a backbreaking, dirty job, but he thought that if he started with the least popular work, he'd stand more chance of finding a vacancy. Tanners used urine for soaking the fresh hides—it turned them a soft, creamy white—and dog or fox shit for tanning them. It wasn't most people's first choice of career.

But when his eyes got used to the dim light, he realized that most of the men working on the hides were fellow farmers. He wasn't the only desperate herdsman with the same idea, then.

"Welcome to the perfume emporium, Bai." Noyen Ji heaved a pail of piss into a wooden butt. "Can we interest you in a bottle of our rose essence?"

"Don't suppose you need an extra pair of hands here, do you?" Bai made a quick mental list of the other workshops he could try next, starting with the blacksmith. "I'm willing to do anything."

"Sorry, friend. You could try the laundry up at the monastery, though."

"Okay. Thanks."

Bai spent the afternoon trudging from building to building, asking the same question and getting the same answer. Times were hard. Everyone was showing up looking for work to tide them over until things took a turn for the better. And each time Bai crossed the square, he noted that the number of miserable-looking animals in the pens was dwindling. He couldn't see the point of getting a few coins for your animals when you could eat them yourself. The fruitless afternoon depressed him so much that he decided to take a break at the inn. He had enough money for a pot of tea, and he could make that last for hours with the free top-ups of boiling water.

In a few hours, he could think of something else. He couldn't go back to Harua and admit he'd failed again. He had to return home with a job.

Yes, tea always made things look a lot brighter. He wandered down the street toward the tattered red silk pennant that flew from the inn's upper balcony, glancing into the windows of the buildings he passed. On one of the walls, there was a peeling and faded poster that caught his eye.

He'd seen it many times before but on this occasion it reached out and stopped him in his tracks. The words on it were printed in very poor Pesan, as if the person who'd made it didn't understand 'much of the local languages. The meaning was clear, though. The image of the smiling, healthy foreigner in his smart military armor, holding out a hand of friendship, was saying what a great career it was in the COG's army, and how welcome Pesangas were to serve in it. There was even a special regiment for them.

I'm too short. And Harua would kill me if I enlisted, anyway.

Bai walked on, somehow feeling the poster was aimed at him personally today. His father had served in the COG forces, and he raised Bai and Seng to understand that soldiering was an honorable living. Pesangas came from a warrior tradition; part of that tradition was to aid allies. The COG was respected, and it hadn't needed to invade Pesang to get the hill tribes' support for its war against the UIR. Bai was shocked when he first heard that nations did that—that they rolled over like beaten dogs and did the invaders' bidding. They should have driven them out. You could only fight alongside those who respected you, and those who you respected in return.

Bai could have used a big dose of self-respect right then. He opened the inn door, found a table, and sat down, suddenly realizing how exhausted he was. A radio was chattering in the background while a bunch of old men gambled with dice.

"Don't tell me, tea and jug of hot water," the waiter said. "But you look like you need a plate of rice."

"I need a job more," Bai said. "Anything going?"

"Nah. I could use someone to wash the dishes when I close tonight, though."

"Okay. Can I sleep on the floor?"

"If you sweep it first."

"Done."

It was a start. Bai hadn't gone looking for work since he was a kid. He needed to get back in the habit, and this was as good a way as any. It didn't bring him any closer to going back home tomorrow with good news for Harua, though. Somehow, he'd set himself a deadline and felt duty bound to stick to it. It was more for himself than for her, he suspected. He sipped his tea and paid no attention to the radio.

He didn't care much about politics, especially beyond Pesang, but the knot of men sitting around the ancient radio set was growing one by one, and they were frowning in concentration. Bai was curious. He listened to the broadcast. It was in Tyran—he could understand a lot of it, even if he found speaking the language hard—and it was talking about the situation in Vasgar.

Vasgar was hundreds of kilometers away, but there was nothing between Vasgar and Pesang except mountains, so that made them neighbors.

"The Indies are going to invade, mark my words," one of the old gamblers muttered. He kept his eyes on the dice. "They'd better stop before they reach our border, though, if they want to hang on to their balls."

"And heads," said another. "They wouldn't get far without those."

Everyone laughed. No army had ever invaded Pesang. They said every foreigner was scared shitless at the prospect of encountering a Pesang hill-man with his machete, and believed they could never hear Pesangas coming until it was too late. Bai didn't quite see himself as menacing, although he wasn't afraid to use his knife.

Did it really matter how tall he was?

No, this was stupid. Harua would go mad if he so much as *thought* about it, but he did. He thought of that poster, and how the white-faced recruiting sergeant had measured him and told him he was just a bit too short, but he couldn't stop thinking that it was worth one more try if the war was coming this close to home again. He'd been a little boy the last time anyone had talked this way.

"Where's the nearest recruiting office now?" he asked, knowing someone would answer.

One of the men sitting by the radio slurped his tea from a saucer. "Paro," he said. "Why, you getting all patriotic?"

The words just fell out of Bai's mouth. He didn't even think about it. "I'm going to sign up."

There was a silence around the room. Bai could hear a dog yapping in the distance.

"Me too," said another man. "In case these Indies get ideas. Anyone know where we can get a ride?"

"My brother drives a truck," said another man. "I'll go get him."

It was that simple, and that impulsive. An hour later, Bai found himself in the back of an open truck, bouncing down the potholed road to Paro with a dozen other men he'd only just met, not knowing if he'd be turned down again, or if he'd be a soldier this time next week, or if Harua would disown him when she found out.

He liked the feeling. It was more than needing the money. He really wanted to serve. It was a matter of pride.

When the truck reached the COG recruiting office, a soldier in armor stepped out onto the street to look them over. He was huge, a head taller than any of them, with very light hair and eyes.

"So you want to be Gears," he said. He spoke pretty good Pesan for a foreigner. "Can you all use that machete?"

Every Pesang male carried one. Each man from the truck drew his from its sheath with a rasp of metal on leather.

"Can you all speak some Tyran?"

Bai plunged in with his best accent. "Sah, yes, we can."

"That's what I like to hear. This way, gentlemen. First thing— I'm a *sergeant*. Sergeants aren't *sir*. We're *Sergeant*."

Bai decided it was now or never. He walked up to the sergeant and craned his neck to look him in the eye.

"Sergeant," he said. "I tried to join before. They said I was too short."

"That was *then*, son," said the sergeant, ushering him into the office. "You're just the right height now."

Harua would kill him. Bai reasoned that she would calm down when she received her first envelope full of banknotes.

It wasn't going to be forever, after all.

CHAPTER 6

He wants to be an engineer? A damned mechanic? I'm glad that my poor father isn't alive to see this. After all the education that Damon's had, all the privileges we've given him— he's a Baird, for God's sake. And a Lytton, too. He has duties. Now go and be a man for once, and tell him that either he joins the army, or he loses his inheritance.

(ELINOR LYTTON BAIRD, WIFE OF MAGISTRATE JOCELIN BAIRD, EXPRESSING HER DISAPPOINTMENT AT THEIR SON'S AMBITION TO STUDY MECHANICAL ENGINEERING)

PATROL VESSEL *AMIRALE ENKA*, PRESENT DAY, 15 A.E.

Muller stuck his head out of the wheelhouse. "Dom? Old Misery Guts is on the blower. Talk to him, will you?"

Dom was leaning on the rail, keeping an eye on the trawlers following line astern in the patrol boat's wake like ducklings. If there was anything in the water to hit, *Amirale Enka* would hit it first. There was a kind of logic to it.

"Okay. Is he mad?"

"Hard to tell. He always sounds pissed off."

Baird was on the foredeck, squatting over a small pile of debris he'd spread on a piece of canvas. He really did look like he was doing a jigsaw puzzle. Sam, still manning the gun, glanced over her shoulder to watch. Dom stepped into the wheelhouse and took the mike from Muller. Yanik the Disemboweler still leaned on the wheel, silent and unconcerned.

"Santiago here, sir."

"Can we rule out a Stranded attack yet?" Hoffman asked. "Folks believe what they want to believe, but it might calm things down here if I could look them in the eye and say it wasn't."

"What, civilian trouble?"

"Yes. What's your ETA?"

"About half an hour. Sorry, sir, the best we can do is guess. Baird says he can't see how the Stranded could pull off an attack like that, no matter how much hardware they've collected. Sam—well, she knows her ordnance, and she says it must have been huge. Mines are a really long shot, but the least *un*likely."

Hoffman went quiet for a moment. "It wouldn't convince me. Sure as hell won't convince anyone else."

"Sir, it'd be better if we *could* prove it was Stranded," Dom said. "Because if it's not, it's something we don't know how to deal with."

"We're going to have to limit where these people fish." Hoffman had heard him, all right. He just didn't want to talk about it on an open channel. "Give them some reassurance. Okay, get your ass back here and brace for diplomacy."

Yanik stirred. "This is what happened to our frigate. Collision— torpedo—grounding—*pah*. Whatever. Ships are not so unlucky all at once, eh?"

Muller rolled the stub of his cigar between thumb and forefinger. He seemed to use it as worry beads more often than he smoked it. "We could always rig a couple of vessels to do a wire sweep," he said. "But yeah, I'd rather find out what we're dealing with first."

Baird got up from his jigsaw of destruction and swaggered into the wheelhouse.

"I found a tooth," he said. "Human molar."

Dom waited for him to make some crack about putting it

under his pillow. He didn't. He seemed really *puzzled,* and that rare condition shut him up in a way nothing else could. It was as if he just couldn't believe that he didn't have an answer.

"No similarity between the two attacks, then." Dom kept thinking about the families who would be back in Pelruan now, numb with shock, sobbing their hearts out or refusing to believe their men had gone. He remembered every time he'd felt that way, but he couldn't re-create the sensation, and he wasn't sure if that troubled him or relieved him. "We found big chunks of hull and other debris where *Harvest* went down."

"Did we keep all that?"

Muller nodded. "It's on a trailer in one of the boat sheds."

"Okay, I'm going to take another look at it. The answer's staring us in the face."

Whatever that answer turned out to be, it wasn't going to be good news. Dom could see that even before *Amirale Enka* passed the channel marker buoy. When he checked out the jetty through his binoculars, he could see a mob of civilians milling around Michaelson, and at least two squads of Gears who looked like they'd formed a cordon. He expected to see Marcus, too, but he didn't. As the vessel slowed to enter the small ships' basin, Dom picked out Cole in the growing crowd. Cole—good-humored, funny, but very, very *big*—was good at calming folks down just by standing there.

"Shit, I hope they don't think we're landing bodies," Dom said.

Baird shrugged. "Soup, more like."

"Ever consider social work as a career?"

"Yeah, it was that or the diplomatic service." Baird gave Dom one of his wary looks. "You got to stop imagining how bad other people feel, Dom. Look after Santiago, Private D. You've got enough shit on your plate."

Okay, that's the Baird version of sympathy. He does try. He fails, but he tries.

The crowd stayed on the other side of a chain safety barrier as *Amirale Enka* came alongside and Gorasni seamen jumped onto the quay to secure her lines. Michaelson stood by one of the

bollards with his arms folded, looking up at the boat. He was waiting for Muller to report, Dom realized. He didn't address the
Gears at all.

"Well, this is all going *swimmingly*," Michaelson said, watching the crew drop the brow onto the quay. "But at least we didn't
misplace a frigate."

"Damned if I can tell you what happened, sir." Muller cocked
his head in Baird's direction. "But maybe he can."

Baird was already halfway down the brow in his rush to get on
with solving the problem. For a moment, Dom envied him; he
was totally self-contained, immune to grief, and satisfied by making broken things work. He was perfectly evolved for this bleak
postwar world. Now that Dom thought about it, he could never
recall Baird having a nightmare. Most guys had them, some frequently, some not, and in crowded barracks it wasn't something
you could hide; but Baird always seemed to sleep soundly.

"Let me take a look at what's left of *Harvest*," he said. "In case
we're blaming our nice Stranded neighbors unfairly."

Michaelson watched him go. "He doesn't think it's Locust,
does he?"

Dom shrugged. "I don't want to say it. But the grubs had
barges, remember. And that leviathan thing. We found them in
the underground rivers."

Sam walked up to Dom. "You can't cross an ocean in a barge.
And from what you told me, you'd see them coming anyway."

"*Excellent* point, Private Byrne." Michaelson was quite the
charmer. Even Sam didn't take offense when he checked her out.
"But I'm not ruling out anything. If you'll excuse me, I'd better go
and see just how far out of favor the navy is with the Chairman
now."

Lewis Gavriel pushed through the line of Gears and caught
Dom's arm. The poor bastard was mayor of Pelruan, a COG civil
servant marooned here since the Hammer strike fourteen years
ago, and he'd never even seen a grub. Now he was watching
his quiet island bombed, colonized, and generally fucked up by
his own species. Irony probably didn't cover it.

"Dom, can you tell me *anything*?" He was a nice guy. Dom wanted to help. "Casualties in double figures probably doesn't look as bad to you, but we're a *small town*. A few thousand people. We all knew those men well. Folks are angry."

Dom wasn't sure that he would have given Lewis someone to blame even if he'd known the answer, much as he wanted to. It would just cause too much trouble.

"I *saw* it," he said, "and I still don't know what happened. I'm really sorry."

Fate saved him, or so he thought. Marcus's voice interrupted over the radio.

"Dom, Sam—on me. Get over to the main gate for some assertive community mediation."

Sam swiped Dom's shoulder as she passed him. "Come on, Dom, it's kicking off."

He shrugged helplessly at Gavriel. "Got to go." As he turned, he caught sight of Marcus at the far end of the jetty. That explained his great timing. "If I hear anything, I'll tell you. I swear."

The collective mood of a mass of human beings was a weird thing. It made Dom edgy. On their own, people were generally reasonable, open to suggestions to move along or calm down. But in groups, they seemed to forget they ever evolved speech or opposable thumbs, and turned into one single dumb, bad-tempered, irrational animal. By the time Dom caught up with Marcus and Sam, the number of civilians milling around seemed to be growing, and there was a real smell of aggression.

Dom had policed food riots in Jacinto. He knew that smell of *mob*. And he never wanted to face down civvies again. Almost all the folks here were from Jacinto, though, the *old* Jacinto, so why the trawler incident had riled them was anyone's guess.

"Not a good day to be Stranded," Marcus said. "And they're not too crazy about us, either, thanks to Trescu."

"Why?"

"He shot a prisoner."

"Dead?"

"That's the usual outcome."

It was going to turn into a cage fight. Two tribes of people with grievances against each other, crammed into the same space; Dom's stomach knotted. The grubs had always been outside the gates. There'd always been a line between sanctuary and battle-field before.

By the time they reached the main gates, Dom could already tell that things were getting out of control. The line of trucks, junkers, and farm vehicles stretched far enough up the approach road for him to see it even over the sea of heads and helmets. At the front, behind the ironwork gates, Hoffman and Prescott were talking to the civilians outside. They were from Pelruan. Dom recognized them.

"Shit," Marcus muttered.

Dom's autopilot sent him hurrying to back up his old CO. It was a reflex now. "Blockade or lynch mob?"

"Shit either way." He checked his Lancer. "Dom, you sure that boat didn't get blown up by Stranded?"

"Sure as I can be. How the hell would they manage it? Even we can't mince a vessel into small pieces like that."

"Just checking."

They got to within a few meters of the gates. Hoffman had never been to charm school, but that probably worked better with the locals than Prescott's silky line of patter. At least the colonel sounded like he meant every word. And he did.

"You're not coming in," he said to the farmer at the front of the angry crowd. "And you're not going to block this access. God-damn it, I'd put a round through any of those bastards as soon as look at them, but that's not how we do things. Wait for one of our route-proving APCs to deploy, then turn your vehicles around and follow the 'Dill back home. You hear me? Go home."

Prescott opened his mouth to speak but he was drowned out by the shouting from the convoy.

"We didn't invite you here," someone yelled. "And we didn't invite the scum you've given houseroom to."

Other voices joined in. "We don't give a shit *who* you are. You've screwed this place in a matter of months. *Months.*"

The Vectes locals had never encountered a grub, and that gave them a different take on threats. Dom just prayed that nobody started shooting. The press of bodies on both sides of the gates was increasing and if things got uglier, people would get hurt. Sam was maneuvering herself into a position where she could get a clear shot. He didn't know whether to block her or not.

"Don't start that shit again," Hoffman snarled. "The whole *world's* screwed, and a lot worse than *this*. Go home. I know you're mad. *I'm* mad. But leave it to *us* to deal with it."

Marcus sighed and shouldered his way through the other Gears to step in front of Hoffman. Dom saw them exchange a glance. For a moment Dom thought Marcus had just decided to shield Prescott or something, but then Marcus hauled himself up and stood on one of the buttresses to get his head above the crowd. He held up his hand. He didn't do that very often.

"Hey!" he called. "Just listen. You know me. I'm telling you that trawler wasn't sunk by Stranded. We don't know what the hell did it. That's a good reason for going home and locking your doors *right now.*"

There was a silence that lasted maybe five seconds, an eternity in this situation, broken only by muffled barking from inside the vehicles. They'd brought their dogs along too. Dom saw Prescott twitch as if he was going to dive in and fill the gap with some bull-shit. Marcus just looked at him, *that* look, the one that shut *anyone* up, and Prescott seemed to change his mind.

Nobody moved. But somebody in the line of vehicles spoke.

"You wouldn't lie to us, Fenix?"

Marcus had a way of getting everyone to listen. They probably had to strain to hear him. He just dropped his voice way down.

"No," he said. "You need to know the truth. We might have bigger problems than just a few assholes. Go home, and let us do our jobs."

It took a few more seconds, but the silence became more ragged, and people started shuffling and generally calming down. There were no more shouts. Dom heard engines starting somewhere down the line.

"Wait for the Armadillo escort," Hoffman called. "I don't want any more casualties, you hear me?"

Everyone started moving away from the gates. Prescott caught Marcus by the arm, and for a moment Dom thought Marcus was going to deck him. Prescott, as cocksure of himself as any man could be, stopped in his tracks.

"Are you insane?" he demanded. "You could have started a panic. Why tell them there's an unknown threat out there?"

Marcus gave him the slow stare. Prescott let go of his arm.

"Dynamic risk assessment, Chairman. Better than having a riot."

Dom hung back with Sam for a few seconds, ready to wade in, but Prescott said nothing and walked off. Hoffman confronted Marcus.

"Think I couldn't handle it, Fenix?"

"Don't carry the can for Prescott," Marcus said quietly. "Makes it harder to get civvies to listen to you next time. Let them focus on the Chairman. It's his job to be disliked."

The set of Hoffman's jaw softened. Dom knew the old man well enough to know when he was taken by surprise.

"Okay, carry on saving my ass," he said at last. "Three times, and you get to keep the trophy."

"Nice job," Sam said as Hoffman walked off. "He respects that."

"Terrific." Marcus's attention was already on something else. "Ahh, shit. What *is* this, fight night?"

There were still a lot of people hanging about, some of them Stranded women and kids who'd accepted the amnesty. A gaggle of them had blocked the path of a bunch of Gorasni troops. Dom didn't know what the uniform was—militia, maybe—but it didn't seem to matter to the Stranded. They were spitting mad, and Dizzy Wallin was standing between the two factions making take-it-easy gestures.

"You murdering assholes!" one of the women yelled at the Gorasni. "Why don't you fuck off back to your own country?"

"Ladies, let's remember we got *young 'uns* around," Dizzy said.

"And you fellas—you wanna be seen fightin' with *girls*? Everyone just *relax*."

"Shut up, *garayaz*," one militiaman snapped. It was one of few Gorasni words Dom had picked up: *heap of shit*. "You're one of them."

Dizzy took a step back. "That ain't nice."

"Here we go," Marcus said.

Dom, Sam, and Marcus started a slow jog across to the argument, but it all got out of hand in seconds. One of the women gave a Gorasni the finger. The Gorasni lunged at her and almost hit one of the kids, a girl about ten. Then Dizzy stepped in to defend the kid, a bunch of Jacinto civvies dived into the melee yelling abuse at Dizzy, and punches were being thrown, all in the five seconds it took for Marcus to cannon into the ruck and force everyone apart. Sam got a smack in the face as she pushed the Stranded women away.

Dom didn't see if she threw a punch back. He was hit from behind—could have been accidental, but he didn't care—and the next thing he knew he'd pinned one of the Jacinto contingent against the nearest wall. The yelling stopped.

Marcus had one of the Gorasni in a headlock.

"Don't piss me off," he said. "I missed my anger management class today."

Dom let the civvie go and stood back. Dizzy still shielded the terrified kid, and this was the first time Dom had seen him lose that permanent patient good nature. Maybe the risk to the little girl had done it. Dizzy had two teenage daughters, and they were his life.

But he turned on the Jacinto civvies, not the Gorasni.

"We *fought* for you," he said, like the idea appalled him now. "I *abandoned my girls* for you. Damn it, I busted my ass killin' grubs, and I still ain't *human* enough for you? You ain't worth it. All you see's this damn hat and a bit o' dirt, and we're all the same. All assholes. Vermin. Well, fuck you."

Dizzy ran out of steam and let the kid rush back to her mother. It was so unlike him that even Dom was lost for words for a few moments. The man didn't seem so much angry as hurt. But the outburst put a stop to the fight. Sam moved in.

"Come on, Diz." She draped her arm around his shoulders. "Let's go and have a glass of your vintage kidney-killer. I'm choosy who I drink with."

Marcus stood glowering until the crowd slunk away. Dom sloped his Lancer on his shoulder, waiting for the next flashpoint.

"One big happy family." Marcus's shoulders sagged as if he'd taken a big, silent breath of despair. "Better check if Baird's come up with the goods."

There were bound to be tensions when you were rebuilding a whole planet, Dom thought. Relief at simply surviving didn't last long. People only seemed to unite when there was a clear threat to rally against.

Maybe Baird could put a name to one for them.

BOATHOUSE 9, VECTES NAVAL BASE.

Baird had never failed in his life. He aced every exam; he invented gadgets while waiting for the average kids to catch up with him on the page. He had never doubted his own abilities.

Until now. *Now* he was wondering if he was half as smart as he thought he was. The wreckage from *Harvest* was spread out on the floor, each section roughly where he thought it would have been before it blew up, the way accident investigators sometimes reconstructed Raven crashes.

Not that we didn't know what caused them. Ninety-nine times out of a hundred—Reavers, Brumaks, and grubs that got lucky.

There was a lot of boat missing. All he had was a few sections of hull, splintered and peppered with bullet holes.

Something wet splatted on his head. He looked up; a couple of seabirds had taken to roosting in the rafters. He was too engrossed to bother shooting them, and just moved position to sit on a crate out of the birds' range.

"Sit there long enough and you're gonna be caked in bird shit," said a voice behind him. It was Jace Stratton. "You think the Stranded got some tech we don't know about?"

Baird didn't turn around. He'd never been sure what to make of Jace. The kid was all right, a solid soldier, and maybe that was all he needed to know. Baird could also tell that Jace thought he was a dick, but then most people did, and Baird hadn't given a fuck about anyone else's opinion for a long time. Trying to please people never paid off.

"No, I don't," Baird said at last. "Because if they had, they'd have used it by now. And if they have fancy tech, they'd had to have stolen it from us. There'll be a boring reason for all this."

"What's the connection, then?" Jace asked. He didn't take the unspoken hint to get lost. "The two trawlers, or the latest trawler and the frigate, or all three?"

"Damn, I forgot to pack a forensic engineer." Baird slid off the crate. It was giving him a cramp in the ass anyway. Jace was a useful sounding board if nothing else. "Got any ideas? Don't think it makes you my boy detective sidekick or anything."

Jace gave him a yeah-whatever look and stood studying the pieces. The biggest section of hull, about the size of a couple of lunch trays, was still attached to part of the keel. Jace lifted the chunk of white fiberglass composite and flipped it over in his hands.

"I know how to do this," he said. His voice echoed in the cavernous space. "I've seen it on TV. They lay out the bits and try to reconstruct it."

"Man, the benefits of education."

Jace just gave him a look and carried on. Baird awarded him points for persistence. All that was left of *Harvest* was this glass fiber and plastic — no machinery, no bodies, no nets, no fabrics. If they'd recovered the engine or any of the fuel system, Baird might have been able to rule out a fuel explosion. You couldn't smash a trawler to bits just by shooting it up. It would have taken more than that to sink *Harvest*.

He picked up one of the smaller pieces and examined the edges, and realized he couldn't tell the difference between scorching caused by burning fuel or by the heat of an explosion. The ragged edges didn't clue him in, either.

"Which way around does this go?" Jace said. He held up a chunk of flat glass fiber composite peppered with bullet holes, then flipped it over. "This way or that?"

And that was the best damn question anyone had asked in a long time.

"Good point." Baird took the section out of his hands and tried to work out which side had been in contact with the water. There wasn't enough curve in the sheet to work out which part of the hull it came from, and both sides looked pretty shitty with encrustation. "There's more crap on this side, so I'm guessing *this* way up."

The ragged bullet holes had to have a direction.

Baird took off his glove and eased a finger into one hole to see if splinters snagged his skin. Yeah, he could feel it. When he pulled back, his finger slipped out easily. He tried it a few more times with another hole. When he held the sheet under a light and tilted it carefully, he could see a slight bowing around the holes.

"Shit," he said. "The shots came from inside the hull. Not from outside. It wasn't shot up from the outside while it was capsized, then."

"Is that a big deal?" Jace asked. "Doesn't tell us much."

"It tells me plenty."

"Okay, pirates might have boarded the boat. And they might *not*. You know how everything goes to rat shit when the shooting starts in confined spaces. How many of our guys got killed by friendly fire? Do these fishermen generally go out armed?"

Yeah, Jace was right. It didn't prove anything. But that was another good question nobody had asked before.

"Let's ask them if they went out cannoned up. It's not like they've got a lot of firearms washing around up there."

Jace nodded. "They're boarded, they squeeze off a few rounds, they hole their own vessel. Game over."

"But what blew the shit out of it?" Baird examined the splintered edges of the sheet. It had the same feathery tear lines he would have made if he'd ripped up fiberboard. The splaying suggested the force of the blast went outward. "You got to do more than hit a fuel line. It's not like the movies. You need a buildup of flammable vapor or something to ignite and explode."

"Hey, is this going to be the multiple factor thing you go on about? You know—it's never one thing that causes *catastrophic failure*. It's a lot of them all at once."

Jace was really getting into this. Baird felt chastened by the realization that Jace listened to him and *learned*. That didn't happen too often.

"Could be," Baird said. "Doesn't explain the confetti today, though. Or a steel-hulled warship having a negative buoyancy moment."

The doors creaked open. Marcus and Dom ambled in, followed by Trescu and Hoffman. The colonel was wearing his keep-this-asshole-away-from-me look.

"I'm charging admission," Baird said.

Marcus contemplated the wreckage. "Got anything?"

"Something we should have checked earlier. Shots fired from inboard to outboard."

"And?"

"Probably followed by an explosion inside the vessel. Can we skip all the movie scenarios? They didn't just put a hole in their own fuel line. Something else went wrong."

Trescu wandered around with his hands clasped behind his back as if he was doing an inspection.

"I'm a rational man," he said. "Very big ocean, very few vessels. Three sink in the space of a few months. All very different. Random statistical clusters are for clerks. So I will assume a common element until proven otherwise. Yes?"

"I thought your frigate holed herself on an underwater obstruction," Hoffman muttered.

"Indeed she did," Trescu said mildly. "But how did the obstruction get there?"

"Where? You don't have an accurate last position for her."

"That," Trescu said, "is why I am keeping an open mind about exonerating our *garayazka* neighbors too soon."

"If they'd done it, Commander, they'd be ramming it down our goddamn throats," Hoffman said. "It's not them. That much I'm sure of. Maybe there's another pirate contingent. They're always having territorial disputes."

Nobody said *grubs*. Nobody needed to. The new answers had just thrown up more questions.

"Screw this," Baird said, embarrassed that he hadn't solved the puzzle completely. He found himself checking Marcus's expression for signs of lost faith. However much people disliked Baird, he knew that they trusted his expertise. "If there's some shit out there, let's go find it. I'll volunteer. Got another tub you can do without?"

Trescu stared at Baird and Baird stared back.

"You Gears go out every day with the fishermen. Where is your new strategy here?"

Hoffman seemed to have had enough. "The trawlers can fish closer to the island until we get a handle on this, with a couple of Gears embarked on security detail," he said. "*Inside* the maritime exclusion zone. I think we can trust En-COG to maintain that. And if you happen to remember any little details about your frigate's demise, Commander, don't forget to tell us, will you?"

Hoffman turned and strode for the doors. It was a pretty eloquent command to follow him and get on with something useful. Baird piled the pieces of hull back on the nearest pallet and left with the rest of the squad. Trescu headed off on his own toward the Indie submarine *Zephyr*, probably to polish his jackboots or something.

"If they had a submarine, we'd have detected it by now," Dom said. "I mean, that's the only thing that could take out *Levanto* without being seen, right?"

"Don't believe all that submariner bullshit." Baird liked tinkering with the systems in *Clement*, but he had no illusions. "They can't find half as much as they let you think they can."

"Yeah," Dom said, "but they can blow stuff up okay. That's how this crap started, remember. If *Zephyr* hadn't torpedoed Darrel Jacques, we'd have a treaty with the gangs now and *he'd* be keeping them in order."

Baird decided that Dom had spent too much time wandering around Stranded camps looking for Maria. He'd picked up a bad dose of tolerance for them. Jacques would have turned out like all the rest, and nobody really knew how many Stranded were still scattered around Sera.

The COG was just a small city now. The last thing it needed was to make concessions to criminals.

"That's *our* job," said Baird.

FUELING PIER, VECTES NAVAL BASE: NEXT DAY.

Bernie's heart sank as she picked her way down the slippery steps of the pier wall and looked at the trawlers bobbing beneath her on the swell.

She really didn't feel up to being bounced around in a noisy tin box that stank of fish and fuel oil. She wished she'd let Hoffman reassign her. But that was more than an admission of defeat. It was a surrender to old age. The moment she accepted lighter duties, she would begin that slow—or not so slow—decline into frail senility. She didn't want to hang around and fade.

"Where's the puppy, Boomer Lady?" Cole leaned on *Montagnon*'s rail. "Thought you two was *inseparable* now."

"Whining his head off in one of the old fuel compounds with half a sheep carcass until I get back."

"You sure that ain't Baird?"

"No, Mac's the one with worms." She saw Baird tinkering with the trawler's winch mechanism. "A mother always knows."

Baird straightened up and fixed her with his blank look. "Talking of parasites, has Trescu the Terrible beaten anything useful out of that Stranded brat yet?"

"Why ask me?"

"Hoffman tells you everything, Granny. I mean, I used to think

it was your joints creaking when I passed your quarters, until I realized it was mattress springs . . ."

There's a lot Vic doesn't tell me. She let the jibe pass. "I suppose
we'll know when we stop finding bloody big craters in the roads."

Bernie jumped down onto the concrete platform that ran just
above the low watermark. Marcus stood with one boot on a bollard, looking like he was getting ready to slip the lines on *Coral
Star.* Dom and Sam were rostered to go with the smallest boat,
just known as M70. It needed a quainter name, Bernie decided.

Marcus gave her a glance, made no comment about being last
to muster, and waited for her to negotiate the shifting gap
between the boat's ladder and the pier wall. She pulled herself up
through the gap in the side rail and stepped straight into the
wheelhouse.

Aylmer Gullie, the elderly skipper, sat in the cockpit seat with
a mug of something steaming in his hand.

"Okay, Sergeant Fenix, slip the lines." There was a loud thud as
Marcus jumped across from the quay. Gullie pulled back the
throttle. "You really think this is going to be any safer?"

"Maybe not," Marcus said. "But at least we'll know more if
we're here instead of watching you detonate from two klicks
away."

"Optimist." Gullie winked. "Don't worry, we're staying
inshore."

Inshore for Vectes meant twenty kilometers, the limit of the
island's volcanic shelf. The three trawlers chugged out at near
their top speed, a modest eighteen kph, and there wasn't a lot for
Bernie to do except walk around the limited deck space and keep
a lookout. The four crewmen were busy below. She sat forward of
the brightly painted derrick that made the trawler look like it
would capsize at any time, and regretted having so much time to
think.

*What the hell is so bad that Vic's taking this long to tell me
about Anvil Gate?*

The worst thing was that she'd started imagining just what he'd
have to do to make her despise him. She'd killed two men the

hard way in absolute cold blood. Her threshold of unforgivable was set generously high.

Not violence, then. Something small. Something cowardly. No, that's not Vic. Foul temper. Thoughtless, sometimes. But cowardly? No.

Marcus wandered out and looped an arm around one of the derrick supports. He stood there for a full fifteen minutes, staring out across the waves in total silence.

Eventually he murmured, "Shit." But he said it to himself, not as a cue for her to ask what was bothering him. There were moments when she wanted to ask him how he handled what Hoffman had done to him—utterly out of character, unthinkably callous—but she knew Marcus too well to have any hope of an answer.

He stood there for another fifteen minutes, still silent, then turned and went aft.

What the hell do he and Anya say to each other?

Bernie forced herself to change the subject. It was nearly two hours into the trip before she heard enthusiastic chatter behind her and saw one of the crew training his field glasses on a flock of seabirds diving and dipping into a patch of water.

"More oilfish, I'll bet," he called to her. "Look out for bubbles over the side."

The hunt for the shoals did a good job of distracting her. Ten minutes later, *Montagnon* shot her nets and dropped to a sedate trawling speed. They were in business. *Coral Star*'s crew came up on deck and Bernie had to move back to the wheelhouse.

Cole flashed her on the radio. He didn't travel well. "Can I throw up now, please, Momma?"

"Try to miss the fish," Bernie said.

There was still no sign of trouble. There hadn't been any signs that *Levanto* was heading into danger, either, but the trawlers were inside the MEZ and that meant they had the comfort of a Raven patrol with a working sonar buoy, and CNV *Falconer* doing the rounds. This was as safe as it got in a job that was risky at the best of times.

At least Gullie was good company for a man who really did know far too much about fish.

"You any good at salting fish?" he asked her.

"Not two tonnes of it."

"I think it's going to be more like twenty. I can feel it in my water."

He probably could. When *Coral Star* drew her nets an hour later, Bernie went outside to see how good his guess was. A straining net emerged on the end of the cables as the winch whined, a bulging ball of glittering scales and draining foam.

For once, no gulls hovered around shrieking and trying to grab their share. They'd shifted their attention to the other trawlers.

Odd. Really odd.

"See?" Gullie said. "Chock full."

"The birds don't seem impressed."

"Ingrates."

The catch was mostly small, iridescent oilfish. Bernie wasn't squeamish about killing what she ate, but watching the squirming mass of fish, eels, and slimy things she didn't even have a name for suddenly made her feel sick. They were struggling to breathe, suffocating in air, flapping around in their death throes. When she killed an animal, she made sure it was *fast*. It was the only decent thing to do. Marcus watched, frowning, but that was no guide to what he was thinking.

"You okay, Bernie?" Marcus asked.

"I'll have the beef today," she said, turning to the rail to look away at the horizon. There wasn't a lot of room to avoid the bloodless carnage. "*Really* well done."

It was just as well Dom wasn't standing next to her. She'd showed him how to wring a chicken's neck when he'd been in her survival class during commando training. God, he was a kid then. *Seventeen*. The poor little sod had looked at that chicken with such horror that she'd been sure he'd pass out. He carried that big fuck-off commando knife that he didn't think twice about using in combat, but there he was feeling guilty about a chicken. He did it, though, and he ate it. He did it because he had to.

Poor old Dom. We never know what's going to be one step too far for us. We balk at the damndest things.

Maybe Hoffman's memory of Anvil Gate was something small but unerasable like the damn chicken, a substitute for something far darker.

He'll tell me. Got to be patient.

Bernie wasn't paying much attention to what was happening behind her. She could hear the trawler crew chatting, and the wet slapping noises as they sorted the catch into different buckets. Five or six hundred meters to starboard, she could see Cole leaning over the rail of *Montagnon* as if he was going to throw up again. Baird was scanning the sea through binoculars.

Well, back to canine patrol tomorrow . . .

"Hey," said one of the fishermen, the kid they called Crabfat. "You think this is what Cole got excited about when we caught that shale eel? Remember how he told us not to touch it?"

"Shit," Marcus said. "*Shit.*"

The hair on Bernie's nape rose instantly.

"Not you as well." Gullie laughed. "Plenty of sea life glows. It's dark down there, and they—"

"Get clear. I said *get clear.*"

"God . . . what the hell's *that?*"

Bernie swung around and saw what Marcus and Gullie were looking at. In the mound of fish, she could see a misshapen coil of scaly flesh that she would have taken for some kind of eel if it hadn't been rippling with blue light.

It wasn't the lights that scared the living shit out of her. It was the fact that the thing was changing shape as she watched it.

It sprouted a distorted limb, then another. Her eyes met Marcus's for an awful second.

The gulls spotted it. They bloody well knew.

"Get off the damn boat." Marcus grabbed Gullie by the collar and shoved him toward the stern. "All of you—get off the fucking boat—*jump!*" He opened the radio channel. "Dom, Baird—steer clear. We've trawled up a frigging Lambent."

They were in the middle of the ocean. The only place to run

was over the side. Gullie scrambled over the gunwale and his three crew didn't even stop to argue. They dropped into the water. Bernie did what she was trained to do—she stayed put. How big was this bastard? Could they save the boat? Did it have a blast radius?

"Bernie—get out. Go on." Marcus caught hold of one of the net lines and hitched it to the winch. "I'll try to dump it overboard again."

The Lambent eel was thrashing around now, shooting out tentacles and wrapping them around anything it could grab. One just missed her and whipped around one of the derrick's stanchions.

"Yeah, I don't think it's going without a fight." She revved her Lancer's chainsaw. "Is it killable?"

"Don't." Marcus ducked as a tentacle lashed past his head. "They explode."

"Shit. You'll never dump it."

"Just *go*."

"Set the bloody throttle to full speed and jump. Sod the boat."

Everyone came on the radio at once. The Lambent eel seemed to be growing by the second. It was thrashing so violently that it was scattering dead fish everywhere, carpeting the deck. Marcus vaulted over the tool locker and disappeared into the wheelhouse, and a few seconds later *Coral Star*'s engines roared into life. The boat shot forward, but trawlers weren't built for fast getaways.

"Marcus?" He hadn't come back out. She edged past the eel with her back to the rail, feeling her way along with both hands. "No heroics. I mean it."

She got to the wheelhouse door just as Marcus burst out of it. He crashed into her like a thrashball player and sent them both over the port-side rail into the water. For a moment, she was floundering in the muffled green gloom, propeller noises burbling in her ears, and then something jerked her head above the water and she took a gasping breath. The explosion shook her right through to her gut.

"Shit—" Marcus said.

The last thing that crossed her mind before the sky fell on her was that the trawler wasn't nearly as far away as she'd hoped it would be.

The column of water crashed down like a collapsing wall. She didn't know if she went under for seconds or minutes, only that when she bobbed up again, Marcus still had a grip on her webbing. Her hand felt instinctively for her rifle. It was still on its sling. If she'd been wearing full armor and not just torso plates, she'd have gone down like a stone.

"Everyone okay?" Marcus yelled. "I said, *is everyone okay?*"

"We see you, baby," Cole said. "Swinging by to pick up passengers."

Bernie trod water, looking around for the trawler. She couldn't see a damn thing except the bobbing heads of the trawler crew and *Montagnon* bearing down on her. *Coral Star* had vanished along with the Lambent eel.

Gullie swam over to Marcus. "Is that it? Is that a Locust?"

Marcus spat out some water. "I've never seen *that* before," he said, "but it's Lambent. Whatever Lambent are, the grubs were fighting them in their tunnels and *losing.*"

Gullie just tipped his head back, eyes shut, and floated. "And now they're here. We were safe. The Locust couldn't tunnel out here. But you never told us they could *swim.*"

"We didn't know," Marcus said sourly. "Now we do."

Bernie's stomach kept churning. The depth of the shit they were in suddenly hit her. The Stranded were the least of their problems now, and Vectes was no longer an ocean away from the horror of the mainland.

The nightmare had decided to follow them, except it was far worse. This was a life-form even the grubs were scared of.

"Yeah . . . shit," Marcus said again, as if he'd heard her thoughts.

Montagnon came up on them and cut her engines. Bernie grabbed the scrambling net and got halfway up to the gunwale, but Cole had to reach over and haul her the rest of the way by her belt. She flopped onto the deck at Baird's feet.

"Well, that fits my theory," he said cheerfully. Bernie decided she'd kick the shit out of him when she stopped shaking. "*Harvest* hauls up a glowie in the nets, they try to shoot it, it blows up— mystery solved. Same for *Levanto*."

"I'm so happy for you, Professor. Really."

Baird held out his hand to pull her to her feet. "Could it sink a warship, though?"

Gullie, wringing wet and white with shock, stared at the position in the water where his livelihood had vanished in a ball of smoke and flame. "How big do those things get?"

Marcus took out his earpiece and shook the water from it.

"Brumak size," he said. "At least. The size of a tank."

It was the last time anyone was going trawling for a long while.

CHAPTER 7

All civilian vessels are confined to inland waterways and five hundred meters from the shoreline until further notice.

Martial law is now in place under the terms of the COG Fortification Act.

All residents must observe a curfew between the hours of 2000 and 0530 unless the subject of a farming exemption.

(By order of the office of
Chairman Richard Prescott)

PELRUAN—NEW JACINTO ROAD.

"I want this kept quiet," Prescott said. "I want to know what we're dealing with before we start panicking the civilian population."

Hoffman pressed the mute button on the radio mike and was glad he was halfway to Pelruan, unable to grab the Chairman and shake the shit out of him. Where the hell did Prescott think he was? He couldn't even keep the lid on everything back in Jacinto, where he had every line of communication buttoned down and every citizen wholly dependent on the COG for protection, food,

and information. Vectes was a much looser, more free-range animal, impossible to rein in. The news was already out. Hoffman
was on his way to Pelruan to do his hearts-and-minds act.

Anya's knuckles were white as she gripped the steering wheel.
"Count to ten, sir," she whispered.

Ten. That was counting enough. Hoffman released the mute
key.

"We *know* what we're dealing with." Hoffman shut his eyes.
"*Goddamn Lambent.* And there's no keeping that a secret. The
fishermen know. They *saw* it frag their boat. They radio home.
They *talk.* What the hell do you want me to do—shoot them all
to shut them up?"

Prescott paused. Maybe he was considering the retort as a vi-
able option. Hoffman wouldn't have put it past him.

"I'm giving an order to restrict and jam all nonmilitary comms
channels," he said at last. "We don't know who or what might be
out there monitoring us now."

"Chairman, the people here live in isolated communities.
They *need* their radio net."

"They can relocate to New Jacinto."

Even loyal, tolerant Anya rolled her eyes at that. Hoffman decided to pick his battles, and this wasn't one worth fighting—yet.

"And the farmers? You want to move them in, too?"

"Every farm and settlement has at least a squad of Gears bil-
leted there. They can make supervised use of the secure military
net."

There were a dozen reasons why that was going to make matters worse. Hoffman saved them for later. He could waste time arguing with this asshole, or just get on with his job and beg
forgiveness later.

"Very well, Chairman. Hoffman out."

The Packhorse rattled north. Anya didn't say anything for a
while, but Hoffman could see she was fretting.

"Do you think he realizes how much we depend on locals calling in incidents when they're out working?" she asked.

"No. Does he know how many radios we can support on the
military net?"

"I don't think so."

"Good. I get the feeling we'll have a *lot*." Hell, nobody in Pelruan would be communicating with Stranded. It was hard enough to get them to mix with the Jacinto population. He'd give them free access to the COG's channels. "No point pissing off these people any more than we have to. If we stop them talking to each other, they'll just take to the roads, or bypass us in ways we might not know about."

Anya smiled. "Good thinking, sir."

"I don't disobey orders often."

"Ah, you're not disobeying now. I distinctly heard him say, 'supervised use of the secure military net.' Control routes all, hears all. I think that qualifies as supervision."

"What is it with you CIC kids? Mathieson's turned into a politician, and now you."

"I was thinking," Anya said, "that I was a frontline Gear now."

"So you are."

"I'm fit enough to resume patrols, sir."

"I need you on civilian liaison right now."

"Don't you think you should put Sergeant Mataki on that for a while? She understands rural people. They respect her." Anya paused. "And she's been blown up twice in one week. She's not sixteen anymore."

In all the years Hoffman had known Anya, she'd never said a word out of line or argued about anything. She never griped, sulked, or criticized. A quiet rebuke from her felt like a hard kick in the ass.

"I know," he said at last. Pelruan was now visible in the distance, a neatly maintained little fishing town still living in an age the mainland had forgotten a whole war ago. "I know what I ought to do. And you know how she'll react."

"If it were me, sir, I'd stop her."

Even in the privacy of this vehicle, she didn't spell it out to him. But Hoffman could read a whole extra layer of meaning in there. *Don't let it happen again. Don't let her end up like Margaret.* If only he'd stopped his wife from storming off in the run-up to the Hammer strike, she'd have survived. He didn't. Margaret was in-

cinerated with all the other millions of unlucky bastards. Anya
had spent the final hours before the launch calling around every
vehicle checkpoint in Ephyra to try to find her.

Anya knew, and understood.

"Thanks, Anya," he said. "Good advice."

Lewis Gavriel was already waiting outside the town's assembly
building when Anya brought the Packhorse to a halt. He was with
Will Berenz—his deputy—and a group of about fifty people.
Drew Rossi, the sergeant responsible for the town's Gears detachment, walked forward to intercept Hoffman as he got out of the
vehicle.

"Sir, is it true?" he asked. "Is it Lambent?"

"Damn well is, Drew."

"Shit."

"How are they taking it?"

"You have to spend fifteen years with grubs for neighbors to
grasp it. I don't think they understand at all."

"I'm not sure I do, either, Sergeant. Okay, let me talk to
them."

Hoffman was going to level with them whether Prescott liked it
or not. There was no reason not to.

"Have you heard from your boats?" he asked, knowing they almost certainly had. "Everyone survived this time. But you can't
go out fishing now."

Gavriel looked shell-shocked. They all did.

"Is it true?"

"What, that your trawlers were blown up by Lambent? Yes. It is."

"They're Locust, then. You know how to deal with them."

"Lewis, I have no goddamn idea *what* they are, only what they
do. Nobody knows the first thing about them. Except the grubs
were at war with them underground, and we never knew until we
sank Jacinto."

It was a hell of a lot for anyone to take in, let alone people
who'd been cut off from the rest of Sera since the Hammer strike.
Hoffman could see the complete bewilderment on their faces.
They couldn't even manage to be angry. They looked like scared

kids waiting for Dad to tell them he'd make everything okay again.

Berenz broke the stunned silence. "I never thought I'd say this, but I wish it had been the Stranded."

"So do I," Hoffman said. "Because they're *killable*. Last Lambent we killed—well, we *think* it was Lambent—took a Hammer of Dawn laser to finish it. That's what sank Jacinto."

"Oh God . . ."

"No bullshit, people. Every time we see one, it's a different shape or size. And don't ask me why they detonate. I know as much as you do. If it wasn't for some of the Gears running into them under Jacinto, we'd know even less."

"Why have they come here?" Gavriel asked. "Or are they everywhere, and we just happened to be unlucky?"

"If I knew that," Hoffman said, "I'd have a better plan, but I don't. Not yet." He looked into their eyes and suddenly felt like an utter bastard. This was an old COG outpost, and these folks had grown up thinking the COG was invincible. The last few months had proved to them what a delusion that was. "But the best I can do is this. Any of you want to take refuge in New Jacinto—I'll make damn sure there's room for you. If you want to stay here, I'll ship in more Gears. And if you need me to do any damn thing at all, you *call me direct*. Got it? Lieutenant Stroud will make sure of it."

Anya had her arms folded, feet apart. She didn't stand like the old Anya now, no casual hand on hip. She stood like a Gear. Damn it, she stood like her *mother*.

"There's nothing to suggest they'll come in close to shore," she said. "They've all been trawled up as far as we can tell. So as long as you don't put to sea, you'll be okay."

"But fish is a big part of the food supply here," said one of the women. "Our farms are keeping *you* fed down south. How are we going to make up the shortfall?"

It was just the start of a long chain of consequences that Hoffman could now see unfolding before his eyes. *Food shortages. Hoarding. Us and them.* He had to nip this in the bud.

"We've had a lot of practice at managing food supplies," he said. Damn, these people needed an officer assigned to them permanently, not just to make things happen but to give them some confidence that they weren't going to get screwed over any more than they had been already. He *needed* these people. He needed their cooperation even more than he needed the Gorasni fuel. They were the ones who knew how to live off this island. The Jacinto civilians were all city folk. "You'll have a member of my staff assigned to you to make sure you get a fair deal."

It was the kind of thing Anya could handle. Hoffman stopped short of dumping the job on her there and then, but his mind was already made up. This was made for her. She could play frontline Gear, too, but she'd also do what she did best—organize, deploy, and reassure.

"What about the curfew? And the radio blackout?" Gavriel asked. The crowd behind him was gradually growing as more people seemed to notice the COG command had come to town. "Is that because of the Lambent, or the Stranded? The no-go areas were bad enough."

"I'll talk to the Chairman," Hoffman said. *Why the hell am I doing this? Why aren't I just relaying the orders?* It went beyond his pragmatic need to keep this town sweet. He knew it. "Leave it with me. You'll get your radio net."

Anya gave him a wary look as they got back into the Packhorse. They were four or five klicks down the road before she said anything at all. Maybe she'd worked out that she'd be spending more time in Pelruan than at the naval base, and she'd see even less of Marcus Fenix.

"Are you okay, sir?" she asked.

"Why?"

"I didn't realize you felt so responsible for Pelruan. You seemed quite agitated."

So maybe it's not about Marcus. And maybe I'm the one with the issues.

"We can't leave this to politicians." He realized that sounded like he was plotting a coup. "Anya, you're the right person to take charge of the town. Will you do it?"

"I'll do whatever you ask me to do, sir."

"You can say no."

She hesitated just that fraction of a second too long. "I'll do it."

"It's not a soft girly option. You'll have command of a couple of squads."

Hoffman let that sink in. Anya just nodded.

Yes, he was worried about Pelruan. And the worry sprang not just from necessity, but from the last time he'd been responsible for the day-to-day survival of a city.

Not Jacinto. Whatever I felt, I was never alone in Jacinto. Anvegad—that was different. That was desperate. That was all down to me.

"Thank you, sir," Anya said. "I won't let you down."

On the way back to base, they had to stop to let the route-proving vehicle pass them. One of the giant grindlift derricks had been fitted with a chain flail and drove the main roads twice a day to clear any explosives. Dizzy Wallin brought the juggernaut to a stop and stuck his head out of the cab.

"All safe behind, Colonel," he called. "Trust ol' Betty. She don't miss a thing with her new grass skirt."

"Thanks, Wallin." The height of the cab gave the man a good view over the countryside. "Anything happening on the ground?"

"Just those Indies out lookin' for the gang."

Hoffman bristled. "What Indies?"

"Ol' piss-and-importance Trescu and his heavies." Dizzy sounded as if he thought everyone knew, but then his expression changed. "They're out in the woods with that kid. Nial. He was leadin' 'em somewhere."

Trescu hadn't said a damn word about it. The last thing Hoffman knew was that Trescu was still interrogating the teen-ager and had agreed to hand over whatever intel he got. The bas-tard had lied. *Surprise.* Hoffman wondered what had made the Gorasni extra negative about Stranded, because this went far be-yond the COG's dislike of them. After the sinking of the *Trader*, his was starting to look like a concerted purge.

"Thanks for the heads-up," Hoffman said. Dizzy saluted, fore-finger to the battered rim of his nonregulation hat, and the derrick groaned on its way. "At least someone keeps me in the loop."

"What are they going to do with that boy when they're finished with him?" Anya asked.

"I don't plan to leave that to Trescu," Hoffman said. "Screw humoring him. He's not a law unto himself, no matter how many damn imulsion rigs he's got."

This was how things went to rat shit; a blind eye turned here, a concession made there, and questions not asked. Human civilization was fragile enough as it was. Private armies like Trescu's were the road to anarchy, and Hoffman had to assert his authority before things got out of control. Prescott had to be made to see that.

Hoffman was still fuming silently, watching the countryside passing by, when Anya started to brake.

"Someone up ahead, sir. Gorasni."

The Gorasni had set up a roadblock. Hoffman could see it clearly, a token effort of branches and a few strands of razor wire across half the width of the paving. It wouldn't stop a Packhorse. Who the hell did these needledicks think they were?

"Stop twenty meters back, Anya, just in case." Hoffman felt for his sidearm. Common sense said he didn't need it, but instinct said he did. "If they don't pull that goddamn junk off the road before we get there, that is."

As the Packhorse slowed, it was clear the three militiamen weren't going anywhere. Anya brought the vehicle to a halt. Hoffman got out and strode up to the first Gorasni, a square-looking middle-aged man with sergeant's stripes on his sleeve.

"Get this off the road." He was so close he could smell the man's breath—onions, tooth decay, and whatever the hell these people rolled for a smoke. "*I'll* tell you where and when to place checkpoints."

The sergeant didn't blink. "Commander Trescu said we were to stop traffic entering this area for the next hour."

"Commander Trescu can kiss my ass. This road remains *open*." Hoffman never reminded anyone of his rank. It was the resort of an officer who couldn't command. A man had to *show* his authority. "I'm getting back in that vehicle, and if you haven't pulled that garbage off my goddamn road by the time I start the engine, I'll be driving *over* you."

Hoffman was pretty sure they understood Tyran well enough to get all the nuances. He marched up to the driver's side and opened the door.

"Move over, Anya. And get ready to duck."

From that moment on, he couldn't back down. He started the engine, engaged the clutch, and moved off. The Indies just stood there. Hoffman accelerated.

If he hit them, it was too bad.

The roadblock loomed in the windshield. His instinct was to brake, but he just put his foot down. The last thing he saw seconds before the Packhorse thumped into the barrier and smashed it to one side was the Gorasni jumping to safety.

He almost expected shots from behind. He didn't bother to look in the mirror.

"Assholes," he said. "The next man who calls them *Indies* is on a charge. They're not a separate state anymore."

"Well done, sir." Anya flicked the radio control and held the mike where he could grab it. That girl could read his mind. "You'll be wanting this."

Hoffman could hear sustained rifle fire in the distance. It didn't sound like Lancers. He'd have known if there'd been a contact on that scale anyway, but nobody had given Trescu clearance to deploy men. This had to stop.

"Mathieson? Get Trescu on the radio for me."

"Wait one." The link went silent for a few moments. "Sorry, sir, he's not using the kit we gave him. He's on his own net. They've got a transmitter on board one of their ships."

Hoffman almost spat. He wasn't going to tolerate two armies here. If Trescu wanted to play soldiers, he could do it where Hoffman could hear it and see it. Gorasnaya was part of the COG now.

That was the deal.

"Jam it," he said. "Shut that damn thing down."

TRAWLER *MONTAGNON*, APPROACHING VECTES
NAVAL BASE.

The mood on board *Montagnon* had shifted through shock, relief, and anger, and had now dried to a shade of shaky, hysterical humor.

Surviving close calls had that effect on everyone except Marcus, Baird noted. He just sat on the tool locker listening to the comms channel. If they ever built a statue of him, that was the way Baird was sure it should look; finger pressed to his earpiece, staring into mid-distance, and frowning. From time to time he made a noise in his throat like a disgruntled dog.

"Told you there was glowies down there, didn't I?" Cole said to Gullie. They were all sitting on the deck while the crew sorted the catch very, *very* carefully. "And you laughed your ass off."

Gullie clutched a mug of hot broth. "I'm sorry. We just never saw these things. How did you live with these monsters coming up under your streets for *fifteen years?*"

"That was grubs. They don't explode much."

Baird joined in. "Unless you make 'em. Then they blow up just *great.*"

He moved over to Bernie, trying not to look as if he was fussing over her. Without armor and the extra bulk of a rifle and webbing, she looked pathetically thin in her wet fatigues. She reminded him of a waterlogged bird huddled on a branch waiting for the rain to stop. She was just an old woman; he couldn't believe she'd ever knocked him down with a single punch. Even her Islander coloring had drained out of her. Her skin looked more gray than brown.

"Hey, Granny, you're not going to die on me, are you? Fishing you out of the water's getting to be a habit." He waited, but she didn't bite back. "Who's going to bitch at me when you're gone?"

"I'm okay," she said. "Hot shower and a night's kip, and I'll be fine."

"I hope *kip* means sleep. Because you're in no shape for anything more athletic."

Cole sat down next to her and put his arm around her shoulders. "Doc Hayman better check you out, Boomer Lady."

"Look, I promise I'll stay alive until we hold Andresen's funeral," she said. "Okay?"

That shut everyone up like a smack in the mouth. Marcus's voice suddenly carried across the deck.

"Shit," he said. "That's all we need."

"What?" Bernie asked.

"Some clusterfuck ashore." Marcus stood up slowly. "A disagreement with our Gorasni citizens."

"Riot?"

"Hoffman and Trescu. I can only hear one side of it. Michaelson's blocked the entrance to the tanker berth with *Falconer* to stop their fuel freighter leaving for the rig."

"Wow, war on the high seas," Baird said. "Are they bored or something? Did they miss the message about seagoing Lambent? Maybe we better repeat it in capital letters."

Marcus got back on the radio. "Let's see if Hoffman wants us to do anything special."

"In a trawler? Yeah, let's bombard them with shrimp and force a surrender."

Dom's voice emerged from the wheelhouse radio. "This is M-Seventy. Anyone want to tell us what's happening?"

Montagnon's skipper, leaning against the open wheelhouse door, picked up the mike. He'd learned all the Gears' technical terms. "Shit, as usual," he sighed.

Baird grabbed a pair of binoculars and looked north from the bows. He could now pick out the carved frieze on the signal tower at the naval base, which meant they were less than thirty minutes out. *Falconer*, the NCOG's fast patrol boat, was sitting in the entrance to the fueling berth.

"And we were all getting on so *well*," Bernie said.

Cole stood up to look. "So do we raise the alert state from *damp pants* to *urgent change of underwear*?"

Marcus looked like he'd made contact with Hoffman. He said "Why?" a couple of times and then "Understood." Everyone turned to see what he had to say next.

"It's just a pissing contest," he said, sounding almost disgusted. "Hoffman jammed the Gorasni transmitter to force them to use our net. Michaelson's stopped their tanker leaving for the imulsion rig until they let us fit an NCOG transceiver in it. He's citing safety issues."

"Why'd Hoffman do that?" Cole asked.

"Because Trescu's not been sharing intel. He went hunting for the bombers on his own."

"Shit, we never used to be this *sensitive*," Baird said. "How come we all got so petty so fast?"

Cole sat down next to Bernie again and nudged her. "Remind me who we're supposed to be fightin' today. I get confused."

"Did he get them, though?" Bernie perked up a bit. "I can see the problem for Hoffman with Indies going off the grid, but did Trescu do us a favor and slot any?"

Marcus shrugged, silent.

"What about the kid?"

"Eight's a kid," Baird said. "Fifteen is adult."

Gullie interrupted. "The Lambent," he said. "Forget the Stranded. What about the Lambent? What are we going to do about the *Lambent*?"

Nobody answered for a while. Baird hated displays of ignorance, and thought the man deserved a rational response.

"Treat 'em like stray mines," he said. "Fishing boats were always catching unexploded mines back on the Tyran coast. It's a risk you have to set against all the times you *don't* find one in your nets."

That was sensible and honest. It didn't answer any of the other questions milling around in Baird's mind, but he'd take this apart and put it back together a piece at a time, like he did when he was a kid dismantling anything he could get his hands on. He'd work out what was going on.

There's always a reason. There's always a method. There's always an explanation.

Montagnon and M70 chugged into the base. The surface of the water was iridescent with a thin layer of fuel, and it hadn't

been that way before the Gorasni imulsion tanker arrived. Filthy
Indie slobs; they were flushing their tanks inshore. Chemical hazard regulations had gone down the lavatory a long time ago, but
Baird thought the Indies would at least understand that this was a
fishing community, and everyone had to eat whatever swam in
that shit. Gullie looked over the side and shook his head.

"At least the Stranded didn't do *that*," he said sadly.

Marcus peered over the side and frowned. "I'll have a word
with them."

Baird was expecting some sign of trouble on the quay, but it was
all very quiet when they stepped ashore. Major Reid met them.
That in itself said that the big boys were busy elsewhere.

Reid was an asshole. He had the kind of petulant face that
Baird could have punched all day without getting bored. If
Hoffman dropped dead, this was the guy who'd take command —
or else it'd be Major McLintock, another rectum on legs. Baird
would almost have taken a bullet for Hoffman to avoid both options.

"Fenix, Mataki — Hoffman wants you in his office for a debrief,
seeing as you eyeballed the thing. He says get yourselves checked
out by the medic first." Reid looked them over critically. "Did you
recover any parts of the creature?"

Marcus fixed Reid with the cold blue stare. "We were kind of
busy not getting our guts scattered everywhere."

"We don't have the lab equipment to examine that shit anyway," Baird said, and walked past Reid. "Did you want souvenirs?
I'll grab some next time."

"Corporal, where do you think you're going?"

Baird turned, still walking. "Until the next patrol? Got to be
some 'Dill that needs servicing."

"You, Santiago, Cole, and Byrne — civil order patrol." Reid was
the admin boss, good at organizing food supplies, which was
probably why nobody had fragged him when Hoffman wasn't
looking. But he wasn't the kind of guy you'd die in a ditch for. He
never quite got the hang of inspirational orders. "We need boots
on the ground at the north perimeter to reassure the civvies."

Dom appeared as if the mention of his name had conjured him up. "More explosions while we were away?"

"No," Reid said. "More hassle between the various contingents inside the wire. Keep a lid on it."

As soon as the Jacinto population had landed, the race had been on to build new housing. People crammed into ships and barracks that were never designed to hold a city's worth of people, and they had to be decanted fast before disease and overcrowding got the better of them. Baird thought of New Jacinto as an organized shantytown, a growing sea of basic wood-frame houses stretching out from the northern wall of the naval base and pushing the city limits further every week.

But however instant New Jacinto was, however much a fresh start—the first thing it acquired was neighborhoods. Baird found it funny that no amount of encouraging people to mix or taking trouble not to call the former Stranded "Stranded" changed one damn thing. The ghetto lines were drawn by the inhabitants.

The line he walked now was between the few hundred Stranded—ex-Stranded—and a mix of huts and emergency tents that housed Old Jacinto locals. The Gorasni refugees were located on the western edge of the shanty. The main road was a run of trackway laid by the combat engineers, an interesting mix of scavenged wood, metal, and plastic planking. Baird paused to admire the ingenuity.

That's where I should be. In the Corps of Engineers. As long as I get some frontline action, too, of course. There's only so many latrine blocks a guy can take.

"I think they've done a good job." Sam took the other side of the trackway, turning to walk backward a few paces every ten meters or so. "I've lived in worse."

Dom ambled ahead. Baird noticed that he didn't stop to coo over kids now. He just turned away. "You know what would help? Putting more civvies on food production. Get them out digging and planting. Useful. And makes you feel good."

"I'm still gonna take up fishin'," Cole said. A Stranded woman was hanging out washing on a line strung between the huts. A snot-nosed toddler clinging to her legs stared suspiciously at the Gears. Cole waved. "All them streams we got here. Gotta be fishin'."

"What's in the center of the island?" Sam asked. "Looks interesting from a distance."

"The dead volcano," Baird said. "Forest. Caves. Probably full of undiscovered species that Mataki will shoot and eat before anyone knows they exist. She's a one-woman extinction machine."

The patrol was almost at the perimeter gate now and Baird was bored shitless already. It was like doing a square search without anything to look for. When they reached the fence, they'd turn ninety degrees and work back again. When he spotted an old man trying to start a portable generator, Baird leapt on the chance with relief. He didn't even need to look. He could *hear* what was wrong with it.

"Hey, here's how you do it," he said, whipping a screwdriver out of his belt. He couldn't bear to see people fumbling around with stuff they obviously didn't understand. "Look. Take this plate off, and you've got this fuel injector. It's just a car engine. *Look.*"

The guy was Stranded. Baird didn't notice or care right then. He caught Dom giving him a you're-okay-really look, and he squirmed. He wasn't being noble. He just had to stop and fix shit in the same way that other people couldn't walk by a crying child or a wounded animal.

Because I can do this. That's all.

He started dismantling the generator. "This needs a workshop, Granddad," he said. "See, this is what happens when you let these things idle too much. Cylinder pressure's too low, the piston seals leak, and then—ah, forget it. Just remember that it leads to smoke and shitty starting."

"Baird, nobody here's got a clue what you're talkin' about," Cole said. "But it sure sounds convincin'." He watched Baird for a while and then jerked his head around to stare back up the trackway to the gates. "We got visitors."

Baird stopped and looked. It was one of the Gorasni utility vehicles, a cross between a Packhorse and a flatbed truck. Baird could see a Gorasni militia guy in his faded black battledress standing in the back, holding on to the slatted sides of the vehicle as it rumbled slowly down the trackway toward the squad.

"Shit, what are they doing in here?" Dom whispered.

Sam slid her Lancer forward on its sling very slowly as if she was getting ready to aim. "If they start throwing candy to the crowd, I'll know to lay off Dizzy's brew."

But it didn't look like a goodwill operation. Baird watched the reactions of people who were behind the truck. As it passed, they took a step back as if they'd seen something they weren't ready for. One or two shook their heads and went back into the tents.

It wasn't until the truck reached the row of huts that marked the boundary of the Stranded zone that Baird realized why. He worked it out a few seconds after the Stranded women started yelling to one another and pouring out of their homes.

The militia guy on the flatbed unbolted the side slats and let the panel drop. It was Yanik. Baird hadn't recognized him with his cap on. And he was standing in a pile of bodies. They were laid out neatly, stacked like logs, but there were eight or nine of them, and they weren't taking a nap.

"Oh, fuck," said Dom.

One of the Stranded women started screaming. Yanik—a nice guy, a *funny* guy—touched his cap to Baird.

"Never let it be said that we are *savages*," he said, giving one of his buddies a hand up to the truck. "We let them bury their dead. Which is more than they ever did for us."

Then the driver got out. The three Gorasni started tipping the bodies off the truck and dumping them—still neat and lined up—onto the grass border on the Stranded side of the trackway. Women were sobbing; the old man with the crapped-out generator stumbled across to the pile and sank to his knees next to one of the bodies. They were all youngish men, and when Baird made himself look, most of them had a single shot to the head.

"Should we be doin' somethin' about this?" Cole asked. "This ain't right."

Nobody knew what the rules were now. Prescott had let the

Gorasni clean up the problem, and this was what it looked like up close; rebel Stranded, shot and shipped back to the camp where their families had taken amnesty.

But it was a war, whichever way Baird looked at it. The Stranded wanted to fight the COG. The Gorasni just didn't fuck around with rules like the COG did.

The Stranded crowd was right on that edge between silent, shocked disbelief, and an eruption into grief and outrage. The old guy was slumped on all fours over the body, like a dog standing guard over its dead master. He looked as if he didn't have the strength to stand up.

"This is my son," he said. His voice shook. *"This is my son."*

Baird was the corporal here. A riot was a couple of seconds away. All he could think of was to get the Gorasni out of the camp, to remove the focus for a flashpoint.

"Yanik, you better run, man," Baird said. "Get out of here before this goes to total rat shit."

Sam and Cole moved instantly to block the Gorasni from the Stranded. Dom went over to the growing crowd and started calming them down.

"Folks, let's stay cool," he kept saying. "Stay cool."

Baird watched for a moment. What *did* you say to the families and friends of men who'd turned Andresen—and DeMars, and Lester—into frigging ground chuck? Did you say *sorry?*

No. You fucking didn't. Because you weren't.

Baird could hear a weird chorus of disjointed sobs and shouts that was starting to merge into one voice and getting louder, a curse and a scream and a threat at the same time. Yanik slammed the truck door behind his buddy and put one boot on the flatbed to jump on board.

"You look at me like I am a *grub*," he said to Baird. "Like I kill for no reason. One day, Blondie-Baird, I will tell you what the *garayaz* did to us at Chalitz, and you will see things another way. We are the last Gorasni. *The last.*"

The truck revved up and shot off in reverse—very nearly in a dead-straight line—to swing around and head out through the gates again. Baird looked over his shoulder for the first time since the truck had stopped. That told him how much he trusted Jacinto folk not to mess with Gears. There was a crowd watching, all right, silent and apparently unshocked.

"We oughta at least help the ladies," Cole said. "They didn't blow anything up, did they? Shit, there's *kids* lookin' at all this. Let's get some tarpaulin or somethin'."

"Yeah, comforting the widows is really going to go down great with most of the people standing right behind us."

But Baird went to do it anyway, because it upset Cole. He didn't get far. A Stranded woman—thirty, maybe, all hate and tight lips—blocked his path.

"And you can fuck off, too," she snapped. "We don't want your help."

Sam herded the Jacinto locals back from the trackway. "I think it'd be a good idea to go inside," she said. "Help us out here. Move along."

All Baird could do was call it in and wait with the squad to make sure nothing kicked off while the bodies were carried away. Where were they going to bury them? Maybe it was a cremation. He didn't ask—he wasn't designed for this kind of touchy-feely shit, and he knew it. Dom, Mr. Sensitive, didn't seem to be handling it any better, though. He stepped back to stand with Baird.

"I never heard of Chalitz," he said quietly. "Must have been bad."

"Dead's dead." Baird put it out of his mind right away. He could do that a lot more easily now. "And we're not. I'm going to do whatever it takes to stay that way."

SERGEANTS' MESS, VECTES NAVAL BASE.

Bernie's debrief hadn't taken long. There wasn't much she could tell Hoffman about the Lambent life-form, and she felt ashamed. She saw the enemy and she didn't evaluate it. That was sloppy.

"Didn't see much myself," Marcus said, arms folded on the bar. "Don't beat yourself up."

Bernie couldn't remember the last time she'd had a drink with Marcus. He wasn't social. It was more of a brief, disjointed conversation that just happened to be in a place where alcohol was served.

"At least they're getting smaller. Not Brumak-sized this time." She checked her watch. There was condensation inside the glass after the morning's dunking. "Maybe they'll be a unifying influence and stop the Stranded cutting our throats."

"Yeah, Trescu's boys get to the point."

"Prescott should have shipped the Stranded out right from the start."

"But he didn't. So we make it work."

"You're a kinder soul than me, Marcus."

Marcus snorted. It was as near as he ever got to laughing. "I take people on an asshole-by-asshole basis."

Bernie drained her glass. "Got to go."

"You on watch?"

"Hoffman."

"Ah," Marcus said, not looking away from the Locust cleaver hanging on the wall behind the bar. Andresen had built this bar with Rossi. Baird had taken the cleaver from a grub the hard way, and given it to Bernie. Everything in this mess had cost blood. "Ah."

"When you're my age, waiting looks bloody stupid," she said. "Grab some life, Marcus. You'll never get those years back."

He just grunted. He knew what—and who—she meant. "Uh-huh."

Bernie wasn't sure who she felt worse for, him or Anya. She headed over to the HQ building, wondering if things would have worked out differently if Helena Stroud or Adam Fenix had still been alive to nag their offspring into common sense. From outside the building, she counted the floors up and windows along, and saw that the light was still on in Hoffman's office. She'd haul him out.

The back stairs creaked a lot, but it was still more discreet than going via the main staircase. She got to the landing and went to push the door open, but the raised voices stopped her in her tracks.

Shit. He's got someone with him.

Bernie dithered, wondering whether to come back later. But she hung on. There was a row in progress. The longer she stood there, the less she felt she could leave. She waited, not even sure why, and stepped into one of the alcoves next to the door.

Prescott was in there, letting rip.

"What in the name of God were you *thinking?*" he snapped. "You can't just shut down their comms system. You have no authority."

"I have *every* damn authority." Hoffman's voice had sunk to that strangled growl that said he was close to losing it. "I'm the chief of staff. We have *one* army and *one* navy. We do *not* franchise the defense of this state to a bunch of animals settling their own private vendettas. I don't care if they've got fuel rigs coming out their asses. Either I command *all* our assets, or I command *none.* Your call, Chairman."

"Are you threatening to resign?"

"I can't do this job if you keep cutting me out of the loop. Stick to policy and objectives. Leave the operational shit to me."

There was a long silence, about five seconds. Bernie wondered if the next sound she was going to hear was the crunch of bone.

"I hate to be dissident, Chairman, but I'm with my red-faced colleague on this." It was Michaelson's voice. Bernie hadn't even realized he was in there. "It's simply unacceptable to allow the Gorasni to operate an army within an army. Or a navy, come to that. The deal was refuge in exchange for fuel, and our condition was that they join the COG. This isn't even about their behavior with the Stranded."

"They've destroyed three explosives caches and killed fifteen gang members in the last twenty-six hours," Prescott said. "I don't recall you making that much progress."

"I don't torture kids," Hoffman snarled. "And I don't dump

bodies back on the widows. That slows things down a little, Chairman."

Michaelson cut in. "We have to bring them into line. If we don't do it now, it'll just escalate. You'll lose control."

Bernie had to hand it to Michaelson. He knew how to grab Prescott's attention. He was a much more political animal than Hoffman, more inclined to play that game and enjoy it. Hoffman just lost patience. He wanted to storm the beach and take it.

Too honest, Vic. Prescott's going to chew you up and spit you out.

"Very well," Prescott said at last. "And what if Trescu denies us fuel?"

Michaelson actually laughed. "Chairman, he has an isolated rig, no air assets, and the whole Gorasni population is living within our borders. Am I missing something?"

"Goddamn it, can't we concentrate on the urgent issues?" Hoffman interrupted. "*Lambent.* We have Lambent in the middle of the ocean. Not back on the mainland, *on our doorstep.* I can put Stranded bombs on hold for a while, and even Trescu, but we have to pay attention to what we've found."

"I'm more interested in what sank Trescu's frigate," Michaelson said. "Because exploding luminous eels don't quite answer the question."

"You get the intel," said Prescott, "and come to me with a threat evaluation. By the way, I want a personal security detail— I need to be able to walk around New Jacinto without dodging stones from malcontents. I refuse to give in to hooliganism."

The floorboards creaked as someone walked toward the door. Bernie pressed herself flat in the alcove and held her breath, feeling a complete fool and wishing she'd just knocked, embarrassed herself for two seconds, and walked away. But she hadn't.

The door swung open and Prescott breezed past, heading for the stairs. He didn't see her. Now she had to wait for Michaelson to leave, and he could stay chewing the fat with Hoffman for hours. The door was slightly ajar and the voices clearer.

"Asshole," Hoffman muttered.

"Don't worry, we'll handle him. Give him his personal protection Gears and let him play statesman with Trescu. Keep him busy."

"Why the hell isn't he more focused on the Lambent?"

"Politicians. Short-term thinking and feuding tribes—*that's* his stuff. Once he smells intrigue and horse-trading, he's hard and blind. Can't see anything else."

"I'm going to waste a shitload of energy butting heads with him. I plan to do as I see fit until he shoots me."

"Get some sleep."

"Don't tell me it'll all look better in the morning."

"In the morning," Michaelson said, "I'll get Garcia to take *Clement* out to mooch around. That's what submarines are for."

Bernie thought Michaelson would never go, but he swung the door open and trotted down the stairs, whistling. She gave it a few moments before knocking on the open door and walking in.

"Good timing," Hoffman said. He locked his papers in the ancient safe set in the wall before switching off the desk lamp. Then he reached into the desk drawer and took out an unlabeled bottle of clear, straw-colored liquid. "Wallin's special vintage. I don't know who needs a drink more, you or me."

"I was eavesdropping," Bernie said. "I thought you ought to know."

Hoffman steered her back toward the door. "That saves some time."

"I *saw* the bloody thing, Vic. Remember the horror movie where the shape-shifting fungus took over Ephyra? Well, it was like that."

"Think I'm overreacting?"

"No, you're reacting like Marcus."

"Being an uncommunicative asshole and neglecting my woman?"

"Very funny." Now she *knew* Hoffman was shitting bricks. He never joked. "Look, I don't know how many billion cubic meters of ocean there are out there, but it's a lot, and the last place we saw Lambent was under Jacinto, so even I can do the sums. Either they're on the move and they know where they're going, or they've always been around here. Neither answer cheers me up much."

"Me too," he said. "That's my conclusion. But what's really keeping me awake is that frigate. And knowing Trescu is a secretive bastard with an agenda just makes me wonder what he's not telling me."

They climbed the brick steps to the sentry post on the top of the naval base walls, a sheltered spot built into the stone when the base was constructed centuries before, and settled down for a quiet drink. The post had a great panoramic view of the ocean. It was also impossible to walk past by accident.

Hoffman handed her the bottle for the first swig. "You're confined to base, by the way. Sorry, Bernie."

Her gut churned. She took a mouthful of the moonshine and gulped it down. It had a faint hint of aniseed. "How long?"

"Until Doc Hayman passes you combat fit." He took the bottle back. "Two close calls in a week. They say it comes in threes."

"Okay."

"You're taking it better than I expected."

"I did a few years in support before they let me serve frontline. I didn't enjoy it much." She was on her second gulp of Dizzy's moonshine now. No, she wasn't taking it well. She just hadn't started arguing yet. "I won't enjoy this, either. But I can always go walkabout again if I get bored."

"The hell you will." Hoffman grabbed her arm a little too hard. That wasn't like him. "You'll stay put. Shit, woman, you know what happened with Margaret. I can't go through that again. You'll damn well stay where I can keep an eye on you."

"You could have said something like that forty years ago."

"Okay, I *didn't*." He lowered his head for a second, as if it hurt to be reminded that he'd run out on her. It was water so far under the bridge that she'd all but forgotten it herself. "But I'm saying it now."

Bernie suddenly found it all very funny, and it wasn't down to Dizzy's moonshine. She went to wipe the neck of the bottle on her sleeve before taking her turn with it, and then decided no bacteria could survive that stuff. She'd probably caught every bug that Hoffman had by now.

She wiped the bottle anyway. "As Baird would say, this is so classy."

"I misplaced the mess crystal." Hoffman folded his arms and stared out to sea. Like Marcus, he had two accents—his natural one, and the one he'd learned in uniform. Marcus switched from posh kid to grunt. Hoffman went from NCO to officer. "You want to see the wine list?"

The bottle went back and forth a few times in silence. The night was pitch-black, so clear and moonless that Bernie could pick out the navigation lights of the radar picket ship about fifteen kilometers away.

So I'm grounded. But it's because he cares. Can't have it both ways. It's not forever, is it?

Eventually the pinprick red and green lights in the distance swapped sides, and Bernie thought she could see the mast light. Whichever ship was out there had turned 180 degrees. Then her perspective shifted, and she realized she was looking at something else entirely; it was two ships a long way apart, but almost aligned. The mast light belonged to something else. She couldn't tell if it was background or foreground.

"Vic, can you see that?"

He squinted. "Don't worry. It's a ship."

"I know that. Don't ours always run with nav lights?"

Hoffman grunted and fumbled in his pocket for his earpiece. "Control? Hoffman here. Who's monitoring inshore traffic? I want to know what's under way due south of the channel buoy."

The pleasant haze from the moonshine evaporated from Bernie's head as fast as it had settled. She snapped back to full alert and put in her earpiece.

"The radar picket's diverted to intercept an unidentified craft, sir. Unarmed cabin cruiser, thirty meters, not responding to challenges. Do you want me to patch you through to the ship? It's *Scepter.*"

"Yeah, and check that Captain Michaelson's aware." Hoffman grumbled under his breath. "We're not exactly on a shipping lane here."

"Refugees?" Bernie asked. She put the stopper back in the bottle. "People do pass by here from time to time even if they don't land."

"That's another complication we don't need." Hoffman looked away for a moment. "Control? Thanks . . . put him through . . . Lieutenant, what's that vessel doing?"

Bernie eavesdropped on the channel again. The voice sounded very young. "Sir, we're coming alongside now. She appears to be drifting. I can hear her engines on idle, but there's nobody on the bridge. Wait one while we get a searchlight on her."

"You make damn sure she's not booby-trapped with a few tonnes of explosive," Hoffman said. "This isn't a good week for maritime safety." He turned to Bernie. "Don't we *ever* learn anything about Stranded?"

The CO of *Scepter* came back on the radio. "Colonel, the vessel's holed above the waterline—there's a four-meter chunk out of her bow. The deck's buckled, too. Can't see much else until it gets light, but she's taken a pounding. No visible charring or smoke damage yet."

Bernie found herself going through a checklist of trouble. Pirate attack? No, they'd take the ship too, if only for scrap and cannibalization. Collision? It was a big, empty ocean, but then people did stupid things in ships. Maybe the screw had fished up another Lambent life-form and blown a hole in their cargo hold. They'd have abandoned ship in a hurry, just like she had. Nobody stopped to shut down the engines when they were trying to get away.

"I think it's deserted, sir."

The radio popped slightly as another call sign joined the net. "Michaelson here. We're scrambling a couple of Ravens—don't board until they're on station. Like the Colonel says, it might be another Stranded surprise party."

"I'm going to armor up," Bernie said. She could hear the

Ravens starting their engines. If there was going to be trouble, there was always the chance that there'd be coordinated attacks from the land side. "We're never going to have that chat about Anvegad, are we?"

"Oh, we will." Hoffman got to his feet and dusted down the seat of his pants. "Let's get this squared away first. I'll be in CIC."

By the time Bernie had done the round-trip back to the sergeants' quarters and put her armor on, more Gears and sailors had emerged from the messes to watch from the jetty, although what the hell they thought they could see in the middle of the night was anyone's guess. One of the Gorasni men was talking to Baird as if they were old buddies. Bernie headed for the CIC building for no better reason than wanting to know what was going on, and found Hoffman talking via the loudspeaker to Michaelson in *Sovereign*. He had both hands flat on the chart table and he didn't look up.

"Might have been caught by the current, of course," Michaelson said. "It probably wasn't heading this way."

"Got light from the Raven, sir." That was the CO of *Scepter*. "We're boarding now."

Scepter went quiet for a long time. All Bernie could hear was the occasional aside from Michaelson to one of his crew, and the intermittent chatter of helicopters as someone at the incident location switched a mike on and off. CIC was silent. The three junior officers on the night watch sat listening, and that ten minutes—Bernie checked the rusting metal face of the wall clock—felt like it dragged on for days.

When *Scepter*'s CO suddenly came back on the radio and broke the silence, everyone flinched.

"Sir, there's nobody on board," he said. "There's stuff scattered everywhere, and what looks like blood on the bulkheads, but no bodies. No obvious signs of firearms being used, either. I'm not sure what to make of this, but—well, the rummage team says there's a tree trunk rammed through one of the transverse bulkheads, at an angle from the main damage."

"Say again?" Hoffman said.

"A tree."

"Damn, we should have sent a bot to relay images. What do you mean, a *tree*?"

"I haven't seen it, sir, but PO Hollaster says it's like a gnarled trunk of a creeper, only much thicker, and it's splintered at the bottom like it was torn off. No roots. And the hole in the bow is caved in, suggesting a shaft punched through it and up through the deck."

Bernie could see that everyone else was just as bewildered as she was. She couldn't even begin to imagine a logical explanation for that. She waited for one of the NCOG people to suggest something technical known only to seagoing types that would clear up the whole thing for the landlubbers, but they said nothing.

"Well, we're rather short of wooden warships these days," Michaelson said at last. "So there goes the only possible theory for a freak collision. I'm damned if I can explain this at the moment, gentlemen, so let's get off that ship, tow her to the two-kilometer anchorage, and have another look when it's light."

Hoffman scratched his scalp with both hands.

"A goddamn *tree*?" he said again. "A wooden beam? A battering ram?"

"Am I the only one worrying about the blood and absence of bodies?" Bernie asked.

"A tree," *Scepter*'s CO said. "Really. It's some kind of weird tree."

CHAPTER 8

It is in the best interests of the region to have a stable and se-cure Vasgar. For that reason, and that reason alone, the Union of Independent Republics will send a peacekeeping force to provide support and protection for the Vasgari people to enable them to resolve their constitutional crisis without foreign interference.

(DANIEL VARI, CHAIRMAN OF THE UNION OF INDEPENDENT REPUBLICS, IN THE 62ND YEAR OF THE PENDULUM WARS)

HOWERD COMPANY, 26TH ROYAL TYRAN INFANTRY, FORWARD OPERATING BASE TYRO, WESTERN KASHKUR—32 YEARS EARLIER.

"They're running late, Fenix," said Colonel Choi. He sipped his tea. "I expected them to invade weeks ago."

Adam Fenix checked out the aerial recon pictures, trying to pin them flat on the wall while the permanent, infuriating wind snatched at the paper. Tyro was a collection of temporary huts clinging to the slopes of the mountains that separated Kashkur from its neighbors on three sides. At this time of year, the wind never gave up for a moment. If there was a crack in the building, it would find it. It had.

"So what's the delay at our end, then?" Adam asked. "If this is

from the Furlin border, the Indie cav and heavy artillery could be
at the first crossing point tomorrow. These images are about four
hours old, yes?"

"Politicians."

"The Chairman was talking tough about defending Vasgar's
neutrality only an hour ago, on the radio."

"Oh, that's *talk*," Choi said. "Not *do*. And I thought you were
one of the great intellects of Tyrus, Captain."

Adam took the comment as a joke, nothing more. "I can
see we're going to fling poor old Vasgar from the sled to divert the
wolves, then."

"Neutrality's a bitch, isn't it? No enemies, maybe, but no allies,
either."

"Hasn't the interim government asked us for help?"

"Do we seriously want to be first to walk into a country that's
ripping itself up? No, the Indies can have that privilege. We'll end
up with a whole new theater to fight—that's a long border to defend. If we just let the Indies walk in, it won't make it any easier
for them to reach Kashkur. Anvil Gate can just shut down the pass
and pick off the Indie armor at leisure. All we have to do is stop
the Indies moving through Shavad."

"Very economical."

"We'll need everything we've got to hold *this* end of Kashkur."
Choi stared into his teacup. "Is this sediment something I should
worry about?"

"It's spices, sir. The locals put spice in everything."

"As long as it's not your ambitious lieutenant trying to poison
me to create a vacancy."

"Stroud wouldn't bother with poison." Adam kept a straight
face, partly because it was true. "She'd just put a round between
your eyes. Very forthright, our Helena."

Choi paused for a moment and then bellowed with laughter.
"Good-looking girl. Has she said who the father is yet?"

"No, sir, and I don't think that's any of our business."

"Must be hard for a woman to leave a small child behind
under those circumstances."

"It's hard for a man, too." Adam went back to the map on the wall and tried to see the swirls of color and contour lines in three dimensions. "I'll start moving the company down to Shavad now."

"Change of plan. You'll be shutting down the imulsion pipeline and making sure supplies stay rerouted north the moment Furlin crosses the border. Then, if need be, you reinforce the Kashkuri forces in Shavad."

The big picture was suddenly clear. "We're cutting off Vasgar?"

"Exactly. No fuel—so the Indies are going to have a tough time resupplying. If necessary, we'll destroy that section of the pipeline and make it permanent. But in the meantime, just implement the contingency plan. Shut down Borlaine and Ecian Ridge, and open the emergency pipeline at Gatka."

It was an interesting way to receive a change of orders. Adam saw the map in a whole new light. He'd already started working out the logistics of who and what he'd need to cut the supply—three teams of engineers, three infantry platoons to guard the pipeline hubs just in case the UIR managed to insert special forces—before the very obvious realization sank in. There were millions of neutral civilians who were going to be plunged into even worse chaos than an occupation.

"Just as well this isn't later in the year," he said. "I'd hate to see a Vasgar winter during a fuel embargo."

"It's not going to be too clever in the summer, either. But disgruntled civvies will give the Indies something extra to worry about." Choi stood up. "Time you got going. I want your teams in place tonight. We haven't warned the imulsion companies, just in case they talk, so they're going to be very surprised to see you. They're going to be losing a lot of revenue."

Revenue? Of course. Life goes on. Companies need customers, bills need paying.

Adam sometimes wondered how he failed to factor commerce into warfare. He'd have to watch out for that blind spot.

"So we're commandeering pipeline hubs now, sir."

"You got it, Fenix. Can't rely on civilians to cooperate even in a war. It's gone on too long. No sense of crisis—unless they're the ones in a combat zone." Choi got up and looked out the window, then checked his watch. "Mustn't keep the chopper puke waiting. He has a tendency to show his displeasure with bouncy landings. I'll call in at twenty-five-hundred."

Adam saw Choi off at the landing pad. The clock was ticking. He had less than a day to roll into three imulsion hubs, tell the operators that they were shutting down an entire country's supply, and keep that supply shut off until further notice. Military objectives were clear-cut. He approached them knowing he was going to take fire and give as good as he got. But this was one of those operations that was fraught with delicate problems, because it involved civilians, *allied* civilians.

If they don't cooperate, it's going to get . . . unpleasant.

Choi's aging Tern helicopter dwindled to a black spot against the backdrop of mountains. Adam knew he had an audience peering from the barracks windows and standing around in workshops and doorways. He had to turn around and look. He knew everyone was expecting an order to move down to Shavad to join the rest of the battalion on the front line.

"Captain?" Helena Stroud walked up to him. "Shall I get the staff and NCOs together for your briefing?"

Helena was an unnerving combination of a beautiful face, a wonderful actressy voice, and the eye-wateringly profane vocabulary of a drill sergeant. Adam had fully expected her little girl's first word to be *motherfucker* rather than *Mommy*. As Choi had correctly judged, Helena was ferociously ambitious and as hardcharging as any of the men, and Adam didn't expect her to be his lieutenant for long. Complicated bets were already being laid in the sergeants' mess back at HQ as to when she would make captain, then major, then colonel, and how many medals she'd be awarded while doing it.

"It's not what we thought," Adam said. "We're cutting off the imulsion pipeline to Vasgar."

He expected her to react as he did; uneasy, and wishing he was doing some clearly defined fighting. But Helena was always up for any challenge.

"That'll be a nice change of pace," she said cheerfully. "We'll need some clankies for that. Let me see if I can rouse them from their oily slumber. Briefing in the canteen tent, sir, fifteen minutes?"

"Very good," he said. "I'm glad you're relishing this, Stroud."

"I'd rather be brassing them up, but a girl can't always have it her own way." She walked off briskly in the direction of the company office. "Maybe we'll get some decent contact later."

When Helena said fifteen minutes, she meant it to the second. Adam saw the flurry of activity between the huts as he gathered up his maps and made hurried calls. By the time he got to the canteen tent, she had all the NCOs and officers sitting on benches, the company's detached squad of 2 REE clankies—men from the 2nd Battalion Royal Ephyran Engineers—with schematics pinned to an easel, and a chalkboard awaiting Adam's attention.

It would have irritated some officers, but Adam was already used to Elain's rigorously organized approach to life, so he simply felt reassured to have a fiercely competent female on his staff. One of the corporals tossed something small and brightly colored in Helena's direction and she caught it one-handed. She held up a pair of pink knitted baby bootees.

"Oh, Collins, bless you! That's a *very* sweet thought." She flashed him that luminous smile. "Anya's nearly three now, but I'll put these away for *her* daughter."

"Or your next one . . ." someone said.

Everyone laughed, including Corporal Collins. "My wife's a very slow knitter, ma'am. Do what you can."

Helena stepped aside to let Adam start the briefing. He clipped the central Kashkur map to the board and penciled circles around the imulsion facilities.

"We have some asset denial to carry out, ladies and gentlemen," he said. "By twenty-five-hundred tonight, we need to have these imulsion pipeline hubs secured in preparation for shutting them down. Yes, this *is* in allied territory. No, the imulsion companies haven't been warned, for opsec reasons. So expect this to be *challenging*."

The assembled Gears looked at him in silence as if thinking through the likely course of events. It wasn't what any of them usually did. Eventually someone spoke.

"But doesn't it take days to shut down a pipeline, sir?"

"It takes days to shut down *production* safely," Adam said. "All we're doing is rerouting the flow. "We shut the imulsion spur pipelines supplying the two Vasgari refineries, and reroute the output into the west. That means closing Borlaine and Ecian Ridge, and opening the pumping station at Gatka to divert the stream. Either way, the Indies won't have access to fuel if and when they roll across the orders, and they'll have to ship it in, which is going to seriously crimp their logistics."

"Technically simple, sir," said one of the engineers. "But also a big and provocative step to take, because we're depriving a whole country—a *neutral* country—of essential power."

"The Indies might not think we'd go that far this early."

"But the Vasgari power stations run on imulsion too. They'll lose electrical power in days."

"That's the idea. Let's get this done, Gears."

Adam knew all too well what would cascade out of this. Once Vasgar used up its imulsion reserves, not only would the traffic stop and the factories grind to a halt, but the lights and refrigeration would go off too.

And the hospital power supplies. And the water-pumping stations. And everything the civilians rely on to live.

"Doesn't Anvil Gate get its fuel from the Vasgar side?" Carmelo was one of the transport engineers. "Who's resupplying them?"

"It's all brought in by the same road anyway, so we can just as easily get tankers down to them from the nearest Kashkur depot." Adam reminded himself that he needed to talk to the garrison commander, just a courtesy to let the man know what was going on in his backyard and that someone was taking care of the smaller detail for him. He'd be busy preparing for the Indie advance. "All they have to do is sit tight and lob some heavy ordnance down on any Indie foolish enough to try to beat history."

Foreign invaders had always met the end of the line at the Anvil Gate garrison. Nobody had tried to fight through that pass from the south for more than a century. Adam tried to recall any army that had managed to fight its way past Anvegad, and he couldn't think of one. They'd always been forced back to try another longer, more troublesome route.

The UIR would meet the same barrier to its ambitions—if it didn't run out of fuel first.

"Okay, be ready to roll by sixteen hundred," he said. "It's two hours overland to Borlaine, and they won't be expecting us."

"Lieutenant Stroud can give them a big smile and grab them by the nuts, sir," Carmelo said. "That usually works."

Again, everyone laughed. They weren't disappointed that they weren't going into battle yet, and they had that unquestioning optimism that 26 RTI—the Unvanquished—always seemed to radiate.

It might have been the momentum of an undefeated tradition. It might have been that this particular company knew their captain's reputation for meticulous planning. It might also have been the aggressive certainty that Helena Stroud could inspire out of thin air.

Adam Fenix took the logical view that it was a combination of all three, and decided not to look closely at the ratio.

ANVIL GATE GARRISON, ANVEGAD, KASHKUR:
0530 NEXT MORNING.

"Well, that'll teach me to keep my mouth shut."

Pad Salton walked up and down the elevated gantry that ran from the main gun emplacement to the observation post, a metal bridge with a thirty-kilometer view across two countries. He was checking out the best sniper positions. With this terrain, he was spoiled for choice. Hoffman leaned on the rail, finding himself torn between his usual anxious impatience to fight and get it over with, and wondering what the hell had gone wrong.

"Bit pessimistic, Pad," Hoffman said. "Assuming they'll get close enough for you to slot one."

"Your pessimism, my optimism, sir."

"You know the range on those guns? Fifteen thousand meters. You'll have to get the bus to even *see* the Indies."

"Yeah." Pad braced his elbow against the brickwork and sighted up his Longshot. "But some bugger always gets through. That's why you've got me."

Nobody had tried to take Anvegad since the days of horse cavalry. The Indies were either crazy, pulling a flanker, or just anxious to grab Vasgar now that its government had fallen apart. The place had plenty of heavy industry further south, and—Hoffman tried to recall his briefing notes—iron deposits that probably made it worth the Indies' time even if they didn't get to take Kashkur.

Hoffman watched the activity directly below the bridge. Sander, cautious to a fault, had decided to rush in extra supplies and munitions just in case the campaign dragged on. Gears were already muttering about being stuck here beyond the planned end of their deployment, and the gunners were moving 150 mm shells on hand trucks through the narrow alleys and passages to makeshift shell stores. It was just getting light, and the fort-city was speckled with street lamps and illuminated windows below him.

"Is he expecting a siege or something?" Pad asked.

"I'd rather he was the nervous type than the sort that thinks it'll all be over by dinner."

"You still talk like a sergeant, you know, sir." Pad scoped through with his Longshot again, this time in the direction of the supply route to the north, a narrow road that squeezed through a steep gorge. It was a perfect killing zone for a sniper. "And I mean that in a *good* way. Oh, look, more trucks."

Hoffman checked the road through his binoculars. Headlights bounced in a procession in the distance. "So how far do you think the Indies will get, Pad?"

Pad shrugged. "Have to work on the basis that they'll roll up to the front door. When do you think they'll find out we've cut off the imulsion?"

"It'll be a while yet." Hoffman looked at his watch. "The Indies are probably going to cross the border in the next hour. But you can't keep something like that quiet for long with the number of people involved. If they don't have agents this side of the border, I'll be amazed."

"And the refinery's going to notice the flow's stopped."

"Pretty fast, yes."

"Bit shitty not to warn them. They won't be joining the COG in a hurry after this."

Vasgar had made its choice, but its neutrality hadn't kept it out of the war. Hoffman really had expected the COG to rush to its aid and pour in more Gears it couldn't spare, but so far it hadn't; Ephyra had learned its lesson about overstretch. That made him feel better.

Can't go running into every damn skirmish and wiping these countries' asses for them. Costs too many men.

"I'm going to check the teleprinter." Hoffman didn't like standing around doing nothing. "See you at breakfast."

Anvegad was a city of early risers, but the place was a lot busier a lot earlier than usual. Hoffman passed Byrne's girlfriend, Sheraya, in the delivery bay. It was a cobbled courtyard just wide enough for a modern truck to back into. She looked as if she was arguing with a driver, but it was hard to tell because the language always made Kashkuris sound as if they were about to punch your face in. It was just the combination of expressive hand gestures and harsh consonants. She was probably just telling him that his bread rolls were the finest in the land and asking how his mother was.

She caught Hoffman's arm as he walked by. "Lieutenant, the driver says the bakery hasn't received all its flour deliveries today. That means he's only delivered half of the garrison's order. He promises it'll be back to normal tomorrow."

"We can live with that, Miss Olencu," Hoffman said. "But feel free to scare him some more."

Sheraya didn't crack a smile—so she probably *was* berating the

guy—and went back to the high-volume, rapid-fire discussion.
She earned her pay, that girl. Hoffman imagined himself struggling to learn the language well enough to argue and negotiate
without starting a riot, and decided that interpreters were a
budget item worth every buck.

When he got to the small admin office that doubled as the ops
room, he found Sander sitting at the desk, gazing alternately at
the phone and the radio transceiver while both remained stubbornly silent.

"No news, then, sir?" Hoffman glanced at the desk. Sander's
sketchbook lay open with a half-finished pencil drawing of the
view from the north side of the city, looking down that deep
trench of a gorge. The lines were light and feathery, ready to take
a wash of paint. "Real news, I mean."

"I'm waiting on a few messages. Confirmation that Indie troops
have crossed the border, and that Captain Fenix has cut off the
pipeline. As soon as I've dealt with the priority traffic, I think we
should let the Gears call home to reassure the families. You know
how comms goes to rat shit when a new game kicks off."

Sander was definitely a planner. Hoffman checked the
overnight telex messages, looking for something from Margaret.
But there was nothing, and he had a sudden urge to write a letter,
a *proper* letter, the kind every Gear left for his family just in case
things ended badly. Hoffman had never written one for a wife before; parents and sweethearts, yes, but never anything serious like
the last words to a wife. He knew he was going to sweat over it.

"We're short on the bread delivery today, by the way," he said,
putting the task out of his mind for the moment. "Thought you
ought to know. The bakery driver says he'll make up the shortfall
tomorrow."

"That's okay. We're stocked up on everything now—call me a
worrier, but I've had so many shortages with supplies and victual-
ing in other garrisons that I grab as much as I can, when I can."
Sander reached across the desk and took his sketchpad in one
hand, frowning at the drawing. Hoffman realized it was the captain's safety valve rather than trivia that got in the way of his job.
Sander didn't drink. He *painted*. "I've run out of burnt umber.

I'm going to have to make some myself now. Not sure if there's any clay around here, though."

"I suspect Miss Olencu can procure some for you, sir."

Hoffman wandered outside again and stood on the ramparts, scanning the plain below with his field glasses. The constellation of lights that marked the imulsion refinery across the Vasgar border were gradually fading from prominence as the sun rose. About ten minutes later, Hoffman's radio crackled. It was Sander.

"It's a go, Victor. Just heard from Captain Fenix. He's shutting down the pipeline."

Hoffman found his stomach knotting. He was five hundred klicks from the advancing UIR forces, but it still made his adrenaline pump.

"They've invaded, then."

"Token resistance at the border crossing, but the Indie armor is rolling in. I think the imulsion companies put up more of a fight when Fenix told them to stop supplying Vasgar. Much bleating about loss of revenue and who was going to compensate them."

Ungrateful assholes. "I can't see Vasgar being able to pay its fuel bills now anyway."

"As of now, we're on REDCON three. Alert-thirty. We've been authorized to open fire on Vasgari positions when we make enemy contact."

Well, that made life easier; no messing around waiting for the Indies to open fire first.

They'd take a while to get to the northern border, though, if they were going to get this far at all. They had a whole country to work through. There was no telling what the shreds of Vasgar's government, its army, or even its disgruntled citizens might do to throw a spanner in the works. Hoffman wasn't counting on a magnificent Vasgari resistance, but there'd be fighting of some kind.

He slung his binoculars around his neck, snapped the bayonet on his Lancer, and went back down to the barracks. The ready-state siren went off, echoing around the walls.

Somehow that made it all more official. Anvil Gate was ready for war.

It was a small garrison, just a hundred Gears plus a few thousand civilians living beyond its walls in the city. That was all this place had space for; a few humans to keep the big guns company and eke out a living from them. And this was what they'd all drilled for from the time they'd arrived at Anvil Gate, but doubted they'd use this time, or on their next deployment here, or even the next. The absolute emptiness of the rocky plain below the fort just added to the sense of unreality. The never-ending war was still a whole country away.

Hoffman did his rounds, driving around the city to see how the locals were reacting. They didn't seem overly anxious. Their history was one of sitting tight and waiting for the invader to exhaust himself on this stubborn rock. As Hoffman passed the small bar where Sander liked to eat and take coffee, the owner waved casually to him as he leaned against the door frame, waiting for breakfast customers.

"Maybe you get to fire the guns this time, Mr. Lieutenant," he called.

Hoffman slowed a little. "I hope you remember your emergency drill. The Indies might bring some big guns too."

The café owner laughed. Taking Anvegad was about the same as walking straight up to a man with a loaded rifle trained on you and trying to disarm him. The garrison could watch the enemy approaching before they even came within range of the battery.

There were no surprises.

Back in the NCOs' mess at the base of the main gun emplacement, Pad and Byrne were listening to both radios—the broadcast service as well as the COG military net. Hoffman could see the frowns of concentration as both men switched their attention from one to the other, fingers tapping their headsets occasionally.

"So what else is happening?" Hoffman helped himself to coffee. He really couldn't face Pad's hot sauce this morning. "Or are we the headlines?"

"It's all about Shavad," Byrne said. "We've sent in tanks. That'll keep the Indies busy."

"Break out your knitting. We could be waiting some time."

Hoffman decided to ask. "I saw your woman this morning, Sam. Are you two serious?"

Byrne looked baffled for a moment. He had a broken nose that made him look a lot more aggressive than he was. It was the result of a dumb accident in a truck, but most people didn't get as far as finding that out.

"Yeah, sir, I am," he said. "She's expecting."

Hoffman couldn't manage annoyance. There wasn't a regulation about it, although Byrne should have told him in case it caused trouble with the locals.

"I suppose you want permission to marry while deployed, then," he said.

"Now that you ask, sir, yes."

Sander wouldn't object. He was about to become a father himself. And there was nothing whatsoever to be achieved by telling Sam he had to wait.

"Go ahead," Hoffman said. "Although what a smart girl like that sees in you, I have no idea."

Pad mopped at his plate of eggs and lethal Islander sauce. "It's his dazzling intellect, sir."

"Has to be."

It turned into an uneventful morning. Hoffman was beginning to think the border incursion was a feint to take the attention from Shavad, where the serious fighting was taking place, but at lunchtime the local radio station—the one that Sheraya had to translate for Captain Sander—reported that UIR forces, Furlin's Third Infantry, had reached Oskeny. The city was fifty kilometers inside the border. There hadn't been more than a roadblock erected by the local police chief, and it hadn't worked.

Hoffman had everything to think about and nothing to actually do. He checked the fuel tanks deep under the fort that supplied the generators—full to the brim, enough for two weeks' continuous running—and climbed to the gun floor of the main emplacement.

The artillery boys were on defense watches, sitting on their rickety metal seats and staring past the huge barrels of the twin guns while the radio chattered. Every damn position had a radio of some sort tuned to the Ephyra World Service. They looked like they were waiting for a movie to start.

"This is weird," said the sergeant. "Can't remember the last time I could actually see the target."

"Well, with optics . . ."

"We don't get to do much direct fire anyway, but this is like being a helicopter gunner—look down on it, point at it, blow the shit out of it. They've got no cover out there. Fish in a barrel."

"Yeah, that's why nobody's tried to move through Anvegad for quite a few years."

Hoffman walked the whole perimeter of the fort, some of it along the top of ancient walls, some of it in alleys that hadn't seen daylight for the best part of a thousand years. The fort was a fascinating warren. It was also oddly relaxed. Every time he got to a vantage point to check out that spectacular view, there were still thousands of square kilometers of absolutely nothing.

Later in the day, just after lunch, the flour delivery truck arrived and groaned its way up the steep access road. There'd be extra bread in the morning after all. Anvegad went about its business, and not one shop closed for the day. Hoffman and Sander eventually met up in the observation post.

"The refinery's shutting down," Sander said. "Big argument between the acting president and the Chairman. They really weren't expecting us to choke the supply."

Hoffman snorted. "It's the first thing any sane commander would do."

"Everyone's too comfortable with the war. They reach a stage where they think everything is a bluff to achieve something else."

"Unless they're the ones getting their asses shot off," Hoffman muttered. "No hidden meaning there."

Sander nodded. "No. Definitely not."

It was about 1600 hours when a muffled *whump* shattered the quiet. Hoffman couldn't work out which direction it had come from, but that wasn't the sound that grabbed his attention most.

The *whump* was followed by a slow rumbling noise that gradually built into a roar. The rumbling was so loud that it almost drowned the next *whump*, and the next.

"What the hell is that?" Sander said.

There was nothing, absolutely *nothing*, in a two-hundred-degree arc in front of them. Then the comms net came to life.

"Sir?" It was Byrne. "Sir, possible contact north of the fort. In the gorge."

Hoffman went pounding down the stairs to the next level, where he could look out to the fort's back—the road into Kashkur. A pall of smoke rose from the gorge and spread out, or at least he thought it was smoke.

"Shit, sir. Look at *that*."

Hoffman stared, trying to work out what he was seeing. Sander was right behind him. His first thought was that shutting down the imulsion supply had left flammable vapor in the pipeline, and somehow it had ignited. It was always possible. Pipes developed leaks, and when the pressure dropped and the thick fluid ran away from cracked metal and perished seals, accidents could follow.

It was a damn big explosion.

"Where's the goddamn road?" he said.

It was like a kid's puzzle. *What's the difference between these two pictures?* Hoffman stared, and like all familiar things, the view looked wrong but it took him a few moments to pin down exactly what had changed.

He couldn't see the road, or at least part of it. There was just jagged gray rock and dust, as if the mountains had taken a few steps to the east. The rest of it carried on to the north across more rugged hills, but the section he could normally see from this window had disappeared.

No road. The road's not there.

"It's a landslide," Hoffman said, stunned. "What the hell did that?"

Sander sounded as if he'd gulped in air. "That's thousands of tonnes of rubble. I counted three explosions."

Sam Byrne's voice came over the radio against a background of vehicle noises and shouts. "I'm going out to check, sir. I'm taking one of the ATVs. Stand by."

"Salton, get your squad and give him some fire cover until we're sure what we're dealing with," Hoffman said. "I'm coming straight down."

Hoffman wasn't the only one trying to get to the main gates of the city. The streets and alleys were packed with civilians trying to work out what had happened. He pushed his way through the crowd, yelling at them to get the hell out of his way.

"Sir! Over here!" It was Carlile, one of the combat engineers, driving a small ATV. "Get in."

Hoffman scrambled into the cab. "That's got to be the pipeline."

"I don't think so, sir." Carlile drove at speed down the winding track into what looked like the tail end of a dust storm. "I heard explosions—detonations. Timed. Regular intervals. That's the sort of shit I use, sir."

The main road—the only road—through the pass was three hundred meters from the base of the ramp. As soon as Carlile steered right and joined the road, the scale of their problem became painfully obvious.

The pass was a narrow gorge between two big, rocky cliffs that were getting on for mountain-sized. That morning, it had been a deep-cut V shape.

Now it wasn't. It was a wall of rock at least twenty-five meters high, and the road had vanished beneath it. Carlile stopped the ATV, put on his helmet, and jumped out with Hoffman. The avalanche debris was still clicking and moving as the rock settled.

Hoffman leveled his rifle and waited for shots. But it was a lot of trouble to go to for an ambush. Pad emerged from the side of the road and jogged over to them. The debris shifted as he passed, sending him sprinting to avoid further rock falls.

"The whole road's blocked," he said. "They brought the whole hillside down. From what we can see up top, it's taken out a two-hundred-meter stretch, at least."

"They?" Hoffman said. "You think it's enemy action?"

"Bloody sure of it," Carlile said. He went as if to climb up the artificial hill that had formed in less than a minute, but stopped as the rocks shifted again. "Look at the slope up there."

Hoffman followed where the engineer pointed. He could see it now. The top of the cliff looked as if it had sheared off.

"Could be a fluke," Carlile said, "but if I was going to do a spot of counter-mobility and pack explosives into a hillside to bring it down, that's what it would probably look like afterward."

It wasn't imulsion vapor, then. It wasn't bad luck or shitty timing. Hoffman began wondering how long it must have taken someone to pack those cliffs with enough explosive to change the map of Anvegad.

"Shit," he said. "The bastards have cut us off from the rest of Kashkur."

CHAPTER 9

Where's the nearest land when you're at sea? It's always in the same position—right under your hull, buddy.
(CPO FRANK MULLER, NCOG, INSTRUCTING GEARS IN THE ART OF
AVOIDING RUNNING YOUR VESSEL AGROUND)

TWO-KILOMETER ANCHORAGE, OFF VECTES NAVAL
BASE: PRESENT DAY, 15 A.E.

"Wow," Dom said, looking up from the Marlin. "That's the weirdest damage I ever saw."

The deserted cruiser rode at anchor, a sensible distance from the shore. Nobody knew what the hell had punched that hole in her. In daylight, the massive void in her bow and foredeck looked even less explainable to Dom than it had the previous night.

Marcus brought the Marlin alongside and cut the engine. He stood at the helm controls, studying the daylight slanting through the ruptured bulkhead. "So what can ram clean through a hull at that angle?"

"Had to be low in the water to slant up like that." Dom secured the Marlin's line to the cruiser's ladder and reached for the handrail. "If I was guessing from scratch, I'd say she steered onto a reef in heavy seas and skewered herself on a freak chunk of rock, then the swell took her off again."

"And then there's the *tree*," Marcus said.

"Look, I said *guessing from scratch*."

"And the blood."

"Okay. I get it."

The name painted on the bow was *Steady Eddie*. If there'd been a home port named on there, it had been worn off or scraped clean long ago. Dom pulled himself onto the deck and powered up his Lancer's chainsaw. The navy salvage crew hadn't found anything on board last night, but that didn't mean there was nothing here, because they'd just done a quick search of the main compartments in the dark with a flashlight. Dom couldn't begin to piece this together. So he'd assume the very worst until proven wrong.

And he wasn't afraid. Not even nervous. That struck him as weird, because any sane man needed a little spark of fear in an unknown situation, but he didn't have it. It was like it just didn't matter anymore, as long as it was him going in first and not Marcus.

So that's where I've gotten to. Always had to have a purpose. Used to be the family. Then it was finding Maria. Now it's all about keeping Marcus alive.

Dom decided he felt a lot better. He'd forgotten he'd thought he had nothing much left worth living for.

"I'd call this a motor schooner," Marcus said. "This cost a *lot* of money once."

She must have been a beautiful vessel in her day; she was a vintage design, more like a yacht. But now she was a scruffy heap, even without the recent damage. Her wheelhouse was rotting and her glass was cracked.

But she had a deck-mounted machine gun. Every fancy cruiser needed one, Dom thought. It looked in good condition. Whoever had owned her had clear priorities.

"Start from the bow and work back," Dom said. He aimed down into the hole in the deck as he peered in. It was a huge well, nearly the entire width of the deck at that point, and the splintering flared upward. *Steady Eddie* had been struck from beneath the bow, not from above. Whatever had hit her had taken a chunk out of the chain locker as well. "Upper deck, then down below."

"Aye, skipper," Marcus muttered.

"You could live on a boat like this."

"Or die on one." Marcus studied the hole, then dropped his legs through and lowered himself to the deck below. "Yeah. Shit. Blood."

"*Literally* shit?"

"No. Literal blood, though."

Dom dropped down after him. The hole in the boat's side matched the gap in the deck, as if whatever struck had gone in at forty degrees. If it had entered a meter lower, the boat would have sunk. The sun lit up the lower deck, revealing a bulkhead sprayed with blood.

"Now here's the freaky detail," Marcus said, prodding something with the tip of his chainsaw. "One for Baird to chew over."

There really *was* a huge stalklike object embedded in the transverse bulkhead behind him.

It had lodged in the doorway of the compartment, at an angle from whatever had gone through the hull. Dom had never seen anything like it. But they were in more southerly waters now, and he didn't know much about the kinds of trees growing around the islands. This one looked more like densely packed creeper instead of a conventional tree, as if the stems had coiled together to form a solid, gnarled mass. He decided it was probably tropical. It also looked as if it was long dead, although there were no signs of decay.

And it was as hard as concrete.

"Never seen wood like that," he said.

Marcus tilted his head slightly as if to get a better look. "Me neither."

If it hadn't been for the sprays of blood, Dom would have settled for the explanation of a freak grounding in a storm, a million-to-one accident as the boat smashed down onto a sharp outcrop on an island.

Yeah, weird shit happens. But somehow I don't think this is going to be it.

The chaotic state of the interior didn't prove a thing. Clothing and equipment, including a harpoon with the shaft still attached to the line, were scattered everywhere. Dom worked his way aft. Although there was no more serious damage, there were bullet holes in the deck and halfway up the bulkheads, as if someone had been firing down at something and missed.

It looked like the damage that had been done to *Harvest*. But there were plenty of possible reasons for loosing off a few rounds below deck besides hauling up Lambent marine life.

Marcus checked another compartment and disappeared into the gloom.

"Well, they weren't unarmed," he said.

"What?"

"Look." Marcus stepped back out and let Dom peer inside. The compartment was stacked with boxes of ammo, plastic-wrapped rectangles that were probably explosive, and loops of wire. "Might be part of the resupply chain to the gangs back on Vectes."

"Might just be routine precautions, given the freak show around these waters."

Marcus shrugged. "Let's check out the wheelhouse."

They came up on deck at the stern hatch. When they looked over the side, a rainbow layer was drifting on the water surrounding the boat.

"She's leaking fuel," Marcus said. He opened the wheelhouse door and stepped in. "Nice comms fit. No expense spared."

Dom poked around in the console and pulled out some dog-eared charts that had been folded carelessly. Then Marcus checked the radio and turned the dial; it was still switched on, just as the engines had been left running. The crew didn't seem to have had the time to shut the ship down before abandoning her.

Marcus looked at the preset channel controls on the radio, picked up the mike, and pressed the first one.

"This is *Steady Eddie* calling," he said. "Anyone out there looking for this boat?" He released the receive button and waited for a moment. "This is *Steady Eddie*. Position . . . just south of Vectes."

Marcus paused again, frowning. Dom felt the hair on his nape bristle. Then the speaker above the windshield made a loud clunk.

"Who's that?" a man's voice demanded. "And where the hell *are* you? We've been searching for you for *three days*."

"Jackpot," Dom said quietly.

Marcus took a breath. "This is Sergeant Fenix of the Coalition of Ordered Governments."

"Ahh, *shit*. You assholes again."

"Let me guess. Lesser Island Free Trade Association?"

"Don't dick with me. Where's the crew? Have you murdered them yet? That's what you usually do."

Word got around, then. The Stranded bush telegraph had a bigger range than Dom had imagined.

"The boat's wrecked," Marcus said. "We found it. We want to know what happened to it, not claim salvage."

The channel went silent for a few moments.

"Every time we lose a ship, it's you bastards sinking them," the voice said. "Cut the crap."

"Not this time. You've got bigger problems out here." Marcus waited, but there was no response. The channel was still open, though. Dom thought he could hear breathing. "Fair enough. You want to talk—you know where we are. Fenix out."

Marcus put the mike back in its cradle and tried the ignition. The engine spluttered but then ran smoothly. He shut it down again.

"It's safe to bring it in," he said. "Then Baird can pick it over."

"We need a biologist." Dom climbed down into the Marlin and slipped the line. They headed back to the naval base. "Not an engineer."

"Baird did okay with his grub theories. He was usually right."

Dom wondered if Marcus would ever say that to Baird's face. Baird still bitched about Marcus making squad sergeant instead of him, but Dom knew it was just griping for the sake of it. Baird was happy as long as everyone accepted that he was smarter than the rest of them. He hadn't shown any signs of enjoying authority when he led the squad on that refugee camp patrol, so Dom wondered just how much he really wanted it. Baird looked out for Cole, and he even managed to show some concern for Bernie in small doses, but it was beyond him to care much about those outside his small circle. And he seemed to know it. Dom was convinced that Baird had been deliberately insubordinate to sabotage every promotion he'd had in the past, to make sure he was busted back down to corporal every time. He just needed the reassurance that people thought he was good enough to be a sergeant. He didn't actually want the emotional responsibility of being one.

Marcus gave Dom the fixed stare. "What's the joke?"

"What? Oh, Baird. I'd miss the cabaret if the asshole got himself killed."

"First time I've seen you amused for some time." Marcus sounded almost relieved. "He has his uses."

An impatient Baird was waiting for them when they landed. "You didn't bring me back samples? I could have gone with you."

"Relax, they're bringing the whole boat back," Dom said. "It looked like it was running arms and ammo for the Stranded, so they must have been landing it here in inflatables or something."

"Whoa, retribution. That gives me a warm glow. So *is* it a tree?"

"Maybe. Weirdest tree I ever saw, if it is. More like a giant vine—a stalk."

"So we're four vessels down in freaky circumstances in a couple of months." Baird nodded, looking satisfied. "I say it's glowies. Can't all be down to shitty seamanship."

Marcus didn't look convinced. "But the last boat didn't blow up. What's the tree got to do with it?"

Baird shoved his goggles farther back on his head with that know-all expression. "I'll work it out."

It took Michaelson's salvage team an hour to bring *Steady Eddie* into the naval base and berth her securely. By that time, Michaelson was pacing around waiting to board her. Trescu stood farther along the quay, talking to one of his submarine crew. Maybe he was getting edgy because *Clement* had gone out to do some active pinging and she hadn't reported in yet.

Baird headed straight for the hole in the deck with a handsaw and came out five minutes later with a small chunk of the unidentified stalk. He held up the saw in disgust.

"That stuff's like heavy-gauge steel," he said. "Look what it's done to my saw." He jumped back onto the quay and handed the chunk to Trescu. "Sure you didn't find any of this when your frigate went down? Or are you still too shy to talk about that?"

Trescu didn't seem offended by Baird's tone. Either he cut Baird a lot of slack for being useful, or he regarded him as an insect hardly worth reacting to.

"We found very little debris apart from what would have been on deck," Trescu said.

"Are you sure you gave us the right search area?" Michaelson asked.

"Why would we lie to you?"

"Probably the same reason that we tend to assume we control everything. Unconscious cultural habit." Only Michaelson could get away with saying that. It took a bit of charm. "*Clement*'s taking a look along this boat's likely course, but it would be *very* helpful if we could pin down the last location for *Nezark*. Because Commander Garcia hasn't found that geological formation your people reported."

Trescu spread his arms. He really did look surprised and indignant. Dom believed him.

"Why would we invent such an insane excuse?" Trescu asked. "You don't believe me? Very well. Take *Zephyr*. Take the crew who did the sonar search. Check for yourself. The best location we have is that sector we gave you." He took a step toward Michaelson. "I have no explanation. I *want* one. *Nezark* wasn't a disposable wreck, and her crew were not faceless strangers. We grieve too, Captain. The COG has no monopoly on civilized sentiment."

Michaelson nodded politely. "Let's look again, then," he said. "Full sonar and aerial sweep of that whole section of the grid. With our best teams."

"Do I get to go with *Clement*?" Baird asked. "Ravens—been there, done that."

Dom took it as read that Baird was automatically included in *best*, and so did he. Michaelson slapped his shoulder.

"Of course, Corporal. I'm counting on you to find out what's sinking these vessels before I lose my whole damn fleet."

NCOG SUBMARINE CNV *CLEMENT*, AT LAST REPORTED POSITION OF GORASNAYAN FRIGATE *NEZARK*, NORTHWEST OF VECTES.

Baird had been allowed to tinker with *Clement's* systems— encouraged to, even *bribed* to—but this was the first time he'd been out on a patrol.

He'd earned the right as far as he was concerned. He'd built a towed side-scan sonar for *Clement* by cannibalizing a fish-finder taken off one of the trawlers. If there was anything worth seeing down there, this baby could image it clearly enough to see the frigging whiskers on barnacles.

But he didn't want to look too excited. A guy needed to preserve some dignity. He squeezed into the torpedo compartment and listened to the rumbling, humming, and whining all around him. She was running on batteries now, two hundred meters below the surface. It was the most perfect machine he could imagine.

"Baby, you're lookin' *radiant*," Cole said. He kept hitting his head on the deckhead pipework. He wasn't a submarine-sized guy. "That imulsion rig's gonna know you've been cheatin' on her with a sub."

"You know me. I'm shallow. I go for looks every time."

"Well, now it's dived, it don't make me puke like most ships do, but I ain't gonna get serious with this lady anytime soon."

"Cole, you know what this is? Forget the water. This is as near as we get to a *spaceship*. The most complicated weapons platform ever built. Even counting the Hammer of Dawn. Operating under the sea is harsher than orbit, man."

Cole just looked at him straight-faced for a moment, then burst into raucous laughter. "When they gonna make a full-size one?"

Baird didn't find submarines claustrophobic. They were just

cramped, no worse than some of the spaces ashore that he'd had to live in. Everything was made to fit. Things stowed away or folded back into bulkheads or doubled up as something else. It was like heavily weaponized camping. Yes, he loved it. He even loved that weird smell.

In the control room, things were even more cozy. Garcia stood hunched over the sonar operator, studying the screen with one of the Gorasni crew, Teodor, while another Gorasni stared at the charts with apparent disbelief. They were doing a parallel search of the seabed in a fifteen-kilometer square from the position in *Nezark's* last radio message.

"You sure?" Garcia asked Teodor.

"Sure. Your chart is wrong. Your position is wrong. *Crappy.*"

The helmsman looked up from the yoke and gave Garcia an eloquent roll of the eyes. Teodor turned to his colleague and they exchanged a burst of Gorasni.

"Much as I hate to argue, we're exactly in the square you designated," Garcia said. "We can still triangulate off the Hammer satellites when we surface. We know where we are."

But Teodor was distracted by whatever his buddy had said. He tapped on the side-scan sonar display and made a look-at-this gesture. The other guy quickly folded back the edges of his chart so he could lift it to show Teodor, managing to look both dumbfounded and angry at the same time. The chart was overwritten in thick black pencil.

"Janu knows where he was, too." Teodor took the dog-eared, folded chart and thrust it at Garcia. "And *that* is where we find the new rocks. *There.*" He turned to the sonar screen. "And they are not *there.* Rocks don't go home. They stay."

"So explain why we find the right spot and the rocks are *gone,*" Teodor said. "Lava eruptions, quakes—all leave marks, yes?"

Baird thought the obvious answer was that a tired, panicky navigator had recorded the wrong position. Garcia had simply plotted the speed and time—assuming they'd given him the right numbers—and drawn an arc from Branascu, then looked at the broad corridor the Gorasni ships would have taken.

The search area didn't look too far out to Baird. But even a frigate was a small object to find in an ocean.

Garcia looked frayed. "Look, let's surface again and see if the Raven's found anything useful."

"Sir," said the sonar operator, "the seabed here isn't the same as on *our* charts, either. Look. That is *not* flat. It's a convex mound. Lots of debris on it."

"And where is this bulge?" Teodor asked. They all looked at the Gorasni chart. "Same as the place we marked *rocks*."

"All stop," Garcia said. "David? Plot me a square search out from that position. Chief—periscope depth."

"'Course, that don't explain where the rocks *went*," Cole said to Baird. "We goin' up top now? I'm just gonna find a sick bag. I'll be layin' down with the torps if you need me."

"We're just coming up far enough to raise the radio mast," Garcia said. "Michaelson and Hoffman really need to hear this. Brace for a rerun of all the you-must-be-mistaken conversations."

It took some believing, Baird had to admit. When *Clement* came up to mast depth, Gettner flashed the sub first. She must have been dunking her sonar buoy.

"KR-Eight-Zero to *Clement*. Problems? Result?"

"Here's the edited highlights." Garcia squeezed the mike handset so hard that his knuckles went white. Baird watched him defocus for a couple of seconds as if he was rehearsing a form of words that didn't make him sound like a total dick. "We found the location but the rock formation was gone. Moved. Collapsed. Whatever. We're starting a square search for the wreck now. Here's the start position."

Gettner paused for a beat. "No shit."

"Okay, sounds impossible, but Corporal Baird's sonar confirms the seabed's changed."

"Fair enough. I've seen two cities sink into holes. Nothing surprises me now. Gettner out."

Garcia shrugged. "She took that pretty well, all things considered. Now let's talk to the boss fella."

Michaelson took it without comment. Baird eavesdropped for

a while as Garcia traded speculation with him about grubs collapsing bedrock underwater. The search resumed again, this time with some expectation of an answer. Baird went back to keep an eye on the sonar display.

"I'll tell you when we find something," the operator said, his eyes not moving from the grainy image forming by sections in front of him. "Why don't you go look after Cole? I don't know why you keep dragging the poor guy to sea. You know he chucks up all the time."

"Because if you run into some serious shit out here, Cole's the guy to get you out of it," Baird said. *Because we're a team. Because he's my buddy.* "Sick or not."

He almost hoped the sonar operator would need a break and leave the monitoring to him. But the guy was glued to the seat. Baird retreated to the tiny chart table and waited for Cole to come back to the control room. Teodor and Janu squeezed in next to him, resting their asses on a locker and keeping out of the way of moving traffic. Baird, a man who liked to maintain his personal boundaries, wondered if he'd really be cut out for submarine duties.

It was almost getting to the frustrating stage when the sonar guy twisted in his seat to call Garcia.

"Sir? Look at this. This has to be *Nezark*. Looks like a hull to me."

Teodor shot off the locker as if he was spring-loaded. There were so many bodies crowded around the screen now that Baird couldn't get a look in.

"Very clear," Teodor said. "Is a Gelen. Look at profile. Very easy to identify. Hey, there are holes in the hull! I can see *holes*."

"There you go," said Garcia. Everyone stood back and Baird finally got a look at the elusive display. Even if he said so himself, it was pretty damn good. The frigate looked like a detailed brass rubbing, heeled over to one side, with two massive puncturelike gashes in her port side below the waterline. "Better call in."

The sonar guy still had his gaze fixed to the screen. "Sir . . ."

"What is it?"

"Sir, weird shit. There's something moving."

Baird thought he meant marine animals. There was a lot of stuff swimming around out there, as noisy as a tropical jungle over the hydrophones. Baird had never seen a biologic on this sonar so he got up and took a look.

Okay, so the imaging wasn't as great with a moving object in real time. But he could see that the disjointed outline wasn't a whale. And it sure as shit wasn't a shoal of fish. It took him a moment to make sense of what he was seeing, but it looked like an invisible hand was filleting the seabed, ripping its backbone out like a zip. Beneath the boat, something was erupting out of the mud and rock, leaving long spines behind it.

Garcia grabbed the mike. *"Emergency surface."* He seemed remarkably calm given what Baird could see. "Surface, surface, surface. Blow tanks."

Someone hit the alarm. It sounded three times, and suddenly the boat was filled with the noise of compressed air purging the ballast tanks. The deck tilted under Baird's boots like a surfboard at forty-five degrees. He grabbed the nearest solid object that wasn't a handle or a valve. Pencils and other loose objects skidded off the chart table and bounced along the deck.

Cole was probably washing down the torpedo compartment decks with puke by now. It was a white-knuckle ride.

The surge to the surface felt like it was never going to stop. Baird's gut floated, gravity free, and then came crashing down through his pelvis as *Clement* breached like a dolphin doing tricks and smacked down hard into the sea again.

"Helm, full ahead, flank." That was Garcia-speak for *get the fuck out of here.* He looked at Baird as if he expected him to shed some light on the completely unbelievable. That was what happened when you acted like you knew it all. "Seismic. Has to be. Lava. Fault line."

"That's *biologic*," Baird said, not sure if he was going to wet his pants or ask Garcia if they could do it all again. "It's alive."

"I go look," Teodor said. "You open the sail? Yes?"

"I'll go look."

Baird headed for the hatch. He'd climbed up to the small open bridge enough times to know the drill, but never after surfacing when the sea had drained out of it. It was cold, wet, and slippery; even without his armor, it was a tight fit. He got a foothold on two metal ledges that folded down on either side, and braced his elbows on the top edge.

Was there anything out there?

It wasn't easy to spot things on the surface unless the sea was like a millpond. Today it wasn't. But that wasn't going to be a problem.

A hundred meters off the port bow, maybe less, something punched through a mat of white foam.

It was a fucking stalk, just like Dom had said. A gnarly, weird-looking *stalk.*

No, it made even less sense than that: it was a stalk stretching out like some big, brainless arm, and *things* were spewing out of it, *things* with six big, jointed, crablike legs, things about the size of a dog. One of the things at the tip of the tree paused like a diver waiting to launch from the top board.

It was luminous, and not in a good way.

Glowies. More glowies. Different *glowies. Oh . . . shit.*

Baird ducked down into the sail. He didn't think to jump below and shut the hatch. He yelled to the deck beneath.

"Hard to starboard. *Go on. Do it!*" He stuck his arm down into the well, hand outstretched. "And somebody hand me my frigging rifle. *Now.*"

KR-80, ON PATROL, *NEZARK* SEARCH AREA.

"You know when I said nothing would surprise me?" Gill Gettner banked the Raven and dropped so low that Dom was sure she was going to tip everyone out of the crew bay. "Wrong. Wrong, wrong, *wrong.*"

Dom clung to the safety line. *Clement* was a lonely black shape in the sea below, trailing an arrow-shaped white wake. Something was on an intercept course with her, but it was hard to work out what it was or even its size from this angle. It was only when the Raven leveled out five meters above the water and came up on *Clement*'s stern that Dom realized what it was.

Barber leaned out of the bay to get a better look. "Well, *there's* something you don't see every day."

"No shit," Marcus muttered.

Tree had sounded almost funny when they salvaged the abandoned cruiser. Now it wasn't funny at all. *Clement* turned in a shallow arc and the grotesque stalk missed her bow by a few meters. Dom could see things clambering over the stalk like swarming insects, but they must have been at least half a meter tall. One leapt for the boat's casing. It landed on the sonar dome at the bow. *Shit. Am I hallucinating, or is that thing glowing?*

Baird was in the foxholelike well of the submarine's bridge, his Lancer braced on the rim. He opened fire as the thing—six legs, scuttling like a spider—charged down the length of the boat's casing. The muzzle flash was suddenly overwhelmed by a ball of light and a loud explosion.

Gettner veered to port. "Shit!"

"He's okay, he's *okay.*" As the Raven swept past, Dom could see Baird reloading and then frantically rubbing something out of his hair one-handed. "That's got to be Lambent. How many different models do those things come in?"

Baird pulled his goggles into place, looked up, and made a gesture that could have been anything from *get clear* to *don't leave me here, assholes.* Gettner looped around and came back down the line of the boat's course, bow on.

Submarines were blind. *Clement*'s eyes were now just Baird and Gettner. Marcus moved up to man the door gun.

"KR-Eight-Zero to *Clement,* any damage?" Gettner turned and kept pace with the boat, holding position aft of the sail. "I'm looking at one live Baird and the remains of a . . . an exploding giant crab."

"Garcia here, Eight-Zero. We're okay. Hull seems intact. What did we avoid?"

"A big stalk of something that just punched out of the water. I don't know where the glowing crawlies came from—on it, in it, no idea."

"Yeah, I'm fine, assholes." Baird's voice cut in, shaky and pissed off. He still had his Lancer ready as if he expected a second wave any second. Dom gave him a thumbs-up. "Thanks for asking. This is how I love to spend my day."

"We see you, Baird," Gettner said. "You want to give us a sitrep, or just bitch all day?"

"It must be like coral," he said. "Rock hard and full of individual polyp things. Except it grows about a zillion times *faster* than coral. You want to fly over and take a look? They're still all sitting on that thing like—"

Gettner cut him dead. "*Clement!* Steer one-eighty! Hard over!"

Dom saw it a heartbeat later. Something shot along under the water, broke the surface, and shaved across *Clement's* bow. It was another stalk. He heard the shout—might have been Baird, might have been Garcia—and saw the boat roll. Whether she turned in time or was struck a glancing blow, Dom didn't know. He heard Marcus suck in a breath.

Submarines weren't built for surface stability. *Clement* heeled, then righted herself. But the polyps had a foothold on the hull. Its curve and the slick of seawater left them scrabbling for purchase, but they hung on, a carpet of the things, clinging to the sonar dome and the forward hydroplanes. They seemed to be timing their charge.

Baird opened fire again. "Close the hatch," he yelled. "I said *close the frigging hatch!* Dive and drown these things. Otherwise they'll blow like mines."

Garcia cut in. "Get below. *Now.*"

"Yeah?" Baird emptied a clip into the first wave of polyps and detonated them. The boat shook. More swarmed up. "I turn my back—they'll come straight down on top of me."

"No heroics. Get off the bridge."

"*What* fucking heroics?" Baird sounded enraged. "Tell Gettner to earn her pay and get me out of here."

Gettner dropped closer. Dom kept an eye open for new stalks but held his aim. Marcus swung the gun, trying to get a clear shot, but he could only aim down at the hull.

"Shit."

"Yeah, don't be tempted to open up with the gun yet, Fenix," Gettner said. "Heavy caliber—I don't know if those boats can take sustained fire."

"Understood." Marcus still sighted up on the submarine. "Major, you up for a winch rescue?"

"You bet. Any polyps that climb up the cable—bat them out." The Raven lifted a few meters. "Baird, you picked the right day to drop the armor. Ready when you are."

Baird picked off a polyp trying to climb the sail. It blew out a chunk of the anechoic coating as it exploded. "Okay, shut the hatch and crash-dive, or whatever the order is. Garcia? Just do it."

"Yeah, do it," Gettner said.

"Dom, take the gun." Marcus moved in and started prepping the sling and winch with Barber. "If we hang around, we'll get one of those stalks up the ass."

"I'm estimating they can reach at least fifteen meters out of the water," Gettner said. "Trust me, I'm going to bang out fast."

What if those polyps could swim? Dom watched them clinging to the submarine. They were pretty chunky. Maybe they'd sink.

As soon as *Clement* flooded her tanks and sank beneath the surface, they slipped off the casing and thrashed around in the sea. Dom trained the gun on them as Baird kicked free from the bridge and trod water for a moment. He was now ringed by a ragged fringe of floundering polyps, any one of which could have gone off like a depth charge.

"Remember—the downdraft could trigger them," Gettner said. "I don't want to scrape Baird-burger off my undercarriage."

Barber kept his eyes on the water. "They aren't mines."

"Nat, they're *Lambent*. They could do any damn thing."

"Okay, right . . . right . . . overshot, move back . . . got it."

Baird was now directly underneath the Raven, battered by the downdraft in the middle of a disk of foaming water. He raised one arm with an OK gesture, diver-style. His left hand still gripped his Lancer, held above his head.

"Let's go." Marcus squatted on the edge of the deck with Barber, guiding the sling in one hand. "Yeah . . . steady, Major . . . steady . . . okay, he's got it."

Baird struggled to get the sling under his arms for a few seconds. He should have dropped the rifle. Dom was ready to tell him to jettison the thing, but Baird wouldn't have listened anyway. The polyps swept closer to him on a wave, looking far from dead even if they weren't efficient swimmers.

Everything blows up in our faces now. Used to be that everything burrowed underneath us, buried us, dragged us down. Now it's all explosions.

The cable went taut. The winch started whining. "Got him, Gill," said Barber.

Dom had stopped thinking about the submarine. He was too busy watching the polyps thrashing toward Baird's legs while he kept his peripheral vision tuned for movement under the surface, for signs of more stalks erupting. One of the polyps managed to slap its legs down on the water and jump a meter. It grabbed at Baird's boot and hung on.

Baird yelled in pain. For a terrible moment, Dom expected the polyp to detonate and take Baird's legs with it, and nobody could do a damn thing—not even shoot at it. Then Baird kicked, it dropped, and it exploded as it hit the surface. Baird was lost for a second in a column of water.

"Hey, you assholes trying to use me for frigging *bait?*" he yelled. "Winch me up!"

"He's okay," Marcus grunted. "Normal for Baird."

Dom was itching to sink the polyps. "Can I fire now?"

"Knock yourself out."

Machine-gunning the creatures in the water felt surreal. Dom had to give some of them a second pass to get them to detonate, but where they'd drifted into a mass, a single exploding polyp set off a chain reaction. It was like watching a pyrotechnics show.

Marcus hauled Baird inboard across the deck by his belt.

"Yeah, spread 'em around, Dom." Baird rolled over on his back, gasping but not too exhausted to bitch. "I mean, they might have eggs or something, like coral polyps. Help 'em spread."

"You're welcome."

"My frigging ankle hurts. It got me."

Gettner's voice rasped over the speaker. "Hey! I can throw you back *anytime*, motormouth. Fenix, radio ahead and warn Doc Hayman that Baird might have brain damage. Because I swear I just saw him risk his self-obsessed ass to save his buddies. That says frontal-lobe trauma to me."

"It's a nice boat," Baird said defensively. Dom watched his embarrassment, the telltale roll of the head. "I want it in one piece."

"Sure you do," said Marcus.

Dom was pretty sure that the first non-Baird thing that went through Baird's mind was saving Cole. If he thought any wider than that, then the man was changing. Or maybe Dom had read him all wrong. It was a crazily brave thing to do, whatever the motive.

"They'll let you keep playing with the boat, I'm sure," Dom said.

"Hey, I rebuilt their comms and towed array. They'd peel grapes for me if I wanted. If we *had* grapes."

Gettner interrupted. "Serious moment, guys. Is he fit enough for me to hang around here? Because I can see something. Look at the water. Follow the line from the main stalk."

Dom couldn't see what she meant until the Raven gained altitude. A streak of shadow grew under the surface as the growth continued underwater, heading southeast. While Dom watched, another stalk erupted from the sea a few hundred meters ahead of the last one.

"Wow, is that part of this one, or what?"

"If it isn't," Marcus said, "maybe they're erupting all over the region."

Barber marked it on the folded chart resting on his thigh. "Better put out a shipping warning."

"Hey, Nat, we've got one ahead," Gettner said. "Look."

She turned the Raven so Barber could see from the crew bay. Dom watched his expression behind his goggles as he refolded the chart and looked at the next grid. His frown got deeper, he started licking his lips a lot, and then he sat back with his hands flat on the chart, staring into the mid-distance for a moment.

"If I draw the proverbial line through these points, you know what it intersects with?" he said at last.

Baird unstrapped his boot and nursed his injured ankle. "This isn't going to be a fun quiz, is it?"

"No, it's not," Barber said. "The damn things are on course for the Emerald Spar field."

Marcus pressed his earpiece. "Control? This is Fenix. We might need a hand at the imulsion rig."

Dom had reached his crisis overload for the day. Whatever came down the pike next, however bad, however crazy—it wasn't going to shift that needle beyond the end-stop.

The harder they fought, the worse things got.

IMULSION PLATFORM EMERALD SPAR, 350 KILOMETERS NORTHWEST OF VECTES.

Gettner touched down on the rig's helipad, muttering to Barber about loads and return trips.

Baird could hear her. She was already planning for the worst—the evacuation of the platform. Judging by the welcoming committee that met the Raven, though, the rig crew weren't planning on going without a serious fight. They were, as Bernie would have said, seriously *tooled up.*

"Is that hardware for the stalks, or us?" Baird asked.

Marcus shrugged. "It's their home. How far would you go to defend yours?"

"Mine was demolished by grubs. Like yours."

"Yeah. So it was."

Gradin and six of his crew waited at the edge of the pad, armed with an array of weapons that Baird had to admire. It included a grenade launcher, a flamethrower, a harpoon gun, and a Locust Hammerburst.

Grubs. Baird almost felt nostalgic about them. Nice big targets, predictable things that he knew how to fight. Things that relied on dry land, just like he did. After fifteen years, he had the measure of them. Now he was dealing with glowing monster eels, ship-killing giant stalks, and dog-sized exploding polyps, all of which sounded like interesting novelty acts until he started adding up the casualty list.

His ankle was giving him hell. He was parked somewhere between angry lashing-out aggression and the shaky aftermath of being too scared to think straight. When he jumped out of the Raven after Dom, he realized—again—that his armor was still on board *Clement.*

Gradin shook Marcus's hand. "So is it our excellent cuisine or witty conversation that brings these *stalks* to our door?"

"We're still working that out. You can evacuate. Gettner can take you off the rig."

"And leave you to defend the platform?" Gradin took a step forward and did a theatrical count of heads. "I make that four, unless your Raven flies itself. We stay. Everyone here can use a weapon, including our wives."

Marcus didn't even try to argue with him. "Fair enough. We've got extra squads inbound, but until the cavalry shows—better get started."

"So tell us how to fight these things."

Baird was the world expert on stalks and polyps by default. Everyone looked at him expectantly.

"It's an emerging field of research," he said. "As in—we met the assholes for the first time a couple of hours ago. They blow up when you hit them. Or when they hit you."

Gradin sighted up on an imaginary target somewhere past Baird, then lowered his rifle. "Good. That is all I need to know."

"About knee-high. Six legs."

"Walking mines."

"*Running* mines. Lots of running mines, and they use the stalks like siege ladders."

Gradin shrugged. "We keep them clear of the vapor venting system, then. Or else we all end up orbiting with your Hammer satellites." He looked out to sea. "So this is all *Lambent*."

"Probably. They were the ones the grubs were fighting a war with." Baird had a feeling that he'd overplayed his expert card. "We can't keep up with the different shapes they come in, so here's the rule — if it looks weird or glows, blow the shit out of it. We can worry about accidentally plugging endangered bioluminescent species later."

Gradin gave him a look that could have been amusement. "We take your advice."

Gettner and Barber stayed with the Raven while the others climbed down to the drill deck. The platform was a lot of real estate to cover with just fifty people; Baird suspected that wasn't even enough personnel to run the drilling operation safely. In the canteen, a team of surprisingly cheerful men and women were laying out ammunition and medical supplies in what looked like a well-practiced drill. They seemed to have a plan for sieges.

"You've played this game before," Dom said.

Gradin shrugged. "We're a fat target marooned in the middle of nowhere. Yes, we're ready. Stranded, exploding monsters, marauding COG — we repel all boarders. That was a joke, by the way. We joke."

"Yeah, I knew you didn't mean it about the Stranded."

"Where is your big thrashball star?" Gradin asked.

"Probably still throwing up all over a submarine," Baird said. He'd kept trying to raise Cole on the radio, but *Clement* was obviously still below mast depth. "You'll have to make do with us puny guys."

"You want someone to take a look at that leg?"

"Not until it falls off." Baird paused. He could go through the motions, he supposed. *Diplomacy. Yeah. How hard can it be?* "Thanks."

The ankle injury worried Baird. He kept unfastening his boot to take a look, and it wasn't so much the pain as not knowing a damn thing about those polyps. He was checking to see if it was glowing. He felt stupid for even thinking it, but after the weird shit he'd seen in the Locust tunnels—the luminous mucus on the floor that he'd stopped Dom from handling, and the grubs that looked a bit shiny, too—he was half-expecting to morph into some grotesque mountain of exploding meat like that Brumak did.

Shit.

"You want some pain control?" Marcus said.

Baird had to come clean. Marcus had seen all the Lambent variations too. "Just checking I'm not glowing in the dark."

"You're the one who was always bitching about having no flashlights."

"Just saying."

"Don't worry. I'll shoot you if you light up."

Marcus could say shit like that and not sound remotely callous or glib. Baird couldn't. He knew it. He fastened his boots again and then began worrying about what to use for body armor instead.

Gradin stepped up onto a bench at the front of the canteen and let out one of those piercing forefinger-and-thumb whistles that Baird couldn't do. That got everyone's attention.

"People, Eugen is filling the standby tanker to capacity so we can ship out as much fuel as possible. A precaution." Gradin pointed to the northwest quadrant of the platform. "The landfall—if it happens—is likely to be on the helipad side, but these stalks can shoot up anywhere. So *two* lookouts per flank, and one depth-charge launcher. Keep the polyps from exploding near flammable vapor."

"Do we begin shutting down the whole platform or not?" asked one of the men.

"No time. Drilling is suspended. That is all we can do."

One of the women was loading spare ammo clips with rounds and didn't look up. "Are these things quick?"

"Yeah," Baird said. "They are."

"Can they swim?"

"No, but they don't drown fast, either."

The name tab on the woman's overalls said DERSAU A. "So. I treat them same way as cockroaches. Flamethrower, maybe. Works really *good.*"

"At a distance, yes . . ."

Marcus looked up as if this had rung a bell with him. "What's the lowest flashpoint imulsion you've got here?"

"Flashpoint, or *fire* point?" Gradin asked.

"You read my mind."

"We prerefine some grades that will burn. Two-edged sword, of course."

"Do it to them before they do it us."

"This is how Gorasnaya waged war in the Silver Era." Gradin looked amused. "Stand on the castle battlements and rain fire on the unwary. We enjoy this."

"It'll be a party," said Baird.

They really need me here. I can rig stuff fast. This is what I was born for.

The platform had plenty of spare pipe sections and conduit. It took Baird, Eugen, and the drill crew half an hour to divert the outflow from one of the storage tanks to a network of hoses around the platform. Wherever those stalks came up—*if* they came up—their little polyp buddies would get sprayed with flammable fuel and torched.

It might not get here, of course.

Who was he kidding? He'd seen enough of the Locust to know that if shit was feasible, then it was a dead-cert fucking guarantee to end up in his lap. The glowies wouldn't be any different.

He looked up at the crane arm that jutted from the side of the platform. The remains of the Stranded pirate still hung there, a keep-clear warning in any language, but it wouldn't make one damn bit of difference to those dumb stalks.

Now it was a matter of waiting. Baird wasn't good at that. He walked around the topside gantries, checking for missed angles and vulnerable pipe runs. The platform would go up like a bomb if too much vapor escaped into a closed space and ignited. He was standing on the helipad trying to devise ways to use the flare-off as a giant flamethrower when Dom wandered up to him, Lancer clutched across his chest.

"Just as well we're quick learners," Dom said.

"Humans. Great at inventing things to fry each other. Shit at being harmless."

"Always good to hear an outsider's view on us." Dom seemed to be waiting for a retort. "Don't worry, I bet Cole's fine."

Baird still didn't take the bait. He didn't feel he had to now. He watched Gettner jump down from her Raven, walk around checking its skin, and then sit behind the door gun facing out to sea. He wondered if she'd ever been a deck chief and missed letting rip with that gun. Everyone needed a weapon in their hands. Gettner struck him as the kind who missed hers.

Marcus joined the staring-out-to-sea committee. "Listen," he said.

The chatter of Raven rotors drifted in and out of Baird's hearing on the wind. That definitely boosted everyone's spirits, although the Gorasni had seemed up for a good fight anyway. A cheer went around the platform.

"*Now* they earn their fuel!" someone yelled.

"Yeah, it must look that way to them," Marcus said.

Dom glanced at him. "You going soft on Indies?"

"They're not Indies now." Marcus turned to face the direction of the sound. "And none of them ever shot at you or me."

Three Ravens appeared as black blurs on the horizon to the southwest, instantly reassuring. Ravens were air support, replenishment, and a ticket home. It was going to be a tight fit on that landing pad. As the first bird came into land, everyone took refuge from the downdraft and rotors by withdrawing to the deck below. Baird waited for the engines to cut, but the Gorasni guys went straight back up top. He could hear their loud cheers.

"Must be the mail drop," Dom said.

But when Baird climbed up to take a look, he could see what had prompted the cheering. Miran Trescu had stepped out of one Raven followed by a squad of Gears. With body armor and a custom assault rifle, he looked like a seriously hard bastard.

"No Prescott, then?" Baird said. "Surprise."

The Gorasni rig men were slapping Trescu's shoulder and pumping his hand. He'd made their day. This guy wasn't a desk jockey. He looked like he loved his job.

"See," Eugen said to Baird, grinning from ear to ear, "this is why we follow Trescu *anywhere*. No figurehead. No manager. A *leader*."

Baird looked anxiously for squad mates. Sam was swapping ammo with Jace. Even Drew Rossi had shown up, and that told Baird something; this wasn't just a case of throwing the best guys at the job in hand. It was a training acquaint for the future. Hoffman had sent the guys who would lead squads the next time the stalks appeared after this.

Baird couldn't see Bernie. But he did hear a loud, bellowing laugh.

Cole stepped out of a Raven with a navy kitbag over his shoulder, walked up to Baird, and dropped the bag at his feet with a clatter of metal.

"Baby, I turn my back for one minute and you're gone," he said. "Put your damn plates on. You look like a *civilian*."

"Yes, Mom." Baird could rely completely on Cole, maybe the first and only person in his life who was always there for him with no questions asked or conditions set. He opened the bag and took out his armor. *Clement* probably hadn't even reached port yet, which meant Cole had been airlifted off the casing. "Bernie sent you to nag my ass off, did she?"

"She says she always *knew* you were human, deep down."

"I just didn't want to lose our last sub on my watch, okay?"

Cole wasn't letting up. "Well, the sub *thanks* you, and so do the crew that was shittin' themselves when that dose of crabs showed up."

Yeah, I did something that Marcus would do. Does that make me a different person? I don't even know why the fuck I did it. I don't like losing. I knew Cole was relying on me. Does it make me an asshole because I wasn't thinking of the other guys first?

"Yeah, whatever. Where's Bernie, then?"

Cole shook his head. "Hoffman grounded her. Says she's gotta take desk duties until she tests fit again."

"I bet that went down well."

"It's gonna take him more than flowers to smooth over Boomer Lady, that's for sure."

There were eighteen extra Gears on the rig now, plus Trescu. Yeah, Bernie wasn't essential, and she wasn't a lucky charm. Everything she touched lately detonated under her. Baird still felt bad for her. He didn't like being left behind when he could do something useful, so he could imagine how she felt about it.

"She can take her killer puppy for nice long walks," he said. "Savage a few Stranded. It'll do her good."

Two of the Ravens took off again to monitor the progress of the stalks. There was nothing to do but stand here and wait for the things to hit or miss the rig. Baird switched his radio to the pilots' channel and listened.

It was half an hour before he heard the words he'd been expecting.

"Shit . . . that's *fast*. Four-Seven-One, you see that?"

"Confirmed. I'd say that's multiple stalks, not one with branches."

"Everyone's an expert," Baird muttered.

Marcus shook his head slowly. He must have been listening in on the comms net too, but then he always did. Trescu walked up to him, looked him in the eye in total silence, and nodded once. Then the Gorasni leader strode into the center of the helipad and proved he'd once been a drill sergeant.

"Emerald Spar!" Trescu roared. "Stand by to repel invaders! This rig is *Gorasnayan soil!*"

CHAPTER 10

Individually reliable, collectively disciplined.
(CHAIRMAN RICHARD PRESCOTT, DESCRIBING THE COG'S VISION OF
THE IDEAL ARMY)

IMULSION PLATFORM EMERALD SPAR, 350
KILOMETERS NORTHWEST OF VECTES.

"You think these things put out runners, like plants?" Kevan
Mitchell stayed on the radio, giving a running sitrep from the
Raven as it kept an eye on the stalks' progress. "It sticks up a
branch every so often like it's checking its bearings. No polyps.
Maybe it's looking for somewhere dry to off-load them."

Dom could follow the progress by sight. The helicopter moved
in odd lurches, hovering for a moment and then darting forward.
Its searchlight played on the water below. Even in the afternoon
sun, Dom could see it.

The Raven was coming at the imulsion platform head-on. The
Lambent stalk—or stalks, however the thing propagated—was
making straight for the rig.

"I'm going to give it another rattle with the gun the next time it
pokes its nose above water," Mitchell said. "But that's made sweet
fuck-all difference to it so far."

Sorotki cut in, probably aware that everyone was listening to the radio chatter. "Heads up, people—*Clement* and *Zephyr* are both back on task. *Falconer* is steaming in our direction, ETA four hours. *Centennial* is about thirty minutes behind her."

Four hours sounded as good as never to Dom, but he put it out of his mind. All the Gears were at their action stations, lined up on the stalk-facing side of the rig on both main decks. Between them, some of the platform crew stood at the safety rails with an assortment of heavy weapons. The woman with the flamethrower—her name was Aurelie like her grandmother, she told Dom—had a good clear space to herself. Nobody fancied being panfried if things got out of hand.

But they were all sitting on a powder keg anyway. And the incoming trouble was an enemy that self-detonated. If there was a worse place to fight these things, Dom couldn't think of one.

"This is going to be like a mycelium," Baird said.

"What?"

"Fungus," Marcus muttered. "Most of it's below the surface. All we see is the bit aboveground."

Dom got the idea all too quickly. "No point pissing away ordnance trying to stop it, then, is there?"

"You never know." Marcus raised his binoculars to his eyes. "You just never know."

A burst of fire out to sea got Dom's attention. Everyone held their breath and strained to watch. The Raven fired a couple of belts into the water, but then peeled away fast when a long projection of stalk shot up from the surface, dark gray and peppered with glowing patches. Everyone watching let out a collective gasp. The things could reach a lot higher than they thought.

"Okay . . . can't stop the stalk *that* way," Sorotki said, dead calm. "We'll save the ammo for its little shiny friends."

The fuel tanker that had been moored at the platform had taken on its maximum load of imulsion, and was now a few kilometers out heading for Vectes. Dom watched it for a few moments, half-expecting it to suddenly disappear in a ball of flame, and then his radio crackled.

"Hoffman to Emerald Spar."

Marcus responded. "Receiving you, Colonel."

"Late to the party—apologies, Gears. Had to tear myself away from the Chairman's valued advice. I'm inbound."

"Fenix to Hoffman—bad timing, Colonel. Suggest you stand off and observe."

Dom didn't hear Hoffman's response. He could imagine the old man chafing at the bit to grab a rifle and fight, especially as Trescu had rushed to the front line. Hoffman had his faults, but hiding behind his gold braid when there was real soldiering to be done wasn't one of them.

"I reserve the right to ignore that if I see you getting your asses kicked," Hoffman replied. "Standing by."

Cole chuckled to himself. "The man's *savage*."

"What's the old folks' equivalent of a midlife crisis?" Baird asked. "Senile crisis?"

Cole didn't seem to be listening. He kept flicking the controls on his Lancer one-handed, pistol-style, eyes fixed on an imaginary point just beneath the approaching Raven. "I never played against psycho glowie crabs before. Let's do it."

Suddenly the time in front of Dom collapsed into a fast count-down. The Raven was nearly at the rig.

"*Stand to!*" Trescu yelled.

Marcus raised his Lancer. "Hold this platform, Gears. *Hold it.*"

From this angle, Dom couldn't see what was happening under the surface. His pulse was pounding in his ears.

"It's reached the rig, it's *at the rig*," Sorotki said.

Dom braced, waiting for the shaft to burst from the water right below him and shower the platform with polyps. They'd be in his face right away. He'd be aiming short bursts, trying to detonate them before they got too close. He'd be—

But nothing happened.

Two seconds . . . three seconds . . . and nothing had reared up in front of him. He looked around. Everyone in the line was look-ing over the side, rifles angled down, lost for a few moments.

"It's gone *under!*" Sorotki yelled. "Shit, it's under the rig."

For a stupid, *stupid* moment, Dom really thought the thing

had just missed them, oblivious, following a blind course set by some unknown instinct, and that it would carry on until it hit something else. Then he felt the vibration in the soles of his boots.

It was like a heavy wave hitting the structure. Dom held his breath for a second, then he heard more thuds and tearing metal. Sorotki's Raven looped back from the north.

"It's still under the rig," he said. "It hasn't come out the other side. It's gone—"

"*Up*," Marcus said.

From the deck below, the lookouts started yelling.

"It's come up through the bottom deck! *Polyps!* They're coming out everywhere—"

Automatic fire rattled somewhere below. Dom, along with everyone else, rushed to the ladders to head off the polyps. The things had bypassed their first line of defense in a matter of seconds. The hastily constructed lace of hoses and pipes full of flammable fuel designed to roast the creatures as they climbed onto the platform would be no damn use at all.

And the lowest deck was where the lifeboats launched.

It was just as well nobody was planning to leave this rig before the polyps did.

Boots didn't help much on thin metal ladders. Baird gave up and jumped the last two meters to the main deck with Sam and Cole right behind him. The noise—rifle fire, clanging metal, shouts, Ravens at a hover—was deafening. He had to cup his hand over his ear to hear the radio.

"Where's the stalk come up? Where is it?" If it had ruptured a vapor tank, the platform was already in deep shit. "Anyone know?"

"Under the drill," someone said. "In the well bay."

Automatic fire and shouting was coming from every part of the rig. Baird tried to remember all the exits and ladders opening from the drilling modules. He couldn't. He just ran for the center of the rig, found an open hatch, and aimed down it.

"Clear." He climbed down backward, expecting something

to snatch his legs from under him at any second. When he hit the deck, he could see along that exposed side of the platform. The external doors and hatches were all shut. If those things were coming up *inside* the rig, then they'd have to find some way to get *out*, too. "Hey, they'll be crap at opening doors. No fingers."

"How are we going to know if we're near a vapor leak?" Sam said. "This whole place smells of imulsion."

"Just shoot the frigging polyps," Baird muttered. "Because if they blow, they'll ignite it a lot better than we ever will."

Cole put one hand flat on the metal bulkhead as if he was feeling to see if it was hot. "Hey, we got some puppies in there scratchin' to come out. Feel it?"

Something—lots of somethings—was banging and scrabbling against the metal from the other side.

"Told you." Baird stepped back to the rail, facing the doorway. "No thumbs."

Sam stood to one side and Cole to the other, Lancers ready. "In three . . ."

" . . . two . . ."

Cole reached out and slipped the catch. " . . . *go!*"

The door burst open. Glowing polyps spewed from the opening like an avalanche of lightbulbs and meat. Baird saw the crossfire as Cole and Sam fired into the scrambling mass, and he stared into a sea of fangs that seemed to stand still like a freeze-frame. All he could take in was those open maws. His finger tightened on the trigger by pure reflex as the things exploded and spattered his face. He didn't dare stop. It took a real effort to break off and reload. The polyps seemed to keep coming from nowhere, and then, as suddenly as they'd boiled out, they stopped.

Sam held up her hand to check fire and stepped through the door. There was a long, rattling burst, followed by a few small explosions and a flare of yellow light. Then she came out again.

"Clear," she said, reloading. "Next?"

As they moved along the walkway, the firing and yelling continued below them. When Baird reached the end, he could see a carpet of polyps moving like a solid mass up the stairway from the

deck below. The crazy Gorasni woman with the flamethrower—
Aurelie—was clambering down a ladder running parallel with
the stairs. The whole rig was a mesh of interconnected gantries
and steps linking the different modules. That was as handy for the
polyps as it was for everyone else.

Aurelie looked up at Baird. "You stand clear," she called. "I use
this anyway."

And she did. She hooked her left arm around the ladder and
leaned away from the bulkhead, somehow managing to take most
of the weight of the flamethrower nozzle with her right hand. It
wasn't a smart weapon to use one-handed. She didn't have much
control over the jet direction when it ignited, and that flame shot
a long way.

A *frigging* long way.

Baird and Cole jumped back, just escaping the arc of flaming
fuel. Baird heard her yell something. He thought she'd fallen, but
when he looked again she'd managed to aim the jet and was playing it on the polyps that were at the top of the column trying to
scale the stairs. They burned, but they didn't burn easy. They
hung on. It looked as if it was going to be a race between who let
go first—or who cooked first.

Cole leaned over the rail and fired into the flaming mass of
legs. Maybe it was the heat congealing their proteins, but they
didn't burst apart like a shot pumpkin this time. Then one of
them detonated. The stairway and a section of the gantry bolted
to it—probably rusted through at a critical point—fell away from
its supports and plunged into the sea beneath, taking the polyps
with it.

Aurelie was left hanging on the ladder, flushed and breathless.
There was nothing beneath her now, and if anyone on the other
side of that section needed to escape, they were out of luck too.
The only way was back up. That was no easy climb with a red-hot
chunk of metal in one hand and an arm numb from gripping the
ladder.

And then it got a whole lot harder. The gantry above her
suddenly filled with a jostling mass of polyps.

"Hang on, baby," Cole yelled. He climbed up one of the safety rail stanchions to swing onto the deck above. "Keep your head down. Pest control's comin'."

Baird watched the polyps turn like one animal and make a rush for Cole. But there was nothing he could do to give him covering fire. Baird was below the edge of the deck, and now Cole was between him and the polyps. Cole waded into the mass of scrabbling legs like weeding a patch of grass, standing his ground and firing down just a meter or two from his boots.

Baird climbed after him. When he hauled himself onto the walkway, Cole was busy kicking away a wounded polyp while he reloaded. It didn't seem to have enough strength left to detonate itself.

"These ain't fun," Cole said. He stepped over the debris, almost skidding on bile-green slime. "You still there, lady?"

Aurelie was clinging to the ladder. It took both of them to haul her onto the deck and not lose the flamethrower over the side. She dusted herself down and pointed to the bridge between the drilling section and the treatment modules.

"There are many coming up through there," she said. "The stalk split the bulkhead. I go in—then I can keep burning them. But I need cover."

Sam jogged down the gantry and grabbed Baird by the shoulder. "Marcus is in the well bay. He says the polyps are still coming up the stalk—how many of those things does it carry?"

"Shit, how do I know? It's our first date." Baird had to assume the stalk could disgorge an endless stream of polyps. He pressed his earpiece. "Hey, KR units? Any of you able to fly low and look under the rig?"

"We're having so much fun with the door guns," Sorotki said. Baird could hear the hammering bursts of gunfire in the background. He wasn't sure where the Ravens were directing their fire, but wherever it was it meant the polyps were swarming over open decks now. "Let me tear myself away for a moment."

"Can you see the stalk?"

Baird couldn't even tell where Sorotki was now. He ran back to the end of the walkway and turned onto the next section, stopping to look over the side every few meters. He found himself looking down on the strobing rotors of a Raven wreathed in spray thrown up by the downdraft. Sorotki was almost sitting on the water.

"I see it," Sorotki said. "Still wedged in the deck."

"Try blowing the shit out of it. Break it off. Take their ladder away."

"Those things still coming out, then?"

"Yeah. Just a few." The firing around Baird seemed to merge into a continuous barrage. "Look, just shoot, will you? Cut it off."

"It'll just grow a new one."

"Do it." Baird tried to raise Marcus. "Marcus? Baird here. We're trying a new tack. Two-Three-Nine's going to try to pulp the stalk from the side. Keep your head down in case of freak ricochets."

"Understood."

"Where are the rest of—"

Baird was silenced out by a sequence of loud bangs. Then there was a much louder bang, a longer booming explosion, and a ball of flame shot out horizontally at the accommodation end of the platform. Metal creaked and groaned. Baird felt a jolt through the soles of his boots.

"Ahh shit," Marcus said. "What was that?"

"Something blew out a compartment near the living quarters." Baird could see a steady stream of smoke. "We've got a real fire now by the look of it."

Gradin cut into the comm circuit. "I've sent a damage control team to deal with it. If the rig burns, the polyps will be *academic*. And so will we."

"You handle the fire, we'll handle the polyps," Marcus said. "Sorotki? Mitchell? Do what Baird says. Sever that stalk."

Baird was at the instinctive reaction stage now. His mouth was dry with terror, but the rest of his body carried on with business as usual, doing split-second things he couldn't have managed if he'd stopped to think about them rationally. There was something even more devoted to preserving Baird than Baird himself. It was that primal part of his brain that really didn't give a shit about his mind or his soul or anything beyond keeping the meat alive.

The small remaining scrap of Thinking Baird observed that reflex with amazement every time. He decided that was how those frigging crazy Raven pilots functioned most of the time.

Smoke and flame belched from the rig just fifty meters away from the hovering Raven. Sorotki was still holding the helicopter steady just above the water. Metal structures could have fallen and shredded his rotors, another explosion could have sent him crashing into the sea, and there was no telling what could burst from the water and take him down with it. But he just seemed to park in midair while Mitchell got a steady lock on the stalk.

Baird could see the rapid muzzle flash as Mitchell fired between the platform's legs. Sam elbowed Baird to get his attention.

"Hey, we're not out of polyps yet. Move it."

"Yeah, okay. Lead me to 'em."

Cole jogged up to them. "Somebody oughta check those lifeboats are still around if this all goes to shit."

There was another loud boom. A hatch just in front of them burst open, maybe from the shock wave, and more polyps spilled out. Baird decided he'd take grubs any day. Even a tank-sized Corpser was somehow less hideous. It was the fact that these things *swarmed*. They were knee-high and they just kept coming, blindly single-minded, triggering some primal dread of being drowned in a wave of exploding meat.

Sam took out the first rank. The three of them were getting into a routine now, like an old-style rifle platoon forming ranks and reloading while the other sustained fire. Polyp debris spattered the metal walkway. When the firing stopped, Baird's ears were ringing.

"Stalk down." That was Mitchell's voice in his earpiece. The Raven lifted and circled. "I think I've put a few holes in the rig, but the stalk's pulped now."

"Okay, let's mop up the stragglers," Sam said.

Firing continued from all directions. As they worked their way along gantries picking off the remaining polyps, the noise thinned out and became more sporadic. Voices started calling in on the comm net.

"No more polyps coming through," Marcus said. "How are we doing?"

"Running out of targets." That was Rossi. "Everyone okay?"

"Two rig crew missing," Jace said. "Hey, can anyone give us a hand with this fire?"

The accommodation section was now belching black smoke. The threat had shifted from polyps to something that had previously held the top award for Worst Possible Shit to Happen on a Rig. Baird hoped all that flammable fuel Marcus had piped to the decks to repel the polyps wasn't leaking.

Hoffman's voice cut in. "Is the platform secure? Can't see anything else moving from up here."

"Just finishing up," Marcus said. "KR units, stand by for casevacs."

The relative quiet that suddenly fell across the rig was weird. Baird could hear the whoosh and thump of the waves again, and metal clanging as people ran along gantries. Raven engines faded in and out on the wind.

Then there was a dull, echoing thud. Baird thought it was something settling from the damage, maybe the fire spreading and buckling plates, but then he heard Marcus, and knew it wasn't.

"Shit," Marcus said. "Stalk! We got another stalk! More polyps, coming through the other side of the well bay!"

So Mitchell was right. There was another stalk to take its buddy's place.

"Shit," Baird said, and ran for the center of the platform.

Dom never paused to consider what would kill him first, a polyp or a vapor explosion. He was living a second at a time, unable to think outside the moment until the mass of polyps he was firing into finally slowed or stopped.

The creatures boiled up through a buckled sheet of steel and met a hail of automatic fire from Marcus, a Gorasni driller, and four of the roughnecks. Dom wasn't surprised to see Trescu burst into the compartment and open fire as well. It just seemed a regular thing for the guy to do.

But the polyps kept coming. Every minute or two there was a long pause, as if the stalk had run out of ammo, and then it would start up again. Dom had lost track of the time. Hours, minutes? Minutes. Maybe fifteen. Maybe thirty. He couldn't stop to check.

"Where else are they getting in?" Marcus yelled, reloading. "Can we get a fuel hose down here and burn them out?"

"They burst one of the vapor tanks," the driller said. "Yeah, you kill them. You kill us, too. The whole damn rig."

Another explosion shook the metal grating Dom was standing on. The polyps rushed out of another gap in the deck. It was now impossible to tell what damage was down to exploding polyps igniting gas leaks, and what was part of the chain of disaster set off by the initial fire under the living quarters. All anyone could do was stand and fight and try not to die. The thickening fog of black smoke made that a challenge.

"Where's all that smoke coming from?" Marcus yelled.

Dom couldn't tell if it was drifting or if they were right underneath the seat of a fire. "Dunno. But we can't stay in here much longer without breathing apparatus."

Marcus emptied another clip into the bottomless well of polyps. While he was reloading, one of the things got its front legs over the edge of a deck hatch. Dom moved to fire just as Marcus put his chainsaw down through its head. It went off with a loud bang, throwing him back a couple of paces, but he kept his balance and opened fire again.

Apart from an occasional shout of "Gangway gone!" nobody was coordinating the defense of the rig now. Nobody could see what the hell was going on. Dom wondered why the Ravens weren't taking over, but then it occurred to him: they couldn't see much from the air, either.

For a few moments, the flow of polyps stopped. Dom risked looking into the opening, and Marcus called across the compartment to Trescu.

"We'll need to evacuate if these assholes don't call it a day soon." Marcus wiped sweat from his nose with the back of his glove. "The smoke's going to choke us either way."

Dom expected Trescu to spit defiance and swear he'd die before he'd abandon the platform. But he didn't.

"If Gradin tells me the fire has spread, then I shall order it." Trescu stepped back and cupped his hand over his ear as he tried his radio. Another explosion—much bigger, much louder— shook the rig. "Gradin, this is Trescu. Is the fire contained?"

Dom didn't hear the answer, but he saw the look on Trescu's face. The man put his hand on Marcus's back to get his attention.

"Get your people off," he said. "There is still gangway access to the lifeboat under the flame boom. That will take thirty."

"Yeah, and your guys?"

"Very well. We go too."

It was an instant decision. They used the lull to run, dog the doors shut from outside, and head for the boats. Even in the fog of smoke, Dom could now see the state the platform was in.

Everywhere he looked was burning. The smoke was black and chokingly bitter, and he couldn't stop himself breathing it in. Out of nowhere, a memory stopped him in his tracks: Maria, worried, scolding him for not wearing a helmet with air filters, telling him he had to at least cover his face with a scarf if he was going to go out into the ash-clogged air after the Hammer of Dawn had incinerated most of Sera. Dom shut it out of his mind and tried to concentrate on working out which end of the rig had the free-fall lifeboat. He was totally disoriented. He simply followed Marcus.

Astonishingly, some of the platform's systems were still working. The immediate evacuation alarm started that bowel-gripping *honk-honk-honk* as he jogged along the walkways, spitting to clear his mouth of the acrid smoke. Polyps could have been lurking around the next corner, but they seemed the least of his problems now.

Marcus ran along ahead of him, grabbing rig crew by their collars and hauling them away from the flames.

"Leave the thing!" he yelled. "You can't save it. Get to the boats. Jump. Anything. Just get off while you still can."

Dom found himself counting as he went. He knew how many men and women were on this platform. He knew two were missing. So he counted every individual he saw and subtracted one from the total, and then shoved the person down the nearest intact ladder toward the boats or an open deck where a Raven could hover. It was completely pointless; he couldn't work out how many survivors were left to evacuate, but it made him feel better trying. He was just one of a dozen Gears still on the rig struggling to evacuate everyone.

And some Gorasni still refused to give up.

Gradin was playing a jet of water into an open compartment, but it looked like steam was coming straight back out. Dom didn't even know what was burning in there or if seawater was the right thing to use. But even if it was, Gradin might as well have been pissing on it. The whole platform looked red-hot. Marcus caught Gradin's arm.

"You're done here," he said. "Trescu called it off. Let's go."

Gradin shrugged him away. Dom could feel the heat on his face even though he was a few meters away from the door. "I will *not* abandon this rig. You go."

"It's just a fucking piece of metal," Marcus said. "It's not *people*. You can't rebuild *people*." And he knocked Gradin flat with a single punch.

The guy fell back and hit the deck. Marcus had only stunned him, but it put Gradin off balance long enough for Marcus to grab him bodily and heave him over his shoulder like a firefighter.

The enclosed boat hung on ski-slope rails, ready to free-fall into the sea. Marcus managed to run for the boat under the flare boom and force Gradin through the open hatch.

Dom found the hull was full of exhausted, wet, grimy people. It could take a few more, though. The boat wouldn't have to wait long to be picked up. Marcus tried the radio.

"Anyone still on the rig—either jump *now* or get down the lifeboat at the flare end. I'm counting down two minutes. *Run!*"

He waited for responses. But there was always the possibility that someone's radio had gone down, and most of the Gorasni didn't have earpieces anyway. "Are all Gears accounted for?"

Hoffman responded. "All off the rig except Baird, Cole, Santiago, and *you*. We've got a few more civilians to winch clear."

Trescu appeared at the end of the walkway, smoke-stained and disheveled. He was leading a guy with bad burns to his face and hands. Dom was about to risk running back into the smoke to find Baird and Cole, but they emerged from the smoke haze a few meters behind Trescu.

"We *go*," Trescu said. "While we still have the light to find people in the water. Get ready to launch, Fenix."

It was a brutal choice, but Dom knew it was the only one they could make. Dom thought about the stalks and wondered if everyone who escaped was only postponing the inevitable. A stalk could skewer a small lifeboat like a kebab.

"Who's driving this thing?" Marcus said.

"Me." Baird stepped through the hatch and sat in the helm position. "Always wanted to try this. Move over, Indies."

The more flippant Baird was, the closer he was to pissing his pants. Dom would have to explain that quietly to some of the folks on board, because they'd lost buddies—maybe even wives. He waited with the hatch open until the two minutes were up and nobody was responding to last calls. When he squeezed into a seat, he found it was missing a safety harness, but he was ready to take a few broken bones if it meant getting out of this inferno.

"Hatch secure." Marcus was already in the second helm position, watching for Baird's cue to release the hydraulic mechanism that would send the boat shooting away from the rig. "Okay. Lower away."

"Sure. Easy does it." Baird reached for the handle. The seats all faced aft. This was going to be a crash dive. "All that shit's for *davits*."

It was a long way to plummet. Somehow, it was even weirder falling backward. Dom's stomach caught up with him as the boat hit the water and he cracked his elbow hard against something. It hurt worse than anything he could remember for a very long time. But it beat being burned alive, or worse. There *was* worse, he knew.

How much more? How many more times are we going to scrape through?

"Baby, that's *enough* of the high seas this week . . ." Cole muttered.

Baird seemed to have taken over as skipper. He started the engine after a few stalls, and the boat chugged away. But even with the hatch shut, the light through the porthole was still visibly yellow from the flames.

"Far enough," Marcus said. "Let's see where we are."

The stern hatch opened onto a small platform, just big enough for two or three people to stand very carefully in quiet seas. Marcus stepped out onto it.

"Ahh . . . *shit.*"

Marcus had turned that one word into his own complete language, depending on tone. There was a dismissive *shit,* a regretful *shit,* and even a pleasantly surprised *shit.* But this was his weary, distraught, can't-stand-another-death *shit.* Even Dom had to listen hard to get the right translation. He got up to look at what Marcus could see.

Emerald Spar was almost completely engulfed in flames, trailing long palls of black smoke in the wind. The ships heading from Vectes wouldn't have any trouble finding it now. The rig was one big smoke flare. Now that it was getting near dusk, the fire could probably be seen for kilometers, too. Five Ravens hung around the platform, one of them still winching someone to safety. Dom couldn't tell if they were plucking people from the water or the burning rig. Every time Dom saw a Raven pilot hovering above flames, or taking fire, or getting into some seriously lethal shit to haul someone to safety, he wanted to hug them and tell them that he loved every last damn one of them. Yes, even that snarly bitch Gill Gettner; he loved them all.

"Baird, get back over there and let's see what we can do," Marcus said quietly. "The Ravens can't take them all."

There were only a few people left to pull from the water. One of them was Aurelie. She'd lost her flamethrower, which was just as well, and she submitted to Cole wrapping her in a stained emergency blanket. There was no sign now of stalks or polyps.

"How long is that going to burn?" Dom asked.

"We stopped pumping." Gradin looked terrible. "But we didn't complete a shutdown. If the seals hold . . . it'll burn itself out."

The platform was sagging visibly now. Another gangway collapsed into the sea. The whole rig was falling apart, sinking piece by piece, and for Dom it was one reminder too many of watching Jacinto vanish under the water.

He turned his back on the destruction and leaned on the lifeboat's canopy. "Sometimes I think we're going to sink the whole planet."

"Or blow it apart," Baird said. "Look, what's the common factor here? Why are these things coming out to sea?"

"Who cares?"

"Us. Either they hate us, dumb as they are, or there's something that draws them to us. Ships. Rigs."

"Engine noise? That travels a long way in water."

"Hello, submarine? Stealth? Low cavitation props?"

"Okay, what, then?"

"Fuel. Imulsion. They're following the imulsion."

"The first trawler wasn't running on imulsion. That was some vegetable oil."

"You sure?"

Dom wasn't, actually. He looked at the pretty spectrum of colors shimmering on the waves in the fading light. That stuff got everywhere. It leaked from ships. It was dumped from tank-flushing. Its more volatile fractions dispersed on the breeze.

Imulsion traces crisscrossed the ocean.

And at least one big imulsion trail led to Vectes, to all the vessels that came and went, from the naval base to the fishing grounds to the imulsion platform.

It was almost dark now. Dom still had his back to the burning rig, watching the reflection on Baird's goggles.

"Whoa," Baird said, looking past Dom. "Photo moment. One to show Prescott, so he can kiss his new empire good-bye."

Dom shuffled around to look back at the rig. He turned just in time to see another explosion send a ball of searing yellow flame into the sky. Then there was another, and another, and a fire-cracker sequence as the smaller tanks ruptured in the fierce heat. When the loud boom died away like the echo of an artillery bar-rage, another sound drifted across the water, quieter but more disturbing.

It was almost like an animal. It started as a low moan but then rose up the scale to painful peaks before falling back to rumbling agony again.

It was the creaking and tearing of metal. The platform was col-lapsing.

The rivets and welds of its framework were gradually giving up under the stresses of buckling, red-hot metal. The whole struc-ture lurched as something gave way and half the topside slid into the sea, sending up clouds of steam. There was a crack almost as loud as the last explosion before the rest of the rig dropped like a beaten man falling to his knees.

Then the rig vanished.

Dom stared at the clouds swirling on the surface for a while. He couldn't tell if they were just steam or smoke from the burn-ing fuel floating on the waves.

But Emerald Spar was gone. Like Jacinto and Tollen, it had simply drowned. There was a long silence across the water. All Dom heard was the lapping of the waves on the hull and the sound of Raven engines, followed by Baird swallowing.

"Man, that breaks my frigging heart," Baird murmured. He meant every word. Dom saw his lips set in a thin line. "Fantastic engineering. *Fantastic*. Just fucked in a couple of hours by things that probably don't even understand what it is."

It was Sera's fate in a nutshell. Dom couldn't bring himself to berate Baird for focusing on the loss of objects and not people. For some reason, he kept thinking about a Pesanga Gear who gave up his place in a boat so that Dom could see Maria and the kids again. It was after the raid on Aspho Point. The guy didn't make it. Dom tried hard to recall his full name. All he could manage was Bai.

People—no, grieving for people just hurt too much. Mourning machines was bad enough.

"Fuck 'em," said Baird, to nobody in particular.

CHAPTER 11

The backbone of military aviation will always be rotary, and tactical airpower must remain in the hands of ground commanders. Fixed-wing costs too much to do too little—I see no reason to waste any more taxpayers' money on the Petrel strike-fighter program when we could spend that on helicopter-launched missile systems. These birds represent better value and can do everything we need, and do it better in most cases—transport, combat, observation, maritime, and special mission. We do not need to fragment our defense strategy by creating a separate air force.

(GENERAL JOD LOMBARD, GIVING EVIDENCE TO THE COG DEFENSE COMMITTEE ON THE LACK OF NEED TO CREATE A SEPARATE AIR FORCE AND EXPAND FIXED-WING PROCUREMENT, TWO YEARS BEFORE ACCEPTING A SEAT ON THE BOARD OF HELICOPTER MANUFACTURER AIGLAR)

COG GARRISON ANVIL GATE, KASHKUR; 17 B.E., 32 YEARS EARLIER.

Hoffman paused on top of the mound of rocks to look up at the approaching helicopter. It had taken the COG HQ at Lakar an hour to get a bird in the air, but at least it was one of the new Ravens. Hoffman knew he was going to spend a lot of his career looking up at the undercarriage of one of those.

It circled for a while before the pilot came back on the radio.

"Yes, you're up shit creek," she said. "This is going to take more than a shovel and a bucket."

"I'm glad you came all this way to tell us the goddamn obvious." Hoffman didn't like the way the rubble under his boots shifted from time to time. "No signs of any infiltration out there?"

"Negative. It's like the end of the world between here and the next city—just scrub and goats. Do you need any immediate assistance? Any casualties?"

"Don't let me keep you. Our phones are out and we can't move vehicles, but apart from that it's a goddamn vacation."

"Sorry, but it's going tits up at Shavad. They need every helicopter they can get. If Shavad falls, you're going to get pretty lonely out here."

"Okay, we'll wait for the heavy engineering boys."

We just have to sit here and blow away anything that comes from the south. And that's what we'll have to do until the road's open.

The Raven banked away and vanished. Carlile, the combat engineer, was making his own plans to clear the gorge. He clambered over the stone and then gestured to Hoffman to climb back down. It was scarier than being shelled. Every handhold felt like grabbing thin air, and the constant rumbling and clicking threatened another collapse. When Hoffman's boots hit the road, he was more than relieved.

"Is anyone under that?" he asked.

Carlile studied the dam of rocks, fists on hips. "If they are, then we won't know for a while. We need one of the big obstruction-clearance vehicles to even start to shift that. A Behemoth."

Hoffman visualized the map, and the lowlands that ran the width of Kashkur like the mountains' skirt.

"That's got to come across from Lakar. A bit close to Shavad for my tastes."

"Yeah." Carlile caught his breath. Sweat dripped off his chin. "That's going to take four days, maybe five. I'll get on it."

Hoffman had put his priorities in immediate order. The first worry was security—who was out there, whether this was the first attack of many, and whether there were casualties. Gears had set up machine-gun positions on the fort walls to handle any close-in defense. So far—apart from the landslide—there was no sign of enemy activity, but Hoffman couldn't imagine any enemy going to the trouble of altering the landscape and leaving it at that.

So being cut off wasn't top of the list at the moment. Anvegad— both the city and the garrison—had two weeks' supplies at any one time. People here, civilian and military, were used to being stranded by the weather or just not getting supplies on the day they were expected. It was nothing to shit bricks over yet.

Why now, and what's coming next?

"This would have taken them some time to set up."

"Oh, definitely, sir," Carlile said. "It's thousands of kilos of explosives. And to ship that in without being spotted, they'd have to do it on foot over the hills a load at a time. Then they've got to bore holes and set the charges. It's a long job."

"UIR spec ops pros, or local sympathizers?"

"Hard to tell. It's the level of blasting skill that civvies in the mining industry have."

Hoffman had to assume the road had been cut for a reason, not just because it was as close as the bastards could get to the garrison.

No point relying on Intel for help. We'll have to go look for these assholes ourselves. If they're not already back across the UIR borders by now, of course.

"Well, we won't get any assistance from Vasgar, so we're stuck here until this road's open again." Hoffman kept a wary eye on the craggy slopes above as he moved back to the ATV. Pad Salton was perched high on the rocks with his sniper rifle, providing overwatch. "I'm just waiting for the next incident."

"Look on the bright side, sir. If we can't get anything south to the fort, the Indies can't get anything through going north."

"I'll cling to that small mercy, Carlile. Thanks."

Hoffman walked back up the access road, stopping every so often to look back at the landslide. He'd always been security conscious, even for a Gear, but now he was fixated on who might be out there watching.

We'll need tighter security now. The locals won't mind being stopped and searched when they go in and out.

As he walked past the sentries at the city gate, crowds milled around trying to get a look at the destruction. The air was hazy with rock dust. A line of Gears and the local constabulary was stopping anyone from going outside the walls, on Captain Sander's orders, but there was nowhere worthwhile to go anyway. Outside was definitely not the safest place to be.

Sander called to him from across the square. The captain was talking to a couple of the councilmen, no doubt doing his we've-got-it-all-under-control act. He was good at civilian liaison. Hoffman felt a little ashamed for thinking of Sander as a soft college kid who was more interested in painting than being a soldier, because he was actually proving to be a reassuring and steady presence for everyone.

And he had the sense to stock up to the rafters on supplies. Smart guy. Clairvoyant, even.

Sander exuded concerned calm as Hoffman approached the group. "Lieutenant, Alderman Casani is making sure all the residents are accounted for. What's the update on the road?"

"The sappers say it can be cleared with a specialist excavation vehicle," Hoffman said, remembering to start with the can-do part of the news. *Civilians need to hear that.* "It'll take a few days to get earth-moving equipment down from Lakar, that's all. The phone lines might take longer, but we've got radio comms."

Casani was a sober-looking, thin guy in his forties who looked like he should have been running an investment bank rather than this lonely outpost. "People will be sensible," he said. "This is no different from being snowed in."

"Snow doesn't set out to kill you, Alderman." Hoffman didn't want these people to get complacent. "We're on a war footing now. People have to take precautions, however well-defended this city is. Anyone who can close the road can do a hell of a lot worse if they put their minds to it."

Sander's fixed calm flickered a little. "We'll step up patrols, Alderman. But I have to ask you to activate the civil emergency procedures. Restrictions on movement, management of resources, cooperation with our security measures. Purely as a precaution."

"But when the road is open again," said Casani, "there will still be the UIR on our doorstep and the need to watch our neighbor suspiciously."

"Yes, things have changed," Sander said. "They changed the minute the UIR sent forces across the Vasgar border. We'll all have to live with that."

Casani did a little nod, as if the reminder of the invasion south of this border was an explanation for everything. Maybe the reality hadn't sunk in. "This city understands its responsibilities, Captain. You will always have our full cooperation."

Hoffman and Sander made their way back to the garrison. Most of Anvegad's five thousand inhabitants seemed to have taken to the streets to try to get a glimpse of the damage or chat about it. Every damn surface was covered in a layer of dust. It was starting to settle, crunching under their boots like a dusting of dry, gritty snow.

"Usually," Sander said, "civvies get a little wobbly when a big bomb goes off next door. These people just seem curious."

"Anvegad's never been captured. Makes folks feel bulletproof."

"That's preferable to panic at the moment." Sander was in the process of moving operations from the main admin block to the gun emplacement itself. One of the engineer corporals was busy unplugging a radio kit when Hoffman got to the top of the stairs. "I'm sending out a forward controller just in case. Damn bad timing to piss off the Vasgari while we still need to move around out there." He started taking stuff down from the walls. "Give me a hand with the maps, Victor."

If Hoffman was going to nitpick, Anvil Gate wasn't the best garrison for a modern army. It was all narrow passages and steep stairs, five floors built entirely around those huge guns, like a keep in the center of an ancient castle. Anvegad itself was the castle grounds, just as narrow and crowded, a city built when the idea of fuel-driven vehicles was witchcraft. But the guns—big artillery didn't change much. That was why Anvil Gate remained.

A hundred Gears could hold it. A bigger force would logjam itself trying to move around.

"Very cozy ops room, sir." Sergeant Byrne squeezed past him in
the passage on the ground floor, scraping his rifle along the stone
walls. "The maps are a nice touch. Makes a man feel at home.
Maybe some cushions, though."

"You're nest-building," Hoffman growled. "You sure it's Sheraya
who's pregnant?"

"I suppose this postpones the wedding."

"The hell it does, Sergeant. Do it *today*." Hoffman didn't mean
it to sound ominous. It wasn't. He just knew how army life got in
the way of everything else, and why it mattered to grab these
things when you could. "When you get a lady knocked up, you
don't keep her waiting for the ring. Okay? That's an order."

"The aldermen are going to be too busy, sir."

"I'll see that they find you one with ten minutes to spare for a
ceremony. You can save the celebrations for when we're not spitting dust everywhere."

Sander must have heard the exchange. He looked up from the
desk, radio in one hand, as Hoffman came in.

"You're a sentimental man after all, Victor."

"I want his mind on the job. It's one less thing for him to worry
about."

"I know the feeling. If you want to send a message to Margaret,
by the way, you might want to take your own advice about sooner
rather than later."

Hoffman's reflex reaction beat his private wishes to the punch.
"If the men can't send personal messages via operational
channels, sir, then I won't, either."

Sander just blinked for a moment as if he'd taken that as a
rebuke. It wasn't. Hoffman decided not to dig a deeper hole by
explaining that.

Margaret will understand.

"Okay, all we can do is wait, then. We'll run patrols along the
Vasgar line, but not across it—yet." Sander turned to look at the
sector map behind him, a maze of tightly packed contour lines.

"It's at times like this that a man needs a Pesang detachment. Those little chaps can get to places even the damn goats can't."

"It won't be long, sir. A week."

"You think the Indies are going to wait that long?"

"They sound pretty busy at Shavad."

"Maybe so." Sander looked around the room that now resembled a frontline trench on the Ostri front thirty years ago. The air smelled of musty canvas and wool, and almost every centimeter of the planked walls was covered with charts, lists, and—yes, Byrne was right—paintings of the fort. "But we'll see them coming, that much we do know."

Hoffman was used to the waiting game. He grabbed some rations, stuffed every spare pocket with ammo, and went up to the gun floor to sit at the back of the chamber. A couple of ammo crates and a few folded blankets with that dusty, flat smell of graphite lubricating grease—that was all he needed to get his head down and have a short nap when he needed to.

"Captain kicked you out, sir?" the artillery sergeant asked.

"Can't bear sitting on my ass and listening to a game on the radio, Evan." Hoffman took his notepad out of his belt and flipped over a clean page. He'd write that letter to Margaret. "Got to watch the action."

"It'll be *way* over there. Even if they're not going to give us forward air control, we can still manage direct fire. We can see for ten or fifteen klicks easy enough if the visibility's okay."

There were ten gunners on this crew. All except Sergeant Evan had ear defenders parked around their necks like ancient torc necklaces. Hoffman had never been this close to guns this big. He started scribbling.

Margaret, if I don't come back from this deaf, I'll be damned lucky . . . but this is if I don't come back at all.

It never felt real, that line. However many times he'd written that last good-bye to anyone, it always felt theoretical. He wondered if one day it would seem solid and inevitable, and then he'd know that somehow fate was giving him a big hint that this was it.

Hunting around for the right words took more time than he expected. He didn't look up until the radio—his and everyone else's—changed from routine voice traffic to something more urgent.

"KR-Five-Three-Zero to control . . . four Indie artillery units and an infantry company moving north out of Porra, *fast*. Five-Three-Zero out."

Porra was a hundred kilometers south of Anvegad. The Indies didn't need many men to take the refinery, and it was the first target anyone would secure. Hoffman decided he'd have treated it as a priority if he'd been in their position in case the staff or the garrison tried to sabotage it.

"Here we go," Evan said. He looked at his watch. "I give them two hours, max. Now, with the right wind, we could probably hit the refinery from here. Just about."

Sander's voice cut in. "Let's keep Anvegad's unbroken record, Gears. All garrison personnel, go to REDCON One."

The garrison sirens were tested every month, and every crisis had its own voice. REDCON One started like a deep intake of breath and then rose up the scale to a series of ear-busting blasts.

"Adrenaline's brown," said Jarrold, the gunner in charge of the shell hoist. He was Pad Salton's age, maybe eighteen, maybe nineteen, but looked a lot younger to Hoffman. The shells were monsters that made the munitions for the smaller guns that Hoffman had seen earlier—the "One-Fifties"—look like Lancer rounds. It all added to the impression of Jarrold as a child playing with oversized adult things. "But ours is bigger than theirs."

"Remember that if they get close in, Private, ours are going to be all pretty well the same size."

That was the point of the big guns—to stop the enemy from getting too close. Guns had a minimum range as well as a maximum. Under a certain distance, they'd have to rely on close-in weapons. But the Indies were coming for the refinery. Hoffman knew it.

"It's five hundred meters, sir," Jarrold said. "And at that range, we could just as easily stroll out and punch them in the face."

"What is?"

"Minimum range."

It was still surprising how fast arty trucks could move on an open road, especially when they met no opposition along the way. Hoffman put away his letter and stood at the observation platform, focusing the range-finder binoculars on a point far beyond the refinery.

"Make the most of it, sir," Even said. "Because once we've got something to shoot at, we'll be needing those."

It was mid-afternoon when a message was passed from Battalion HQ to alert Anvil Gate that the UIR column would reach the refinery in two hours.

At least Hoffman had a good idea now of why the Indies had put so much effort into blocking a route that conventional military wisdom said they needed.

They couldn't take the garrison. But they probably didn't want COG reinforcements diverted east through Kashkur and down through the pass to close in on them in a pincer movement. They wanted to concentrate on Shavad and keep a single front.

That way, they could work their way through Kashkur to the imulsion fields, and eventually Anvegad would be irrelevant. They were playing a more patient game than Hoffman had thought. He stared into the distance at the point he expected to see the UIR appear.

But he could be patient, too. And, after centuries of standing guard at the gates of Kashkur, so could Anvegad.

SHAVAD, NEAR THE SOUTHWEST KASHKUR
BORDER.

If the war ever reached Ephyra, then it would look like this, Adam realized.

Shavad had the same elegant, tree-lined avenues and fountain-filled squares as the Tyran capital, the same colonnaded public buildings. The style was more oriental and exotic, but the city was the heart of a modern province where people liked shopping and theaters and clean trains that ran on time. The people were just like Tyrans.

Yes, it would be just like this. And that scared him.

He tried his radio again. This time the channel was working. "Gold Nine to Control, we requested casevac an hour ago. I've got Gears down, a lot of them Tango-One—they can't wait for you to finish your coffee break. What's happening?"

It took a few moments for the controller to respond. Adam counted three incoming shells in that time, one so close that he felt the brick dust sting his eyes a few seconds later as the blast washed down the road.

"Control to Gold Nine, you're not the only company taking heavy casualties." The controller sounded fraught. "We've lost five Terns to ground fire during attempted extractions—you suppress the Indies behind the lines, and maybe we'll have something left flying to send you."

They seemed to be everywhere. It wasn't just the artillery, tanks, and missiles from across the river that were tearing the guts out of the Shavad defenses. On the north side, the fragile front line of the city itself, COG ground forces were getting hit in the back from snipers and mortar fire. Adam could only think that the UIR had been slipping special forces into Kashkur for months ahead of Vasgar's collapse.

And I bet they engineered the end of the Vasgari government as well.

"Control, we need some routes cleared, too. We can't get the ATVs out to the north."

"Roger that, Gold Nine. I can divert a Behemoth for you. One hour, maybe two. It's leaving Lakar soon."

Adam took off his gloves and spat on his fingers to try to wipe the grit from his eyes. He always hated wearing goggles, but now he was going to make a point of finding a complete helmet. His eyeballs felt scoured; his mouth was caked with dust and grit.

It had now taken him half an hour to move less than a hundred meters down the road. Every time he tried to make a dash for the next available cover—a doorway, basement steps, a burned-out truck—a hail of fire drove him back. A mortar blew tiles off a nearby roof, raining shards on him. The Indie barrage had changed the landmarks of the area so much in the last couple of hours that he had to check his compass to make sure he was still heading the right way. He didn't recognize a single major building along the river now.

But he had to move. He couldn't cower here all day. He took a deep breath to steady himself and then ran for it, moving in short sprints from cover to cover. Eventually he reached the end of the street and crouched by the corner of a building to peer around it.

He could see the river that wound through the center of the city—promenades along the banks, elegant stone balustrades now smashed to rubble, polished brass flower troughs that had been ripped apart like paper. The waterfront walk was now a shooting gallery. Nothing could move along that route.

Adam couldn't see if all the road bridges across the river had been blown or not. The COG was relying on sporadic intercepts of the UIR comm net to work out where the Indies could and could not go. Three bridges seemed to be impassable, but the fourth, the one closest to him, was stubbornly refusing to collapse into the water. Two of the Sherriths' tanks had been pounding it for a couple of hours with little success, although the barrage was forcing the UIR advance to try elsewhere. Their infantry had been forced to trickle across a narrow pedestrian bridge five kilometers west.

But they kept coming. It was like trying to stop a leak, watching the water rising, and every time one crack was plugged another opened. Adam took a breath and slipped back into the shadow of a collapsed hotel awning.

How can it be this hard to move across one block?

He retuned his radio to call Helena. "Lieutenant, any luck?"

"No, sir. Looks like they've got a couple of guys up in the museum—I can't think of another building where they could put a forward observer. I swear there's sniper fire coming from there, too."

"No joy on the casevac, either."

"Why the hell do we spend so much budget on those things?"

Helena sounded as if she was choking back an expletive. "Case-vac's going to be impossible anyway until we take out some of the Indie positions on this side of the river. Can we get around to the back of the museum via the promenade?"

"No, the Indies are lined up along the south bank like they're waiting for the regatta to start. Ideas?"

She paused. Adam could hear the steady rattle of fire in the background and a lot of shouting about applying pressure. It was the combat medics trying to give Gears first-aid instructions while they were tied up on other casualties.

"I think we can get into the museum at third-story level," she said.

"How?"

"The gap between the exterior walls is four meters."

"And you think we can breach it without being seen."

"Ladder, smoke grenade, speed."

Adam thought of all the lectures he'd attended at the academy, all the strategy theories and lessons from history played out with wooden blocks on table-sized maps. In the end, battles came down to solutions held together with string and individuals snatching flimsy opportunities.

"Okay, I'm heading back. We've got one chance at this."

"Teale's dead, by the way, sir. Sorry."

That made twenty-two KIAs out of a company of ninety men and women. Adam had lost Gears before, but not in those numbers and not in a matter of days. He added Sergeant Teale to the list of personal letters he'd have to write as soon as this was over. Maybe he'd phone the families instead, if the lines weren't down. His father had always told him that he had to be man enough to do that, or he wasn't fit to be an officer.

"Okay. I'm working my way back now. Don't start without me."

As he moved down the street, he felt like the last human being left on Sera. He couldn't see another Gear out there. The explosions and gunfire were just disembodied sounds not related to the people who were making them.

Where are the civilians? Where are the people who live here? Where do they go?

They'd melted away before the COG moved in, or so it seemed. He wanted to believe that the Kashkuri forces had evacuated everybody, but you could never completely clear a capital like that. In the basements and hidden places, terrified families huddled and waited. He knew it.

But there was nothing he could do about it, so, just as his father had taught him—by advice and example—he simply shut it out of his mind and focused on the next task.

The building they'd taken over on the southwest corner of the square had turned out to be a dental surgery. Adam thought that was a wonderful stroke of luck at first, as good as finding a ready-made first-aid post, but apart from a cupboard stacked with local anesthetics, hypodermics, and dressings, it was short of most of the things they needed for emergencies. It was still better than treating badly injured Gears in filthy streets, though. He did a discreet head count as he went around from room to room at the back of the building, and it wasn't encouraging; there were more than twenty wounded. The medic had moved them into groups according to their severity, waiting for the helicopters. Anyone who wasn't T-1 or T-2 and could hold a rifle was back fighting.

Down to half a company. God . . .

He *had* to get them casevacked, if only to free up the Gears taking care of them.

Corporal Collins was in the upstairs office with a light machine gun resting on the windowsill. He'd pushed filing cabinets across the windows, leaving himself small gaps to fire through like crenellations.

"Rough out there, sir," he said. "There's as many of the bastards behind us as there are in front of us."

Adam edged to the window with his back to the wall and studied the reflection in the framed dental school diploma above the desk on the opposite side. The museum was on the northeast corner of the square, five floors and a lot of windows that gave whoever was in there a complete view of anything that moved below or out on the road.

"Top floor, roof?" he asked.

"I think so. I'm sure I caught muzzle flash. There's a sniper there if nothing else. But I'm betting the FO's up there too. Look at the skyline. The only high building that hasn't been creamed."

Adam imagined long, case-lined galleries in the museum, thousands of years' worth of artifacts and history. It was irrelevant. It would break his heart, but it was a case of saving objects or lives. He did what he had to and got on the radio.

"Gold Nine to Green FDC." For a moment, he couldn't believe the next words would ever escape his mouth. But they did. "Can you target the National Museum?"

The Sherriths' fire direction control could have been anywhere now. "FDC here, what do you need?"

"We think they've put their observer on the museum roof."

"Shit, half the Indie army must be inside Kashkur. Let me get a range on that and warn off aircraft. Wait one."

Every sword had another edge. Adam despaired of ever getting a Tern or a Raven to land. But the observer had to be put out of business.

"They're a liability," he said.

"Sorry, sir?"

"One for the mess over a beer when we get back, Collins." Adam was fascinated by the theory of warfare, but the reality depressed him, not because it was violent but because it was executed so badly. It didn't have to be this primitive, this wasteful of life and property. "I'm going to find Lieutenant Stroud. Keep your head down, Corporal."

"Always do, sir."

Helena had a plan by the time Adam caught up with her, one that involved an extending metal ladder. She was standing in what had been the waiting room of the surgery, bracing the lowest rung on her knees and seeing how far she could push it out single-handed. At the far end of the long room, Sergeant Fraisen was trying to guide the other end onto the edge of a table. Adam could guess what Helena was planning.

"Are you going to use *that* to bridge the gap between the buildings?"

She put the end of the ladder on a low table. "I am. Like this."

The ladder was stretched out like a gantry now, resting on two solid supports. Helena stood on it and walked across unsteadily like a tightrope walker in need of more rehearsal.

"You won't be able to do that ten or fifteen meters off the ground," Adam said.

"I used to do it on a log over water in basic training, sir. But I can crawl, too."

"Well, you won't be crawling anywhere yet. I've asked the Sherriths if they can hit the museum roof. I'm waiting on their response."

"And if that fails?"

"*Then* we can try your lunatic idea. Put a credible plan together and convince me."

Adam realized he'd fallen instantly into accepting that she was going to breach the building if push came to shove. That was Helena all over. She wanted things done, and she wanted them done *now*. And she never seemed to trust anyone to carry out her plans without her personal supervision.

Adam had a certain sympathy for her impatience. His own frustration was a lack of intel; there was no aerial recon worth a damn. Helicopters, even the expensive new Ravens, were vulnerable overflying infantry and armor. All Adam knew was what he could see with his own eyes, and what he was told over the radio by other commanders who had as limited a view as he did.

There had to be a smarter way to do this after sixty years. His grandfather would have recognized most of the doctrines, and probably even some of the technology.

Whoomp.

The building shook and plaster snowed from the ceiling. For a moment he thought it was an Indie special forces team breaching the building, but it was a mortar, and he felt ludicrous relief. *Just a mortar. Good God, man.* There were still piles of old-fashioned sandbags out on the street, five deep and twelve high, doing nothing much of use. When it got dark, he'd retrieve those and try to reinforce the surgery position as best he could.

He was only supposed to hold the Indies off until the big guns and even bigger guns came down from the north. It wasn't meant to drag on like this. He wasn't supposed to be surrounded. He ran his palm over his face, forehead to chin, and his hand came away with a thin streak of blood.

Nobody told me I was bleeding, either.

Helena crouched beside him. "Sir, we can move along the alley at the back of this block, come out in the northwest corner at the theater, and enter its basement via the scene dock doors. Then we go to the top floor and traverse the gap to the museum. That brings us out on the third floor. From there, we go up the stairs to the roof. How does that sound?"

"*If* we need to."

"Okay, *if* we need to."

Helena exuded confidence. She always did. It wasn't cocky bravado; she simply seemed to know that she was going to succeed, and the possibility of failing wasn't an issue for her. Where Adam would have looked at the downside, she seemed to see only the up.

Outside, the sporadic thump of shells sounded like a very slow racketball game in progress, the slight variation in pitch creating an impression of something being batted back and forth across the river. The automatic fire barely seemed to pause to draw breath. Adam went to check on the wounded.

"Vallory isn't looking too good, sir," said Kinnear, one of the medics. She was repacking the man's leg wound, a deep shredded hole just above the knee. "He needs blood. Look, I'm willing to call in an ATV and try driving him out of here."

"You won't get a hundred meters," Adam said. Kinnear would have to drive west along the river without the cover of buildings, in full view of the Indie tanks lined up on the other side. "Can you hang on until we've shut down the FO on that roof?"

"Can do, sir." She didn't sound convinced. Adam got the feeling he'd have another death to explain to a wife before the day was out. *I'm sorry we lost your husband, ma'am. We were just waging war the way our fathers did.* "Anyone found some morphine yet?"

We've just grown too used to this. Satellite recon and targeting, that's what we need. Fast fighters to deliver payloads accurately. Better still—satellite weapons platforms that can take out a single building without Gears needing to storm it like a damned castle.

Adam had the ideas. He knew he could make them work. He just had to survive long enough. He certainly had the incentive now.

His radio popped. "Green FDC to Gold Nine."

"Go ahead, FDC."

"One nasty surprise coming up for the museum," he said. "Duck and cover, just in case . . . all call signs, clear Gorlian Square, repeat, clear Gorlian Square."

The sniper had already made sure there was nobody near the museum, but Adam didn't have the disposition of all his Gears at any given time, only the squad or platoon leaders. He radioed them anyway.

Helena flattened herself by the window to watch. "I hope their insurance covers this, sir."

There was no replacement value for unique cultural treasures. Adam had joined the ranks of history's despoilers, the thoughtless vandals he once so despised, and the ease with which he'd done it appalled him.

"I've just given the order to wipe out three thousand years of culture," he said.

Helena huffed to herself. "I worry more about the orphans of Gears than a few old vases."

Adam took it as a deserved rebuke, said nothing, and crawled outside the front door behind the cover of a retaining wall to observe. He didn't even hear the first shell. But he saw it, all right; it landed on the elegant steps that ran the whole width of the museum frontage, bringing the lower half of them down like an avalanche.

"That's his ranging shot, I hope," Helena said.

The next shell took out a row of windows on the second floor.

"Well, I think our chum probably knows we've pinged him now," Adam said. "He'll move, at least."

"Maybe he won't, sir. And we won't know unless the Indies suddenly keep missing."

"What about the sniper?"

"We've got helicopters inbound. We'll find out the hard way."

The artillery shells carried on biting chunks out of the museum. Helena was right; it was just *stuff*, things, inanimate objects. And the steady chatter of Tern rotors was getting closer. He'd done what he had to do.

COG GARRISON ANVIL GATE, KASHKUR.

"If you were them," Captain Sander said, "what would *you* do?"

Hoffman braced his elbows on the sill of the observation post window and tried to steady the binoculars. The Indie column was visible only by the distant plume of dust it kicked up into the still air like a curl of smoke.

"Depends how they think it's going at Shavad. If they overrun Kashkur, they'll be more concerned with stopping us from sabotaging the refinery as we retreat."

"Didn't think the Unvanquished did that."

The 26th Royal Tyran Infantry had never retreated or surrendered; the motto on its cap badge—*Unvanquished*—had to be maintained. Hoffman left definitions of victory to the historians.

"We're not the only regiment in this fight," he said.

"I asked Choi if we could take out the refinery now. It's in range. He said no."

There were a couple of thousand workers at the refinery. It was almost as much of a city as Anvegad was. Hoffman found himself calculating the speed of the Indie advance against the time it would take for the staff to evacuate the refinery.

"The refinery's probably not going to put up a fight," he said.

"Would you, if you were sitting on millions of liters of fuel? Even if they've piped most of the stores out by now, it's still a bomb waiting to go off."

"Of course, they might even be *pleased* to see the Indies."

"So where's the damn aerial recon?" Sander got on the radio again. "Just one Tern. Is that too much to ask?"

"Yes," Hoffman said. "It probably is right now."

"Okay, we wait." Sander had a channel open to Battalion Command, keeping up as best he could with the situation in Shavad. "And we'll be doing this without air support."

Hoffman listened in for a while. Every helicopter in the region was being pulled in to support 26 RTI and the Sherriths, half of them on casevac. Given the shit the Royal Tyrans were in, Hoffman couldn't feel shortchanged. Frustration was starting to get to him. He'd never been used to sitting on his ass and listening to a battle he wasn't actually taking part in.

And those are my buddies out there. I'm going to have a lot of funerals to attend.

Kashkur was just one theater in a war that spanned most of Sera. If he listened to the international radio stations, Shavad wouldn't even be in the top-ten news stories today, so Anvegad — a choke point that no commander in his right mind would ever try to attack — was one of those stories that would never be told.

"Sir, I'm going to get back to the platoon." Hoffman adjusted his cap. "Shake out a patrol and find some better observation points."

"Mountain men," Sander said. "You really need mountain men. I'm going to request some Pesang support if this looks like it's going to drag on."

Hoffman made do with what he had and sent Byrne out with a squad to set up observation points five kilometers south, where the terrain was still rocky enough to enable men to move between cover. An hour later, the gunners and Byrne's patrol got on their radios almost simultaneously to say they'd spotted the first UIR vehicles.

"Definitely heading for the refinery, sir," Byrne said. "Six self-propelled guns, a dozen tanks, some APCs, and some big unarmored supply trucks. Oh, and a low-loader with tarps all over it.

Maybe that's carrying a track-laying vehicle. Bit thin on the ground for a serious attempt to break through the pass, actually."

"Not banking on the refinery fighting to the last man, then."

"If the rest of Vasgar rolled over, then why should they die in a ditch for a few cans of fuel? They're only civvies."

The wait-and-see was getting to Hoffman. But there was no point doing anything else. If the Indies showed signs of moving north of the refinery, then the vintage guns would see them off. Hoffman did his rounds again, checking on the machine gun and antiaircraft positions and noting how few civvies were on the streets.

It was hard to draw a line to mark where the garrison ended and the city began, other than the security checkpoint on the gates of the vehicle compound.

"Lieutenant." Sheraya Olencu stepped out from between the columns of the council building as he passed and walked along with him. "Is there anything else you need me to do?"

Hoffman thought of Sheraya only in terms of dealing with local procurement, handling the traders and drivers who kept the garrison fed and supplied. Then it struck him that she might well want to be around Byrne if the shooting started. She was pregnant. He had no idea how that was affecting her, but it made sense to him that she'd be anxious about separation at a time like this.

"Did Sergeant Byrne do as I ordered and get the alderman to marry you two?"

"Yes." Sheraya lowered her eyes. "He always follows orders."

"Thank God for that," Hoffman said. "Look, I'm going to risk the captain's wrath and say this—I'm giving you permission to stay within the garrison if you feel the need. Special circumstances."

She slowed her pace a little. "You're a considerate man, Lieutenant. Is it because you miss your own wife?"

Hoffman hadn't thought of himself as considerate or even sentimental, but he certainly missed Margaret. "When there's a war on, I don't believe anyone should put anything off longer than necessary."

"There's *always* been a war on. Even my grandfather can barely recall a time when Sera was at peace."

"Well, the war's right here, right now." Hoffman wished he hadn't put it that way. "Or as close as it'll get for Anvegad. Come on. You can sit in the mess until Sam's off duty."

Sander wouldn't mind. There'd been a time when Hoffman would have objected to having wives inside the garrison other than in designated married quarters, but he couldn't work up any outrage at the bending of regulations these days. He was starting to feel agitated about the road being blocked. It was the same feeling he got when he had to sit down with his back to a door. He wanted to turn around and face it.

He stopped Carlile on the way through the vehicle compound. "How are we doing on the bulldozer, Sapper?"

"It's not left Lakar yet. Shavad might need it for the next two days, apparently." Carlile looked irked. "Fucking typical if you don't mind my saying so, sir."

"Well, we've got two weeks before we need to resort to cannibalism," Hoffman said. "I need to get up to speed with what's happening there."

"That's your regiment, isn't it, sir? Two-Six RTI."

"Yes. It is."

"The engineers out there say the Indies put special forces behind the lines into Kashkur before they invaded Vasgar, judging by the amount of sabotage the lads are dealing with. Apparently they've got snipers all over Shavad."

"You hear more than I do."

"That's only because I've been stuck on the radio trying to get Lakar moving."

Hoffman climbed back to the gun floor and looked out over the plain again from the observation position. Sander stood on the opposite side of the chamber, field glasses pressed to his eyes.

"Frustrating," he said. "They're just in range. But I can wait."

"Cheer up, sir. They didn't get their hands on the imulsion supply."

"It's only a matter of time before the power stations start run-

ning out of fuel. That's going to put some pressure on them."
Sander lowered the glasses and glanced across at Hoffman. "No
word from Lakar?"

"They haven't dispatched the bulldozer yet. Carlile says it's
had to divert to Shavad. Like the Ravens."

"Damn. We're not a priority, are we?" Sander took out a small
pad and started sketching. "I'll have an entire mural done before
they pull their finger out and get around to us."

It was late afternoon, all long shadows and a blue haze on the
mountains, before the knot of UIR vehicles around the refinery
showed signs of movement. Hoffman watched, noted, and calculated.

Evan slapped the part of the gun barrel he could reach like he
was patting the neck of a racehorse.

"They say that an Indie guard post and a COG one faced each
other across a border for ten years and didn't so much as exchange
a shot," he said absently. "I forget where it was. I bet they did, too."

Sander had been leaning against the wall. He pushed himself
away and stretched his back. "Just going to put a call into Brigade
Command about the Behemoth," he said. "If we lose Shavad,
they'll need this route open one way or another."

He turned toward the steel door that led down the stairs. As he
got halfway across the gun floor, Hoffman heard a shout from the
ramparts.

"What the hell's that?" Sander said casually, looking out. "Oh,
shit—"

The gun floor was engulfed instantly in a blinding yellow light.
Hoffman heard the whoosh of a backdraft, two loud bangs like
a car crash, and the air around him exploded. Something hit
the back of his head; his mouth was filled with a searing pain,
he could taste blood, and he suddenly felt the cold stone floor
under his cheek. He couldn't hear a thing. He couldn't move.
He was sure he was flailing his arms, trying to get up, but he wasn't
moving at all. Then the sound rushed back in and all he could
hear was the garrison siren, panting screams, and a strange, gong-
like sound. Everything else was just muffled underwater noises.

But he could see. Now he was looking up into Evan's face, a mass of blood and pale gray dust. The gunner was leaning over him.

"Sir! Come on, get up! Fucking rocket—they're behind us! They're fucking well *behind* us!"

Someone pulled him upright. He felt like he was spinning on a fixed point, about to keel over again. He fell against Evan. As he looked around, trying to work out what the hell had happened, he saw the mess all around him—blast marks, blood, an armor backplate, black fabric. Someone had been hit.

"He's dead," Evan said. "Captain's dead, sir. Come on. *Out*."

Hoffman knew he was concussed because he kept wondering why nobody had fired the guns. Evan pushed him through the door and he nearly fell over Jarrold on the way down the stairs. He ended up sitting on the step, distantly aware of yelling and noise wafting in from the city.

"Hit my head," he said. *Sander's gone. Shit, he's gone. He's dead.* "What the hell was that?"

"Someone out on the rocks," Jarrold said. "This side of the city. Some bastard put an RPG through the observation window. Shit, sir, it's a miracle we got out alive."

Hoffman found his mouth was working even though he didn't feel it was connected to his brain. *Rocket attack in confined space. Yeah. Why am I still alive?*

"Are we still under attack?"

"Dunno, sir."

Hoffman tried to press the button on his headset, but missed. It took him two stabs with his finger to activate his radio.

"This is Lieutenant Hoffman," he said. "Byrne, Salton—get out there and find who fired that. Gunners—I need a crew to check the main guns, *now*. And somebody monitor the refinery, because I can't see straight."

It wasn't even his voice. It was drill, and ten years of taking incoming fire, and the instinct that said if he didn't get a grip of this then nobody else would. He knew he was hurt; he knew Sander was dead. He just needed the autopilot Hoffman to carry on while he tried to reconnect all the torn, loose, and terrified parts of himself.

Two things preoccupied him for the next few minutes, and neither was urgent, he knew.

One was that the glass of his watch was broken, and he couldn't see the second hand. The other was that he had no idea what he was going to say to Ranald Sander's pregnant widow.

CHAPTER 12

In order to preserve our existing stocks while we find a new source of imulsion, only vehicles, vessels, generators, and machinery capable of using alternative fuels will be operated until further notice. All nonessential travel and non-mains power use is now restricted to vehicles and devices rechargeable from the hydroelectric supply. This ban will be enforced under the terms of the Fortification Act. Please cooperate fully with requests from COG personnel.

(EMERGENCY ORDER FROM CHAIRMAN RICHARD PRESCOTT TO ALL

VECTES INHABITANTS)

NEW JACINTO, VECTES: THE MORNING AFTER THE
DESTRUCTION OF EMERALD SPAR: PRESENT DAY,
15 A.E.

Bernie found it hard to tell what hit people hardest when they heard the news about the imulsion platform.

The mood around New Jacinto felt like a communal bereavement. Even Mac trotted along beside her with his head lowered. She walked through the construction sites and new dirt roads that now stretched a few kilometers out into the farmland to the north, and tried to work out if this was the point at which the Old Jacinto population, the folks who'd stoically endured unending grub attacks and privation for fifteen years, would finally snap.

It wasn't about the fuel. They didn't give a shit about shortages of things they'd never had much of anyway. It was about hope being dashed again and again. There were only so many times you could take something away from people, hand it back, and then snatch it away again. It broke them. It made them shut down.

Whatever the Lambent were, they were worse than the grubs. And they were out there somewhere, in forms and shapes that people couldn't even begin to guess at.

I really thought it was over. I really thought the worst monsters we had to face from now on were going to be human.

"Hey, dog-lady!" The shout made her turn. It was the Gorasni sailor called Yanik who seemed to have struck up a rapport with Baird. Friendship was too strong a word. "The shit gets deeper, yes?"

"I'm really sorry about your mates on the rig," she said carefully. It wasn't the time to mention fuel shortages. "Poor bastards."

"So what use are we to you now? No fancy frigate, no imulsion, and your doctor thinks we are all murdering scum. The old Pelruan soldiers cross the road to avoid us. I think our wedding is over."

"Honeymoon," Bernie said automatically. "The phrase is *the honeymoon's over.*"

The conversation had turned very awkward very fast. Mac must have sensed her shift of mood, because he stood growling at the back of his throat in his let-me-kill-him pose—ears forward, lip curled back, eyes fixed on the threat. Bernie held her hand against her leg and snapped her fingers to distract him.

"You think it is?" Yanik asked. He didn't seem bothered by the growling at all, or maybe he had a lot of faith in her ability to control Mac. "Because Trescu is now in trouble, I think. And that is *not* good for anybody."

Nothing was clear-cut for Bernie these days. One thing she'd accepted as an inarguable fact since childhood was that the Indies were the eternal enemy. The Pendulum Wars had become so embedded in every state's culture that she'd been a Gear for a couple of years before she even started to ask herself why any South Islander—conquered and colonized nations, not willing volunteers—would see the COG as the natural good guys. But the UIR were a bunch of empire-building shits, too. Who could you trust? Well, she thought that she couldn't trust the Stranded, either, but then Dizzy Wallin showed up and took that certainty away from her as well.

At least I know the dog isn't cooking up a scheme. That's something.

"I don't know what Prescott thinks," she said. "But we're all in the same shit together. And we're probably better off having you here than not having you, imulsion or no imulsion."

Yanik clapped her on the shoulder and nodded at the two rifles—one Lancer, one Longshot—slung over her shoulder. Mac rumbled a warning again. "Good. I know I get no bullshit from you. You know how to deal with *garayaz*."

He gave her a finger-to-brow salute and walked on through the construction site toward the naval base gates. Mac watched him for a few moments as if he was debating whether to go and sink his fangs in his face after all, just to teach him not to touch his pack leader.

"Come on, Mac," Bernie said. "Just because we've got monsters, it doesn't mean the Stranded have taken the day off. *Seek!*"

Bernie wondered if Yanik thought she was a reliable guide to COG attitudes because of Hoffman, that she knew more of what was going on than the rest of the Gears. They didn't miss a damned thing, these people. But that was what came of living in a big village. Everybody knew your business sooner or later. A close community had its downside.

At least she had the time and the reason now to take Mac out tracking on foot. As Baird put it, "asshole hunting" was best done quietly and without a vehicle anyway. As soon as they reached the exclusion zone roadblock, Mac bounded ahead. The Gear on the checkpoint paused to chat to her.

"What the hell else is out there?" he said. "How long do you think we've got before that stalk thing gets here?"

"No idea," she said, realizing that she felt increasingly pissed off at being out of the loop. "No bastard tells me anything."

Mac led her through the woods for a couple of hours, and if there hadn't been that growing list of crises jostling for attention at the back of her mind, she would have been as near to contented as she'd been for a long time. It was even quieter than usual. Most of the Ravens were grounded today—at least Baird kept her informed, even if nobody else bothered—and she couldn't even hear the occasional grinding sounds of Packhorses in the distance.

Well, Pelruan's okay. They learned to live without imulsion years ago.

And I suppose it means that the navy's buggered. Can't run a warship on vegetable oil.

Mac came cantering back to her with his follow-me face on, tail thrashing. She put her finger to her lips.

"Sssh. Good boy. Show me."

And Mac did exactly that. He trotted off, head down, and led her through undergrowth to a tree-covered, barely visible path crushed by recent and repeated foot traffic. The battered vegetation and the various stages of wilting told her that the route had been used over the course of a few days.

Still worth staking out, then.

Bernie rubbed Mac's head and gave him a snack of dried rabbit meat as a reward before finding a ledge further up a nearby bank to give her a better view of anyone moving along the path. Making a sniper hide was easy out here. She just eased herself into the bushes, made the ground comfortable with her jacket, and settled down prone with the Longshot propped on its bipod.

She could wait for days if she had to, but she didn't expect it to take that long to get some trade. It was only a hundred meters to the path; a Longshot was overkill for that range. This wasn't going to be the old Pendulum War days when she'd lay up for a week in a scrape to finally drop a target a thousand meters away. Mac flopped down beside her and rested his chin on his paws, occasionally looking up at her as if he was waiting for a sitrep.

It's going to be hard to hand that dog back to Will. It really is.

Mac just happened to be the one dog out of all Will Berenz's animals who took a shine to her. He accepted her as his new pack leader and he did whatever she asked, sometimes working out what she wanted even when she forgot his special commands. She found herself rehearsing how she would ask Berenz what she would have to barter to keep him.

It was a few hours before she got the first indication that someone was coming. Mac, head still on his paws, pricked up his ears. She put her hand on his back to keep him down. Eventually she heard what the dog must have reacted to; the slow swishing sound of someone picking their way carefully through grass and bushes. It took a few moments of scoping up and down the path before she saw her target flash across her optics. At that moment, another Bernie took over.

She'd developed her own concentration technique during sniper training. She imagined what her target would go on to do next if she didn't take him—or her—out with one shot. It always worked.

When she settled on the movement, it turned out to be a man of about forty with a rifle across his back, carrying a box with rope handles. He kept shifting it—holding it in both arms one moment, pausing to switch to the handles the next—and that told her it was heavy, possibly ammo. He couldn't move fast and had to wade through the vegetation.

Swish . . . swish . . . swish . . .

Okay . . . is he alone?

If she'd interrupted a supply column, she couldn't shoot and run from this position, so if there were others coming she'd have to leave it and just trail them at a safe distance to locate their camp. This wasn't a great place to start a firefight.

I ought to let him pass and track them anyway.

The man's head was in her crosswires now. She had to make the call. This was a decision she'd made maybe hundreds of times in her service career, but it was still something of a gamble every time. And she very rarely thought about her target in human terms, but today—she did.

Okay. End it now. He'll never know he's dead. Not hours of bleeding out. Not running for his life. Just gone, just like that.

Bernie exhaled, held that breath, and squeezed the trigger. *Crack.* She saw the spray of blood as the man dropped instantly. Relief flooded her gut. Mac flinched at the sudden noise but stayed put.

"Good boy," she whispered. "You're the best spotter I ever had."

She got to a kneeling position and waited a few moments to be sure there was nobody right behind the guy. Then Mac jumped up and stood staring down the slope to the left, hyperalert. He was a great spotter, all right; there *was* someone else out there. And they couldn't have failed to hear that shot.

Shit. Bang out, engage, or lie low?

Bernie reloaded the Longshot just in case, then took up the Lancer. Two younger men were moving at a crouch along the path, pausing to check around them every few meters. One had a handgun and the other a hunting rifle. They moved right up to within a few meters of the other man's body, and Bernie braced for the reaction when they finally fell over him. They'd freeze. They'd look. And that was the window she had to drop both of them.

Now they were almost in front of her. They still hadn't spotted her. They still hadn't found the body, either, but there was no way they could miss it if they carried on. She exhaled slowly.

Wait. Wait.

But something subconscious took the decision, not the sniper part of her brain at all. *Them or me. Simple.* Bernie opened up with the Lancer from the cover of the bushes and put five or six short bursts through the two men at chest level. Then she hunched down as flat on her knees as she could, waiting again, listening to crows squawking high in the canopy, wondering if a small army was now heading her way.

But nothing came. Eventually she got up, legs shaking, searched the bodies—definitely dead, no awkward coup de grâce needed—and took their weapons.

The box was full of ammo, but it was too heavy to carry with all the extra firearms. She dragged it into a well-hidden spot she could find again for recovery later. Every round that she could scavenge counted.

That's drill for you. That's years on the clock. I evaluate the risks, take what's useful, cache the ammo. But I never used to think about the who and the why of dead men.

"Home, Mac." She could hear her own voice shaking and made an effort to steady it before she pressed her earpiece. "Mataki to Control—enemy contact in grid. Charlie Seven, three hostiles, all dead. I'm on my way back in."

Mathieson responded. "Roger that, Mataki. You just doing a little opportunistic hunting?"

"You could say that."

"Byrne says she can swing by with the bike and RV with you."

What am I, the charity case now? "I've got the dog with me."

"Can he ride a bike?"

Mac looked up at her with sad brown eyes: *Don't do that to me, Ma.* "It's okay, Control, I'm making my way to the main road. I'll be a couple of hours at least."

"Leave your channel open in case we need to locate you. Everyone's *jumpy* at the moment. Don't want any friendly fire on my watch."

Bernie didn't think any Gear had reached that level of *jumpy* on Vectes. "Got it, Control. Tell everyone not to open fire on the harmless old bag lady and her mongrel. Mataki out."

Bernie picked her way through the woods, putting her trust in Mac's ears and nose. Yes, you really *could* trust a dog. Mac would go all out to defend his pack—her—and it probably never crossed his mind that a human might not put everything on the line for him. She decided to spoil him rotten when they got back to base. He could sleep on her bed and eat her dinner, and maybe Baird's, too. The dog deserved it.

And I shot those guys.

The two extra rifles weighed heavily on her. She longed for a hot bath and a longer sleep. At least there was plenty of water and electricity thanks to the river, even if the COG was now reduced to running vehicles on cooking oil.

What was the point of capping them?

I mean, beyond orders, why? They're a minor irritation compared to what's waiting out there. Did I do it for Rory Andresen? For me? What?

Mac stopped and waited for her to catch up, tongue lolling. He seemed relaxed. As long as he stayed like that, she was sure she wasn't about to run into any more Stranded. But she kept her Lancer powered up and a round chambered in her Longshot, just in case.

I don't know how many people I've killed in my time. I actually can't count them. And that's never bothered me until now.

Bernie gave up trying to work out why—not guilt, not pity, nothing obvious like that—and wondered if it was just some primal realization that she was helping the world run out of humans, even if they were the worst specimens of the species.

"Hey, look—*road*," she said. They'd come out of the woodland on a slope above the main route to Pelruan. Mac stared up into her face, all unquestioning devotion. "You're a great guide dog, too. Who's a clever boy? Yeah, *you* are. Come on. Dinner."

She could hear a Raven in the distance as she kept to the cover of the hedgerows. Her reaction was to look up from time to time just to see where the helicopter was heading, but as this one got closer, she could see it was covering a narrow search pattern. Her radio clicked.

"Hey, Mataki, where are you?" It was Gill Gettner. "I've got a rough fix on you from the transmitters, but for fuck's sake come out in the open so I can see you."

There's a surprise. "Roger that, Major."

Bernie wasn't expecting to be extracted. She broke cover cautiously and dropped to one knee while she waited, just in case some arsehole was out there waiting just as patiently as she had to claw back a little revenge. The Raven landed close enough to sandblast her face. Nat Barber beckoned from the crew bay.

"Is this a lift home?" Bernie ducked her head and ran to the chopper. Mac slunk behind, not used to those rotors and smells and terrible noises. "What a kind and well-brought-up young man you are."

"Shit, Bernie, look at all that firepower on your back. Someone piss you off?"

Bernie picked up a hesitant Mac and shoved him bodily onto the Raven. "Yeah, my estrogen flatlined. Come on, help me stow this stuff. I had to cache the ammo."

"Did you get their gold fillings as well?"

"Bugger. Knew I forgot something." She fastened her restraints, clipped Mac's collar to a safety line, and sat him between her knees. "So what brings you out this way at a time of fuel crises?" A thought crossed her mind, and she wasn't amused. "Hoffman?"

"No. Fenix requested we haul your ass back to base after we dropped off supplies for Anya." Barber always was an open and honest soul. "He says to save your ammo for the glowies."

"*Shinies*," Gettner said. The Raven lifted and banked steeply, making Mac scrabble for a grip on the deck. "I prefer *shinies*. And don't let that dog pee in my bird."

Gettner and Barber were usually a double act of vitriolic commentary, but they were definitely forcing the banter today. Bernie wondered how bad it had been out on that rig.

"Too late," Bernie said.

"The piss?"

"Too late to save the ammo."

It was probably too late for a whole lot of things now, but all Bernie could focus on was the next twenty-six hours. Anything after that was a renewable daily bonus.

ADMIRALTY HOUSE, VECTES NAVAL BASE.

Hoffman had already seen how Prescott conducted himself at the end of the world—twice.

The man had held his nerve through the Hammer of Dawn

strike, and he hadn't batted an eyelid when Jacinto was sunk. Hoffman wondered what it was going to take to make the sweat bead on that aristocratic top lip.

He couldn't decide if Prescott didn't know enough to be scared, if he knew something nobody else did, or if he was just missing a pair of adrenal glands. Whatever it was, he sat at the long meeting table in the sail loft as if it was another emergency management meeting of the kind they used to hold weekly in Jacinto to measure just how deep the shit was getting.

Trescu, not one of life's nervous types, looked a lot closer to the edge than Prescott ever had. Despite himself, Hoffman found something to admire in the guy's willingness to roll up his sleeves and do the tough jobs. One moment, he'd blown a prisoner's brains out; the next, he'd turned around and calmly faced an all-too-possible death to save the team on that rig. The only thing that seemed to scare him was losing his people. Gorasnaya, a proud nation for a thousand years, was now a dwindling village. Hoffman realized that was worse than galling for the Gorasni; it was a collective death, an extinction, a reflection of what now faced all of humanity.

I know how it feels, Trescu. You wake up sweating because you might screw up and the human race goes extinct on your watch. Now place your bets on the odds of Prescott putting his ass on the line for us.

"Losing the supply is a major blow," Prescott said. "I admit that. But it's something we can deal with in time. What will it take to restore the wells?"

Trescu's face was covered in small marks as if he'd taken a shrapnel blast. He nursed a badly burned hand under the table and probably thought Hoffman hadn't noticed.

"Would that be before we stop the Lambent, or *after?*" he asked quietly.

"For argument's sake."

"I have no idea how damaged the wellheads are. We would need divers with special equipment for that, or a remotely controlled deep-sea bot. And once we evaluated the damage, we would need to use the most advanced engineering techniques to rebuild the entire platform." Trescu leaned forward and folded his arms on the desk, slipping his injured hand out of sight. His voice suddenly hardened. "And in case it has escaped your attention, Chairman, none of those things exist on Sera any longer. So my technical assessment is that we are completely and utterly *fucked.*"

Hoffman reached a decision at that moment. It was something he never believed he was even capable of thinking.

I can't just be a good loyal soldier and obey the Chairman. I can't do this any longer. We have to have a plan for when the wheels come off this damn thing completely.

And they would. As the remnants of the world lurched from crisis to crisis, it always felt like this had to be the rock bottom. But it never was. There was always some new depth to plumb.

Trescu knew it, too.

He turned his head very casually and met Hoffman's eyes for less than a blink, and leaned back in his seat again.

"Well, I understand that," Prescott said. "Your tanker crew did well to get that last consignment off the rig. That buys us some breathing space. The question now is how much of our resources we devote to reconnaissance off the island. We could wait and see what comes our way. We could also expend a lot of irreplaceable fuel gathering intelligence. But my biggest concern is that we have no idea how many forms these Lambent have evolved into, or how to kill them effectively."

The bastard was always good at restating the obvious. Hoffman decided to embroider reality a little. It was better than asking permission from a man who really didn't seem to be on the same page as everyone else.

But he's not stupid. What's he up to?

"I've got Ravens out doing an aerial recon on the course the stalks were taking," Hoffman lied. Well, he'd have them airborne again inside the hour. "Whatever we learn from that tells us how long we might have. But we've got to assume that they'll reach us sooner or later. We have to be ready."

"Give me a plan."

"I don't know what we can do to stop the stalks, but we know we can kill polyps," Hoffman said. "I'm thinking in the same terms as I would for human infantry—obstacles to slow them down and concentrate them in a kill zone while we pick them off. The problem remains—how many of them can a stalk disgorge? And is this aquatic, or is it a land-based organism? We need to work out what kills most for least effort."

Trescu sat in silence, just staring at the charts on the wall for a while.

"Commander?" Prescott said.

"Stranded," Trescu said.

"What about them?"

"Make them do something useful. They have enclaves on the mainland. We know these vermin stay in touch with one another, so who better to tell us about any stalk incursions there?"

"And they're going to cooperate fully after the recent unpleasantness with your people, are they?"

Trescu raised an eyebrow. "Even *garayazi* recognize that what kills us will also kill them. And to defend this island, we will need them to work with us, not against us."

Trescu rarely suggested anything that he hadn't already thought through to its logical conclusion. Hoffman had seen enough to know that. But he'd given up wondering if the guy had an agenda beyond keeping his people alive, because even that was starting to look massively ambitious now.

"Just spit it out," Hoffman said. "Are you saying we should recruit them for however long it takes, or just ask them nicely not to bother us while we're fighting something worse than them?"

"I don't know." Trescu shrugged. "I think I mean that we should talk to whoever runs the biggest gang now and explain what's going to overrun us *and* them if we fail to pool our resources."

Prescott did his unimpressed gesture, that slight backward tilt of the head so he could look down his nose at someone without needing to stand up to do it. Hoffman struggled daily to find something human to like in the man.

"They'd use this as an opportunity to undermine us," Prescott said. "They see themselves as the alternative future for Sera. If we go cap in hand to them and say we need help to deal with the Lambent, they won't be able to focus on the size of the threat. Only what leverage they can gain from it."

Takes one to know one. Hoffman had reached the stage where Prescott's objection to anything became a powerful incentive to do it. He made a mental note to be careful of that, because that asshole could spot any pressable button in others. He'd use it.

"If it only succeeds in making them crap their pants and leave the island, that'd be a plus," Hoffman said.

Prescott didn't forbid him to make contact with the gangs. In fact, he didn't say anything. Hoffman hated it when he couldn't get a definite answer out of him. He waited for one anyway, but it was Trescu who broke the silence.

"Either way, Chairman, we have to fortify the island." Trescu pushed his chair back with a definite gesture of this-meeting-is-over. "I would like to discuss operational detail with Colonel Hoffman later. Now I have to explain myself to Gorasnaya. Many of my people thought I was insane to bring us here and surrender our fleet and our fuel. I must persuade them that schisms and power struggles now will be the end of us."

Prescott understood that, if nothing else. Hoffman could see the change in the set of his jaw. It would have been fascinating to carry on watching these two maneuver and double-bluff each other, if only there hadn't been an unknown quantity of goddamn Lambent waiting out there to kill every last human on Sera.

"I'll walk with you, Commander," Hoffman said. "Just don't expect me to take a bullet for you."

Trescu held the door open for him. "Colonel, I would never presume such a thing."

Outside, Royston Sharle, the emergency management chief, was waiting to see Prescott with Aleksander Reid. Hoffman exchanged nods with them as he passed. Reid shuffled his papers and managed a smile at his superior.

"Three more Stranded," Reid said. "I have to say that Mataki's a game old bird. You Royal Tyrans really are hard as nails."

"What?"

"She slotted three Stranded transporting ammo. Gettner's just brought her back."

Damn. Bernie certainly picked her moments. It was the worst possible time to piss off the gangs. As soon as the dismay crossed Hoffman's mind, he despised himself—how could he even *think* that? Andresen and the others not even cold in their graves, and here he was, worrying about offending these motherfuckers? He was inhaling too much around politicians. *Screw that.*

"Gettner can head back out and get me some aerial recon," Hoffman said. "And I want your projections of fuel use on my desk by twenty-three hundred."

"Very good, sir." Reid nodded. That was the smart response. "Of course."

Hoffman and Trescu headed down the stairs in total silence and were halfway across the parade ground before either of them said anything. Hoffman was still working out how to broach the subject of making sure things got done the army way.

Trescu slowed down to a leisurely pace.

"So . . . you don't like Major Reid. You don't like Prescott. You don't like *me.* I don't like Prescott, and I certainly don't like you. But I *trust* you, Hoffman, and I do *not* trust him. Better a bastard I can trust than sociable company who would put a knife between my ribs."

"I'll remember to get that put on my gravestone." *Shit, I've got more common ground with an Indie psychopath than my own head of state. Fine. That's what it's going to take.* "I'm up for telling the gangs what's coming and striking a deal until we get rid of the Lambent."

"It took fifteen years to deal with the Locust, so this might be a very long-term plan," Trescu said. "But let us live in hope that we can get on with killing each other again soon."

"There's regular anti-Stranded sentiment, and then there's the extra-strength version. What's your problem, Commander?"

"If we ever return to the mainland," Trescu said, "I shall personally show you the mass graves at a Gorasnayan town called Meschov. Or Chalitz. Or a dozen other places where we buried our women and children."

It was one of those answers that cut any further questions off at the knees. But at least it was an indication that Stranded could organize themselves well enough to fight a tough enemy. It was just their bad luck that they'd picked on the Gorasni.

"Okay," Hoffman said, making a mental note to look up *Meschov* as soon as he got a chance. "When the recon information comes back, we put a plan together. In the meantime, we make contact with the gang chiefs, and then Prescott can disown us if the civvies object to the plan."

"Mine won't. There are murmurs, but they'll follow me in the end. And remember we still have two Stranded prisoners."

"That's not going to bring the gangs to the table. Not now."

"I wasn't thinking of hostage tactics. Not this time."

Trescu nodded politely and walked off in the direction of the camp that was still effectively a separate state, whatever Prescott thought. Hoffman went to CIC and sat gazing at the sector chart on the wall, trying to imagine how the hell he could fortify an island against something that could punch its way through ships' hulls and seabeds.

He moved over to sit at the comms desk and picked up the mike. He really needed to know how far this stalk had traveled.

"Hoffman to KR-Eight-Zero. Where are you, Gettner?"

The response was instant. "Threatening a technician in the machine shop, sir. I need a fuel-line part, and I need it now."

"Well, when you've beaten it out of him, take a bot and get back on recon. Find that stalk and send me back some images."

"A *bot* would be Jack, then. He's the only one still running." Gettner broke off for a moment to savage the technician. "Colonel, we've still got the extended range fuel tanks. Want us to take a look at some other dry land and see if this thing has come ashore anywhere else?"

Nobody had been back to the Tyran coast since the evacuation of Jacinto, or even overflown other islands. It hadn't been worth the fuel when all resources were needed to build a new home on Vectes.

But Hoffman needed to know if the stalks could spread ashore, and how. So far, they'd only emerged at sea. It would also provide a handy lie-detector test when he came to talk to the Stranded gangs.

"Do it, Major," he said. "And no dumbass risks. Take Delta with you."

KING RAVEN R-80, NORTHWEST OF VECTES: DELTA SQUAD ON RECON.

"Do they know?" Baird asked. "The pirate demographic, I mean. Do they understand what skewered their boat?"

Marcus leaned on the starboard door gun as the Raven combed the featureless carpet of choppy white waves beneath the Raven. "Depends how much they get to hear from their buddies inside the wire. Because they weren't taking any advice from me."

Baird thought that was one more reason why Prescott should never have given the assholes an amnesty. Even if they'd been searched for weapons and radios going in, it was impossible to maintain that level of security. Gears on watch got tired and bored. Components got smuggled in one at a time. People sneaked out. It just wasn't possible to lock down New Jacinto.

When we were surrounded by grubs back home, nobody wanted *to sneak out.*

"So even if they know it's not us sinking their boats, what difference does it make?" Dom asked. "It's not like they're an armored division whose ass we need to kiss to help us out."

Cole was scribbling on a scrap of paper spread on his knee, occasionally pausing to tap the end of a stubby pencil against his chest plate while he pondered something. He was still writing letters home to a dead mom. Baird wondered what it felt like to have that kind of bond with your folks. It had to hurt. He was glad he'd got all that dependency shit out his system when he was a kid.

"Beats having them in our hair when we're busy with glowies," Cole said.

"Shinies," Gettner said. "Hey, come on, Delta. Concentrate on the search. Nat, are these bearings right?"

"'Fraid so." Barber was on the other door gun. "That's where it was."

There wasn't a trace of the imulsion rig visible, not even much of an imulsion slick. Baird felt a glimmer of hope that the wells had somehow been capped, although he was sure the Gorasni guys had said they'd only stopped pumping, because that gave him hope. In time, he could rig a bot to dive and investigate. Much later, he might even be able to work out how to rebuild the rig.

Come on, who the hell am I kidding? Where am I going to find that kind of heavy engineering now? It's not going to happen in my lifetime.

The realization depressed him more than he expected. He tried to work out if it was any intelligent man's reaction to the loss of the COG's only source of imulsion, or some sort of sentimental attachment to a clever piece of engineering, or just . . . shit, he didn't know *what* it was, or why it had hit him now so many years after civilization had gone down the lavatory. He pulled his goggles over his eyes and busied himself staring at a zillion square kilometers of nothing.

Dom nudged him. "You okay, Baird?"

Shit. So I tell a guy who had to put his wife down like a dog that I'm upset about a piece of metal. Yeah, that's going to help squad relations a lot.

"Just wondering where the next barrel of imulsion's coming from," Baird said, feeling the strain of unfamiliar tact.

"The mainland."

"Well, first there's getting there, then there's dodging glowies, and then there's the Stranded that'll probably be all over the first rig we find, and then there's extracting it and shipping it back. But yeah, apart from that, it'll be a breeze."

Dom opened his mouth slightly as if he was shaping up to say something, then folded his arms and carried on looking out the door.

Cole folded his letter carefully and slid it into his belt. "Damon, baby, you want a colorin' book? I know you get antsy on long rides."

"Hey, you kids in the back," Gettner said. "Any of you bothering to check the chart as we go? I can't do every damn thing."

"You lost, Major?" Baird asked.

"Let's put it this way," she said. "I'm continuing on the bearing the stalks took—"

"Yeah, I'm sure they always travel in a straight line . . ."

"—and I don't think there should be any landmass up ahead. Not that those two clauses are related in any way."

Gettner was looking dead ahead. Everyone in the crew bay was looking at roughly a 120-degree arc on either side. Marcus hung on to the grab rail and leaned out of the gun door to get a better view.

"Looks like an island to me," he said. "Because the chances of it being a bulk container are about zero."

"Glad I'm not hallucinating. Because that's definitely not on the charts, and I'm not off course. We've still got enough Hammer satellites working to get an accurate fix."

Dom folded the chart into a manageable size to study it. Baird, impatient, leaned over him.

"Let me take a look." There was always a simple answer to this kind of thing. "See? This is the edge of a tectonic plate. That's how new volcanic islands get formed—the plates move and magma squirts up to the surface. All these island chains, right down to the South Islands, were formed the same way. Happens all the time."

"How come I haven't seen one before?" Gettner said.

"Okay, maybe not every day. But it's not a mystery. Eruptions happen."

"How long do those things emit smoke once they break the surface?" Marcus asked, checking out the horizon with his binoculars.

"No idea. Can you see smoke, then?"

"No."

"I'm going to take a look anyway," Gettner said. "Crazy not to."

There was still no sign of stalks or polyps. Baird gave the chart back to Dom and got up to lean out of the bay door, trying to work out how the things decided where to go if they weren't attracted by imulsion pollution. If they were, then they should have been partying on the site of the sunken platform. The idea that these glorified vegetables might be following some kind of plan creeped him out more than the grubs ever had.

"So what makes glowies glow?" he said. "We definitely saw glowy Locust in the tunnels. And all that luminous snot moving around. But the stalks and the polyps don't look like anything I've seen before."

"Least we know why the Locust Queen was getting her panties in a bunch about 'em," Cole said.

"I hate it when I think of all the things I could have asked her."

Cole tapped his pencil on his armor again and went back to the paper. "It's not like she was holding a news conference or anything. We were trying to avoid losing vital organs at the time."

"You think we could have done a deal with them? You know— ganged up with them on the glowies, and lived happily ever after?"

Dom looked up, and Baird knew he'd somehow said the wrong thing.

"You think you could stop talking shit for five minutes?" Dom asked him quietly. "Just for once?"

Baird couldn't see Marcus from this side of the Raven, but he could hear him. It was just a gravelly sigh. Baird took the hint.

"Yeah, definitely an island," Gettner said. "Nat, prep Jack for me. Postcard time in about ten minutes. Get me some good recon images."

"Can we name it?" Cole asked.

There was a sudden silence. Cole wasn't joking. Baird felt the atmosphere shift ever so slightly in the Raven, from that mock-aggressive familiarity of guys who'd spent way too long cooped up together, to a kind of . . . *awkwardness.* He was going to fill the silence with something smart-ass, as he always did out of habit, but then he realized what had shut them up. What did you call a new island, a new species—a new *anything?*

You named it after someone.

And everyone had lost someone they probably wanted to commemorate—except him, of course, and he was glad to be spared all that shit. Dom's wife, Marcus's dad, Cole's entire family but probably his mom—yeah, the whole squad was thinking it would have been nice to permanently honor the dead. Gettner and Barber probably had the same thought, too, although Baird didn't know who each of them pined for.

"Let's see if it's a pile of shit and trouble first," Baird said, trying to be helpful. "Might not want to name it at all."

See, I can do tact. I can do diplomacy.

"Can't see any forest," Barber said. "Jagged outline. A lot of haze."

"Rock." Marcus moved off the gun and stood in the crew bay watching the island through binoculars. "Baird's right. Gray rock."

"Hey, look at the gray crap on the water, too. Pumice. Yeah, recent volcanic eruption."

Marcus made another noise in his throat, not his multipurpose grunt but an involuntary reaction as if he'd been caught out by something.

"Ahh *shit,*" he said at last. "You see that, Barber?"

Barber adjusted the lens on the camera. "Fuck. Yes."

"Come on, share," Baird said.

They didn't have to. In less than a minute, the Raven was close enough to the uncharted island for Baird to see exactly what Marcus meant.

It was a lifeless mass of charcoal-gray rock about eight or nine kilometers wide, its surface rough and jagged. At first Baird thought two twisted shapes that rose above the general mound were just lava outflows that had cooled in freak formations, maybe because pumice had already been washed away from around them. But then the picture fell into place, and he knew he'd seen those organic-looking gnarled shafts before.

"Frigging *stalks*," he said. "Wow, they don't hang about."

"Another reason to avoid sitting directly over the island," Gettner said. "Although if those things are on the march, we know they can reach up from the sea anyway."

"Of course," Baird said, knowing this wasn't going to cheer up anybody, "maybe they're showing up everywhere."

"Any polyps?"

"Can't see anything. Just stalks."

Barber released Jack from its housing. The egg-shaped bot hovered at the open door, mechanical arms unfolded. This was definitely a recon job for a remote.

"Can I add to the general misery?" Barber asked. "Does it look to anyone else like those stalks have come up *through* the lava, not *over* it?"

"Yeah," Marcus said. "It does." He turned to the bot. "Go on, Jack. Take a look. Be careful."

The bot moved out of the Raven's bay and headed for the island. Gettner could see the images that Jack was relaying to her monitor, but everyone else had to sweat it out.

"Just stalks," she said. "Not doing anything, either. No movement, no polyps, nothing. Oh, wait—no, that's a seabird." She took the Raven high above the island, banking slightly. "No obvious vent or smoke, but hey, these outflows can just erupt right under you without warning and it's endex."

"I'd be more worried about the killer coral from hell," Baird said. "If you get a spike of that straight through the fuselage, we won't be going home anytime soon."

"I'm just seeing dormant stalks," Gettner said. "Hey, Marcus, Nat, want to check? Look. They're just sitting there."

"Yeah, but does that mean they're *dormant*?" Baird asked.

"They're not spewing shinies, and that's dormant enough for me, Corporal. What am I, emeritus professor of fucking botany or something?"

Baird flinched inside. What *was* it with all these damn women

Gears? They were spitting venom the whole time. Even Bernie could strip paint with her stream of abuse when you somehow got on the wrong side of her. The only woman who didn't rip you a new one for no damn reason was Anya.

"Just saying," Baird said, determined at least to have the last word and not slink away. "We don't know what their life cycle is. We don't even know if they always go around holding hands with the polyps. Maybe the polyps just use the stalks for transport when they get a chance."

"Does it matter?" Dom asked. "They're all Lambent."

"It matters if we want to find the best way to kill them."

"I'm going to update Control," Barber said. "Wait one."

Gettner took the Raven down a little lower to fly along the coastline, and for a moment—a dumbass moment—Baird almost asked her to winch him down to the surface. Nobody had ever set foot on that ground before. It was as new as land ever got. Then he thought better of it. On the north side, steam or white smoke was still venting from a hole on the shoreline. There were no more stalks. Maybe they'd found the place too dauntingly barren as well.

"Keep an eye on the fuel," Gettner said. "One more trip around the harbor, then we move on."

Barber cut in. "Hey, Gill, listen around channel fifty. It's breaking up, but I think we've picked up interference from the Stranded long-range net."

Marcus perked up. "Can we get a fix on their transmitter? Been quiet for a long time."

"Let's swing by and pick up Jack. Then we can try getting a bearing."

"It beats going back empty-handed," Gettner said. "Fuel permitting, I think we should check out the mainland on the next sortie. Concentrate on where this stuff is making landfall, or else we'll be chasing our own asses all over the ocean."

Baird settled down at the comms position in the tail of the Raven and eavesdropped while Barber searched for a clearer signal. Occasionally, he heard broken bursts of crackling conversation that sounded like the skippers of boats confirming their positions.

"So they're keeping mobile," Marcus said. "How we doing, Barber?"

Gettner turned the Raven a couple more times until Barber seemed satisfied he had a location.

"It's only a hundred kilometers or so off our course," he said. "Got to be worth the fuel. Twenty-, thirty-minute deviation, tops."

Baird had never thought of the Stranded gangs as much more than scavengers with a few fast patrol boats and—somehow—access to fuel, preying on the regular Stranded living in isolated outposts across the islands and coast of the mainland. They were parasites on the backs of other parasites. How many Stranded were out there?

Maybe there's more of them than there are of us. But they're scattered. You can't live that way. You've got to have numbers. You've got to organize.

"Imagine living at sea most of the time," Dom said, like he was talking to himself. He almost sounded wistful.

Cole still looked a bit green around the gills. "Baby, that's my worst nightmare. Or living in a Raven. The Cole Train's strictly land-based."

Baird lost interest in the sea beneath and went back to checking out the maps, trying to imagine where he'd go if he was a stalk and what might lead him there. He was still churning over the imulsion trail theory and wondering if it was just coincidence—it could have easily been discharged effluent that the things were following—when Marcus and Dom both drew in a long breath at the same time. Baird looked up, expecting more evidence of stalks.

Barber sighed. "Holy shit. *Holy shit.*"

They'd found the Stranded transmitter, all right. The only question was which vessel out of the fleet below it was located in.

The vessels below weren't warships, but that didn't matter. They were a mix of freighters, leisure craft, powerboats, small tankers, tugs, and even a car ferry. They were keeping station just like a proper fleet, and there were a hell of a lot of them.

"It's like the En-COG fleet review," Gettner said. "In the days when we had a real navy."

Baird started counting. There were at least a hundred.

"So guess what course they're on," Gettner said. "Go on. *Guess.*"

CHAPTER 13

Civilization is the silk coat on the back of the beast, easily torn away by the first cold wind.

(KASHKURI PROVERB)

ANVIL GATE GARRISON, KASHKUR: 32 YEARS EARLIER.

Anvegad's doctor specialized in fractures and liver flukes, two things he saw a lot of in this nonindustrial backwater. He would also treat injured goats if asked nicely.

Now he was trying to stop Gunner Arlen Pereira from bleeding to death. Hoffman watched the doctor shaking his head and probing inside Pereira's open abdominal wound, trying to instruct one of the battery medics where next to try clamping. They didn't seem to be able to work out where the blood was leaking from.

Hoffman sat astride a wooden chair, tolerating first aid from Private Reaves and trying to hold his radio headset to his ear so he could carry on talking to HQ.

"Lieutenant, we're not going to be able to get help to you for a while," said the female major on the radio. "We can't even get a casevac chopper to you while Shavad's going down the tubes."

"I don't need *help*, ma'am," Hoffman said. "This is for your situational awareness. We've got adequate supplies and ammo for the time being. We're not under sustained attack yet. For all I know, it might be a disgruntled local goat-shagger with a grudge against the garrison. But the attack came from the Kashkur side of the border, so this might be Indies inserted behind the lines weeks ago." Hoffman could take the shit as well as any Gear, but he felt angry now on behalf of others. "Captain Sander's dead and his pregnant wife needs to be told. Gunners Dufour, Tovey, and Pole are also dead. We've got eight men wounded, two seriously. *And the fucking road to the north is still completely blocked,* so we can't evacuate the goddamn civvies even if they wanted to leave. Are you clear about the situation *now,* ma'am? *Are* you?"

The major paused, but didn't bawl him out. "I am, Lieutenant. Do you still require a Pesanga squad for recon?"

"What?"

"Captain Sander put in a request for them."

Everyone knew the Pesangs' reputation. This was the kind of terrain they lived in. One Pesang could cover the ground of five Gears. And they were *feared.*

If there were any Indie assholes hiding out there, they'd find them.

"If you can get them here, ma'am, we can make use of them."

"We'll think of something. I'll expect a sitrep from you in ten hours, unless the situation deteriorates."

Hoffman went to stand up. Sheraya and Reaves pushed him back down.

"Nine," Sheraya said. "There are *nine* wounded. That includes you, Lieutenant."

"I've got to go out there." Hoffman felt he shouldn't have been sitting on his ass in the first-aid station. "I've got a job to do, ma'am. Let me do it."

"It can wait a little longer." Sheraya kept looking past him. Hoffman wasn't sure what state the back of his head was in, but Reaves was using a lot of surgical tape. "You hit your head that hard, then sometimes you collapse and die many hours later."

"Fine. As long as I get the time to secure this garrison."

At the makeshift operating table, Dr. Salka's expression was changing to quiet desperation. Reaves slapped Hoffman on the shoulder. "Just as well you shave your head, sir. Makes this sort of thing a lot quicker."

Hoffman stood bolt upright and regretted it as giddiness seized him. He could *not* give in to injury now. He had more than a platoon to run, more than a garrison, even more than a city full of civilians: he had to hold Anvegad. And he didn't know yet exactly what he might have to hold it against.

He put his headset on properly, with the strap around his forehead and the audio bud in his ear. "Salton, anything out there?"

"Negative, sir." Pad had gone searching the slopes around the fort with Byrne and a local man who knew a bit about climbing and had some equipment. "No sign of a vehicle on either side of the pass, either. We should set up an obs post to keep an eye out three-sixty degrees. The Indies over the border might be the least of our worries."

"Do it, Pad. And they're going to send us some Pesang troops." Hoffman steeled himself to check on the gun floor again. "Sergeant Evan, are you making progress up there? Do you need more assistance?"

Hoffman couldn't bring himself to spell it out in front of Sheraya. *Have you finished clearing the bodies? Do you want someone else to do it, so you don't have to see your buddies like that?* He felt he should have done it himself. He hadn't served with them for years, and they weren't his own. He had more distance. The memories that inevitably came back later wouldn't be as bad as they'd be for Evan.

"The guns are okay, sir. They don't dent easy." Evan's voice was a bit shaky, but other than that he seemed fully in control. "No movement at the refinery yet."

"Okay, we continue the lockdown of this city—we are at full defense alert. Ma'am—Mrs. Byrne—I'd like you to get the aldermen together so I can talk to them. There are measures we have to take. I'll send Private Wakelin with you. I want you to have an escort at all times."

Sheraya gave him an embarrassed half-smile. "This is my home, Lieutenant. If I'm not safe here, where will I be?"

"You're safe from your own people, ma'am, but so was Captain Sander until some bastard put an RPG past us when our guard was down."

She just nodded. In reality, there was little that Wakelin would be able to do for her if a mortar or a sniper round was aimed inside the walls, but Hoffman owed it to Byrne to at least show some willingness.

"Lieutenant?" Dr. Salka edged forward, wiping his hands. "I regret I failed to stop the hemorrhage. The young man is dead."

There were routines that Hoffman fell into, officer or not. There were burial details, pay corps and next of kin to inform, ceremonies to be observed, all the tidy bureaucratic closure after losing a Gear in combat. He wasn't sure where—or even if—the locals buried their dead. Maybe they cremated them. Pereira's family would want his body returned home eventually, just like Sander's widow and the others he didn't know much about.

"Reaves, get a mortuary set up and work out where we can dig temporary graves."

"Yes, sir."

It was still daylight. Hoffman was expecting things to get worse when night fell. But he was holding a heavily fortified city with a sensible civilian population that wouldn't present easy targets to anyone taking potshots. It was a matter of sitting tight—and blowing the shit out of anything that moved. There was no more wait-and-see.

Have I missed anything?

Can I do this? Can I really do it?

"Let's work on the basis that we're surrounded," Hoffman said. He took a breath and wondered if he should have warned the aldermen what he was going to do, but he'd have to explain himself later. They'd had the warning siren. They should have been expecting the firing to start. "All fire teams and battery gun crews—stand by."

Evan cut in on the radio. "Sir, we've got Indie tanks moving forward. There's only one place they can be heading. Or they might just be moving into range to shell us."

Hoffman was more worried about infiltration. But he couldn't just sit back and not show these assholes that the COG meant business.

"Start as we mean to go on, Sergeant," he said.

The height of Anvil Gate now came into its own. All Evan or any of the gunners had to do was lay the sights on whatever enemy target they could see below them. They didn't need a forward observer to adjust fire. The Indies could see that plainly, but they came on anyway.

Are they insane?

The border was seven kilometers away, and the first tank crossed it.

"Fire for effect!" Hoffman yelled.

At that moment, the order was all he could recall of fire discipline, the proper procedure for artillery. But he was an infantry grunt and the gunners didn't expect him to do anything other than give them objectives. This was their garrison; he was just there to stop shit happening to them—and he'd already failed to do that.

Should have sent out patrols earlier. Should never have let that bastard get in so close with an RPG. All my fault.

Hoffman knew the guns were about to fire. But nothing could have prepared him for the moment when they did. It felt like an earthquake had hit the fort. And the noise actually *hurt*. It resonated in his chest.

"Shot, *out!*" Evan yelled.

There was a long moment of silence, and then a sound like thunder in the distance.

"*Splash,*" Jarrold responded. "One tank, two APCs destroyed, other targets dispersing."

Hoffman strained to see what they'd hit. There was a distant column of smoke rising, and when it cleared the Indies had spread out into a long ragged line. He had to watch a few moments longer to realize they'd actually come to a halt.

"That's overkill, sir," Evan said. "But they got the message."

The guns were relics almost exactly like the ones on the old COG battleships, a piece of history in their own right. Maybe nobody these days knew what to make of them.

The tanks and other armored units were about 6,000 meters away now. Hoffman saw a flash and a belch of white smoke, and seconds later an explosion shook chunks out of the cliff slope right beneath the observation point. The blast plates on the windows rattled furiously.

Then Anvil Gate's 155 mm guns opened up. The battle had begun. Hoffman had been under fire more times than he could remember, but this was different; this was standing still and taking it, with no chance of moving position or gaining better ground.

But you're on a goddamn peak. Highest ground. Defended by rock. Impregnable.

High or not, the only line of sight he had was from the guns and the other firing positions that were fanned out around 300 degrees of the fortifications. The enemy couldn't see within the city walls without aerial recon, but the defenders couldn't see out, either. More shells thudded into the fortifications, shaving off rocks and making a lot of noise and smoke, but Anvegad stood and shrugged it all off. And it responded in kind, pounding the UIR column with its One-Fifties until a curtain of smoke hung across the plain.

Hoffman checked the terrain from every vantage point, still wondering why the hell a relatively small force like this was bothering to confront the fort head-on. He scanned the horizon, expecting to see a long plume of dust thrown up by more armor approaching from the west. But there was nothing.

Why the hell are they throwing their lives away like this?

Anvil Gate only had to sit it out and smack down anyone stupid enough to get too close. This was what it had always had done, even before the invention of cannon and gunpowder. It had swapped archers and catapults for cannonballs, and then for shells. It was all the same to Anvegad.

Hoffman could see that from the way its people behaved. He

decided against risking the external gantries to move around and made his way down the stone stairs inside the walls of the fort. When he emerged at the second floor, the streets he looked down on were quieter than usual but not deserted. Apart from his Gears and the occasional city official walking calmly between muster points, close to the walls and head down as they'd been told, some civvies were out delivering essentials and wheeling handcarts of produce through the streets. There was no sense of tension or panic at all.

Hoffman thought that was getting close to dumb complacency. Indie gunners would have a tough time getting shells over the city walls, but nobody knew where the guy with the RPG was now. He'd proved he could take an opportunistic shot at vulnerable spots in the taller structures.

The Pesangas can deal with him. Meanwhile—

Shit, I haven't thought about Margaret once. I hope to hell this isn't on the news. She'll worry her guts out.

The steady thump of artillery fire in both directions had suddenly become background noise. But one explosion broke the pattern as he crossed the compound to check on the Sangar manned by his own Gears. He almost dismissed it until the second *whump* a few moments later and the yell of "Incoming! Mortars!"

The explosion threw up a column of smoke and flame, almost as if it had gone off next to him. A rain of debris—fragments of roof slate, hissing metal, wood splinters—hammered down on the buildings around him. He ducked beside the wall and covering his head for a moment, then ran for the nearest Sangar.

He had to scramble up a short ladder to reach it. The three Gears inside were crouched behind the rocket screen, surveying the crags below the walls with field glasses.

"Where the hell did that come from this time?" Hoffman could hear the city's small firefighting force honking its vehicle horns, trying to get through the narrow streets. Many of the city's buildings were made of wood, a tinderbox in waiting. "That's got to be *north* of us."

"It definitely didn't come from the Vasgar side, sir," Dawes said.

Hoffman pressed his radio. "Byrne? Where are you?"

"The monastery tower, sir. I'm moving a couple of small guns up here. It covers our dead area, more or less."

"Well, at least we know what their strategy is now." Hoffman still wasn't sure if his head injury was distorting his take on the situation or if he really had been a dumb asshole not to see this coming. "The frontal assault was to keep us busy while they moved up behind us."

"Yeah, we'll lose some civvies, sir, but they're not going to take the city with a few mortars—not unless we let it burn down," Byrne said, brutally pragmatic. "And half the place is still solid stone, so good luck with that."

"We could really do with a Raven right now. Even a Tern."

"I don't think they'd have much more luck spotting these bastards than we would."

"I'm going to get Carlile to rig some mortar grillage on the key buildings."

"It'll be dark in a couple of hours, sir. Good and bad—if we black out the city, we can move around above cover, but they can still fire on our position and be pretty sure of hitting something."

COG bases got hit all the time. There was a big difference between doing serious damage and actually mounting an assault on a scale that could overrun them. They'd lose a few lives, a few buildings, as Byrne had said, but the city wasn't going anywhere.

And neither was anyone else, not as long as that road was blocked. Hoffman had options, though. He had food, he had water, and he had electric power. And, if the worst happened, the civilians could take shelter in the network of tunnels deep in the rock.

Hoffman could sit it out for a couple of weeks. By then, Shavad would be won or lost, and that outcome was outside his control.

SHAVAD, WESTERN KASHKUR.

The Kashkuri certainly built things to last. The museum in Gorlian Square had lost its impressive steps, half of its stone-mullioned windows, and most of the statues in the second-story wall niches. But it was still standing. Another shell hit the roof balustrade, throwing a small avalanche of masonry onto the square below. Smoke wafted out of broken windowpanes. The east wing was on fire.

If that didn't keep the Indie observer's head down, nothing would. But it was a big, flat roof, and there were still plenty of vantage points left even if the whole top floor was blown away. Until someone took a look from the air, Adam Fenix wouldn't know if the casevac flight was going to get his Gears to hospital or be brought down in flames.

"We've got to go with it now." He turned to Helena. "You handle the Terns. Get those Gears ready to move." He radioed the FDC to pause the guns for a while. "Gold Nine to FDC—check fire. Inbound casevac. Check fire."

Helena was on the radio to the Tern pilots, one hand cupped over her earpiece and the other holding binoculars to her eyes as she scanned the front elevation of the museum. If the Indie observer wasn't incapacitated yet, he'd hear the guns fall silent, and the sound of helicopters, and he'd know he had a target on the way in. And if he did—then the Terns had to get in and out fast. Adam started thinking how they could be better protected against ground fire, and added it to his list of projects to deal with if he survived this campaign.

Of course I'm going to live. My boy can't grow up without a father. No Indie's going to do that to him.

It was that kind of silly death-denying logic that most Gears went through at times like this. Adam looked at Helena Stroud, single mother, and was reminded that kids grew up without fathers all the time.

"T-Five-Twenty to Gold Nine, we'll be on the ground in two

minutes—if we can find a parking space." The Tern pilot was circling, looking for a level surface to set down in the sea of rubble that had once been a pretty square with gilded fountains. "Let's do it."

Adam had moved two mortar teams to the north of the square. He'd thought that the Terns might come in behind them, on the riverbank side, so that he could make sure the museum observer was distracted during the casevac. But unless they flew dangerously low between the buildings, they'd probably take fire from the Indies across the river. He had to leave it to the pilots' skill and judgment. They could see what he couldn't.

"T-Five-Twenty to Gold Nine—critical cases on the first bird, maximum six."

"Roger that, Five-Twenty." Adam signaled a squad to move out and secure the landing zone. They'd only be able to land two birds at a time, and that was pushing the available space. "Keep your eyes open for Indies on the museum roof."

"Not a lot of it left, Gold Nine . . . let the looting begin. Save me a few Silver Era funerary urns."

Adam couldn't take his eyes off the museum. Even when the first Tern touched down, he found himself looking down the sights of his Lancer, checking the building's facade window by window, as if he had a hope in hell of seeing anyone before they got off a shot or a grenade round. He talked of snipers and observers; but the reality was that he had no idea who or what was in there. The Indies could have inserted a dozen machine-gun crews, one man and one component at a time slipping into Shavad over a period of months. They'd had intelligence agents in Kashkur for years, just as the COG had them in UIR territory, unseen and unacknowledged.

Wounded Gears were waiting in the open even before the first Tern touched down, the worst cases shielded bodily from the downdraft by their comrades, and, Adam had to imagine, from possible sniper fire. He found himself wondering if he would put himself between someone and a bullet like that, because he'd never consciously done it. It shamed him for reasons he couldn't yet understand. The Tern lifted off, didn't take a direct hit from an RPG, didn't burst into flames, and headed north to the field hospital at Lakar, out of range of the Indie guns. Adam let himself breathe again. The other Tern, which had been hovering behind the shattered stump of a block of apartments, moved in to pick up the next batch.

The Indie guns were still hitting the same targets they'd been pounding half an hour ago. They seemed to have moved on from this part of the city.

Maybe that meant their observer was out of action.

The second Tern took off and the last two landed. They were too close together for Adam's peace of mind. He found himself existing solely for the moment when they were clear and away. Then Helena moved, and for a moment his attention was broken.

"Bastard," she muttered, dropped to one knee, and aimed somewhere along the museum frontage. "*Bastard.*"

He didn't see what had caught her eye. He only heard her short burst of fire, almost simultaneous with a rocket streaking past just above head height. He had no idea how it missed the Terns. He could have sworn it actually passed between the two sets of rotors. Automatic fire started up from the window above his head, so Collins must have seen whatever Helena had spotted, and then the mortar teams joined in. It bought the Terns the time they needed. Adam gave them time to clear, pulled everyone out of the square, and got back on the Sherriths' FDC.

"This is Gold Nine to FDC, resume—adjust fire, grid Alpha Eight, seven-one-five-zero-zero-three, over."

"Grid Alpha Eight, seven-one-five-zero-zero-three, out."

It took about ten seconds for the next shell to find the museum and pound it. By then, the Terns were gone. The museum was still substantially intact. Smoke belched from the windows on its northeast side.

"We have to check he's not still functioning in there," Helena said. The Indie had become a man, no doubt one they all had an individual image of in their minds, when he could easily have been a squad. "Permission to go in and clear the building, sir."

"I should have worried about collateral damage a few hours ago," Adam said. "But we can't keep shelling the building and hoping we got him. Okay, lead on."

"I can do this. You worry about holding the road."

Adam knew he should have hung back, but part of him wanted to see how much damage he'd done. One day, he knew, he'd look back on this battle and feel appalled that he'd destroyed something precious and irreplaceable. He would understand that human lives came first, but he would mourn for the loss of knowledge all the same.

"Helena, I know you can do it," he said. "But so can I. You're going to get yourself killed one day if you don't learn to stand back."

"If I do," she said, "it'll be because something needed doing."

She moved off, working her way up the right-hand side of the square. Adam gestured *follow us* to Rawlin and Collins.

"We should have bribed Timgad Company to lend us Mataki," Helena said. "She'd have dropped him by now. I swear that woman could shoot the balls off a gnat at a thousand meters."

"Well, we didn't, so we're down to house-clearance tactics now." The four of them stacked around what was left of a door to the right of the main entrance. "Okay, big floor space, not many walls—open galleries. No idea where the stairs and exits are, so this could be a slow job. In three—two—go."

Adam usually started at the worst scenario and scaled down. He expected to meet fire. He didn't. But what he saw stopped him in his tracks for a moment.

"Oh God." Helena said it for him, and looked up into a halo of daylight. "What a mess."

The museum was a shell.

The exterior walls were almost all that was left in most places. It looked like a thrashball stadium, an empty amphitheater. Its floors had mostly collapsed, leaving splintered ledges along the walls. Adam could see the sky through at least two gaping voids. Then he looked down and realized what he was about to step on. In the glittering carpet of broken glass and shattered plaster, the contents of the display cabinets lay everywhere.

They were just . . . objects, nothing more; not people, not alive, and of no practical use at that moment for an army trying to hold back an invasion. But Adam felt as much anguish and guilt as if he'd slaughtered a nation. There were canvases torn from their frames, fine oils depicting the ancient nobles of Kashkur; there were shards of porcelain, exquisite shields skinned with beaten silver, tapestries, crude clay pots, and hand-illuminated manuscripts that were now charred and smoking. Kashkur had ruled an empire long before Ephyra had even been a village. He tried not to let the shock distract him when there could have been Indie crosshairs centered on his forehead, but he felt he was watching the end of the world.

"Mind the glass," Helena whispered, pragmatic to a fault. "But he'll hear us coming anyway."

Adam couldn't see any flames, but he could certainly smell the smoke. The fires seemed to be confined to the wing at the far end. It smelled of scorched paint. As he kept to the wall, looking above, he could hear creaking—maybe the floor joists starting to give way, maybe someone moving around.

They said this was once a palace. Well, it's not very palatial now.

The Kashkuri government was going to be furious. For some reason that worried Adam more than the prospect of someone on the next floor emptying their magazine into him. Helena put her finger to her lips and pointed up, then signaled Collins and Rawlin to cover the stairs. She gestured at Adam, pointing her finger and counting out five: *I'm going up, five floors.*

He trained his Lancer on the gaping hole above. There was so little floor left that nobody was going to be moving around easily. Helena picked her way across the precious debris of centuries and eventually reached the central staircase, then began working her way up along the treads that were still in place. Adam could still hear the occasional creak above his head.

Helena's voice in his earpiece was right at the limit of his hearing. He was more deafened by the artillery than he realized.

"I can see where's he been," she breathed.

There was a loud creak of wood giving way. "Easy . . ." Adam said.

"Wait."

Adam looked to Collins, who just kept his Lancer aimed up into what had been the stairwell. Rawlin prowled carefully around the lobby, watching other doors.

Then the shooting started.

All Adam heard was three bursts of automatic fire, the thud of boots running, and then the overlapping shots of a close-quarters battle, very short, very sudden. The disemboweled palace fell silent. He didn't hear anyone call "Clear."

Oh shit . . .

He motioned the two Gears to stay put and ran up the remains of the stairs. He'd lost the element of surprise anyway. All he could think was that little Anya had lost her mom and he had no idea who would take care of her now. When he got to the top floor, he dropped to a crouch and looked along a gallery where some glass cases still clung to the walls. Reflections moved. He swung his aim, conscious of the gaps in the floor, and saw Helena standing frozen, head turned to one side. Then she swung around a corner—into an alcove, he assumed—and there was another short burst of fire.

"Bitch," he heard her say. "You won't be calling in any more arty now, will you?" Then, almost as an afterthought, she called out: "Clear—one Indie down."

"For God's sake, Stroud, I thought you'd been hit." Now that the adrenaline was ebbing, Adam was a lot more wary of the state of the building. He felt his way along floorboards that moved alarmingly. "Sure we haven't missed anyone?"

Helena was checking through a pile of equipment. There was a woman dead on the floor, no UIR uniform, just dark blue coveralls. She'd been brown-haired and in her early thirties before Stroud had blown half her head off. In the alcove that overlooked Gorlian Square, there was radio equipment, maps, binoculars, and a geometry kit of compass, set square, and protractors that could easily have been a schoolchild's.

There was also a UIR sniper rifle, and that definitely wasn't any kid's.

"One frigging woman," Helena said, exactly as a man might have done if he hadn't had much respect for females. "But I'll have that lovely rifle for Mataki, thanks. She's always complaining about the Longshot being a pain to reload every time. Bribery with a semiautomatic might work."

Helena had her plans, then. Or maybe it was just instinct. Either way, she wanted the best Gears under her. Adam was just doing what he felt obliged and honor-bound to do; Helena was making a career of it as well.

He got on the radio. "Gold Nine to Control and FDC—Indie forward observer in the museum, now neutralized. We're moving on to cover the main road."

"Roger that, Gold Nine."

As they left the ruined museum, he stopped to pick up something that caught his eye. It was a small silver statue of a horse, very heavy, about thirty centimeters tall and inlaid with turquoise and garnets. Adam took a guess that it was from the earliest days of Kashkur's ancient empire. He had no idea what to do with it. He couldn't bear to leave it there to be looted, but he also didn't feel he had the right to take it away, either. He stood looking at it for a moment, lost.

Helena gave him an odd look. "There's a lot of that stuff."

"What's going to happen to it all? Who's going to recover all this?"

"The Indies, if we don't get a move on and finish off that bridge."

"Centuries. *Millennia*. Gone."

"Sir, it's metal. It's a *thing*. Things get remade. Come on." She held up an admonishing finger, almost joking, but he wasn't too sure. "And please—don't start mourning the burned books."

He laid the silver horse back in the rubble. It would be found again and stolen, maybe even melted down, but he simply couldn't walk away with it. "Let's go," he said. The company was now down to sixty or so Gears. Adam regrouped them into two platoons and readied them to move east along the river to the bridge, another piece of Kashkuri construction that just wouldn't yield. He radioed the field hospital at Lakar and checked on the casualties—Vallory had made it, which cheered him enormously—and waited for a sitrep from Control.

The smoke was now a thick fog on the water. If the last bridge was down, he couldn't see it, but he could hear the guns still pounding in a slow rhythm as if they were getting bored with the whole battle.

"Gold Nine, get out of there now," said the controller. "The Indies have taken the bridge. They're moving northeast. You're going to be cut off if you don't fall back now and rejoin the main battle group."

Adam's gut sank. He took a breath before relaying the order. "Change of plan, people. We're rejoining Choi now. We've lost the bridge."

There was an awful silence, the kind you got when you'd lost so many men and women to gain so little. Helena put her hand flat on his backplate.

"No, sir. Two-Six RTI didn't lose it. The Sherriths couldn't hold it. We remain the Unvanquished."

She slung the looted sniper rifle over her shoulder and strode off toward the waiting transport, an open truck filling up with exhausted Gears. Adam didn't think there was a difference. She clearly did, though, and it seemed to improve everyone's mood a little.

Adam's mind was made up at that moment. This was not his calling, but it *was* Helena Stroud's. He wasn't good at this. He didn't have that charisma and certainty that a real leader needed. He fought because he felt it was wrong to let others do the dying, but now he knew he could save more lives by designing better weapons and systems, designing *deterrents* to war, than by being a mediocre infantry captain.

When he finished this tour of duty—if the war went on as it always had—he was going to take the Defense Research Agency offer a lot more seriously.

As he climbed into the truck, he thought of the exquisite silver horse, abandoned to its fate. His father would have been disappointed in him for not salvaging it for the Fenix estate.

DIVISIONAL HEADQUARTERS, PESANGA BRIGADE
OF RIFLES, GULAN PROVINCE.

Bai Tak couldn't recall ever having this much food in his life. And so much of it was *meat*. No wonder the Gears, as the Coalition called its soldiers, were so big.

He sat in the canteen surrounded by Pesang men from all over the country, and simply ate whatever was put in front of him. Some of the veteran riflemen found that funny.

"Ah, you can always spot a new recruit by how fast he gets indigestion," one of them said. His name was Cho Ligan. "And then your pants get too tight. And then the novelty wears off."

"I think it's going to take a long time to wear off for *me*." Bai looked at the chunk of steak left untouched on Cho's plate. "If you're not going to eat that, I will."

"Go ahead."

The only drawback of this new life was that Harua had been furious and had sobbed her heart out when he left for training. It was all too fast, she said. He gave her no time to prepare for him going away. Even handing over the recruiting bounty he got for signing on for five years didn't calm her down, but at least he had the comfort of knowing she had plenty of money to pay for food and to hire some help with the herd. She might even have enough to replace animals that didn't survive the drought. The bounty was a lot of money by Pesang standards.

But he hadn't started really missing her yet. Things just felt strange. He was too overwhelmed and exhausted by all the new things he had to learn to have time to mope around. He was still coming to terms with the rifle they called a Lancer, which was not only complicated but absolutely huge. The one thing he understood instinctively was the bayonet that clipped on to the barrel. Although it was for stabbing, he knew that if he was ever in a tight spot that his machete would serve him a lot better when it came to dispatching an enemy.

"So how long do you think it's going to be before we get to

fight?" Lau En was single, a little younger than Bai, and keen to save enough from his pay to buy a workshop in Paro so he could get a wife with a lot of land. "I don't want to lose my enthusiasm." He nudged Bai and indicated one of the white COG officers making his inspection rounds of the canteen, checking to see that the Pesangas were satisfied with the food. "See him? He knows about ten words of Pesan, so don't ask him anything complicated."

"That's all right," Cho said. "We only speak ten words of Tyran. So we're even."

The canteen was very brightly lit. Bai was used to few lights indoors and a lot of dull, dark wood surfaces, so he thought he might never get used to this bright and shiny COG world. He was scared of leaving fingerprints on everything. But the most foreign thing of all was the television in what the Gears called the *mess*.

Television was a radio with movies. He had a radio at home, and once every couple of years he walked all the way to the occasional theater in Paro when the owner announced he'd found a film to project on the whitewashed wall of his barn. But seeing the two combined in one small machine was something that amazed Bai. The screen was about thirty centimeters across, and the images were black and white, not colored like the movies he remembered, but he still couldn't take his eyes off it. He could actually watch the man who read the news bulletins.

"You'll get fed up with that," Lau said. "It's all bad news. The COG's taking a pounding again. We've had a few bad years."

Bai had to get used to *we* and *us* also meaning people who lived unknown lives in ornate and rich cities.

"Shavad," he said. "I know. Do you think they'll send us there?"

"We'll lose Shavad by the time any of us get deployed. Two-Six RTI and the Sherrith Cavalry have lost a hell of a lot of men. And women. They have women Gears. *Officers*, too."

"Hey, we've *all* got women in command at home, right?" Cho said. "How will we notice the difference?"

Lau was right. It was depressing news from Shavad. The pictures filled in the gaps that Bai couldn't work out from his grasp of the language. He wondered what use he'd be in this kind of war, a man used to oxcarts and no electricity for weeks at a time.

After lunch—he got four meals a day in the COG, another amazing thing—there was more rifle training out on the ranges. Bai wished he'd laid off the second helpings. Lying prone to fire was uncomfortable on a full stomach, but he'd made the mistake and so he would learn from it.

He was secretly relieved when the sergeant halted firing for a moment. He was still partly reliant on the hand signals for drill because he often couldn't follow the different accents among the Tyran-speaking foreigners, but the hand signals were clear. He had no idea why they'd halted firing. It was just a welcome excuse to ease himself off his belly and relax a little. He watched an officer in bulky metal armor plates—a major—stride across the grass to talk to the sergeant, then turn to face the men who were waiting patiently with their unfamiliar Lancers.

He spoke really good Pesan, this major.

"I need some volunteers," he boomed. His voice carried right across the field. "I need six men used to moving around mountains without being seen, men who can track. I know many of you can already do that. But this is in potentially dangerous territory, and you have to be able to live in the wilderness, maybe without support for weeks at a time."

Cho was two positions to Bai's left. He sat back on his heels in one movement and raised his hand.

"Sir, I can do that," he said. "With or without a rifle."

Bai turned his head slowly to look at Lau, just to see if he was shaping up to volunteer. A few more men raised their hands. Bai suddenly had a desperate urge to stick with his new buddies, as well as a powerful sense of missing out on something important if he didn't take part in this.

No point sitting on my backside. If I'm in, I'm in. Whatever it is.

Bai raised his hand. "Sir, I come from the borders," he said. "We had a lot of trouble with Shaoshi raiding our herds. I'm good at ambushes."

The officer smiled. "Ah, you obviously understand what this job requires. Good man. Anyone else?"

Lau obviously didn't want to be left behind. "Me too, sir. I can track. I'm a good climber, too."

The officer rubbed his hands together. "That's what I like about you lads. You're always willing to give it a go. Okay, report to the quartermaster in half an hour and get your kit. You're going straight to Kashkur."

Bai let the words sink in. That was the trouble with volunteering. Sometimes, you just didn't have the full picture first. He made an effort not to let the shock show on his face and got to his feet.

Look, how hard can this be? I signed up on the spur of the moment. All wars are dangerous. Harua isn't going to be any more angry with me than she is now. And this—this is something I don't need to be trained to do. My father said he always volunteered. It never did him any harm.

"You're nuts," Cho whispered to him as they lined up to be issued with their new equipment. "You haven't even qualified with the Lancer."

"The major didn't seem to care." Bai could see Lau ahead of them, being given a huge backpack that looked bigger than he was. "And you're the one who volunteered first."

Lau walked past them with his new backpack. "I think this is a hammock," he said, grappling with the straps.

Seng, Bai's brother, had seen it all and done it all, and often said that people were basically sheep who would follow anyone who looked like they knew where they were going. Bai got the feeling he was more of a sheep than a wolf. But he couldn't back out now. Cho and Lau were going, and a man didn't let his friends down.

He'd never been in a helicopter before. He'd never been outside Pesang. He wasn't even used to the Lancer yet, not in the effortless way he was used to his machete. But an hour later, he was sitting in the open crew bay of an incredibly noisy aircraft he was told to call a *chopper* or a *bird*, with dust and fumes whipping into his face as they flew over the mountains to Kashkur. It was a tiny helicopter, nothing like the big black ones that he'd seen on the TV. It had the words TRAFFIC DIVISION on the side.

He couldn't even get to know the other men on the journey. It was too noisy to talk. He wasn't used to constant loud engine noises any more than he was used to blazing electric lights in every room.

And the damn radio earpieces—they *itched*.

"We've got to report to a Lieutenant Hoffman," Cho said. "At the fort."

"Where are we landing?" Bai asked.

"Wherever the helicopter can set down. The Indies are attacking Anvegad."

"I don't suppose any of the Gears speak Pesan."

"No."

"Well, that's going to be fun . . ."

"They just point us where they want us to go, we look for the enemy, and either draw a map of where they are or kill them." Cho shrugged. "How much Pesan do you need to speak for that?"

Bai hadn't thought much about killing the enemy. It never occurred to him that he might not be able to stomach it, because he slaughtered cattle and sheep when he needed to, and it seemed far harder to him to kill a dumb, innocent beast than someone who would kill you if you didn't get the first blow in. He would know what to do when the time came. His father said there was nothing to it.

"That's Anvegad below." The loudspeaker in the crew bay barely made itself heard over the engine noise. The pilot had that strained, shouty voice. "And if you look to the south, that's the UIR at the refinery. I'm going to set down at the north side of the fort because of the shelling. You'll have to go the rest of the way on foot."

"We just walk in?"

"Use your radios. Just give the fort the call sign to ID yourselves so they don't shoot you."

They said that the Gears used one Tyran word a lot when they were scared, surprised, unimpressed, or generally trying to express strong feeling. In fact, it seemed to mean anything a Gear wanted it to mean.

They said *shit*.

"Ah . . . shit," Bai said.

The helicopter touched down on an outcrop just long enough for them to get out and drag their backpacks after them. Then they were alone, staring out into a smoky violet dusk across a wilderness a lot like home. The fort was a dense black outline dominated by two huge guns.

At least they could see where they were heading. They began picking their way down the rocks.

Cho held up his hand for quiet. "Listen."

Bai could hear it, too; the occasional slide of gravel as someone crept through the darkness. His instinct was to reach for his machete. The six Pesangs settled down into the rock crevices to wait for whoever it was to make himself seen, but Bai wasn't sure if it was going to be the enemy now. He got ready to swing his blade.

Boots. Those stupid, noisy, clumsy Gears boots. He could hear the creaks of the leather straps and the scuff of metal.

A Gear, like me.

Then a huge explosion lit up the sky for a moment. He found himself looking up at a man in full armor about to step on him. Bai caught a glimpse of red hair and a face covered in swirls of blue ink. He almost yelled out. He'd never seen anything like it.

"Holy fuck," said the man. "You nearly made me shit myself. You little buggers really *don't* make any noise, do you?"

Bai didn't yet have the language skills to tell the red-haired tattooed giant that he'd almost shit himself as well. He saluted. He didn't know what else to do.

"Rifleman Bai Tak, sah," he said. "We Pesanga. Six Pesanga. You want help?"

"Bloody right we do, son. Come on. Come and meet the CO. I'm Pad, by the way. Private Salton." He turned around as he led them down the slope and grinned, staring at Bai's machete. "Is it true that once you draw your blade, you're not allowed to sheath it again until you cut some bugger's head off?"

Bai understood most of what Pad was saying, but putting an answer together in Tyran was a lot harder. He just did what everyone did when faced with a foreigner who seemed to be friendly. He grinned back.

"Damn, you love your work," Pad said. "We're going to get on just fine."

CHAPTER 14

I can do business with Hoffman. He would not—could never—lie to me. He enjoys wielding the truth too much. I think he's in love with its power to shock. And he knows that as long as he brandishes it, nobody will burden him with secrets he doesn't want to keep.

(COMMANDER MIRAN TRESCU, JUSTIFYING HIS ALLIANCE WITH
COLONEL VICTOR HOFFMAN TO DISGRUNTLED MEMBERS
OF HIS COMMUNITY)

**KR-80, TRACKING STRANDED FLEET WEST OF
VECTES: PRESENT DAY, 15 A.E.**

"Okay, I'll field this call if you're all out of the office," Gettner said. "But they didn't mistake us for a SAR bird."

Dom listened on the radio. The incoming voice was one he thought he'd heard before, and Marcus's slow blink confirmed it. This was the guy he'd called from *Steady Eddie.*

"I'll talk to him," Marcus said. He took a breath and pressed his earpiece. "This is Sergeant Fenix. Remember me?"

"Hey, COG. Dropped by to strafe us? Or do we need to watch for submarines this time? You're so versatile."

"You need to watch for the things that sunk your cruiser. Who am I talking to?"

"Lyle Ollivar. Remember that guy you torpedoed after agreeing to a truce with us? I took over from him. They wanted someone less trusting in the position."

"Okay, pissing contest over. You know what Lambent are?"

"We hear the name."

"We lose ships to them. So do you. They're the things that make the Locust crap their pants. You want to know how bad things could get?"

"Oh, we know."

Dom looked at Baird for a moment. Did they know about the imulsion rig yet? If they did, did they understand what had actually happened? There was only so much they could glean from whatever got whispered and passed around between Stranded on the island, and they probably hadn't cracked COG radio encryption yet. Baird just shrugged.

"We need to talk," Marcus said. He gestured to Dom to get his attention and mouthed *call Hoffman*. "No bullshit. I'm willing to come to you."

Ollivar paused. "Unarmed."

"If you don't count a cannoned-up Raven for insurance, yes."

Dom gave Marcus an emphatic shake of the head just as Control responded. *You must be crazy. Don't do it.* He moved to the back of the crew bay to get out of audio range. "Control, this is Santiago. I need to speak to Hoffman."

Marcus carried on the negotiation. Dom thought it was a waste of time, but Marcus did things by the book—at first, anyway. He always gave assholes one chance. Maybe it was the right thing to do. For every bastard who killed Dom's buddies, there were many more Stranded who were just pitiful losers, or unlucky like Dizzy, or decent folk like whoever had looked after Maria for years before the grubs got her.

I'll never know who they were. They might even be on those boats down there.

Yeah. My wife was Stranded, too.

Dom couldn't forget that. Today was one of the rough patches he plunged back into—less frequently now, but near-unbearable all the same. It was coming up to the anniversary of the day he'd first met Maria. There were more good days than bad now, but the bad ones still came back with a vengeance, grabbed him, and whispered: *You lost them, all—kids, parents, wife, brother, friends. There's only Marcus left.*

Marcus was still waiting for a response from Ollivar, staring out of the Raven's door. Hoffman came on the radio.

"What is it, Dom?"

"Sir, we've located a Stranded fleet west of the island, inbound. Marcus is talking to their leader."

"They planning an assault?"

"If they are, Captain Michaelson can probably reduce it to driftwood. Maybe landing arms, maybe something else entirely."

"Do you need backup?"

"Not yet."

"Tell Marcus—no deals we can't honor."

"Got it, sir. Stand by. Santiago out."

Gettner cut in. "I can't circle here all day."

"Give him a few minutes," Marcus said. "If he's up for it, can you land me?"

"You're nuts."

"Can you?"

"You can rope down to the car ferry on the edge of the convoy. I can approach that from its starboard side—less chance of being shot at."

"If you're roping down, so am I," Dom said.

Marcus ignored him. "If it goes to rat shit, Major, bang out and get back to base."

Screw that. Dom started laying out two rappel lines on the deck in front of his seat. *He's not going down there alone. Or unarmed. They never notice the knife. They're too fixed on the fucking chainsaw to care about the knife.*

"Okay, Sergeant, how and where are we going to do this?"

"Car ferry. Space to fast-rope down."

"No need to tell you what happens if you live up to my expectations of you fascists and do anything dumb."

Gettner looped the Raven around and came in lower than Dom thought she'd risk.

"Don't hang about," she said. "I don't fancy ditching here when I run out of fuel."

Barber checked Marcus's rappel line and stood ready to give him an assist off the edge of the bay. Marcus's attention was on what was underneath him, not behind, so Dom just exchanged nods with Barber and stepped into position to follow down. It was almost funny that there was no discussion needed. Marcus was doing something sacrificially risky, so Dom was going to ride shotgun, and Barber was going to enable that—again. Marcus could argue the toss about it later with Dom, *after* he didn't get shot or taken hostage.

I'm still a commando. I can do this shit.

Their boots hit the ferry's deck. Marcus crouched as the Raven lifted clear, looking faintly annoyed.

"You ever stop to think that Ollivar might object to two Gears when he thought he was dealing with *one?*"

"He can kiss my ass," Dom said. He noted the welcoming committee of four armed Stranded around the landing area. "What are you going to say to him?"

"That he's in the same shit as we are. See where we go from there."

It took Ollivar ten fuel-wasting minutes to arrive. His powerboat—gun on the foredeck, very snazzy, a real drug baron's gin palace—brought him alongside, and he boarded with the ease of an admiral on a ship inspection visit.

He didn't look like a pirate, unless Dom counted the assault rifle. He was thirtyish and well groomed, like an ambitious middle manager on his day off doing a bit of adventure training. This was the chief of the quaintly named Lesser Islands Free Trade Association.

The fact that kill-crazy Trescu was responsible for the death of his predecessor probably didn't matter much to a man who saw the COG and Gorasnaya as being one and the same.

Well, we say they are, too. What's the guy to think?

"I really hate it when history repeats itself," Ollivar said, apparently unworried by Dom's unexpected arrival. "So why should I give you lying fucks the time of day?"

Marcus shrugged. "We're having problems with the Lambent, and you're going to have them, too."

"Ah, but we're small and mobile, and we can even run to the mainland when we need to, but you've painted yourself into a corner on your little fortress island. Sitting ducks."

Marcus didn't react. He never did. He just had that look that said he was making a note of anything useful, a slow-motion nod. "So you accept that Lambent are taking out your boats, not us."

"We fish too. We've found a couple."

"Stalks as well?"

"The things that keep punching up through the ground? I hear they're appearing all over the mainland now."

"Okay," Marcus said quietly. "So you think you can deal with this."

"We can *avoid* it. That's why we're heading to Vectes, in case you thought we were mounting some armed landing. We're getting our people out while we still can."

"If this shit's spreading, you're going to run out of places to hide," Marcus said.

Dom wasn't sure if Marcus knew something he didn't, or if he was doing something very *un*-Marcus—bluffing. He steeled himself to stand there like the dumb sidekick and not show any surprise. Ollivar stared Marcus out for a few seconds, but he was the first to blink—literally.

"What makes you say that?" he asked.

Marcus didn't so much as twitch a muscle. "We're monitoring the stalks that wrecked our rig. But if you think you can handle it on your own, fine—I'll just thank you for getting your assholes off our case so we can work out how we stop these things." He pressed his earpiece. "Fenix to KR Eight-Zero. Requesting pickup—we're done here."

Ollivar folded his arms, still doing the silent routine. Maybe that was the little tic that showed he wasn't as relaxed about evading the Lambent as he claimed. Marcus hadn't actually asked him to do anything; there was no reason for the I'm-not-playing body language. But then Marcus was just standing there with his arms at his sides, a little awkward, hands loosely clenched. Dom knew that was just because he didn't know what to do with his hands when he wasn't hugging his Lancer—but it might have come across to Ollivar as balling his fists for a fight. Marcus wasn't always easy to read.

"Warn us when you're ready to embark," Marcus said. "So our navy knows you're coming. You know how they are."

"Don't tell me you wouldn't want to blow them all away for what they're doing to your guys."

"Love to," Marcus said. "But I've got bigger problems than you. And you'll all end up dead anyway."

Gettner was now hovering overhead in a fierce downdraft. Barber lowered the sling on the winch.

"Shame about your rig," Ollivar said. "If you've got any sense, you'll fire up that navy of yours and get the hell off Vectes too."

Dom thought about that all the way back to the naval base, arms folded and eyes shut so that nobody would start a conversation with him. He wasn't sure he could face another upheaval. It had been bad enough running from Jacinto to Port Farrall and then to Vectes. There had to come a point where it was better to stand your ground and die rather than wandering the world scared shitless of what was around the next corner. He listened to Marcus talking to Hoffman on the radio, and got the impression that the colonel was digging in rather than thinking of evacuating.

What the hell else could he do with a whole city?

"Okay, Hoffman's glad they're going," Marcus said, taking out his earpiece and scratching his ear. "We got something right. One less variable to factor in. Maybe they'll be kind enough to leave us the rest of their explosives."

"Were you acting?" Dom asked. "With Ollivar, I mean."

Marcus just raised his shoulders a fraction. It wasn't even a shrug. "I can't act."

"That's probably why it convinced me."

"What, that they'll end up as dead as us?"

"Yeah."

"He can chew on that for a while." Marcus got up as the Raven flew low over the base perimeter. Half a dozen of the ancient bulldozers that had been taken out of mothballs to clear land for housing were parked in a line, and Gears were milling around them. "Looks like Hoffman really *is* digging in."

Dom craned his neck. "What exactly are they doing? Did he say?"

"He just said that if it worked at Anvil Gate, it might work here."

Hoffman never talked about Anvil Gate any more than Marcus or Dom talked about Aspho Fields. Dom assumed Hoffman's reluctance was the same as his, born of a necessary thing that neither wanted to recall if they could avoid it. But the decorations and promotions tied to both events made damn sure nobody else ever forgot.

Hoffman had raised the specter himself, though. Maybe that meant he was dealing with his ghosts better than Dom was.

The old man was right. Some things were best faced head-on.

NEW EARTHWORKS, VECTES NAVAL BASE; THREE DAYS LATER.

Ollivar's piss-pot fleet hadn't come inshore yet, but neither had any stalks or polyps. And there hadn't been an incident of any kind involving the gangs. Hoffman felt that the world was holding its breath for some reason.

He hoped that it was just giving him time to complete the fortifications before all hell broke loose. It would make a change to being run ragged by unfolding disasters on a daily basis, always two steps behind where he needed to be. The ditches and pits around the northern boundary of the camp were now extensive enough to give everyone a feeling of security and decisive action, however misplaced that might turn out to be.

What if the stalks come up inside the wire?

What if we can't channel the polyps into kill zones?

What if . . . this is really the time that I fail?

At least Dizzy Wallin was happy. He climbed up into the cab of his derrick—*Betty,* he called it—and started the engine. The huge machine shook convulsively before rumbling into life. Hoffman stood at the top of the ramparts formed from the excavated soil and found himself almost eye to eye with the man.

Dizzy ran his hands over the steering wheel as if he was soothing it. "Mornin', sweetie," he said to the rig. "Did you have a restful night? You ready to do a little work for Dizzy? That's my girl." He rested his elbow on the cab door. "You gotta treat the ladies right, Colonel. Show you appreciate 'em."

Hoffman was pretty sure that Dizzy really was just referring to the derrick, and not taking a poke at his guilty conscience. All the drivers recruited via Operation Lifeboat—Prescott's coyly named project for conscripting Stranded with the promise of aid for their families—had this fixation with their vehicles. Maybe creating a crazy game was the only thing that made the job bearable; that, and drinking, which Dizzy did plenty of.

So what? He gets the job done. Poor bastard. How he kills his liver is his business.

"They're all ill-tempered when they first wake up," Hoffman said. "Best to give them a wide berth until they've had a coffee and put their lipstick on."

Dizzy roared with laughter. "Ain't that the truth. Look, how do you know this trap is gonna work, sir? Maybe them polyp things is just too dumb to follow a trail o' crumbs."

"They'll come at us, Wallin. We're the crumbs." *I've done this before. I've presented my throat to the enemy. And then, when he's come within reach—I've killed him.* "Then we make sure we get them where we want them. We lure them. We herd them. Damn it, we even bulldoze them with Betty. But we get them in a killing zone, and we finish them."

"Betty ain't gonna like that much, sir."

"She's a tough old bird. Most women are. Don't you worry about her."

But even the tough ones sometimes don't make it.

The whole site came to life as drivers, engineers, and laborers showed up to get on with the digging and leveling. Staff Sergeant Parry, the most experienced engineer left in the corps, scrambled up a bank of earth with Royston Sharle to pore over a map.

They knew what they were doing. They didn't need Hoffman around. But he wanted to watch them for a while, just to be reassured that this wasn't an insane waste of fuel and manpower when there was transport to maintain, houses to build, and crops to grow.

If they thought it was crazy, they'd tell him, one way or another. He was sure of that.

"Did you like digging holes in the garden as a boy, Victor?" Michaelson walked along the top of the hard-packed ramp. "I did. Buried my mother's best porcelain teapot as pirate treasure once. She wasn't delighted."

"If you tell me that made you want to join the navy," Hoffman said, "I might have to punch you."

"Have you come clean with Prescott about how much fuel this is going to take?"

"He knows all the numbers. He also knows that if push comes to shove and we *don't* use the fuel—the imulsion reserves won't matter a damn."

"So this is what you did at Anvil Gate."

"It was. Except I didn't dig any holes."

"Somehow the words *booby traps* in the official reports didn't quite give me the full picture."

"I didn't write it. COG Command didn't like my version, for some reason."

Yes, this was one of the ways that Hoffman had defended Anvil Gate. It was more the principle than the exact method, but it was age-old wisdom; if you feared you might be overrun and your outer defenses breached, you needed a way to make sure that the enemy regretted it. Entering your citadel had to mean death.

It was surprisingly easy to fight that way when the time came.

There was a territorial animal inside every human being— sometimes hardly hidden, sometimes so buried that even the indi-

vidual didn't know it was there—that would turn to blind savagery
in defense of its home soil. Hoffman knew it was simply a matter
of releasing it. Enemies pouring over your ramparts was a pretty
good trigger.

"What if the stalks don't show?" Michaelson asked.

"Then we've still got good fortifications," Hoffman said.
"Which won't eat or drink anything, as Sergeant Mataki is fond of
saying."

"Is she talking to you yet?"

"Mataki?" Hoffman was all too aware that Bernie wasn't happy.
He'd have preferred a good bust-up to clear the air, but she seemed
to be at loggerheads with something else, something internal;
age, and her denial of it. If he hadn't known her better he would
have said she was suddenly scared of dying, which was an odd
thing for a Gear who faced it every moment in her job. "She
prefers the company of that goddamn dog. She even lets it sleep
on her bed now. Damn thing growls at me."

Michaelson gave him that indulgent look, an amused kind of
sympathy. "It's tempting to think we know what's best for people."

"That's the nature of command, Quentin."

"As long as we're sure we're not just doing what's best for
us. I wonder how you'll take it when Prescott retires you. In the
not-too-distant future, as well."

"I haven't *retired* Mataki. I've taken her off frontline duties
while she's recovering." Hoffman was still trying to think of a way
to climb down from his position without putting Bernie back in a
job for which she was no longer fully fit. It didn't preoccupy him
as much as he felt it should have. It had become a worry he fitted
in around the main business of the day, and he almost heard
Margaret's voice asking him when he planned to divorce her and
marry the army. "If and when we face an attack, I'll deploy her to
Pelruan to support Lieutenant Stroud."

Hoffman braced for a lecture on sending the womenfolk to
safety, but Michaelson said nothing. He knew all the various his-
tories and complications by now. Hoffman grabbed the opportunity for a change of topic.

"Baird thinks polyps won't climb vertical walls well. So we get them in the pits and we blow the crap out of them. Or we burn them. Either way—they do *not* come out again."

"But we don't know where the stalks will emerge."

"No, but we know the last place we want the polyps to go— toward humans." Hoffman tapped Michaelson's chest with his forefinger. The captain had taken to wearing the lighter naval armor, which somehow changed him from raffish to quietly menacing. The man had commanded amphibious special forces and it suddenly showed. "You just keep them away from the shore side."

"Okay, you've convinced me utterly."

"What else am I going to do, sit on my ass and do nothing because I can't predict what's going to happen?"

"No, I mean it." Michaelson caught his shoulder and turned him around to walk back to the gates of the naval base. "I *haven't* got a better idea. I'm falling back on what I know, just like you. Shore battery. Big guns. Torpedoes. Depth charges. Because nobody's ever had to fight something that can appear pretty well anywhere and dump troops in your lap. It's like fighting ghosts."

It was absolutely the right word, and yet Hoffman found himself hunching his shoulders as if hearing it physically hurt.

Sometimes Hoffman saw the naval base's gun battery as an historic but effective piece of artillery, but sometimes it was a reminder that Anvil Gate had to be faced and put to rest. There was only so long a man could obsess over his past. Everyone here had sleep-wrecking memories that would never leave them, and maybe his would look nothing special if he could experience the traumas of others.

I'm just an ordinary man. I'm not a saint, but I'm not a monster. This is where I stop beating myself up.

If he was going to be doomed to relive the siege of Anvil Gate, then he would make it work for him, not against him. He chose to see it as a training run for an even more critical battle. He would make himself think differently.

Doesn't that make a mockery of all the lives lost? Does anyone

*deserve to burn to death? Does anyone deserve to be shot for trying
to save their loved ones?*

Hoffman decided that ends did justify means, and it was a decision he'd taken unconsciously when he enlisted more than forty
years ago. The essence of soldiering was doing something bad to
stop something even worse. This time, the end was saving what
little was left of his world, and Anvil Gate was helping him do it.

"Yeah, ghosts, Quentin. Goddamn ghosts."

Prescott was holding a public meeting over in the main housing
zone. He expected his minions to show solidarity, even Trescu,
and Hoffman was prepared to indulge him if it meant a quiet life.
He was still the lawful chairman under the Fortification Act,
which had never been repealed. And he still believed utterly in
his right and capacity to govern. Hoffman could see it in every jut
of the chin and squaring of the shoulders. The man wasn't floundering, and he wasn't out of ideas. He wasn't hapless; he wasn't a
clueless bureaucrat. He just seemed to have his mind on something even more pressing. Sometimes Prescott reminded Hoffman of a man who knew he was going to fire his staff, but still
made an effort to behave impeccably right up to the moment he
showed them the door.

He was also a goddamn liar. He lied the regular way, and he
lied by omission. Hoffman still wondered how much classified
material Prescott kept from him. Prescott fed him information
that he desperately needed a crumb at a time even when Jacinto
was facing its final attack, even after the damn city had been sunk.

*He's a politician. He's a politician who still isn't scared enough
to tell me the truth and ask for help.*

There was quite a crowd at the fire muster point. The open
space had become the informal town square in this section.
Prescott walked casually into the crowd, his close protection
Gears a little way behind him, and dominated the gathering just
by the way he stood. The crowd was mainly Old Jacinto citizens,
but there were also quite a few ex-Stranded—what a goddamn
joke—and Gorasni. Trescu arrived late.

"I often wonder who the Chairman feels his security detail

needs to protect him from most." Michaelson feigned a turn to look toward Trescu, but whispered in Hoffman's ear. "The Jacinto mob, the assorted riffraff, or us."

I wish I could find a crass motive. Money. Power. Greatness. Whatever. But he's got absolute power, money means damn all now, and there's nobody left to parade his status to. He really believes it all. He really does think he's been chosen by fate to save humanity.

That was what made a politician really dangerous. There was no common animal motive for the likes of Hoffman or any other man to understand.

"We've faced the unknown before," Prescott said to the crowd. "*Many* times. Things we couldn't even begin to imagine existed. But we survived it all. We've seen nightmarish things, we've come through a terrible war—"

"Ephyra might have come through it," a Gorasni voice yelled. "But the rest of the planet—we *burned*, thanks to you, Mister Chairman Prescott. Even your allies."

"Ahhh," Michaelson said. "I wondered how long it would take for someone to point that out. They did awfully well to ignore that elephant for so long, didn't they?"

Trescu piled straight in. He was just a few strides from the heckler, and he simply walked over and cuffed him hard across the back of the head.

"I don't ask you to forgive, and I don't ask you to forget." Trescu turned to the Gorasni crowd. "But I demand that you focus on what will save our lives. We have a new war coming. You don't need to resurrect another old one."

Hoffman caught yet another glimpse of what made Gorasnaya willing to follow Trescu into a deal few of them seemed to want. Damn it, he *admired* the man. Disliking him was a totally separate issue.

Prescott seemed unruffled by the interruption. "I'm not going to pretend that I haven't had to do terrible things. And I won't lie to you and tell you we'll defeat the Lambent. I don't know if we can, any more than I knew if we could beat the Locust. All I can

do is point to the fact that we're still thriving in the face of overwhelming odds. We can do the impossible."

A handful of people clapped. Then the smattering of applause
picked up pace, and within seconds Prescott was being cheered
by most of the crowd. The bastard had the touch, he definitely
did.

Ends justify means. I shoot people: he lies.

But he hadn't. Prescott had actually leveled with the civvies.

"I've had it with moral relativity," Hoffman said. "Come on,
Quentin. Let's get back to CIC." He beckoned to Trescu as he
passed. "You too, Commander."

One of the windows of the main CIC room looked out over the
sea. Hoffman could see lookouts with their field glasses trained on
the horizon, and two radar picket boats dragging white wakes as
they patrolled the inshore limits. A Raven hovered low over the
water about five klicks out to dunk its sonar buoy. If anything was
heading this way through the water, they'd probably detect it.

Probably.

"No movement with Ollivar's flotilla, then?" Michaelson
asked. "And do you ever leave this office?"

"No to both questions, sir." Mathieson pushed his chair away
from the desk for a moment to grab a pencil from another one. "I
like it here."

"They're waiting for something," Trescu said. "I cannot imagine why."

"I take it you're handing back Nial and his father."

Trescu shrugged. "Not my prisoners. Your call, Colonel."

It was suddenly a tough decision. The Stranded were leaving.
From a security point of view, the bombers would no longer
be a threat, but they were responsible—perhaps personally,
individually—for the deaths of both Gears and Gorasni. Hoffman's sense of justice demanded that they didn't walk away free
men. And yet it seemed pointless to hold prisoners right now.

He found himself almost wishing that Trescu had solved the
problem the 9 mm way and not told him until afterward. And he
wasn't proud that he could even think it.

"Sir?" Mathieson, listening on his headset, beckoned to Hoffman. "Ollivar's vessels are moving into the MEZ. Quite a few
more hulls than we'd imagined—the Stranded contingent here
must be bigger than we thought. He wants to talk to you."

"Tell him to cut the crap and get his people out. That was the
deal." Hoffman dreaded having to let the two surviving bombers
go and then explaining that to Bernie, or any other Gear for that
matter. "Tell him no torpedoes up the ass this time, if that's what
he's worried about."

Mathieson went off the channel for a moment. "Sir, he's insistent."

*One last gloat about the end of the COG. They can never resist
it.* "Very well. Patch him through."

"Hoffman? Tell us where you need us," Ollivar said.

"You arrange your own RV point, Ollivar."

"No, we're landing troops," Ollivar said. "And don't think this
is some heart-of-gold moralizing shit where I do the heroic forgiveness thing because I don't want to descend to your level. This
is just survival. We'll fight those things *with* you, because if we
don't, they'll just come for us after they've wiped you off the map."

Well, shit. Hoffman would need every rifle, lookout, and pair
of hands he could get. His honor didn't feel compromised and he
didn't feel the need to consult Prescott.

*I'm a warfighter. I'm here to win. What else is there to worry
about except whether humankind is still here tomorrow, next week,
next year?*

The only thing he balked at was hearing these scum call themselves soldiers. But he'd swallow that for the time being.

Trescu shrugged. "About time they put something useful into
the fight. Go on. Let them."

Hoffman went as his gut guided him and pressed his earpiece
to answer. "Okay, Ollivar, you might want to spread your vessels
around," he said. "In case we lose the docks. Other than that—
disembark your men at the jetty next to the carriers, and Sergeant
Fenix will meet you. We have a plan."

Michaelson had plenty of free berths. He gave Hoffman a
thumbs-up.

"Oh, good," Ollivar said sourly. "All square-jawed noble infantry stuff."

"No," said Hoffman. "Dirty warfare. As dirty as it gets."

The Lambent were the kind of enemy he preferred. There were no rules of engagement for absolute, literal monsters.

All he had to do was wipe them out and forget they ever existed. They would never nag at his conscience.

NAVAL BASE STORES, TWO DAYS LATER.

They needed anything that would burn.

In a world of desperate shortages, Dom had learned never to throw anything away. There was no garbage. There were only things that had to be reused, from fabric to old cooking oil to human waste for fertilizer. Food scraps went to the pigs and chickens; used paper was pulped and bleached repeatedly until the end product was useless for writing on. Then it would be shredded for insulation or made into ragged, uneven pieces of bathroom tissue. The idea of finding stuff specifically for burning was a whole new habit to learn.

Dom explored the warren of stores cut into the rock under the naval base, feeling vaguely uneasy in the way he did when he entered tunnels. At least he had a rational reason now. The grubs might have been gone, but a stalk that could come up in the middle of a new volcanic island could do exactly the same right here.

"Hey, Marcus? You down here?"

Dom's voice echoed. The tunnels and chambers leading off them were built along the same lines as the ones under Port Farrall, probably because they dated from the same era. There were plenty of old ammo crates that would burn well with a little tar. There would probably be all kinds of stuff soaked in oils and lubricants, too. It would all go up in smoke easily enough.

"In here," Marcus called. "End of the tunnel through the painted doors. Don't go right."

Dom found Marcus in a storeroom lined from floor to ceiling with shelves full of box folders with damp-faded labels on the spine. Marcus was sitting on an upturned box, rifling through piles of papers.

"Archives," he said. "Some of these date back centuries."

Dom peered at the labels along the shelves. The ink on most of them had faded to gray and sepia, and the handwritten dates and titles were sloping and ornate, the formal penmanship of another era. The files were carefully arranged by year.

"Okay, this would burn great," Dom said carefully. "But I'd feel really bad about it."

"Me too. Shit. Imagine what's in here."

It was just as well Baird wasn't down here. The archives were probably full of all kinds of engineering detail. He would have gone berserk at the idea of setting fire to it. Dom felt like a vandal for even thinking about it.

"We could leave it," Dom said. "Loads of wood and other combustibles down here."

Marcus didn't answer. He'd picked up a bound book about fifty centimeters across—an old ledger with a leather cover and a gold-blocked title. When he balanced it on his knee to open it, Dom read VISITOR SECURITY LOG on the cover. Marcus leafed through the pages and then stopped for a moment.

"Shit," he said.

That could have meant anything from the end of the world to pleasant surprise. Dom guessed it wasn't the latter.

"What is it?"

Marcus didn't answer. He just moved on to the next pile of paper, leaving the visitor log open on the floor. Dom squatted to take a look.

It was about halfway down the list, a name written in careful block capitals and then followed by a signature in a different and more confident hand. The date beside it was more than twenty years old.

NAME: FENIX, DR. A.

VISITING: MAJ. SHARMAN, COB 3. EXT: 665.

Dom knew Marcus's father had visited Vectes when it was a bioweapons research facility, and so did Marcus. The mayor of Pelruan had told them. But that wasn't quite the same as seeing your dead father's handwriting, unexpected and out of context. That kind of reminder of the dead punched above its weight.

Adam Fenix's life was a disjointed series of snapshots that Marcus still seemed to be putting together from things that popped up where he least expected them, from small personal stuff like this to finding those unexplained audio recordings in the Locust computer. Adam Fenix never told his son things, and even lied about others—by omission, yes, but that was still lying as far as Dom was concerned, and he knew Marcus felt the same. It was years before Marcus found out why his mother had gone missing. His father had kept it from him. Dom knew the Fenix family as well as anyone could, and it still shocked him that a man could hide so much from his son, his only child. Dom would never have done anything like that to Benedicto. He was damned sure of it.

"You okay, Marcus?" he said.

"Yeah." It was a rasping sigh as much as anything. "Even when he's dead, I still get surprises."

Dom would have torn out the page and kept it if it had been his own father's handwriting. It would have been the last precious link to the man himself, something he had touched and shaped. Marcus just picked up the book, closed it, and put it to one side.

"So what else have we got?" he said, as if nothing had happened. "Anyone collecting the wood shavings from the lumberyard?"

They'd been as close as brothers since childhood. Dom knew Marcus as well as he'd ever known anyone. But sometimes Dom still had to stop himself asking the one question he knew Marcus would never answer: *Do you want to talk about it?*

Marcus never wanted to talk about anything. It would have been pointless to ask. If he needed to, he knew by now that Dom was always there.

"I'll go see what we're piling up," Dom said. "Someone's got to stop them burning the bathroom tissue. A guy has his limits."

Marcus jogged down the passage ahead of him. "Got to brief Ollivar's irregulars with Hoffman."

He disappeared down the dimly lit tunnel. Dom heard his boots clatter up the stone steps to the ground floor.

Reminders of the dead were everywhere, even the ones that you were sure didn't affect you any longer. In the locker room later that afternoon, Dom caught sight of his tattoo in the mirror—a heart with Maria's name on it. Even if he could have had it removed, he wouldn't have. But it felt all wrong now, as if he was still pretending she wasn't dead, like the occasional days when he still felt the urge to do what he'd done for ten solid years—to take out her picture and show it to anyone who might recognize her and tell him that they'd seen her.

There was no single act of closure, he knew. He knew it from the deaths of his kids, and his parents, and pretty well everyone he'd grown up with. It was a gradual process for him. He had Maria's necklace; now he needed to move on another step and deal with the tattoo.

He changed into his civvie clothes and went looking for Sam. She was taking a break in the mess, drinking with Dizzy. It was nice to see them getting on.

"I hear you're pretty good with ink," he said.

Sam gave him that sideways look. "Yes. You want something done?"

"I think so."

"So—traditional Kashkuri stuff? South Islander?"

"Can you change an existing tattoo?"

Sam looked thoughtful. "Possibly. Depends."

"You gonna need some of Doctor Wallin's special anesthetic?" Dizzy held out a small bottle of moonshine. "Guarantee you won't feel a thing if she saws your damn head off."

"I'll get numb later," Dom said. "Thanks, Dizzy."

"Okay." Sam slid off the seat and beckoned Dom to follow. "Better do it now, before we both chicken out. I'll get my stuff."

Dom found a storeroom in the barracks. He didn't want anyone watching, even by accident. He rolled his sleeve back as far as he could and offered his right biceps.

"Okay, you're going to have to talk me through this," Sam said, opening a small bag like a cosmetic case. "What exactly do you want done?"

"I don't know," he said. "But she's gone, and I need to mark that somehow."

Dom knew that Sam's up-yours attitude wasn't the whole woman. Somebody named after a dead-hero father they'd never known would understand all the confusing, painful feelings that Dom still carried around with him. Sam studied the stylized heart and then nodded.

"You ready to trust me on this, Dom?"

"Go ahead."

It took a long time without a powered needle and it hurt more than he remembered. He didn't want to watch her do it, either. When he finally looked, not knowing what effect it would have on him but knowing he wanted *something* to change, it made his throat tighten.

Sam really was good at this kind of thing. Gifted, in fact.

The tattoo and all it stood for had been transformed. If Dom hadn't known it had once been a heart, he would only have seen the angel cradling Maria's name, wings folded, eyes raised toward something infinite and certain.

He couldn't have told Sam what he wanted. But somehow it felt like he'd seen it that way from the start. He'd wear his sleeves rolled down for a couple of days to hide the dressing, not that anyone would have pestered him with questions about it.

"I owe you," he said.

Sam turned in the doorway. "No, you don't," she said. "That's for making my day."

The base was now settling into a quiet waiting game. The sound of vehicle motors and grinding gearboxes continued late into the evening, throwing up a halo of hazy light beyond the ancient walls as the diggers raced to complete the network of pits and trenches. The only ships moving were the NCOG patrols. Even the Ravens were few and far between. Dom sat on a bollard by the jetty, watching navigation lights pass overhead and the black patch of helicopter-shaped nothing as one of the birds blotted out the stars.

"We love this, don't we, baby?" Cole walked up and stood con-

templating the docks with him. "At our best when we're waitin'
for the shit to start. All match-fit and ready to go."

"Wonder when we'll ever shake that off."

"Wonder when we're ever gonna get the *chance*."

"Where's Baird?"

"Weldin' shit. Pipes. So they can flood the pits with fuel and
bake some glowie crab. Man, that boy's creative in all the *wrong*
ways. But I ain't complainin'."

"What are the civvies going to do if it all kicks off? We haven't
got enough spare rifles to arm one percent of them, even if they
knew how to use them."

"Then we better make sure we stop the glowies. That's all we
got."

*No point evacuating the civvies inland, because the stalks can
come up any damn place. No point making them rough it in the
woods, because they'll be even more afraid and disoriented. No
point doing anything except wait—because we just don't know
what's coming around the corner, or even if it's coming at all.*

The next day was quiet, too, and the next, and the day after
that. Dom did perimeter patrols as normal, and rode with the
twice-daily Raven recon flight. *Clement* and *Zephyr* were paired
up now, doing a sonar sweep around the island.

There was no sign of stalks or polyps. It was almost as if they'd
tested out the COG, found they got a kicking, and moved on elsewhere.

But Dom didn't believe that a life-form that could give the
grubs nightmares would quit that easily. The most he could hope
for was that if they were as dumb and instinct-driven as some
thought, then they'd latched on to some other scent. But it would
just be a temporary respite, like all the other quiet moments in
the war.

The bastards were just getting their breath back.

Meanwhile, the coastline to the west was crawling with extra
Stranded. Bernie walked the perimeter with Mac most of the day,
Lancer slung across her chest and her Longshot on her back,
making it clear that it wasn't polyps she was keeping an eye open

for. Dom waved to her from the 'Dill's hatch as it headed back through the main camp. She gave him a meaningful nod.

"I just hope she doesn't cap anyone," Dom said to Baird.

"What?"

Dom dipped down inside the cabin. Baird was driving, listening to two radio channels at once.

"I said, I hope Bernie doesn't shoot any more Stranded and start a riot."

"Killjoy. What else has she got left at her time of life, except mutilating assholes and giving Hoffman a gruesome time?"

"Baird, shut up, will you?"

"Hey, want to listen to the submarine net? I rigged my radio so I can hear their transmissions."

"Damn, you're *stalking* those boats."

Baird just shrugged. He parked the 'Dill in the compound and stayed in the driver's seat, listening to the chatter. Dom decided that was how he coped with being scared—making things and staying busy the whole time, as if that gave him some control over his fate in a chaotic world. Dom hung back for a moment, trying to think of something placatory to say. It was really hard to do the buddy thing with Baird.

"Whales," Baird said.

"What?"

"*Zephyr's* reporting a pod of whales singing on the hydrophone."

"Well, that's nice and relaxing for them."

Baird frowned. He was concentrating on something, not even looking at Dom. Then he sat upright.

"Shit," he said. "Unidentified biologic."

"Stalks?"

"No, something swimming, uncatalogued. They've pinged it with the sonar."

"Isn't that going to piss it off?"

"Pissing it off is better than not seeing it coming." Baird just sat there, listening. Dom watched his expression change. "Squid, maybe."

"Leviathan." A few months ago, a leviathan was the worst thing

Dom could imagine finding underwater. They were another act in the grub freak show, a whale-sized mountain of scaly flesh with teeth and lethal tentacles. Now he was seeing it as preferable to the stalk and polyp combo. At least leviathans stuck to the water. "Hey, they understand how big those things are, don't they?"

Baird fiddled with the radio. The channel he was listening to suddenly burst over the 'Dill's speaker, a conversation between a Gorasni and Tyran voices.

"*Clement*, we still have the biologic. Bearing zero-eight-five, depth sixty meters. Moving *above* us."

"Roger that, *Zephyr*. *Clement* to KR-Six-Seven, unknown biologic approximately ten kilometers south of you. I'm trying to get a side scan. Stand by."

"They ought to make me an admiral," Baird muttered. He'd been bragging all week about how great his sonar gizmo was. "A commodore, at least."

It took a few moments for *Clement* to come back on the net. The voice was Commander Garcia's; steady, but definitely not relaxed this time.

"Well . . . that's a face only a mother could love," he said. "Tentacles . . . whale-sized . . . I'll assume that's a leviathan. Moving north to Vectes. Signal all inshore vessels to return to harbor and stand by."

"Great," Dom said. "Maybe it'll wrestle the stalks."

"Knowing our luck," Baird said, "it'll lose."

CHAPTER 15

Rest in peace, and fear not.

(TRADITIONAL INSCRIPTION ON COG WAR GRAVES)

Bernie checked the Packhorse's rearview mirror to make sure Sam Byrne was still following on the bike. Every time she glanced up, she expected to find that Sam had peeled off in search of something more demanding than guarding a fishing village.

Don't blame you, girl. I don't like being packed off to a safe billet when there's real work I could do, either.

"Going home to your dad, Mac," she said. The dog sat in the passenger seat beside her, occasionally sticking his muzzle out the open window. "He'll be pleased to see you. You'll forget all about me, won't you?"

"Your channel's open," Sam said.

Bernie didn't care. "So I talk to the dog. I get more sense out of him than I do most humans." She switched the radio to standby. "Let's see how Anya's been getting on."

Pelruan depressed Bernie more every time she saw it. It got her down because it was picturesque and peaceful, even with the ditches and razor wire that Rossi's squad had put around its boundaries. It should have been left alone to carry on in happy ignorance in its grub-free backwater. Some Gears—and civvies—felt it was high time the locals understood what the rest of Sera had endured for so long, but some just felt sorry for the poor bewildered bastards.

Yeah, I do. I wouldn't have taken this half as well as they have.

Anya was waiting for her when she drove up to the collection of huts that served as the barracks and admin office. She really did look a lot like her mother these days, especially now that she'd taken to wearing armor. She glanced past the Packhorse for a moment as Sam roared to a halt on the bike.

Bernie opened the vehicle door for Mac. He jumped out and inspected Anya's boots for interesting scents. "How are you, ma'am?"

"All very quiet." Anya kept a wary eye on Mac. "Rossi's a safe pair of hands, so I haven't screwed up and started any riots yet. I hear we've got some interesting wildlife around."

"Stalks? Stranded?"

"Leviathan. Haven't you heard?"

"I've only been monitoring my own channel on the way here." There was no reason for Bernie to be flashed with a message like that anyway, but she still felt discarded and irrelevant. "Anything I need to know?"

"The submarines just pinged one. All vessels have been ordered back to berth and all crews ashore. I've just been recalling the fishing boats."

"I didn't realize they were still working."

"They do some line fishing close to the shore." Anya indicated down the road. "You've got a choice of billet, by the way. Will Berenz or Ellen's bar."

"Well, that's an easy one, isn't it, Mac?" Bernie grabbed her backpack and set off. She knew the way. The dog trotted ahead of her. "See you in the signals office in about half an hour, ma'am."

Sam surveyed the narrow streets between the wooden houses as they walked. "This would really burn."

"What?"

"I always think that when I see wooden buildings. They burn too easily. My mother always told me how Anvegad burned." Sam looked embarrassed for a moment. That wasn't like her at all. "Funny how things take root in your mind."

Hoffman still hadn't finished telling Bernie about Anvil Gate. There was always something that interrupted, and they hadn't had a moment on their own in days. Maybe he'd forget all about it. And maybe Sam knew enough to fill in the gaps.

The older Bernie got, the more the past became her most vivid focus. Maybe the past really did matter that much, or maybe that was just the way the brain aged, giving up trying to access the short-term stuff and seeking comfort and vindication in the memories it had put away safely years ago.

And then there were parts of the past that simply wouldn't let go even when she wanted to run from them. They were all around her now in this tourist-brochure fishing village. There was a war memorial in the middle of the well-trimmed grass square outside the town hall, a square-section tapered granite pillar with the Coalition's cog-and-eagle emblem on top.

Bernie always paused to stand to attention and bow her head at any memorial she passed. Every Gear of her generation did. It was automatic. If she had time, she would stop and read the names carved there, too, because that was the whole point: that these men and women were never forgotten, even if their families and friends were long gone. Names mattered. They needed seeing and saying.

Nobody's ever really dead unless we forget them. That was what Cole always said.

Sam stopped beside her. From the corner of her eye, Bernie could see her shuffle uncertainly, as if she'd never done this, and then follow Bernie's lead. Mac stopped too.

The regiments represented were mainly the Duke of Tollen's and the Andius Fusiliers, with a few NCOG Corps of Marines. Someone had tied a sash in Tollen colors around the column and laid a laurel wreath topped with the Tollen badge at its foot. Bernie had passed the memorial before and not seen the sash, so she wondered if it had been put there for some local anniversary or specific battle commemoration she wasn't aware of. Then Sam nudged her elbow.

"They really don't like the Gorasni, do they?" she said.

It took Bernie a few moments to see what Sam was looking at. Someone had left a card on the wreath, neatly handwritten, and she squatted to read it.

> THE SURVIVORS OF RAMASCU.
>
> WE WILL NEVER FORGET.
>
> WE WILL NEVER FORGIVE.

"Prescott better scrub the joint parade for the Day of the Fallen, then," Bernie said. "He tends to think people can kiss and make up."

Sam stared at the card for a few moments, then saluted and walked away.

"Who did *you* lose?" she asked. "Particularly, I mean."

Everyone had lost almost everybody they cared about. If someone asked that question, they wanted to know which death still gnawed at you most.

"Hard to say," Bernie said. "Depends on the day. Sometimes it's my brother, because we never got on. Mostly it's Gears I served with. I don't have that many special ghosts. I'm lucky."

Sam made a noncommittal *hfff* sound. Yes, Bernie knew she was lucky; she didn't lie awake at night thinking what might have been about the dead. The only thought that plagued her now was dying before she saw things on Sera starting to improve.

"You've spoiled that dog," Will Berenz said, opening the front door. "Look at him. He's put on weight."

"He works hard. He needs to keep his strength up." Bernie bent over and cuddled Mac, then made sure that Sam was out of earshot. "Everything okay here?"

"If you're asking how Lieutenant Stroud's coping, she's very efficient. People here trust her. Good start."

"I realize they're unhappy about the various allies we've had to

make. But there's some serious trouble out there now. We need
every rifle we can get."

Berenz looked crushed, as if he didn't need reminding. "We
were on borrowed time for so long, weren't we?"

"Will, we're going to survive." Bernie gripped his shoulder to
make her point. "I don't know how, but we're going to beat this.
Okay?"

She had no idea why she said that, other than she desperately
wanted to believe it. Everyone on the island had beaten incredi-
ble odds just to stay alive, though. It wasn't unreasonable to think
they could keep doing it.

"Okay," Berenz said. "You'd tell me if we were beaten. I know
you would."

There was a fine line between strengthening morale and giving
people false hope, but Bernie was never sure on which side of it
she fell on any given day. When she got back to the signals office
with Sam, Drew Rossi was monitoring the radio, nursing a cup of
coffee that looked stone cold. They made the drink from some
kind of roasted barley. Bernie wasn't sure she remembered what
real coffee tasted like anymore, but she was pretty sure it didn't
taste like that.

Rossi looked up. "A faraway island's a great idea until somebody finds it, isn't it? And then it's just somewhere you're stuck
with nowhere to run."

"Very uplifting, Drew. You should join Baird's morale committee."

"So what brings you two ladies up here?"

"Banished to the soft option," Sam said. "With the rest of you
girls."

Rossi took it in his stride. He was a likeable man, just another
Gear who took refuge in griping. "No stalks yet, then. So far, the
biggest task is keeping the fishermen inshore. They're sliding further out a few meters at a time."

"Okay, with the assorted wildlife on the loose out there, you're
going to want us on patrol, yes?"

Rossi tapped his temple in a mock salute. "Yes, Sergeant."

"Come on, Drew, I'm not trying to out-sergeant you. I'm just not used to being the spare prick at the wedding."

"Hey, no problem." He cocked his head to one side. "If it was the other way around, you'd stick *him* at a desk, too. We all get to the point where we can't face losing one more person we care about. Shit, even the ones we *don't* care about. Anybody."

Rossi didn't have to say who "he" was. The army was a gossip shop, and the smaller it got, the less escaped its attention. Bernie went off to start the route around town, Sam following.

"I'll monitor the local net," Sam said. "You keep an ear on Control."

There was one advantage to patrolling Pelruan—visibility. It was small, low-rise, and there were a couple of points around the place where you had a panoramic view of the whole town. And there was no underground city of tunnels to worry about, either. If anything popped up here, they'd see it right away.

It's just a question of what we can do about it if it does. Twenty Gears, some dogs, and a mostly unarmed population that's never fought a grub, let alone dealt with Lambent. Great.

To the western side of the town, there was a flat-topped cliff the Ravens sometimes used as a landing pad. The view from there had almost no blind spots. Rossi's squad had built a small observation post up there as shelter against the constant wind. Bernie and Sam walked up the long slope and stood there for a while, familiarizing themselves with the detail below.

Sam turned to face the sea. "Shit. If I turn at this angle, it looks as if there's nothing left on Sera except the ocean."

"Lonely spot."

"Yes." Sam raised her binoculars. "It is."

Life went on below, probably the same as it had for decades except for the defensive ditches and garlands of razor wire put in place to deter a two-legged enemy. Bernie found herself looking south and wondering if she'd ever want to go home to Galangi again.

"Hey, Bernie, take a look."

Bernie turned and followed Sam's line of sight out to sea. She strained to spot the outline of a stalk, but there was nothing like that out there.

"What is it?"

Sam handed her the binoculars. "Line up with the pile of fishing floats on the slipway and elevate fifty degrees. Track right to left."

Bernie didn't see anything at first, then Sam said, "There it is again," and the movement passed in front of her focus.

Something was swimming out there at a leisurely pace, breaking the water in a slow, wavelike motion like a porpoise. It *could* have been porpoises, of course. There was a lot more regular life in the ocean now that most of the human population had been wiped out. Those two ratios seemed to go hand in hand. But the longer Bernie looked, the more she decided it was a single large creature, and it wasn't a whale.

She lowered the binoculars and got on the radio. "Control, this is Mataki at Pelruan. Contact—possible leviathan, two to three kilometers offshore. Might be the same one, if they can move that fast, or it might be its mate. Have you still got a fix on yours?"

"Negative, *Clement* lost contact with it," Mathieson said. "Thanks for the heads-up."

"Okay," Sam said. "I just let Stroud know. She's making sure everyone's back on dry land."

The warning sirens positioned around the town let out three long, wailing bursts, sparking a flurry of activity. Nobody seemed to be out fishing, but crews ran down to the beach to haul the shore-launched boats farther up the pebbles. There was nothing they could do about the trawlers moored in the harbor. The fishermen just had to hope the leviathan didn't venture into shallower water.

Bernie tried to locate the creature again, but she couldn't see it. That was the problem with looking away from the sea for a few moments. Sam shook her head.

"No idea where it's gone," she said. "They must have escaped from the Locust tunnels when we flooded Jacinto. They're making the most of their freedom."

Bernie had never thought about monsters that way before. But half the creatures the COG had come across back on the land seemed to be dumb animals that the Locust had adapted for their own use, all kinds of things that probably didn't have the brains on their own to plan attacks on humans. When she stopped to think about it, it was nightmarish.

Mac was back with Berenz, probably dozing in his kennel or just being a dog with the rest of the pack. She wondered if grubs grew fond of their beasts and let them sleep on their beds—did they even *have* beds?—then set off down the slope to walk around the harbor.

The coast around Pelruan was all headlands and bays, getting steeper and more spectacular further from the town. Bernie was starting to imagine a life where they never went to sea or left the island, a life pretty much like the one she'd known as a child. She stood looking out to sea, ten meters up the beach, and heard a distant helicopter over the sound of the waves hitting the pebbles.

Movement in the water caught her eye. She scanned the choppy water. A column of dark, shiny scales rose from nowhere out of the waves, so fast and silent that she froze for a second and couldn't take in what she was looking at. Then it crashed down on the water like a breaching whale, raining spray on the beach. She'd aimed her rifle before her brain had worked out what the thing was.

Sam inhaled sharply, backing away with her Lancer raised. "Shit."

"Where is it?" Bernie got her voice back. "Where'd it go?"

Leviathans stuck to the water. Dom said they had tentacles, so as long as she kept well clear of the waterline, it was fine. It was okay. It wasn't coming ashore. It wasn't a stalk.

"There." Sam pointed. The tip of a tentacle lashed out of the sea. "Bravo Control, this is Byrne—we've got a leviathan inshore, in the harbor. Anyone got a *really* fucking big harpoon?"

"Bravo Control to Byrne, I'm calling in a KR unit. Stand by."

The tentacle rose out of the water again, and then the head followed. It was the first clue Bernie had that things had gone even worse than horribly wrong. It was bad enough seeing the open maw for the first time. But there were luminous blisters on the thing's face, like lights, and then all the scales shook off the huge tentacle and landed on the shingle like the creature had shaken off a terrible infestation of lice.

Except they weren't lice. They were dog-sized and they scuttled up the shore.

Bernie hadn't seen a live polyp before. Baird's descriptions and the grainy recon pictures that one of the Ravens had taken on the imulsion rig didn't cement the thing in her mind. She wondered what the hell all these crabs were doing coming up the beach, and then reality kicked in. They were knee-high. And even in broad daylight, she could see the luminescence. She opened fire into the seething mass, setting off detonations that splattered the things everywhere. Sam went wide and opened fire to stop them swarming past and surrounding her.

Stalks. They're supposed to come out of the stalks.

Where are the frigging stalks?

"Sam, fall back! Call Rossi!" Bernie wasn't sure if her mike was open or which Control could hear her now. "Tell him the bloody polyps are here, no stalks, just a leviathan—a Lambent one."

Bernie emptied her magazine into the polyps, then turned and sprinted to the quayside to get some height over them, reloading as she went. She was only concentrating on the ranks of creatures right in front of her. She couldn't see if there was an endless stream of them, but she could hear Sam running along the pebbles and firing long bursts. All Bernie knew was that if she stopped and looked away from that squirming carpet of legs and fangs, if she lost her concentration for a moment, she'd be dead.

Suddenly more automatic fire started up from her right. She had to reload, and when she let herself look up for a second she saw Rossi, Anya, three helmeted Gears she couldn't recognize, and a few of the locals with shotguns, all letting rip into the invasion of polyps.

"KR-Three-Three inbound," said a voice in her earpiece.

"Bravo Control, if you folks in the harbor want to thin out, we'll hose them from here."

It was Eldon Rorry and his door gunner, Braley. You could always rely on the Raven crews, Bernie thought. The helicopter banked over her head—low enough for her to see the ammo belt in detail and the reflection off Dav Braley's goggles—and hovered on the seaward side of the polyp invasion. Everyone ran for it. Bernie took cover behind a stack of cable drums that wouldn't have stopped a round at all, and then she saw for herself just how lethal the polyps were.

Braley kept up a stream of fire on the polyps below. But a tentacle rose slowly out of the water. Bernie yelled and waved frantically to get the crew's attention, expecting the tentacle to lift and smash the chopper down into the harbor, but instead it simply flicked as if it was shaking off water. A mass of polyps was catapulted into the crew bay. One went clean through and skidded out the other side, but the rest—

The explosion sent a fireball high into the air.

Bernie's instinct was to duck as metal fragments and whirling chunks of rotor blade shot in all directions. It took her a couple of seconds to look up, hoping it would be a mistake and there'd still be a Raven hovering there, but there wasn't. There was just burning fuel on the water, a lot of smoke, and the tail section slowly turning in the sea before it sank.

But she went on firing. Instinct took over as it always did, and she simply found her targets and killed them until she ran out of ammo and had to reload. She couldn't stop, not even for dead friends.

The firing around her eventually slowed to a stop. The shore fell absolutely silent except for screeching gulls, and she was still too flooded with adrenaline to take in the bigger picture, but she focused on the shocked, chalk-white faces of Rossi and Anya.

"Ahh *fuck*." Rossi turned to Anya. "Lieutenant, we have to sink that leviathan before it lands more polyps."

"Where is it?" Bernie said. "Where the hell has the thing gone?"

It was typical, shitty, rotten luck.

They were ready for an attack at New Jacinto. Now the first strike was at the other end of the island. Baird had been convinced that the assorted Lambent menagerie was following imulsion in the water, and maybe it was, but it had followed it to the least likely place.

I'm guessing. Everyone's guessing. We didn't have a clue what the frigging grubs were or what they wanted—and maybe we still don't. How much can they expect me to work out about glowies?

Nobody gave him a hard time about it. Cole was standing in KR-239's crew bay talking to Mitchell, occasionally patting his shoulder. They hadn't lost a Raven for some time, and the fate of KR-33 seemed to have shaken all the crews as the news rippled around the comms net.

Dom bent his head, straining to listen to the voice traffic as he waited to board the Raven. The alert siren was still wailing at an ear-bleeding volume.

"Okay, they're pretty sure they've killed all the polyps," he said. "No sign of the leviathan. Shit, are these things going to hitch a ride on everything? Are they parasites or something?"

"No idea. Where's Marcus?"

"Over there." The siren stopped and Dom rolled his head in exasperation. "Thank fuck that's stopped. Oh, and don't ask."

"Why?" Baird turned around. Marcus and Hoffman were almost nose to nose, having a heated but low-volume exchange about something. "Okay. I get it."

Baird could guess. He knew the history between those two. It was just a case of working out which of them was telling the other that he couldn't race off and save a woman just because he felt like it. Suddenly they turned away from each other and jogged in different directions, Hoffman heading for the dock and Marcus running to the Raven.

"I'm getting the picture now." Baird climbed into the crew bay and strapped himself in. He had to come up with some answers. He was starting to doubt himself for the first time. "The glowie grubs. The mutating exploding Brumak. Now the glowie leviathan. What's the common thread?"

Cole broke off his conversation with Mitchell and gave Baird his mildly disapproving look. "Baby, I gave up biology class when I was in short pants. Too many dead things floatin' in jars."

"It's *mutagenic.*"

"That don't sound healthy."

"Remember the luminous snot in the tunnels?"

"Yeah, one of my treasured memories."

"I bet it's an infection."

"So what was that glowie shit flyin' around on its own? See, flyin' snot don't sound like *infection* to me. Sounds like a *thing.*"

Cole might have quit biology class, but there was nothing wrong with his powers of observation or logic. Baird couldn't answer that one. Yes, the luminous stuff had evaporated from dead Lambent grubs like some kind of vapor and then shot off at speed.

Air currents. That's all. Just because something moves, it doesn't mean it decides where it's going.

Marcus put one boot on the sill of the bay. "Let's go sink that thing now before we lose it. Hoffman's scrambling the standby squads. That includes Ollivar's men."

"If I was Gorasni, I wouldn't turn my back on them," Baird said.

Marcus shrugged. "Take a look. Side by side."

"All pals together."

"I wouldn't go that far."

The alert siren started wailing again. Dom shut his eyes. "Shit, somebody *turn that thing off.*"

"That's a new alert." Mitchell fiddled with his headset. "Stand by."

Marcus was getting agitated. The signs were subliminal compared to a regular guy's, but Baird had learned to spot them. Instead of getting more restless, he seemed to shut down all nonessential movement and even erase any expression. It was as if he was making a conscious effort to lock down and not let anyone else see he was running out of patience.

Yeah, he's worried about Anya. You're not fooling anyone, Marcus . . .

"Control to all call signs." Mathieson had become the Voice of It's-All-Going-To-Be-Okay since Anya had moved on to infantry duty. He'd really got that tone down pat: calm, even reassuring, but with just enough steel to make it clear that shit was on an intercept course with the fan, and that he was telling everyone the holy truth. It was quite an art. "Message relayed from one of Ollivar's units—leviathan spotted heading south about two klicks off the western coast. All call signs, *stand to.*"

Delta's stand-to position—the place they were supposed to go if an attack started—was at the vehicle compound, ready to mount up and deploy by 'Dill to wherever the stalks first made landfall. Now they were dealing with a thing that was cruising around the coast and would lob its polyps ashore. The whole plan had gone down the pan in minutes.

"Hang on, do they still want us in Pelruan, or has that been scrubbed?" Dom asked. "Control, this is Santiago—what are we tasked to do now?"

"Normal stand-to position," Mathieson said. "Pelruan's clear. The leviathan's coming this way. KR units, get airborne and stand by. Rig drivers—get started."

"That leviathan must be turbocharged." Baird did a quick calculation in his head as he jogged after Marcus. "Maybe it could swim the length of the island in *hours,* but we're talking maybe *thirty or forty minutes* here. Not possible."

"They glow, too," Dom said. "They're not *normal,* Baird."

"Why does no asshole listen to me?"

He thought Marcus was out of earshot, finger pressed to his ear as he talked on the radio. But he stopped and turned.

"Baird, where do you think this thing is going to front up?"

At least Marcus knows who's got the functioning brain in the squad.

"If it does what it did at Pelruan, it'll come into the harbor," Baird said, feeling a little useless now. He hated not having real answers. "No idea why. Maybe it's trying to shed the polyps. Or maybe they'll hitch a ride on anything until it happens to get close to dry land. I can't tell."

"Good enough," Marcus said. "Control—you getting this? They'll probably come ashore over the walls and the jetties."

Hoffman's voice cut in. "All call signs—remember we want to *channel* these things, Gears. If there's more than we can kill out-right, then we channel them to the pits. You let them through. However hard you want to stop them—you *let them through*. We trap them and we kill them. Keep your nerve."

"Where's the other one?" Baird said. "That thing can't do a hundred and fifty klicks an hour. There's *two*. There's got to be two."

Marcus was jogging ahead of Baird. All Baird could see was his back, but he definitely reacted to that, as if he either realized and didn't want to be reminded, or hadn't thought through the tim-ings. He didn't respond for a couple of seconds.

"If it's got a buddy," Marcus said, "there's fuck-all we can do about it right now."

Cole headed Baird off like a sheepdog. "Baby, don't remind him that Anya's in the shit, okay?"

"Hey, we're *all* in the shit. You think this plan of Hoffman's is going to work?"

"Gonna work about as well as taking potshots at 'em one by one until we run out of ammo."

"Who's going to be the lure, then? Us."

"That's the way it is."

"And where's Hoffman when all this is going down?"

"Right behind you, Corporal." Hoffman's bark made Baird nearly crap himself. And it wasn't over the radio.

Baird turned to see Hoffman jogging a few strides behind him, Lancer clutched to his chest, looking homicidal. Baird regarded all officers as parasites, moved rung by rung up the promotional ladder until they couldn't do any more hands-on damage, but

Hoffman was a different animal. It was written all over him: he'd joined the army to fight, nothing more, and the whole officer thing had just ambushed him. He stuck with it because it was his duty. He'd keep on doing it until it killed him. He was Chief of Defense Staff by default because everyone else above him was dead, and rank meant less than nothing these days.

"Beats a desk job," Baird said.

"*Any* day," Hoffman grunted.

Baird took up position on the long quay that ran almost half the width of the base. Ahead of him, the navy's last remaining Raven's Nest carriers stretched along the deep-water jetty like a bridge. Two destroyers, *Fenmont* and *Vale of Dane*, had shifted position and were now sitting with guns aimed west.

Hoffman paced up and down behind the line of Gears, talking to someone on the radio—Michaelson, Baird assumed, judging by what he could hear.

"Then you'll just have to make sure you drive them *away* from the goddamn ships, won't you?" Hoffman sounded more weary than angry for once. "We can't predict which way these bastards are going to run. We'll all have to *force* them."

Everything suddenly went quiet. Baird never liked this lull. His gut shriveled into a hard ball and a burning cold sensation spread through his thigh muscles. It would pass, but he was sure he really was going to piss himself one day just like Cole told everyone he did.

Then the shout went up. Somewhere on the walls above, a lookout yelled: "Contact—one-six-zero, range five hundred meters, too close for the cannon—it's coming around the cliff."

Baird saw the flash from *Fenmont*'s guns even before he heard the boom. He didn't see the leviathan until it reared up again and dived down below the surface. Only parts of it were visible, a couple of undulating humps trailing foam, a tentacle or two as it rolled, even a glimpse of its head, but one thing was clear—it was even bigger than he'd thought, and he'd thought pretty big. *Vale of Dane* put on a spurt and raked the water with her 30 mm close-in defensive gun. For a few moments nothing broke the surface.

Too good to be true. Can't be.

And it wasn't. There was a deep metallic thud followed by a slow grinding sound, and Baird couldn't even tell where it was coming from until *Fenmont*'s bow lifted meters out of the water. She hung there for a second before crashing back down with a groaning, tearing noise. The ship listed to port just as the leviathan surged out of the sea and smashed down onto the deck.

"Don't think a chainsaw's going to work this time," Marcus said. "Let's pick on something smaller."

The leviathan turned toward the quay and plunged under the surface. There were only two options now; to stand and fight, or turn and run. Baird found he couldn't move. The creature rose out of the water right in front of him to fill his field of vision, so close that he couldn't even see the tentacles at its sides. And it stank like the tide had gone out. He heard the wet slaps and frantic scrabbling of polyps, and then the firing started.

It's going to crush me. That asshole's going to flop down on top of me and leave a greasy smear.

Baird opened fire. He didn't know or care if it was going to work. He just fired. The leviathan veered sideways and dived again, oblivious of him.

Now the polyps were all over the jetty, scores of them—no, hundreds. Any plan to drive them toward the newly dug trenches around the base went to rat shit right away. All Baird could do was just keep firing and reloading to hold them off him. He could hear sporadic explosions and screams around him as some polyps reached their targets and detonated. The only thing that stopped him from sinking all his clips into the things was Marcus grabbing him by the arm and shoving him into a run. He tripped over the remains of a Gear, and for a moment he thought it was Cole.

"Run—just frigging *run!*" Marcus yelled. "Get down that trench and just *run.*"

Once Baird started running, his body took over and it wasn't going to stop for anything—not even if he wanted it to. Where the hell was Cole? The leviathan must have come up again with a second wave of polyps, because the firing on the jetty started again. Baird didn't even dare slow down to look over his shoulder. He could hear the things scuttling behind him as he sprinted after the Gears running ahead. Then he was suddenly aware that he was splashing through a stream of fluid that was getting deeper by the stride. The pungent solvent smell of imulsion made him clamp his lips together to keep the fumes out.

Oh fuck. That's my great idea. The fuel flood. Oh shit . . .

It was designed to pump out a controlled spray so the polyps roasted instantly, but nobody was supposed to be running inside the trench. That was planning for you. Plans went belly-up every time. Baird prayed that nobody decided to let off a few bursts until everyone was out of the trench. He didn't want to end his days as a barbecue. In fact, he didn't want to die at all, *ever.*

Despite himself, he turned and took a few strides sideways, just long enough to see a tidal wave of dark gray legs thrashing after him. It was the first time he'd realized Marcus was right behind him.

"Yeah, you seen 'em," Marcus panted. "Pretty. Now get the hell out."

The trench was a couple of meters deep. Baird had no idea where he'd get a foothold and how he'd get up the sides without the polyps grabbing him. But it was that or let the plan fall apart.

Shit. This has to end.

The trench curved around. He had no idea where he was now, but he needed to get out. Then he saw Cole, hands on knees, catching his breath.

"Thought you was never comin'," Cole said, and shoved him up the side of the trench in one smooth movement as if he'd rehearsed it to the second.

Baird pulled himself over the edge and reached down without thinking to pull Cole up. But the arm he grabbed was Marcus's. Cole had scrambled out on his own. There was a rapid burst of fire, and then the loud *whoomp* of igniting vapor. Baird felt the heat sear his face. His eyebrows sizzled, singed by the fire.

And his pants and boots were soaked in fuel. He held his breath, waiting to go up like a torch.

I'm going to die. Oh shit.

"Move it," Marcus said. "Before Dizzy runs you down."

The world started to fall back into place. Baird knew now where he'd come up out of the trench. He was right outside the Gorasni camp. He sat up, looking into a burning pit of thrashing, twitching, exploding polyps. Where the hell had they all come from? There seemed to be hundreds more now. A grinding noise way too close to his ear made him scramble to his feet, and he narrowly missed the mine-clearing scoop of a grindlift derrick.

"Corporal, you better shift your jaywalkin' ass," Dizzy yelled from the cab. "I got *crabs* to clear."

Baird stood back to reload and shift ammo clips into the right pockets, taking stock of the bizarre battle around him. The polyps weren't all charging blindly down the trenches. Dizzy and the other drivers were bulldozing some of the more adventurous ones over the side in drifts, shoveling them on top of their buddies. The things kept detonating, but the rigs could withstand mines. Dizzy whooped loudly every time one went off. The pits of burning imulsion crackled and spat.

"Worked better than I expected," Marcus said.

Baird felt for his eyebrows. "Mostly. Where's Dom?"

"Gone with Hoffman. Come on, the leviathan's shaking off more polyps."

"Shit. We've shown our hand now. They're not stupid—even a frigging amoeba understands that running into flames is a bad idea."

"We'll just have to be smarter than a fucking amoeba, then, won't we?"

Baird took a shortcut through the Gorasni camp with Marcus and Cole, expecting to see the Gorasni settling the score with the polyps for the loss of their imulsion platform. But the men defending the camp were mostly Stranded, Ollivar's army of scruffy assholes. They were great shots, he had to give them that. They were picking off the polyps like rabbits. If he'd been them, he'd have let the Gorasni fry.

Maybe they wanted to save each other so that they still had a sworn enemy left to vent their shit on when this was all over.

It really is going to be over. Isn't it? Another fifteen years of this—no frigging way.

"Tell me there ain't people here," Cole said. He aimed short bursts into the approaching wave of polyps. Everyone was lined up across the main drag through the camp, trying to form a semicircle to stop the things dispersing. There was a whisker between pulling that off successfully and getting in someone else's arc of fire. "'Cause tents ain't brick walls."

One of the Stranded opened up with a Hammerburst. They were sporting a lot of salvaged Locust weapons. "The noncoms shot through when the siren sounded," he said. "Don't worry, you can't wipe out those Gorasni bastards—we've tried."

"I just love it when we all get on so well," Baird said.

"Hey, COG—these things are getting smarter by the minute. Shut up and shoot."

The polyps seemed to be getting the idea in a dumb animal kind of way. Instead of rushing in a mass, falling over one another and presenting a nice wall of meat to target, they started to scatter, racing between the rows of tents. And that was when the tide turned the wrong way. They wheeled around and re-formed behind the line. Half the Stranded turned and formed up into an old-fashioned infantry line to face the choke point of the gate into the camp, and the others broke into pairs, conventional rifle-style.

Baird had now reached the stage where his body was on autopilot—along with his mouth—and he was too busy reacting to crap himself. It was a blessing. It would turn to fatigue and thinking every next shot would be the one he missed, the last one before something killed him. But for the time being, he was coping.

Marcus signaled Cole and Baird to block a row each. "I think they've played this game before," he said.

One of the Stranded heard him. "Seen 'em a few times on land," he called. "Still working out what else they can do. Like how they move around at sea."

"Gee, thanks," Baird said. "Now you frigging tell us."

Then Baird got to see what polyps did when you didn't drop them on the spot. One Stranded yelled, "Stoppage!" His rifle had jammed. His paired buddy was reloading. A polyp jumped him and it detonated like a grenade. It took out both men. There was a second of stunned silence before half the Stranded platoon—yeah, Baird admitted it, he had to think of them like that—went nuts, broke ranks, and charged the polyps.

You didn't get to survive in the wild if you weren't a tough, stubborn animal. Stranded were survivors to a man.

More polyps exploded short of their target, setting tents on fire and scattering wounding debris. Then the things started spitting something—venom, acid, whatever. Baird didn't know, and for once his curiosity didn't force him forward for a closer look.

The battlefield was now all smoke and yelling and an overwhelming need to kill anything that moved and wasn't human. Baird almost didn't hear his radio.

Just as his own name could cut through any amount of noise, so could the word *Pelruan*. Mathieson was trying to free up a Raven and two squads of Gears. One of the Gorasni squads answered instead.

"We go," said the voice. It was Yanik. "You pick us up now. Tell the lovely duchess to hang on."

Sam. It had to be. That was what the Gorasni sailors had taken to calling her, *duchashka.* Pelruan had more trouble, then.

"Hang on for what?" Marcus asked.

Mathieson responded. "Another leviathan. It's hanging around Pelruan. They need some backup."

"I fucking *told you so,*" Baird said to Marcus. "There's *two* of these things."

"Three," Mathieson said. "There's three."

PELRUAN, NORTH COAST OF VECTES.

"Yes, it's back." Sam lowered the binoculars and handed them to Anya. "I swear it's learned already. Look."

Bernie divided up the ammo between the squads with Rossi. Rifles were all they had except for the guns on the garrison's two

'Dills, and those weren't much use against small, fast targets on the ground. She wanted to save those for the leviathan if it got within range. Right now, it was being a sensible monster and keeping its distance.

"That's what freaks me more than anything," Rossi said. "Grubs—you *knew* they could think. But these things—they're just animals. Or *plants*, even, like the damn stalks. What's driving them? What do they want? They're not even eating us."

Anya squatted next to Bernie. "You think we should evacuate the town?"

She should have been asking Rossi. Bernie tried to be diplomatic.

"I don't know what Drew thinks," she said, "but we need to stop those things coming ashore in the first place, or else it won't matter where we run. They'll just spread through the island. Eh, Drew?"

Rossi didn't look up from the piles of clips. "We should at least ask the civvies if they want to leave. I guarantee they won't, but we ought to."

The townsfolk were watching. Only a few of them had firearms, but all those who did seemed to be standing around waiting for orders. They'd been used to taking care of themselves, and however ill prepared they were for the world of grubs and Lambent, they were still willing to have a go.

Among them were the old boys from the Duke of Tollen's Regiment. Bernie knew she was in no position to tell them they were too old. They were in their seventies and eighties; they might not have been fit and athletic, but they still knew how to use a rifle. They probably thought the same about her.

I think they call that irony. I tell this bunch of vets that they're no use now. I hope Vic sees the joke.

And I hope he's alive to hear it.

"You heard who Mathieson's sending us, didn't you?" Anya said. "Gorasni troops."

"Shit." Rossi shook his head slowly. "Well, ma'am, you wanted to hone your frontline command skills. This is going do it."

"I'll handle it." Bernie felt Anya had enough on her plate. Being smart and gutsy wasn't going to be enough to get her through this alone, not even if she could suddenly sprout a dose of her mother's killing aggression. "I get on okay with the Gorasni. It's probably because I know how to castrate farm animals. Always builds bridges, that."

"I can hear a Raven," Anya said.

Mac trotted over to Bernie and stuck his nose in her face. Will Berenz had either let him out on his own, or else he'd been wandering around nearby.

"Hey, sweetie, go home. You can't tackle polyps. Or go sit in the Packhorse." Mac just looked at her with those sad, baffled eyes as if he was waiting for orders in a language he understood. Bernie beckoned to one of the townspeople. "Take him back and lock him up somewhere safe, will you?"

The Raven appeared as a black flickering shape approaching down the coastline. Mel Sorotki's voice came over the radio net.

"KR-Two-Three-Nine inbound, three minutes—Mataki, just tell me you don't have a recipe for these things."

Anya had her intense and slightly defocused look on, as if she was running through the academy theory classes in her head. "Roger that, Two-Three-Nine. Just you?"

"Stroud, we're a one-bird army up here. These Gorasni are hard-core."

"That's what worries me."

"First wars first. Kill the current enemy before the previous ones. That's what I hear."

One of the Tollen vets walked over to Anya and Drew. He wasn't fast off the mark, but he still had that upright bearing and he carried an old rifle like it was still part of him.

"Ma'am." He didn't salute. He came from the era when you didn't salute or return one if you weren't wearing your cap. "Corporal Frederic Benten. We still know how to follow orders."

"And are you still good shots?" Anya asked.

"Yes, and we stand our ground. Partly because we're not so good at the running-away bit these days."

"Good." There wasn't a trace of condescension in Anya's voice. "I want you to form a rank behind the Gorasni, so that if anything gets past them, you pick it off." She gestured. "Three of you on that headland, the rest of you in front of the cottages at the top of the slope."

"Ma'am, *Gorasni?*"

"If they're prepared to get killed defending this town, they're under my command like everyone else," she said.

Benten took it with a grim nod. He went back to his friends, and Bernie watched the news spread among them.

"Shit," Sam said. "Let's hope the old discipline kicks in."

Sorotki landed the Raven and the guy they called Yanik jumped out. He trotted up to Sam and bowed extravagantly.

"My life is yours, *duchashka.* Let us hope it doesn't come to that, though."

Sam gave him her half-smile, the one where her eyes didn't even flicker. "I always wanted a meat shield. Is that it? *Eight* of you?"

"Eight Gorasni equals twenty COG equals fifty trained Stranded. We are *economical* people. Value for money."

"Bullshit," Sam said. "But thanks. And the old boys with the trident badges, the ones giving you the hairy eyeball—they hate your fucking guts. Your guys put their guys in death camps. Be tactful."

Sam could always cut to the chase. Yanik seemed to appreciate it. Sorotki and Mitchell joined the huddle to discuss tactics.

"The leviathan's cruising out there," Mitchell said. "It keeps diving when we get close, but we're up for a strafing run if you are."

"Remember those things can rear a long way out of the water." Anya signaled to the Pelruan locals to move into position. They had no personal radios, so it was back to last-century soldiering. "Don't take chances. Pull back and give us air support here if you don't sink the thing."

"It'll provoke it into shaking off polyps, probably," Sorotki said. "At least that gives us a chance to choose when the attack starts."

Bernie put her hand on Anya's shoulder to get her attention. "I'll go with the locals, ma'am," she said. "That way one at least of us has a radio link to you."

"Good idea, Bernie. And I think they'll listen to you more than me."

It was a shame. Anya was a good Gear. She had all the right instincts, but she was a small, pretty, blond girlie who looked a lot younger than she was, and the old men clearly didn't give a damn that she came from war-hero stock, even if they knew that her mother had won the Embry Star. The doubt was all over their faces.

"Okay, Mel, poke the beehive," she said.

Sorotki had a tough job on his hands. Mitchell was a pretty good door gunner, but they had no idea if a stalk was going to punch out of the water if they ventured too low, or if the leviathan was going to swat them out of the air with a massive tentacle. The Raven circled over the shallows. All Bernie and the others could do was watch. Mitchell was a small silhouette in the open door. Then he opened fire, raking the water below.

The rounds raised a curtain of spray. A few seconds later, a paddle-shaped tentacle like a squid's unfurled from the surface and missed the Raven by three meters. Sorotki banked sharply and gained height, coming back to let Mitchell piss the leviathan off more. Mitchell emptied two belts of ammo into the thing, and it did the job. It did the job really well. The next thing Bernie saw was the tentacle vanish as the Raven shot off toward the beach.

"Incoming!" Sorotki said. "One huge mad thing heading your way, on a line with the slipway."

One of Rossi's squad was on lookout up on the high ground on the other side of the harbor. "No, it's passed the slipway. It's going to hit this side."

"Get out of there," Rossi yelled. "Get back down here."

Being shelled was bowel-loosening, Bernie recalled, but when the shells that landed had minds of their own and charged after you, it was a whole new level of fear. The leviathan crashed down onto the shore. Polyps poured ashore in a weird beachhead landing. Bernie still couldn't tell where the polyps came from—from inside the leviathan, off its back, even out of its arse—but there were a lot of them. She shifted to stand behind the Gorasni positions and signaled to the Tollen vets to stand by. The firing started.

But the Gorasni boys didn't hold a line—they *advanced*.

"I can't do this," Benten said suddenly. "I can't stand with these men."

He raised his rifle. He was definitely aiming at the polyps, but it was clear he wasn't going to back up the Gorasni. The old soldiers were watching him, and they weren't going where Bernie had directed them. For a second she had to look away from the Gears and other men in front of her.

"You'll go where I tell you, Corporal," she yelled. "*Now.*"

"We won't fight alongside them." Benten started backing off to the road to bypass the eight Gorasni. "I mean it. They can die. We'll do this alone."

It was the worst time to lose discipline. "We've got a bunch of Stranded defending the Gorasni camp," Bernie yelled. "That's *after* the Gorasni killed some of them and dumped their bodies in the camp. If that feud's on hold until we stop the polyps, then so's yours. That's an order."

Some of the polyps had broken through. Bernie had no choice. She grabbed Benten and shoved him bodily into line. The Gorasni had turned and were moving back now, drawing the polyps into the more confined space of the street.

"Kill those fucking things." Bernie knew she had to make this stick. "Back up those bloody Gorasni or get out of the way. *Now.* Or I'll slot you myself."

"Then go ahead, Sergeant."

These men were Gears like her. She could only guess what they'd been through at the hands of the enemy. She knew what vengeance and loathing felt like; for one act of violation she'd butchered two men, and done things way beyond a just execution. They'd deserved it. But she scaled that up to spending weeks, months, *years* in a Gorasni labor camp watching your mates worked and starved to death, and probably hoping you wouldn't be far behind them. She had no idea how she could ask these old soldiers to forget that.

But she had to. "You'll do it," she said, "because you're still a Gear."

Benten looked at her with a mixture of real pain and absolute disgust. Bernie was sure she'd have told the Gorasni to go fuck themselves, too. But he stopped, moved back to the Gorasni line, and opened fire.

Bernie felt like shit. But, like the feuds, atonement would have to wait for later.

CHAPTER 16

A dog has a military mind. He respects the chain of command. He needs to know who's in charge for the good of the whole pack, and if there's no leader, he'll take the job himself—because somebody has to. The difference between a human and a dog, though, is that the dog doesn't lie awake at night dreaming of having that power.

(SERGEANT BERNADETTE MATAKI, EXPLAINING HER FONDNESS FOR DOGS)

"You can use one of these, I assume?"

Hoffman handed Prescott a Lancer and watched him carefully. He took it two-handed and tilted the rifle to inspect it, safety catch uppermost, as if he knew what he was doing.

"I was a Gear," he said. "But Lancers didn't have chainsaws in my day."

Prescott rarely pulled the veteran card, which was just as well. Every one of Hoffman's generation had done their compulsory military service unless they were medically unfit. But the Chairman was one of those privileged kids who did the two-year commission so that he didn't look too much like a parasite before his dad whisked him off to groom him for the family firm, the business of politics.

"If you need to use the chainsaw," Hoffman said, "the power switch is *here*. Status indicator—*here*. But I wouldn't recommend getting that close to those things."

"I have my security team. Don't worry."

Hoffman wasn't about to. If anything happened to Prescott, he had a team in mind to run the COG, and it didn't include himself. He wondered if Prescott could grasp the idea of someone who didn't want his job.

"Casualty update?" Prescott asked.

"KIA—ten Gears, fourteen Stranded, five Gorasni. Civilian fatalities—eleven reported, but most civvies are either locked down or they've gone off camp. Wounded—no total yet, but forty combatants have been through ER."

"That's not as bad as I'd expected."

"That's not counting the naval personnel missing from *Fenmont*. Those things aren't done with us yet, Chairman. They've come back for a second bite at Pelruan, and they'll do the same here."

Prescott was fiddling around in his desk drawers as if he wasn't listening. Hoffman found himself fighting a constant urge to grab the man by his collar, shove him up against the wall, and ask him what in the name of God was so distracting that he wasn't pissing his pants about the current situation. And what about Bernie? What about Anya? And Sam—he owed her father better than this. Everything and everyone he cared about was under threat. It had been that way for years, but this was one crisis too many.

"Carry on, Colonel," Prescott said. He finally found what he seemed to be searching for—a small pistol. He put it in his pocket, then locked the drawer. "I'm listening."

The Chairman's office overlooked the base, giving Hoffman a good view of the damage unfolding below. The base and the civilian camps beyond were wreathed in a haze of smoke as the last wave of polyps burned. The creatures were working out how to avoid getting lured into the pits, and everyone with a rifle was back to picking them off individually. The bursts of automatic fire were getting fewer and further between.

"If we can't kill the leviathans before they drop more polyps, the next assault needs to be dealt with differently," said Hoffman. "I'm going to use the Hammer."

"How? Is that wise?"

That's rich coming from you, Chairman.

Hoffman found it interesting that he didn't seem to object to the unilateral decision. "I know the targeting's getting a lot less accurate, but we need a substantial response. It'll mean a lot of physical damage to the base, but it's that or keep burning through ammo."

"But we don't know how many more polyps will show up. They could be a daily feature. Then there are the stalks. They've suddenly stopped showing up. When do we know we've reached the appropriate point to apply maximum force?"

"We don't," Hoffman said. "I'm just being a goddamn soldier. I'm working out how we kill every hostile and neutralize the threat every time. Beyond that—well, that's all I can do."

"Then we need to evacuate the civilians further inland. I'll get Sharle on it."

"We're on an island, Chairman. That limits the advantage of running away. If I knew what this Lambent thing was, I might stand a better chance of beating it. But how come we have only the deadbeats left from the university? What happened to all the smart guys in white coats we used to have, the ones who could do some damn research and find solutions? I'm relying on a handful of intelligent Gears to work this shit out."

Prescott gave Hoffman a carefully blank look. "We didn't get any answers from scientists before, Victor, which is why we deployed the Hammer of Dawn globally. Remember?"

Oh yeah. I remember. I remember trying to locate Margaret, and sending Gears out into black ash as thick as a snowstorm, and finding the survivors sheltering in drains. Nothing wrong with my goddamn memory.

"I'll rely on Baird, then," Hoffman said.

"He's a very intelligent man. I'd really like him on my staff, much as he seems to *enjoy* killing anything that moves."

"Right now," Hoffman said, "I *need* him doing some killing."

Some things had a slow burn time. Hoffman often found himself interrupted by realizations about things that had happened minutes or even days before. This time, his mental tap on the shoulder came from a very routine, apparently unthinking action that Prescott had performed a minute before.

Hang on. Why does he need to lock his drawers? What the hell is there left to hide?

Maybe it was habit. A man didn't change overnight from a culture of secrecy to spilling his guts. Maybe it was time to give him his regular reminder that they were all on the same side.

"I understand," Prescott said.

"Chairman, forgive me for asking this yet again, but is there anything at all that you haven't disclosed or made available to me?" Hoffman hated this verbal sparring. "It might not look relevant to you, but if there's any classified data that even you can't access, it's the kind of thing I can get Baird to pull apart. You'd have shared everything else with me, of course."

He expected a negative response. And he got one.

"If I had anything that could possibly help you to resolve this situation, I'd have given it to you by now," Prescott said.

"Just checking," said Hoffman. *You know I am, too.* "And can I suggest that you relocate for the time being? It might make more sense for you to evacuate with the civilians. They need your leadership right now. We just need to get on with the job."

Prescott stood looking at him. "Very well."

"I mean *now*, Chairman. I might not be able to carry out a rescue if we get another attack, and you've seen how fast things can unravel."

Hoffman got the feeling that Prescott just wanted him to go away. He wondered if the Chairman was waiting to call Trescu—or even Ollivar—and didn't want Hoffman around to hear him. Hoffman was pretty sure that Trescu wouldn't horse-trade with him, but Ollivar was a wild card. The bastard hadn't even told them that the Stranded had come across polyps on the mainland. It didn't fill Hoffman with confidence.

Can't stop Prescott being Prescott. But I'm not going to be dismissed like a schoolboy.

"Good point," Prescott said. He appeared to give up at that point and headed for the door. "I'll stay on the radio, channel fifteen. Keep me updated."

Hoffman followed him down the stairs and went into CIC to talk to Mathieson. But he kept an eye on the doorway to make sure Prescott didn't double back.

"We can't move people far, sir," Mathieson said. "We've commandeered every vehicle we can find, but the majority are on foot. Those who've agreed to leave, that is. A lot have said they'll stay and chance it. They're fed up with running. Even temporarily."

"Damn shame we haven't got an armed population," Hoffman said. He checked again to make sure Prescott had left. "I'm glad we didn't confiscate all the firearms the Gorasni brought in, though."

"By the way, Sergeant Mataki's still operational."

"You can say *alive*, Lieutenant." A thought crossed Hoffman's mind, an uncharacteristic one, and he was ashamed to let it overtake him when he was worrying about Bernie's welfare. *I'm going to take a look in Prescott's office.* "You call me and let me know what's happening at Pelruan, no matter what. Even if I've got polyps crawling up my ass and the base is burning down. Got it?"

"Roger that, sir. Things are quieting down at the moment."

It would only take a minute or two. Hoffman went back upstairs and stood looking at the desk in the Chairman's office. He'd never done anything like this in his life. He hadn't even sneaked looks at other people's private stuff as a kid. But this wasn't about privacy. This was about a secretive asshole of a boss and a civilization teetering on the edge of annihilation, existing from one day to the next. He had to know, if only to enable him to go on working with Prescott without the relationship going totally to hell. He had to be able to trust him.

KAREN TRAVISS

As far as you can trust any politician.

Maybe he was just doing what we were all trained to do without thinking. Keeping firearms secure.

The locks on the old desks here were simple. He took out his pocketknife and unfolded the awl. He wasn't sure how he was going to lock it again, but that depended on what he found, and—

So if I find something that pisses me off, what am I going to do about it? Once I open this, there's no going back.

He opened it anyway. The lock yielded. The drawer contained Prescott's gold watch, a file of papers—the signed paperwork invoking the Fortification Act fourteen years ago which was effectively Prescott's crown and scepter—and a computer data disk with a standard sticky label marked A2897. The paperwork was what it appeared to be, but the disk required examination.

He was committed now. He couldn't put it back and walk away. He took it downstairs to CIC, avoided Mathieson's glance, switched on the old terminal, and tried the disk in the drive. It didn't surprise him that the ancient system couldn't read it. But there had to be one that could, or why would Prescott have kept it?

"Mathieson, I need you to go get a coffee. Or take a leak. Whatever."

The kid knew what that meant. He nodded, averted his eyes, and wheeled himself out the door. Hoffman went to his terminal—the most recent technology they'd salvaged from Jacinto—and tried the disk there. The drive chugged away to itself for a few moments and the screen flickered. But the file name was a random string, and trying to open it prompted the first layer of an encryption dialogue.

What else did I expect?

Hoffman took a full ten seconds to make the decision to put the disk in his pocket. It took another twenty for him to rummage in the desk and find a carton marked DAMAGED DISKS—DO NOT DISCARD.

Everything was saved for another day, in the hope that it could be salvaged or reused somehow. And all the COG data disks looked the same. He just swapped the labels.

Even as he put the substitute disk back in the desk and struggled to make the drawer appear still locked, he wondered what had happened to him—a man so incapable of deceit that fellow top brass never wanted to tell him the serious shit. He appalled himself. It took a hefty blow with the butt of his sidearm to batter the lock into some semblance of being secured again. He'd just dislodged a pin or something, but it would have to do.

But Prescott will know. And he'll come after me, maybe. And what do I say?

I tell him to go fuck himself, and that he forfeited the last of my loyalty when he never told me there was a secret facility at New Hope. That's what I say.

Hoffman's chest was pounding as he walked down the stairs. When he put his weight on each tread, he felt his legs shake. It was crazy. He was a seasoned Gear. But rifling through his boss's desk had reduced him to a trembling pile of guilt.

Quentin Michaelson came to his rescue, even if the man didn't know it.

"Michaelson to Hoffman . . . are you receiving, Victor?"

"Go ahead." Hoffman adjusted his earpiece. "Any good news?"

"*Clement* and *Zephyr* are still submerged. Garcia thinks he's got a firing solution on one of the leviathans."

"Translate that for a Gear."

"The subs have found one of the things idling and they think they've got a good chance of putting a torpedo up its chuff."

"Why didn't they do that before?"

"Ah, gratitude. Because biologics don't move as predictably as vessels, and that makes them hard to hit. Damn it, Victor, we were trained to *avoid* killing sea life."

"If one, why not both?" Yes, that sounded ungrateful. For all Hoffman knew, these were the first two leviathans of a hundred. "But one less leviathan probably means a lot less polyps."

"Garcia thinks both boats will need to fire a simultaneous spread from different angles to catch it off guard. Overlapping fire in three dimensions, if you like. But the other one will detect all that. So it's a case of fire and run like hell."

"We better time this carefully, then. Can Garcia carry on track-ing it?"

"Yes, but if it starts moving, there's no telling if and when he'll pick it up again."

The plan refocused Hoffman on essentials. He had an enemy out there, effectively two amphibious assault craft waiting to land troops. The fact that they weren't human or didn't seem to have any purpose or plan made no difference. Basic principles of war-fare still applied; his job was to prevent the enemy from establish-ing a beachhead, and if that wasn't possible, to prevent them from breaking out.

And then we kill them.

Hoffman felt under his armor for the stolen disk in his breast pocket and went to rally the Gears.

He realized he was automatically including the Gorasni and Ollivar's militia in that group.

It was getting dark now. Some of the wooden houses in the town were burning, and the locals had formed a chain of buckets to put out the fires. Polyps weren't just mines. They were pretty good in-cendiary devices when they blew up near flammable material, too.

But so far, Pelruan was holding on. Bernie seized the lull in fighting to jog back to the compound and retrieve the Packhorse. She drove down the dirt road to the waterfront, passing Rossi on the way. She slowed to a halt.

"Drew, you okay?"

"They're like shrapnel," he said. He had small cuts across his chin. His goggles had protected most of his face. "I frigging hate them more than grubs, and that's saying something. I'm going to get the 'Dill out there."

"How's Silber doing?"

"One of the old boys stopped the bleeding, but he's going to lose that leg. He needs Doc Hayman."

"Let's hope the infirmary's still there when we get out of this shit."

Rossi patted her arm through the open window. "Nice job with the Gorasni thing."

"Yeah, I feel *so* good about treating vets like that. Terrific."

"Mataki, you were a sergeant when I was in short pants. Don't you know by now that nobody's meant to love sergeants? They're meant to be in awe of us."

He jogged away to the first-aid station. Bernie drove on. Human instinct was to find somewhere safe to lay up for the night, but for Gears, it was hunting time. The COG had always favored night attacks. An enemy that couldn't throw light on the battlefield — especially one away from home — was vulnerable to a disciplined force that knew the terrain and had a solid plan.

But if that enemy was naturally bioluminescent, he was doubly fucked. Bernie suddenly found that very funny.

It was probably fatigue lowering her guard, but those wobbling patches of light moving between the wind-stunted bushes on the eastern side of the harbor definitely leveled the playing field. She picked out Sam and Anya behind cover at the top of the beach and drove slowly up to them. Sam was on her rat bike.

Sam revved the bike and braced the butt of her Lancer against her belt. "I bet they wish they didn't glow."

Bernie opened the Packhorse door and nudged Anya to get in. The polyps seemed to be regrouping. "You know that girls' day out we never had because I hit a mine?" she said. "Let's make up for it now."

"I'm in," Sam said. "Better mop up these stragglers before the next wave."

Sam set off along the concrete path toward the bushes, steering one-handed like a cavalry lancer on horseback. Maybe the polyps didn't see in the same spectrum as humans anyway, so operating without lights might have been a waste of time. But it certainly made the bastards easier to see by contrast.

The bike roared and twisted as muzzle flash lit up the under-growth. Sam swerved around, spraying fire. The polyps weren't so bloody clever when they were up against a fast opponent. Bernie decided it was time to risk playing that game in the Packhorse.

And one of the things could detonate under the vehicle, and it's goodnight Mataki. But sod it. I can't keep running around.

"You want to drive, ma'am?" she asked.

"No," Anya said. "I want to shoot."

The Stroud genes were forcing their way out now. The last hour or two had made Anya a lot more confident—and aggres-sive. She was psyching herself up for the next attack, just like her mother used to do.

She's doing fine, Major. I promised, remember? I said that if she ever picked up a Lancer in earnest, I'd make sure she was ready.

"KR-Two-Three-Nine to all call signs." Sorotki was circling overhead without nav or cockpit lights, a wandering noise over Bernie's head. "I can see the leviathan's lights under the water now."

"Stroud here—are you pursuing it?"

"We're going to brass it up as it comes up the beach. It's mov-ing in again."

"Stand by, all call signs," Anya said. "Wait for the Raven."

"Yanik, you okay?" Bernie called.

A voice drifted out of the gloom. "I want a drink. I want to pee. I saved an old soldier from getting *polyped,* and he spat on me. Apart from that, life is *fabulous.*"

In another life and another time, Bernie would have lived hap-pily among the Gorasni. They had that appealingly grim humor, they were good soldiers, and they would fight to the death. But she would never forget the expression on Frederic Benten's face. She had no right to forgive what she'd never endured.

"Glad to hear it, Yanik," she said.

The Raven's engine noise told her it was heading inshore fast. Sorotki, usually a one-man comedy act, sounded pumped up on angry adrenaline for a change. "KR-Two-Three-Nine, following the glowie bastard in—stand by to repel *things.*"

After all the waiting—which had probably only been half an hour, maybe forty minutes—the next assault unfolded on Pelruan in seconds. The Raven's door gun raked the harbor. It was an instant, short-lived fireworks display, a show of muzzle flash and living lights as the polyps were catapulted ashore from the leviathan before they scattered for an attack. The Raven hovered, firing into the water. Bernie saw the leviathan rear and thrash around. Its head was picked out in blue-white points of light. Mitchell was targeting them; she saw the rounds strike. She couldn't hang on to watch the outcome, though, and turned the Packhorse in a screeching tight circle to head for the surreal river of bobbing, scuttling polyp lights.

Anya leaned out of the passenger window, Lancer ready. This was going to be harder than Bernie had thought. APCs like the 'Dill had gun turrets on both sides and a top hatch, but maneuvering a Packhorse for a gunner on the opposite side to the driver—that was another matter.

Point and swerve. That's all I can do.

Bernie drove right at a column of polyps. They scattered. She yanked the wheel hard right, swinging the vehicle's tail around, and Anya opened fire. Something hit the Packhorse's door like clods of mud.

"Gotcha!" Anya's voice was a hiss. "Come about, Bernie. They're going left."

Bernie had to keep moving. If one of those little glowie shits managed to scramble aboard, she and Anya would be dead. She couldn't see the surface she was driving on, she couldn't avoid mud or deep shingle, and she was now totally disoriented because she'd lost a sense of where everyone else was. She could only drive by instinct—and by the direction of rifle fire. Radios didn't help at all.

Anya leaned out further. "Left! Go left!" She fired in short controlled bursts, just the way she'd been trained. Some of the spent casings flew into the cab. One smacked Bernie in the cheek. "Stop! Back up!"

It was like a weird game, except losing it meant dying. Bernie felt the tires bump over something and she waited for a scream or a detonation, but it never came. Anya reloaded as Bernie spun the wheel. She seemed to have lost all sense of fear and caution.

"Ma'am?"

"Keep going! I'm on a roll!"

Anya laid down a long sputtering line of fire through some bushes and wet polyp fragments splattered the windshield. Bernie caught a glimpse of the 'Dill coming at her broadside just in time to accelerate clear. She let the 'Dill move in and paused for a moment to work out where she was.

Above the harbor, the Raven was still at a steady hover and firing. Sorotki and Mitchell weren't giving up yet. Bernie jumped out of the Packhorse to keep an eye out for stray polyps and looked back on the battlefield, and found she was a hundred meters from the harbor wall on the patch of open ground to the west of the town. To her right, she couldn't see far because of the houses, but she could hear the rifle fire; ahead of her was a mass of overlapping fire from both directions. She was expecting someone to get shot at any moment. Then there was a loud *whoop* in her ear via the radio.

"KR-Two-Three-Nine—the bastard's down! Got him!" Mitchell sounded as if he'd caught Sorotki's adrenaline surge. Raven crews were generally flat calm. "Headshot. About five belts of headshots, actually. He's belly up and floating. Not as big as I thought."

"Stroud to Two-Three-Nine—you sure it's not playing dead?"

The Raven lifted vertically. Bernie saw its searchlight cast a fierce white pool on the water. Then it crossed her mind what detonating a Lambent Brumak had done to Jacinto.

But that was with a Hammer laser. That was different.

"Oh, I know when they're faking it . . ." Mitchell said.

Bernie reached for her binoculars and had just lifted them to her eyes when a brilliant flash of light blinded her. The booming explosion seemed to come several seconds later. She heard Sorotki say "Shit!" and for a moment she thought the Raven was going down.

"*Mel!*" Anya yelled.

But the light died away and the Raven was still there. It came .back to hover again. Bernie could now hear dogs howling and barking from the houses.

"Okay, it's definitely not faking," Mitchell said. His voice was shaky. "It just blew up."

Sorotki's usual cheeriness was forced this time. "We'll get a little more altitude before we try that again. Anyone need a searchlight?"

Anya got on the radio again. "All call signs—the leviathan's down. No more polyps. Let's clear up what's left." She bent forward to look out the driver's door. "Come on, Bernie. Let's go."

Bernie got in and started the Packhorse. "You don't want Sam hogging all the big juicy ones, do you?"

"No."

"Good."

"This is weird."

"You said it." A wobbly cluster of lights was racing head-on toward them. Bernie steadied herself to swing the vehicle around. "Okay, ma'am, as they say in the navy—sixty rounds rapid—in your own time—*go on.*"

Bernie had been through the roller-coaster cycle of fear, adrenaline, anger, and hysterical relief so many times that she knew which stage she was at and when she needed to back off. Fatigue didn't help much. She was definitely at the shaky, giggly stage. But Anya was still absolutely bent on destruction. She emptied two magazines before she realized she'd run out of polyps.

"Wow," she said.

The rifles all seemed to fall silent at the same time. There was a lull, and then lights appeared ahead of them—the 'Dill—and Sam's single headlight suddenly came bouncing out of the darkness across rough ground. The only sounds were the surf, the rumble of various engines, and the dogs going crazy.

"You okay?" Bernie asked.

"I'll work that out later." Anya was out of breath. Bernie could hear her swallowing hard. "Stroud to all call signs. Are we clear?"

"Ma'am, all clear this end." That was Rossi. "Just going to drive the course and make sure."

"We glorious sons of the Republic of Gorasnaya have also crushed the enemy in case anyone gives a damn."

"Thanks, Yanik."

Anya waited. The only troops left to report in were the few locals with rifles, including the veterans.

"Nothing moving," Benten said at last. There was nothing relieved or triumphant in his voice; the poor old bugger just sounded resigned. "Permission to stand down now, ma'am?"

Anya, bless her, always knew the right thing to say.

"Stand down, Tollens," she said. "Nice job. Thank you."

The Raven spent a few minutes sweeping the town with its searchlight. Bernie waited, engine idling, just in case some stray polyp had escaped. Anya hadn't called in to VNB Control yet.

"You're *not* okay, are you, Anya?"

"Oh, I'm fine," she said. "That's the scary thing. I want to do it again. I'm not finished. And all this hilarity—I hear it all the time in Control. But now I've done it myself. Tell me it's normal. Tell me I've not got some terrible thing in me waiting to get out and kill and *joke* about it."

"You're normal. We all do it. It's the animal brain taking over."

"I wish I'd known this while Mom was alive." Anya didn't elaborate. "I better let Hoffman know it's over."

She took out her earpiece and picked up the handset mike from the dashboard. Her hand was shaking.

"All done, sir," she said. "We'll sit tight here until we're sure there isn't another leviathan out there."

"Stay put until we've secured the naval base, Lieutenant," Hoffman said. "It's going to get rough down here for a while." He paused. "Everyone's fine."

That was his way of telling her Marcus was okay. Anya hadn't seen him for a while but didn't even mention him, which was a sure sign she was fretting about him. Bernie couldn't stand the avoidance any longer.

"You keep your head down, Colonel," Bernie said.

The mike picked her up. "You too, Sergeant," Hoffman said. "But remember I'm the one with the goddamn rabbit's foot."

Saving Pelruan suddenly didn't feel quite as good as it had a few minutes ago. But Bernie didn't have to explain to Anya. They both understood each other now.

After they'd checked in at the signals office, Rossi organized duty rosters and sent Bernie off for the night. She wandered back to Berenz's house with Sam, feeling like she'd had a wild night that she would regret when she sobered up next morning and recalled her excesses.

"See, even the bloody hound doesn't come out to welcome the conquering heroes," Sam said. "Good night. See you at oh-five-hundred, Sarge."

She was right; Mac hadn't come racing to slobber affection on her. Bernie decided not to take it personally. She'd make her peace with him in the morning.

CIC, VECTES NAVAL BASE.

"I still think it's the only option left," Hoffman said. "We fight or run. And sooner or later, we'll run out of ammo and fuel, and then running won't be possible. Let's end it while the Hammer is still more or less operational."

Dom found it strange to have this kind of meeting without Anya or Prescott around. He knew why they weren't there, but the mood in CIC had shifted; this was a soldiers' gathering, no politics or long-term strategic shit. It was about staying alive for the next twenty-six hours.

And Miran Trescu and Lyle Ollivar were there at the table. Marcus kept giving both of them that very slow head turn, as if he was expecting the worst of them. He probably wasn't. It was just the way he listened. But it was interesting to see the effect it was having on Ollivar. He was getting twitchy.

"So how do we concentrate the polyps in a kill zone again?" Marcus asked. "We baked a few. They catch on eventually. And then there's the Hammer laser. Remember what happened when we lasered that Lambent Brumak?"

It had collapsed the tunneled bedrock of Jacinto. The Hammer and Lambent combo was a city-killer. Dom found himself trying to calculate if a shitload of polyps added up to one Brumak, and what the blast radius might be. He gave up and decided to leave that to Baird.

"Yeah, but they've got one goal," Baird said. "They go after prey. They don't want to steal ships or any of that pirate shit. They'll chase *us*. An orbital laser is beyond their conceptual thinking."

Dom waited for Ollivar to punch Baird out for the pirate comment, but he didn't seem interested. "So what about Marcus's question?" Dom asked. "We sank Jacinto by targeting a big chunk of Lambent meat. If we try that here, we might get the same effect and lose the whole base."

"Valid objection," said Hoffman. "Shit."

Baird was scribbling numbers on a scrap of paper. "Maybe not."

"Not worth the risk if we can kill a leviathan out at sea."

"And then we don't get its polyp cargo, either. So how do we get it to the surface where we want it, and keep it there so we can paint it with the targeting laser?"

Marcus didn't blink. "I'll whistle for it."

Dom didn't care who played bait for the glowies as long as it wasn't Marcus. Shit, he'd do it himself. Why did it have to be Marcus all the time? Dom wondered if what he sometimes thought was Marcus's death wish—or at least not giving a shit about his own life—was actually an attempt to make amends for his father's invention frying the planet.

No. He's always been that way. Ever since we were kids. Always the first to wade in and defend someone. Always the first to throw a punch that needed throwing.

Hoffman looked across at Mathieson. "Lieutenant, get me Captain Michaelson. I want to know what those subs are playing at."

"Are we voting on this?" Ollivar asked. "Because we don't actually give a shit if the COG survives or not, as long as these things are wiped out. That includes Gorasnaya, of course. You can rot in hell too."

"You're welcome," Trescu said.

Hoffman rubbed his forehead, eyes shut for moment. "No vote. My decision. I just want ideas. If you don't have any, shut the hell up and follow the plan."

Dom gave Cole a discreet glance, and Cole just gave him his why-are-we-here look.

Why? Because we do all the weird shit with Lambent. Hoffman thinks we know as much as anyone does. Which is slightly more than jack shit, but not much.

"Okay," Marcus said. "I take a patrol boat out and piss off the leviathan, then slap the targeting laser on it. How I keep it there while the sat platform locks on is the tricky bit."

"Ten seconds," Baird said.

"We'd usually have Lieutenant Stroud to input the targeting coordinates, but she's not here, so Baird can do that."

"Hey, I'm not being left behind here." Baird looked at Cole just for a fraction of a second. Dom spotted it. "I'm the glowie authority, remember?"

"And we can't haul Stroud back just to help us out." Marcus gave Baird his I-mean-it blank stare. "So you'll have to suck it up."

Dom thought Baird was probably more worried about not being around to watch Cole's back, but maybe he was making too many assumptions about the man's motive. Just because he looked like he cared didn't mean that he did. He was certainly pissed off, though.

"Shit, a Raven gunner capped a leviathan at Pelruan, and we can't?" Baird made it sound like a disgrace. "Come *on*."

"Sorotki estimates it was smaller than the ones out there," Marcus said. "Mitchell emptied all the ammo they had into its head. But we might not *get* the head."

Hoffman cut in. "And it still nearly brought the Raven down. We've already lost one bird that way."

Everyone was looking at the clock on the wall. Mathieson was sitting with one hand cupped over his headset earpiece, waiting for Michaelson to tell them what was happening with the hunting submarines.

"Got him, sir." Mathieson switched the radio to the speakers. "He says they're tracking it. Listen."

"Victor, stand by," Michaelson said. "Because once we fire torpedoes—even if they don't hit the thing—the other one's probably going to know all about it."

"Where are they?"

"*Clement* can only detect one at the moment, so it's going for that."

Baird always found the fly in any ointment. "Shouldn't we be out there with the laser ready to deploy *before* they start shooting? Because the first thing that asshole's going to do when it hears its buddy turned to glowie soup is go for the source of the torp noise or head for us, depending on its IQ."

Marcus stood up, like the decision was made. "Tell Michaelson to find a boat he can afford to lose. I'm going to prep the targeting laser. Baird, do your sat coordinates stuff."

Dom jumped up and tapped Cole on the shoulder. "You keep saying you want to take up fishing, Cole Train. Let's go."

"Yeah, if the torps miss, I can always *puke* it to death."

"There's a Gorasni crew out there as well." Trescu got up and headed for the door. "So I take Baird's place."

Hoffman looked resigned to the whole thing. It really was the only option left.

"I always knew a committee could run the COG better," he said wearily. "Okay, do it. The fallback position if the polyps manage to land is that we channel as many as we can into the storage tunnels, seal them in, and pour fuel down there."

"And then," Ollivar said, "hope that there aren't more on the way."

Hoffman went red in the face almost immediately. It was like watching a squid change color. Dom took a step back, ready to jump between him and Ollivar.

"We fight until we run out of ammo or men or fuel or all three," Hoffman snarled. "There's nothing else we can do— except sit on our asses waiting for the right time to pull out all the stops. I have *been there before*, you goddamn parasitic bum. These choices do *not* get any simpler. And we've run out of time for fucking around."

Hoffman pushed his chair back and strode out. The squad followed with Trescu. In the passage outside, Marcus blocked Hoffman's path.

"You should keep Prescott where you can see him, Colonel," he said. "Or is this something else?"

"His job is to deal with the civilians. He can do that just fine with Major Reid." Hoffman pushed past Marcus. "And in case you forgot, one of our duties is to evacuate the civilian government to a place of safety in an emergency. Ten klicks up the road is the safest we can do for now."

"I don't think it's a good idea for you to come on this mission."

"Think I can't hack it, Fenix?"

"If you get killed, then the top command of the COG will consist of Prescott and Reid. Maybe Michaelson will get a look in occasionally, if he's a good boy."

Trescu just gave Hoffman a knowing look. Dom knew they'd never be best buddies. But the two men definitely had an understanding, even if that was a shared contempt for certain things— and people. If Dom hadn't known Hoffman for so many years, and his inability to plot and scheme, he'd have suspected a coup was coming. But that wasn't Hoffman's style.

Dom didn't know if it was Trescu's, though. He suspected it was. And much as he didn't like Prescott, the man was their own, the legal head of state, and Dom couldn't recall him ever doing something that went against the army's wishes. Just being an asshole wasn't a disqualifier. He wasn't a *dangerous* asshole.

"Yeah," Hoffman said at last. "I'm more scared of that than getting my ass shot off."

Hoffman will do the right thing. Maybe Prescott's chickened out and is trying to save his own ass. Okay. I can live with that.

In the end, all that mattered to Dom was that he kept Marcus alive. His best friend was all he had left.

The naval base was now in the grip of a quiet chaos. The evacuation of civvies was still going on and now nonessential military personnel were leaving. Every vehicle was co-opted to do the shuttling. The only stroke of luck in the whole pile of recurring shit was that the weather was mild, and an overnight outside wasn't going to kill people like it would have done at Port Farrall. Dom sometimes thought back to what it would be like there now, whether it would have been smarter to stay put and lose the weakest to cold and hunger instead of uprooting everything to come here.

But we can't do that. That's not how civilized folks do things.

Michaelson stood at the brow of *Falconer* as the squad and Trescu prepared to board. He obviously planned on going along for the ride.

"I did a deal with Ollivar's merchant navy," he said. "Want to see what we've got bolted on the foredeck?"

"Can't wait," Marcus growled.

"I didn't ask what they used it for themselves, of course."

"Go on, sir, show me," Dom said.

Dom still took some pride in being the seagoing Gear in the squad, even if it was from his amphibious landing days in the last war. Michaelson had been around for that, too. He was a lot thinner, grayer, and more wrinkled than he'd been during the landing at Aspho Point, but he hadn't lost that bravado. Michaelson liked a good scrap and would cross the road to find one. Maybe that was why he and Hoffman got on so well.

There had been a 30-mm gun on the foredeck of the patrol vessel the last time Dom had been on board. The other guns were still in place, but this one had been replaced with what looked like a cross between a telescope and a missile launcher.

"Thar she blows," Michaelson said.

Dom took a closer look. "Sir, that's a *harpoon.*"

"Explosive harpoon, actually. I want to think our seagoing Stranded brethren save it for robust negotiations with one another in trade disputes, but whatever they used it for, it might be a way of keeping a Lambent leviathan on the surface for a few seconds."

"Shit, sir, that's going to be hairy."

Marcus strode up to look at it and cocked his head slightly to one side. "Water skiing. Maybe even being dragged to the bottom."

"I'm game if you are, Sergeant," Michaelson said.

"Hell, why not?"

"What did you swap it for?" Dom asked.

"Ten catering containers of canned pork. Don't worry, it was well past its use-by date."

Michaelson seemed in his element. *Falconer* headed south out of the base, trailed by Gettner's Raven, and took up position about six kilometers offshore. Trescu leaned on the rail alongside the squad and they all stared down into the black water to watch for lights, as if being on this relatively small vessel was any protection against a leviathan that could break the back of a destroyer.

Trescu put his hand to his earpiece.

"*Zephyr* is transmitting," he said helpfully. So he still had his comms link to his fleet, then; Hoffman must have gone soft. "She wants to make her move. Captain Michaelson, I suggest we do this *now*. We've lost four hours already. These beasts won't wait forever."

Michaelson pushed back off the rails and slapped Marcus on the back.

"Toss a coin for the privilege," he said.

"It's my job." Marcus took off his armor plates and stacked them. Dom had never known him to do that before a mission. "You get ready to launch the lifeboats. If we blow that thing up, the shock wave's going to rupture every weld and rivet on this tub." He gestured at the armor and gave Dom a meaningful look. "You all might want to consider how long you can tread water in full fighting order."

"Damn," Cole muttered. "Whatever happened to a nice boat trip 'round the bay?"

Michaelson did an after-you flourish of his hand and Marcus

padded along the deck to the harpoon mounting. The leviathan had lights. At least they'd see the thing coming.

If it doesn't come up right under the hull, of course.

"Ready," Marcus called. "Tell the boats they can blow its brains out any time they like."

CHAPTER 17

Your priority is to stop the UIR advance within Kashkur. COG forces hold the central plains of the country and the extreme west, but the UIR is widening its corridors between the areas we still hold. The Anvegad Pass is blocked and must remain so if we are to stop the UIR closing the circle and inserting land forces from the east.

(COLONEL CHOI, OFFICER COMMANDING 6 BRIGADE, KASHKUR)

ANVEGAD, EASTERN KASHKUR: 32 YEARS EARLIER.

Hoffman knew the tough reputation of Pesang troops but he'd never actually come face-to-face with one. Now he was looking at six of them, and he wondered if there'd been a mistake.

They were tiny. They were also very young—most Gears seemed to be, but not *that* young—and the heavy machetes they carried on their belts looked too big for them. They formed up in a line and stood to attention.

Shit. They haven't even got full armor. That's three-quarter grade.

"Sah, we don't speak good, but we understand okay," one of them said. "You give us job, we *do* job."

"I'm Lieutenant Hoffman." For some reason, he took an instant liking to this lad. "What's your name, Gear?"

"Rifleman Bai Tak, Hoffman sah." He turned smartly and indicated each man in the line. "Riflemen—Lau En, Cho Ligan, Jati Shah, Gi Shim, Naru Fel."

Hoffman looked at Pad, realizing that this was all the support Anvil Gate was going to get. "Find these men some better armor, Private. I can't send them out on patrol in their goddamn underwear." He gestured to Bai Tak, tapping on his own chestplate to get the message across. "Heavy plate. You need more armor. And proper boots."

Bai Tak frowned slightly as if he was running through a vocabulary list in his head. Hoffman hadn't realized how little Tyran these men spoke.

"Ah," he said, face lighting up in revelation. "Sah, no more armor. How we move around all quiet?" He stabbed a forefinger down at Hoffman's regulation thick-soled steel-capped boots with their armored greaves. "How we climb in those? We fall and get damn *dead*, sir."

"Good point, Rifleman Tak." So they weren't as green and innocent as they looked. "Okay, go with Private Salton and get yourselves settled in. When you're fed and supplied, come back here for a briefing."

They seemed to grasp things well enough, or at least they all moved fast and gave the impression of purpose. Pad gave Hoffman a knowing look as he followed them.

He drew his finger across his throat, clearly delighted. "I hear they're very light on ammo, too, sir."

Hoffman didn't care how much ammo they burned through. He just wanted the Indies cleared out of the high ground behind him, because they were the ones who were going to drop mortars into the city, pick off his patrols, and harass any relief sent to the fort. They wouldn't bring down Anvegad, but he didn't want to lose a garrison and half the civvies stuck here just to prove a point about the strategic advantages of a gun battery on a mountain.

He hadn't lost anyone yet to the frontal assault. It had all been down to one asshole with a rocket launcher. And that asshole was going to pay for it.

The bombardment from the Indie line to the south was sporadic. There was a lot of activity down there, and the gunners responded with the heavy-caliber belt-fed Stomper and the One-Fifty guns, but the main guns only fired twice. That drove the mobile artillery back a few kilometers.

Hoffman was still trying to work out what the Indies' game was. They weren't keeping up sustained fire, and the shells were either landing short or striking the cliff beneath. The height of Anvil Gate made it hard for them to drop shots accurately. Hoffman suspected that if they'd inserted troops into the hilly country behind the fort, they wouldn't risk shelling their own positions.

They didn't seem to be trying. But there was also the possibility that the commander out there was second-rate, and all they'd been tasked to do was hold the refinery.

Does that solve all my problems?

How long is this going to go on?

Hoffman went up to the gun floor. The place was in almost total darkness except for faint illumination on the controls, and his eyes took a few seconds to adjust. The gun crew were either taking a breather or watching the Indie lines through field glasses. Evan was busy pumping grease into the hoist and loading mechanism.

"Time to hand over to the relief," Hoffman said. "Get your asses down to the medic. Just because you walked out of here doesn't mean you're still okay."

Evan wiped the nozzles of the copper-plated grease guns with a rag. "I think I know what they're up to, sir. Look."

Hoffman steadied his elbows on the sill and adjusted the focus on his binoculars. The knot of Indie vehicles was moving around, and most of them had their lights on. The refinery that had always been a constellation of white, amber, and red stars on the horizon was in darkness, but the damn Indies seemed oblivious of the fact that their vehicles were very, very visible.

"So they're idiots," Hoffman said.

"I wouldn't rule out stupidity, sir, but they know we're stuck here without any prospect of resupply. I think they're trying to get us to piss away our ordnance."

Hoffman thought it over. Whether the Indies intended that or not, it was the reality he had to face. A full magazine and shell store looked comforting until you began an assault, and then it evaporated faster than you ever thought possible. It was early days, but all the supplies *would* run out.

But *inviting* fire? The Indies had lost vehicles. That meant they'd certainly lost drivers. Suicide troops were always a possibility, but acting as live bait with the near certainty of death—sitting there, *waiting* for it—was something very few sane people would do, even Gears. Hoffman had seen men and women do crazily heroic things in combat knowing full well that they stood little chance of coming out alive, but it wasn't calculated and long-drawn-out. They made an instant decision because something *had* to be done; smother a grenade with your own body, drag that wounded comrade to safety from open ground, charge that gun position. It was the moment when self ceased to exist and the only thing the Gear saw was necessity because his buddies would die if he did nothing.

"I don't buy it," Hoffman said. "Nobody sits and fries unless they're religious crazies or something. You remember those Tennad sailors who crewed those little suicide submarines? Ordinary guys. *Sane* guys. The Indies had to weld the hatches so those poor fuckers couldn't change their minds. Because most of them *did*."

"Yeah," said Evan. "I agree. Now watch the lights."

Hoffman took a while to work it out. Vehicles seemed to be milling around, no unusual thing in itself because they were probably ferrying fuel and equipment out of the refinery for their own use. It was a field of moving points of light. At night, it was hard to judge depth and work out the relative positions of whatever was carrying the lights.

It was just that the movement was . . . odd.

It took a few moments to sink in. Hoffman defocused and tried every trick he knew to get his brain to see the movement differently instead of letting it apply the patterns it was used to. Then he saw it, and the whole picture shifted.

"They're moving too precisely," he said. "They're following each other at fixed intervals."

"Now, how many can you see making sharp turns?"

"Shit." Hoffman was suddenly fascinated. "They're making big, open loops."

"Hard tow. Decoys."

"You're shitting me."

Evan chuckled. "I like an officer who talks like I do."

"Okay, two flaws in that theory. One—the lead vehicle has a live driver, and that's the one we're most likely to hit. Two—the vehicles we destroyed earlier were definitely being driven. Separate. Under their own power."

Evan started pumping the grease again. "You can rig a vehicle to push it as well as hard-tow it. We don't always hit the lead vehicle. And the first guys we hit probably just underestimated the range and accuracy of these guns. They got the message fast."

It was still mindlessly dangerous, but there was a chance of surviving. That was enough for some.

"And at night, we don't even know those are vehicles."

"Sappers rig dummy lights to look like any number of installations. It's low-tech and sounds stupid, but at night, it works. All the Indies have to do is keep tempting us to fire."

"And while we're looking that way, we're distracted from what's happening behind us."

"See, they're not as dumb as we think, are they?"

Hoffman wasn't sure he could trust his own judgment now. He should have spotted that right away—hours ago. Nobody would attempt a conventional frontal assault on a battery like this in open terrain. There had to be more layers to it.

Maybe Hoffman was concussed, but Evan had taken a pounding too, and he seemed to be functioning okay. Sometimes there was no excuse for missing the obvious.

"Okay, let's assume that's what they're doing, and hold back accordingly."

"One more thing. The big guns need to be maintained. The more we keep firing without relining these babies, the less accurate they get. They must know that."

"But that's a long time, isn't it?"

"No. It's about three hundred full charge firings, which we could rip through in no time."

"How many on the clock now?"

"Maybe two hundred."

"Replenishment's still going to be our major problem."

"Yes, sir. It is."

Hoffman slapped Evan on the back. "Good work. Now change crews and get some rest."

Hoffman was pretty sure he could work out the tactics now. *Attrition, diversion, isolation.* He wasn't so sure about the intention to keep the Anvegad pass closed to stop COG troop movements out of Kashkur, though—unless control of the fort was part of that.

Either way, Anvil Gate was worth a long-haul effort to take it. He didn't need to guess about that. He just had to sit tight. Geology was on his side. He had power, he had unlimited water, and he had supplies—for the time being anyway. He checked on the briefing room to see how Pad was getting on with the Pesangs, and sat down to call Brigade Control at Lakar.

"Control, we're not going anywhere fast," he said. "Where's the Behemoth?"

"We can't get it to you. The Indies have broken through at Mendurat and they're holding the road. What's your estimate on supplies?"

"Around twelve days food and ammo."

"You're not critical, then."

"That's why I'm flagging up the timescale now."

"We're aware of your situation, Lieutenant. Are you able to hold your position?"

"It's a mountain, more or less. We could hold it dead if we had to. Look, I have five thousand civilians here, and if things get bad, I have no way whatsoever of evacuating them."

Control went quiet for a moment. "We're aware of that too. There's nothing we can do until we regain full control of Kashkur. Keep us updated."

Hoffman began to feel like a nuisance, as if he hadn't really got any problems and Control was just too polite to tell him so. If Anvil Gate had been one fort of many, and not as pivotal as it was, then he would have had a wholly different range of options including abandoning the position. But he hadn't.

He had to plan for the worst scenario. That was what he was trained to do. Anvegad wasn't just an army base, it was a city full of noncombatants. And that changed everything.

But, as Control had reminded him, his situation wasn't critical yet.

If the Pesangs could clear the hinterland of hostiles, then maybe Hoffman could find another way to clear the gorge.

He went back to the briefing room. The six Pesangs were clustered around a map on the table with Sam Byrne who had shown up as well. They were working out positions and the areas they needed to cover. Six men for a huge area like that seemed to be stretching it.

"Don't worry, sah, we do this," Bai Tak said. He adjusted his webbing and penciled something on the folded map in his hand. "At night, *much* better."

While they were talking, there was a distant explosion from the north, a distinct *pomp*. It didn't sound close. Hoffman's first thought was that one of the imulsion fields had been sabotaged, and he went out to the rear gantry to look for a red glow on the horizon. The sky was still velvet black.

He got on the radio anyway. "Anvil Gate to Control, anything going on to the north of us? Maybe fifteen, twenty klicks? Big explosion, but we can't see anything."

"Negative, Anvil Gate. If we get any reports, we'll come back to you."

It could take hours for anyone to report an attack. Hoffman wasn't going to relax yet. He waited on the gantry for a while, wondering if the Indies had developed any night-sights yet and realizing this was going to be a dumbass way to find out, then went back inside. The Pesangs had moved out. He hadn't even heard them leave. It was very hard *not* to hear things out here in this still air.

"The Indies are jerking our chain, sir," Byrne said.

Hoffman sat down and took out his notebook to continue with his letter to Margaret. It was rapidly turning from an emotional last letter to be treasured and reread to a detailed record of un-folding events.

"Got to be," Hoffman said. "They can't smash their way in."

He listened for gunfire while he wrote, and at one point he simply nodded off with his head on his arm. He woke with a pounding headache to find Byrne shaking his shoulder.

"Sorry to disturb you, sir," Byrne said. "This might be nothing, but the baker says his watermill's stopped. The flow's down to a trickle. Carlile's taken a look at the cisterns down below and they're not filling, either."

The river that cut underground and flowed through Anvegad's bedrock had also been harnessed to run waterwheels in some parts of the town. It was a roaring torrent all year; it was one of the things that made Anvegad impregnable, a limitless source of water and power. Rivers didn't stop suddenly like a tap being turned off. If this one had, something was very wrong.

Hoffman was already dealing with an enemy that had cut off his only road access from the north, so the UIR was equally capa-ble of diverting a river the same way. He was fighting engineers now, not troops. That was something he hadn't been prepared for. He felt his scalp tighten.

"That explosion," he said. "I think the bastards have blocked the river."

ANVEGAD HILLS, NORTH OF ANVIL GATE
GARRISON: THREE DAYS LATER.

It was a siege, whichever way you looked at it. Anvil Gate was cut off by road, it couldn't get food and ammunition, and now its water supply had been reduced to a trickle. Bai hadn't expected his war to be like that. But now that it was, he'd deal with it.

He squeezed through the cleft in the rock and looked down

into the mouth of the sinkhole below him. There was still water flowing, but he could see from the ferns and eroded rock left high and dry that the level had fallen dramatically.

"Not much water, sah."

Carlile, the engineer, scrambled up the rocks behind him. "Shit." He looked genuinely shocked. "That's normally a big waterfall."

Well, it wasn't a waterfall now. The river was just a stream that tumbled over the jagged edge and splashed onto smoothly eroded rocks before gurgling into the darkness underground.

"So—how much water we got?" Bai asked.

"About enough for basic survival." Carlile was a nice man. He used a lot of technical words in his job, but he obviously tried hard to find easier ones for Bai. "Some water's still getting through, but not enough. Then we've got the water in the big storage tanks underground—the cisterns. We use it faster than they're filling up. So we're going to have to ration it."

"They blow up the river, like mining?"

"Yeah. You can change the course of a river if you place enough charges in the right place. Like you can blow up a gorge."

"They come back and try to stop all the water, I bet."

Carlile gave Bai a wary look. "Good point. They might."

"Ah, we always have shit like that." Bai was used to disputes over water. "My father—he sort it out."

The Shaoshi often dammed streams from their side of the border and diverted them from Pesang land to irrigate their own pasture. Every so often, it ended in a skirmish and even a few deaths, and then everything would calm down again for a few years. With the current drought, there was no water to steal this year. Harua wouldn't have to worry about that while he was away.

Carlile looked at the machete. "Yeah, I can guess your dad was pretty persuasive."

"We find blocked bit, yes? Then we wait for bastards to come back and teach them lesson."

Carlile chuckled to himself. "Your Tyran's improved a lot in a few days."

It was a case of having to learn. Bai lived in a country where there were at least five languages he had to speak just to get by. He was starting to realize that the COG didn't do things that way, and just settled for making everyone speak the same language. It made sense. But it would never work in Pesang.

The river was fringed by trees, rare and useful cover up here. Bai assumed that whoever was doing the blasting not only knew the terrain like the back of their hand, but was probably still out there now keeping watch. He set off along the higher ground above the old riverbed, trying to keep the course in sight, but the overhangs jutted out so far that it was easier to climb down to the river itself and just walk north along its bed. He clambered down the slope and dropped the last meter onto the wet gravel that now lined the bank. Carlile was keeping up with him pretty well for a man in those big Gears boots, but he was never going to be able to creep up on anyone making that much noise.

When they reached the next rapids—just a pool of foam now, although the eroded rock proved they'd been impressive—Bai stopped to get his bearings.

"Listen." He squatted down, rinsed his face, and drank from his cupped hands before filling his water bottle. "You hear?"

It was the steady rumble and splash of a big, fast river not too far away, as loud as the trucks on the road through Paro. Carlile looked blank and shook his head.

"River," Bai said. "You COG guys, all deaf."

"Too many loud guns for too many years," Carlile said. "You'll be like that one day, too."

They walked for another ten minutes, the steep banks getting higher and deeper as they went, then rounded a bend to see a long, sloping hill cutting right across the course of the river. Bai guessed that hadn't been there a few days ago. The rocks were jagged and free of vegetation even where the water was seeping through them. It looked like someone had blown up an entire cliff to send the rubble plunging into the river.

"Yeah, that work really good." Bai climbed up the dam of boulders and peered over the top. The water had now found a new path south, smashing through trees and flowing into a smaller channel that vanished down a slope into the distance. "Maybe it fall down one day, but not soon."

"Well, we can't shift this without vehicles," Carlile said. "But we can't get them out here."

"No helicopters? Why is nobody coming to help?"

"They'll come," Carlile said. "But it won't be for weeks. Come on, let's head back to base."

Weeks didn't sound hopeful, because Bai was sure that most of Anvegad didn't have that much time. He was used to living like this, just scraping by in a harsh environment and walking a few kilometers to find water. Hunting small animals for food would be relatively easy here. There were even wild goats, a really easy meal for a man with a good rifle. So none of the Pesangs were going to starve to death, and even Gears used to a soft city life could get by. But the civilians would be hit very hard.

Every night now, the Pesang squad went out on patrol. That was their sole task—to catch any Indies operating around the fort. Apart from the pretty spectacular evidence of sabotage and surprise attacks, Bai could tell they were there anyway. They probably thought they were stealthy, but he could smell them and he had a pretty good idea where to look for them now simply by working out the eye lines, the positions they needed to be in to keep an eye on activity in and around the garrison.

Smell and plain carelessness gave them away, too. He found the places they laid up with their rifles and took a leak, because whatever they ate made their urine smell different. He could also smell the oil they used to maintain their weapons. He found the pieces of cut wire coated in bright plastic—just tiny beads, nothing more—that they'd used to lay charges.

They can't be special forces. Unless they're just not very good at it.

Bai had thought that becoming a Gear would be a long, slow training process. He still wasn't fully comfortable with the Lancer rifle, and the rules and regulations were something he'd always have to look up in a book, but the stuff that Lieutenant Hoffman wanted him to do—observe, track, trap, kill—came naturally to him.

Well, maybe not the killing. I haven't killed a man yet. But these guys are out to kill me, so I'll do it when the time comes.

The squad split into pairs, fanning out from the fort on three sides. Bai went with Cho. They'd been out for a couple of hours when he heard the sound of small stones moving. There was a definite crunch and a sliding noise, like something heavy moving on gravel, not the sound of a lighter animal like a goat picking its feet up and placing them carefully. He tapped Cho's shoulder and they both dropped to the ground to wait.

Over there, to the right, Cho gestured.

Bai had to wait a while, but then he picked up movement. Even on a moonless night, there was enough light to see a dark shape that didn't blend in or match the shadows, especially when it moved. It drew his eye.

Yes, it was a man all right. Now that he'd focused on him, he could see the rifle and something else long and narrow on his back. The guy moved into a position that was almost level with the top of the city walls, and began assembling a small mortar.

This was where the difficult choices started. A mortar like that would be ready to fire in a few moments, but Bai didn't know if there were other Indies in the area, and shooting the guy—easy from here, even for him—was going to be heard halfway across the mountains. Cho obviously had the same idea. He drew his machete slowly and gestured to Bai to go around one side of the man while he moved to the other.

Bai definitely couldn't have crept up on the Indie in regulation Gears' boots. He got to within a couple of meters of the man, and even when the guy scanned slowly from left to right, he looked straight at Bai but didn't seem to see him.

It was just a matter of timing.

The machete was a heavy blade. Bai thought it was pretty humane if you put some force behind it. None of this messy throat-cutting business, trying to subdue a struggling man; he was used to dispatching an animal quickly, and a good hard blow would stun as well as slice. The guy suddenly looked to his left, probably spotting Cho far too late, and Bai simply reacted. He was on the Indie in a heartbeat and brought his machete down in an arc with his full weight behind it.

The *thwock* noise was louder than he expected. The handle almost jerked out of his hand, because the man fell with no more than a grunt and the blade stayed embedded in his skull. It was over in a moment. Bai didn't think it would be like that, even though he knew what the blade could do.

But now he had to retrieve his weapon. It took a bit of effort, and he was glad he'd done this at night and not in broad daylight. The blood looked jet-black. Cho dismantled the mortar, slung it on his back, and took the guy's rifle and ammo clips. There was no point leaving the stuff for the other Indies to use. Everything the enemy had to haul up here slowed them down a little more.

And maybe his buddies would find the body. That would say plenty to them. It would tell them who they were dealing with, a corner of the COG that didn't play by their nice city-boy rules.

"You better clean that elsewhere," Cho whispered.

Bai waited until they were some way from the body and in the shelter of a rock before he wiped the blade on a patch of scrubby grass. He rinsed it with a splash of water from his bottle. If he didn't clean off the blood, it would mess up the sheath. For a moment he paused to work out how he felt right then, and although his heart was thumping, he felt quite numb about the whole thing. Was it really that easy? Maybe this was some kind of shock. Either way, he'd done it, and he hadn't lost his nerve.

Is it going to be that easy next time?

It didn't matter. He and Cho completed the rest of the patrol, saw no more Indies that night, and made their way back to the garrison just before dawn. The sentry on the gates just stared at them as he let them in.

"Wow," he said. "Been shopping?"

Cho showed off the Indie rifle and the mortar. It was a sniper rifle, and the guards were so impressed that they went to get Pad

Salton. Within a few minutes, Cho and Bai had an audience, and Pad came to admire the rifle.

"Didn't hear any shots in the night," he said. He winked at Cho. "Have you been saving ammo?"

"Bai got him," Cho said. "No point making noise, is there?"

"And you look like such *nice* little lads, too."

Bai was starting to feel a bit shaky now that he was back in the garrison and no longer pumped up waiting to be shot or ambushed. All he could do was grin. It wasn't because he found it funny, or took it lightly; he just didn't know how to respond to these foreign Gears, and he was almost embarrassed by that. But it seemed to be what they expected—that Pesangs were nice, friendly people who could switch to being unseen, silent assassins in seconds, and who knew no fear. The fact that he was so small seemed to impress them even more. He could guess what they would tell their buddies in years to come.

But I get scared just like you. You think I'm that different?

But yes, he *was* generally happy with life, happy to be making a living for once, happy to have stopped some *Indie bastard*— which he'd first thought was one word from the way Hoffman said it—from launching a mortar into the crowded city. He'd done his job, upheld his honor, and not been killed. He was also going to sit down to a huge breakfast. What was there *not* to be happy about?

And if that image of the little Pesang who would appear out of nowhere and cut your head off made a few more Indies think twice about attacking the garrison—he was happy with that, too.

ANVIL GATE GARRISON: DAY TWELVE OF THE SIEGE.

As the siege started to bite, Hoffman decided that running a city was a far harder job than fighting a war.

Combat was the easy bit. It was anticipating all the little things that made civvies scared, restless, and difficult that took the time.

He walked around the center of the city with Alderman Buyal Casani—driving wasted of precious fuel—and saw all the ways that a community unraveled, even one where the people were used to an isolated life with frequent hardship.

And if I hadn't started rationing food early, we'd be eating card-board now.

Water rationing had become a daily routine, too. As soon as the sun came up, queues started to form at the water tanks on the main streets, with lines of grim-faced people clutching plastic containers and buckets. They got fifteen liters per person per day for all their cooking, drinking, and bathing. Hoffman had settled on fifteen liters on the basis of a desperate call to a refugee agency office in New Temperance. Anvegad had no plan for survival water because it hadn't seemed possible that the river would ever run dry.

Well, it had. It damn well had.

He had to hand it to the Indies; they'd certainly thought this through. It was a very economical siege. They'd gone for the long game and cut the supply chain rather than throw men and muni-tions at it. If anyone ever told him again that army engineers were the tail and not the teeth, he'd punch them into next week. These guys didn't just lay tracks and clear mines. They could actually ruin your entire day without even picking up a rifle.

Very clever. Very effective. Bastards.

And the key to besieging cities was leaning on the civilians.

The shelling was sporadic now, clearly more to create uncer-tainty and fear than to try to destroy the fort itself. Hoffman stopped to watch the water distribution in action. A city official su-pervised the filling of containers and marked the individual's ID card to say they'd had their allocation for the day. No ID card meant no water, and nobody could come back twice. Hoffman liked the Kashkuri, but people were people, and he was wonder-ing when the aldermen would discover the first forged card. It wasn't that hard in a low-tech place like this.

But it was a small city. Most people knew one another by sight, and that was probably enough to deter wide-scale fraud.

I hope.

"I'm disappointed that nobody has tried to clear the pass," Casani said. He was carrying two five-liter containers, just like everyone else in the city. "I realize the Coalition is heavily committed elsewhere, but I feel we have been abandoned."

Hoffman thought it was a good idea not to mention that most sieges he'd studied at staff college lasted years. Anvegad had only been cut off for twelve days. But those long sieges were against cities with porous boundaries, with gates and bridges for people to slip in and out, and even places to grow food. Anvegad was effectively an island with two weeks' grace at any time. The effects hit home a lot sooner.

"Sir, I've made my feelings clear to Colonel Choi," Hoffman said. "But he can't clear the road, and he can't commit a strike force to drive the UIR back. He's more worried about the Indies pushing east within Kashkur. If that happens, it won't matter a damn if we open the road or not. We'll be surrounded."

Hoffman didn't believe that Choi wanted the road cleared at all. The COG probably needed to keep that pass blocked for the time being as much as the Indies did. Hoffman was now wondering when the time would be right to ask the Indies to let the civilians leave. The situation hadn't deteriorated that far yet, but he knew how long these things took to go through neutral diplomatic channels. Then there was the logistics of moving five thousand people across a wilderness to the nearest town.

"People are going to die here," Casani said. "Disease. Dehydration. Starvation. We maintain this garrison. The least COG command can do is keep us alive."

"Do you want to evacuate the city?" Hoffman asked. It was as much Hoffman's litmus test of the man's resolve as anything. "Because if that's what you're considering, I'd better get the diplomatic wheels in motion now."

"No, we intend to stay," Casani said. He actually stopped in his tracks and turned to face Hoffman. The street didn't smell of the usual coffee and baking bread today, just sewage. "This is not some observation post we can choose to defend or abandon. This is our *home*. Would it be beyond your masters to airlift some food?"

"I keep asking. It has to come by helicopter. Their range limits the options."

It was true, but Hoffman also knew that if the will was there, the goddamn supplies would be here in hours. Terns could land and refuel a few hundred kilometers north. He was making excuses for Choi—or Choi's boss, or Choi's boss's boss—and he *knew* it. That walked along the thin boundary of lying. It was a path he never wanted to take.

"Seven hundred calories a day is not enough," Casani said. "Hungry people become restless and difficult."

"But it gives us three times as long to hold out," Hoffman said. "And we're only at the two-week mark."

"You know as well as I do, Lieutenant, that this will *not* be over in weeks."

Casani stopped short of asking how much food the garrison had stashed away as dry rations. Hoffman wasn't going to touch that yet, not for the civilian population. If the garrison was going to fight—and there might come a point where the Indies would try to physically *take* the fort—then Hoffman needed fit men. He wasn't proud of holding out on the civvies, but they had the option of being inactive. His Gears didn't. So they got the food.

But the folk here knew that. They'd get resentful sooner or later.

Sheraya Olencu Byrne wasn't any old civvie, of course, and she ate in the garrison mess. She was *staff*, goddamn it. She was *pregnant*. Hoffman would apologize to nobody for that concession.

He inhaled reluctantly as he walked, aware of the sideways glances that followed him, accusing looks that seemed to say he could perform miracles if he wanted to but he just wasn't trying. The smell was getting to him. Anvegad had always smelled of sewage, but now the smell was becoming a stench. The sewage system needed a minimum flow of water for the ancient drains to be kept clear. And the weather was getting warmer. Casani was right: disease was a real threat.

We never covered shit disposal at staff college. Maybe I'll send a memo to the General suggesting it goes on the curriculum, headed RE: SHIT.

"You're going to have to dump human waste outside the city," Hoffman said. "Which is going to be tough, whether folks throw it over the walls or you organize collections and ship the shit out."

"We are dealing with it," Casani said wearily. "We will drive a truck outside the walls at night and tip it where we can."

Hoffman left Casani at the end of the main street and continued on his own, climbing the levels until he was on the gantries above the level of the ancient walls. It was a no-go area in daylight now. A sniper could have picked him off at any time, but he was prepared to take that risk to get an uninterrupted look at the terrain. There was still no big Indie force massing out there. They knew the range of the main guns, and they had no pressing need to rush into eastern Kashkur yet. They could wait on the outcome of the fighting in the west.

Hoffman climbed down from the walls and wondered what Margaret was doing right then. He imagined her in the middle of a hearing, giving some hapless defense counsel hell.

How often does she think about me?

Hoffman wondered if he had any right to expect her to think of him at all. She wasn't on his mind all the time. That made him feel guilty.

Back in the mess, the off-duty Gears were listening to the radio and eating bowls of chunky soup in grim silence. Byrne ladled it out in carefully equal portions like the head of the household. With Sheraya there, the gathering had the air of a family meal. The soup smelled pretty good.

"Better keep the windows closed," Hoffman said. "Don't piss off hungry civvies."

"Goat," said Gunner Jarrold. "Bai and the lads donated a couple of goats they happened to run into. In the dark, of course. Very discreet. They butchered it before they brought it back."

"As long as we're not eating dead snipers."

"Maybe we ought to spread that rumor and *really* put the shits up the Indies, sir."

"I think the prospect of getting a Pesanga blade through your brain is doing a fine job of that already."

Hoffman had thought six Pesangs weren't going to make much difference, but they punched well above their weight, and often in these unexpected ways. Bai Tak had made his mark from the start as the natural leader, the one ready to have a go and risk anything, as if he was trying to find out just how much he could do. They got a kill most nights and hauled back useful kit. That had to be crimping the Indies' ability to move around out there.

"Sir?" Carlile stuck his head around the door. "Just heard from Brigade. They're sending a Corva down from Ibiri, mixed cargo of water, medicine, food, and some fuel. But that's right on the limit of its range with a full cargo bay."

"Shit, are those old wrecks still flying?" Byrne said. "Well, let's be glad they are."

"Is it going to try to land?" Hoffman asked. The veteran helicopter couldn't airdrop a load here—there was nowhere they could drop anything that didn't involve dodging the Indie guns to retrieve it, if it didn't end up in a ravine in the first place. "Because hovering here is asking for trouble."

"We'll make it work," Carlile said. "ETA two hours."

The world could change in a few seconds. Hoffman allowed himself a scrap of optimism, and didn't call Lakar back to ask them why they couldn't ship out earth-moving equipment if they could get a Corva in the air. Those old crates could carry bulldozers as underslung cargo. But the supplies were the most urgent issue. He'd ask for the engineering kit later.

"Okay, Byrne, let's get some security positions set up. That's a big slow bird coming in. Jarrold, give me suppressing fire just before it lands. Just keep the Indies busy."

Hoffman got up to take a look at the likely landing zone with Carlile, hoping there'd be some goat soup left by the time he got back. His belt was already getting slack, and he didn't have fat to lose to begin with. He followed Byrne along the roof-level gantry and they surveyed the land north of the fort.

It was all slopes. The Corva would have to stop at a hover and roll off cargo. If the bird was going to do that, it might have made more sense to hover over the city itself. Hoffman would talk to the pilot when the guy got to see the terrain.

Byrne spent a while adjusting his field glasses, as if he was working up to saying something. "We're lower on dry rations than I thought, sir," he said. "Maybe I've miscounted the boxes. I'd hate to think of our civvie help pilfering our food."

"They wouldn't," Hoffman said, not believing his own denial for one minute. People would steal anything, anytime, anywhere. At Berephus, they'd had to put armed guards on ambulances to stop the locals from siphoning off the fuel while the paramedics went to haul out bodies. "Capital offense, stealing military supplies in theater."

"Yeah."

Hoffman thought this was as good a time as any to mention his worries. "If we evacuate the civvies, Sam, I want you to go with Sheraya. I want you both out of here."

Byrne walked off along the gantry, head down. Beneath them, a long line of civilians waited for one of the daily bread handouts. Hoffman decided not to tell them there was a supply aircraft inbound until it had been safely unloaded and they were sure they'd received crates of food and not ball bearings intended for some other base.

"That's very generous of you, sir," Byrne said at last. "But she probably won't want to leave her city. And I wouldn't leave fellow Gears in a fight like this."

Hoffman knew that was going to be Byrne's answer. He'd have to find another way to get them out.

In the end, it wasn't possible to keep the news of the airlift from the people of Anvegad. They could hear the old Corva for kilometers, that rising-and-falling groan that Hoffman hadn't heard for a few years. Slow and old, and heavy on fuel; but the bird still flew, and when he saw the wobbly black profile emerging slowly out of the golden haze sitting low on the hills behind the fort, it actually moved him. It was a striking image. He thought of poor damn Captain Sander, and how he probably would have liked to do a painting of it.

"CC-Seventy-Four-Five to Anvil Gate." The pilot was a woman. "I hope you've cleared your pantry. Mom's brought the groceries."

"Not much choice of landing zones, ma'am," Hoffman said. "Steep slopes, lots of loose debris. You want to try for the ground at zero-zero-four-eight-three-zero or hover?"

"I'll land," she said. "It's a little breezy around here."

"You'll hear the arty boys start up soon. Just keeping our Indie visitors busy and out of your hair."

"Thanks for the heads-up, Anvil Gate. I startle easy."

The Indies must have heard the Corva too. Their guns opened up when the helicopter was a few minutes out. It circled over the LZ, kicking up a dust storm, and Hoffman realized it was going to be a pain in the ass getting the crates back into the city. Everything had to go over the walls, a backbreaking task. The best landing the Corva could make turned out to be right on the limit of the slope it could handle.

"Let's get the fuel out first," the pilot said. "I really hate sitting on a firebomb with all this ordnance flying around."

Gears and civilians moved in to shift the metal cans and stack them clear of the chopper. Hoffman watched from the gantry, squatting to minimize his outline, and kept checking his watch. The wind was picking up. The pilot was getting impatient.

"Hey, I'm going to have to turn," she said. "That's one hell of a crosswind. Clear the LZ and I'll come in again."

The dust billowed up as the Corva lifted and climbed slowly to the side. Hoffman was already calculating how much more breathing space the supplies would give them, and how long he would have to eke them out.

That's another month's grace, at least.

He looked up from the manifest that Carlile had scribbled just as a streak of light and gas shot from his right-hand field of vision and hit the Corva square in the flank. He stared, frozen and horrified, at a sky of orange flame.

He didn't even duck. There wasn't so much as a shout from anyone for a long, slow second, that brief moment of disbelief before the reality kicked in. The rotors and burning airframe tumbled down the steep slope and left a wake of black smoke pluming in the air. The Corva was out of sight before two more explosions sent more smoke climbing.

"Shit, shit, shit, *shit!*" Hoffman brought his fist down on the square-section steel rail and kept punching it until he knew he'd done himself some damage. It was pointless to send in a fire-control team. He gave the order anyway. "Damage-control party—medic—get down there."

There was no saving the pilot. The off-loaded fuel was little comfort, and the rest of the supplies had been incinerated. Hoffman felt instantly ashamed for even thinking about them when that woman had just paid with her life for trying to land them. He shoved his grazed fist in his pocket, shaking with disbelief and anger, and went to find where that rocket had come from.

The bastards were still out there, for all the Pesangs' efforts. Hoffman didn't plan to sleep until the last of them were cut down.

And he *meant* cut down.

CHAPTER 18

*We're going to be dangerously low on fuel very soon. I'm going
to keep nagging you about this, because it radically shapes
our options for the future. If we can't fuel the fleet, then we're
stuck here. If we need to run, we can't. If we ever want to return to the mainland, then we have to start planning for that
right away and conserve what fuel we've got left. There isn't a
hope in hell that we'll be able to find a new supply out here.*

(ROYSTON SHARLE, HEAD OF EMERGENCY MANAGEMENT, TO
VICTOR HOFFMAN, QUENTIN MICHAELSON, AND
RICHARD PRESCOTT)

**CNV *FALCONER*, SOUTH OF VECTES: PRESENT
DAY, 15 A.E.**

"They're still there." Garcia never sounded irritable no matter
how many times Dom asked if the leviathans were still around.
"But we're relying on the hydrophones. The side scan's no use—
it's active sonar. Once we ping a leviathan, it knows where we
are."

Dom braced his hands on the wheelhouse console and looked
out into the night. "It might know anyway. We don't know a damn
thing about them, do we?"

"They blow up." Marcus listened to the radio conversation,

frowning at something unseen on the horizon. "That's all the zoology lesson we need."

Falconer had suspended her own hull sonar in case she inadvertently pinged either boat and gave the leviathans a clue. But her engines and prop couldn't be silenced. They were a potential magnet for the creatures. Dom was waiting for them to decide the patrol boat was a soft option and come after it first.

Michaelson let his binoculars dangle from his neck and took the mike out of its deckhead cradle. "*Falconer* to Control, stand by Hammer . . . *Falconer* to *Clement*, *Zephyr*, we're in your hands."

Sometimes you got a Gorasni who was fluent in Tyran, and sometimes you didn't. "*Zephyr* to *Falconer*, we have firing solution. We fire, yes?"

Dom hung around the wheelhouse door. Cole wandered by and nudged him. "What they doin', Dom?"

"I think they're both going for the same one but from different angles."

"And this is shallow, right? Like twenty meters? 'Cos we can hear 'em on the radio."

"*Zephyr* here—we fire first, COG, because we are very close. Short track."

Michaelson opened his mouth for a moment but he never got as far as a response. Dom heard a command in Gorasni, then a snatch of Garcia's voice: "Fire one . . ."

Dom shoved Cole out onto the deck. "Come on, when that hits, one of them's going to—"

"*Impact.*"

Dom was sure he'd lifted clear of the deck for a second. The explosion sounded like it was a couple of kilometers off the starboard bow, and if he'd been fast enough he might have caught the plume of foam even in the dark. *Falconer* shuddered. It had to be a kill.

"Yeah, shallow," Cole said.

"*Falconer* to *Zephyr*, *Falconer* to *Clement*—time to thin out unless you've got a solution on Number Two right *now*."

"*Zephyr* to *Falconer*—its friend must have heard that. *Zephyr* to *Clement*, I hear your tanks—you dive?"

Dom didn't hear whether *Clement* responded. He was focused on what he was sure was going to happen next. That explosion would have rattled even a leviathan's brain. It would either go after a sub, or surface to go after the noisiest, easiest target to find—*Falconer*.

Dom heard a loud splash like someone slapping the water just as he reached Marcus on the harpoon.

Marcus didn't always manage to batten down all his reactions. Dom saw the look on his face—frown gradually vanishing, eyes widening, even a very slight drop of the jaw—and turned to see what he was staring at.

Shit, the thing was *big*. Even in the dark, Dom could see that. The patrol boats's running lights reflected off its wet scales. Even without the points of bluish light, its outline was clear. Marcus fired.

The harpoon went whistling out like a rocket grenade, whipping the line behind it. Dom heard the wet *thwack* on impact. He expected to hear the explosive tip detonate, but there was just a faint, muffled *pomp*, and the leviathan spun around and slapped down onto the sea. Water washed over the deck. The line began paying out at speed.

"Baby, you caught somethin'," Cole yelled.

"Why the hell hasn't the thing blown up?"

"No idea," Marcus said. "Maybe we hit it somewhere that doesn't detonate."

Dom grabbed the ax. "Cole Train, you stand clear of that." He was expecting the creature to dive. If it tried to drag *Falconer* down, he had to sever that cable. "If that line parts, it'll cut clean through you like a damn blade."

"It's holding," Marcus called. The line went tight. "Cole, take over. Just watch the line."

He grabbed the targeting laser and went to the bow. Dom couldn't tell if the leviathan was dragging the boat or not, but either way it was going to be a tough job for the helmsman.

The line paid out to about eight hundred meters. Dom was pretty sure he recalled that the required safety clearance for mine-hunters was one thousand meters. It was all getting a bit too close.

From the slightly elevated bridge, Muller could see more than Dom could from the rising and falling deck.

"It's coming about," he said over the radio. "It's turning to star-board. Still breaking the surface."

"I need it closer." Marcus aimed the laser. "Can you get me in-side a hundred meters?"

Nobody seemed to want to repeat the obvious. If Marcus held the laser on it long enough, if Baird could align the Hammer, if the leviathan stayed surfaced for those essential seconds—then if it detonated like the Brumak beneath Jacinto had, *Falconer* was going to be an instant shower of rusty shrapnel.

But the Brumak was underground. Directed blast and all that shit. Yeah. This blast's not confined.

No, Dom knew zip about explosives on that kind of scale, and he was going to die. At best, *Falconer* was going to be lifted clear by the shock wave and smashed down hard again, hard enough to break her back.

Life rafts. Okay, don't forget. Rafts.

Falconer picked up speed. For a moment, it felt as if they were closing the gap on the leviathan too fast. Dom clung to the rail and tried to look ahead. He was sure he could see the steady, un-dulating movement as the thing rippled along near the surface with its back breaking the water. He definitely felt *Falconer* steer-ing hard to starboard. When he looked back for a moment and the lights caught the water, he could see a U-shaped wake. The boat had turned back toward Vectes.

"I'd take a guess that it's trying to beach," Muller said.

"Baird? Are you ready?" Marcus kept changing position, trying to steady his aim. "You got a lock yet?"

The radio crackled. It took a couple of seconds for Baird to respond.

"Okay, the sats have picked up the targeting laser. Can you ask the glowie to slow down?"

"Helm, give us some slack in that line," Marcus said. "Close the gap. Cole—wind the line back on the winch."

"How much?"

"Until the line goes taut. Then Muller can cut his speed and slow the thing."

"That's going to mean it'll blow frigging *close* to us," Muller said. "I mean *sinking* close."

Michaelson cut in. "Do it, helm."

The engines roared and the line started to sag. When it draped over the bow rail, Marcus yelled "Now!" and Cole hit the winch control. The line wound back around the capstan and went taut. Dom felt the shudder.

"Never done this on a moving surface," Marcus said. "Shit."

"You ready?" Baird asked. "Because correcting this thing manually is a bitch."

"Yeah, let's swap places."

"Come on."

Marcus just grunted. Dom could see the targeting beam hitting a scaly back, but it was bouncing and drifting all over the place.

"I'm ready," Baird said. "I mean, *really* ready."

"I get it, Baird."

Dom could see the naval base clearly now, its jetties and ships picked out by safety lights. At forty klicks per hour, that six-kilometer distance would be eaten up in minutes. They were getting too close to the island. The leviathan plowed on. Dom heard the engines throttle down and the harpoon line creaked alarmingly.

Nobody really knew what a leviathan could do, let alone a Lambent one. It might just have been holding back before showing them just how puny the boat was by comparison. *Falconer* slowed right down, then her engines roared again and it felt like she was turning.

"Fuck," Muller said. "That's full astern. It's got us. We're going to burn out a motor at this rate."

Dom really was ready to part that line. He hefted the ax and positioned himself clear of the arc that the line would whip through when he cut it. *Falconer* seemed not to be making way at all. Then there was a collective shout—the lookouts, Marcus, Michaelson standing at the bridge door—and the leviathan disappeared. The line plunged down into the sea.

"Shit. Lost the contact." Marcus still held the laser on the point where he'd last seen the leviathan, but the beam didn't penetrate far through water, especially water with a lot of deflecting debris in it. "Can we winch that thing up?"

Cole stared at the creaking capstan. "That oversized eel's doin' the winchin', not us."

"In case you've forgotten me, I'm still pretty ready." Baird sounded irked. "Just give me a call when you're through pissing around."

"Cole, jerk its chain," Marcus said.

The winch whined. Dom waited for the creaking to turn into snaps and pings as the line started to part. He was so fixed on the deck hazards that he found himself forgetting that they were tormenting a life-form that broke destroyers and might even blow up of its own accord.

Shit. What if it lets some polyps loose? Can they climb ropes?

He needn't have worried about the polyps. That was the least of their problems. The winch started to smoke, the line groaned, and *Falconer* lurched.

"Okay," Muller said. "Everyone think happy thoughts. Because—oh *fuck*. It's on the move."

"Okay, follow," Marcus said.

"It's on a course for the base. I'm thinking suicide run here."

"Follow it," Marcus said, "but get ready to do a handbrake turn when I say."

"Hey, Land-crab, the navy doesn't do handbrakes."

"Fine." Marcus sounded strained. "Just find some way of dragging that asshole west of the base at the last minute."

Dom decided the ax wasn't going to help much now. *Falconer* picked up speed again. The leviathan was on a collision course with the carrier berth, and *Falconer* was along for the ride whether she wanted to be or not.

CIC, VECTES NAVAL BASE.

Yeah, Marcus was right again.

Baird wasn't good just with big oily hardware; he was pretty good with computers, too. He wondered if even Anya could have handled this kind of target on the fly with a satellite network that was failing one satellite at a time. It was going to be all too easy to steam the water either side of the leviathan and not cook it medium-rare.

Mathieson was watching him intently. He could feel the lieutenant's eyes drilling a hole in him. Baird had to keep resetting the sats' reference times manually because one of them drifted out of sync every so often. The more sats he could bring to bear, the more accurate the firing; and with a target that didn't move in a predictable line like a surface ship, that was going to be tough.

Oh, and then there was the whole diving thing. That was really starting to piss Baird off.

"Baird to *Falconer*—try to keep that asshole on the surface, will you? The sats' laser can't cope."

Michaelson sounded strained but still did the gentleman-pirate act. "*Falconer* to Baird, we strive to please. Sergeant Fenix assures me he has your welfare at heart. Stand by."

And he's going to think I'm an asshole if I don't get this right. Just watch Cole's back. Leave the psycho whale to me.

It was a kilometer out now, its speed about twenty kph. They must have been burning out some of *Falconer*'s motors trying to put the brakes on that. Baird decided he'd have a lot of repairs to look forward to when this was over. Hoffman came thundering up the stairs again and loomed over him.

"If you can't stop that thing," he said, "we're going to have to burn a hundred thousand liters of fuel cleaning up its polyps."

"Yeah, I get it, Colonel," Baird said irritably, not looking away from the display. "I do."

"*Falconer*'s picked up speed again, sir." Mathieson's attention was back on the radar sweep. "She's maneuvering parallel with it and pulling ahead."

Hoffman picked up the mike. "Hoffman to *Falconer*. What are you doing?"

"*Falconer* to Hoffman—if we can't hold it still, we can try to steer it away from the berths."

Baird struggled to keep synchronizing the satellite feeds.

"Five hundred meters," Mathieson said. "*Falconer's* steering wide. It's going to make landfall to the west of us, sir."

"Baird, smoke that thing," Hoffman said. "Even if you haven't got a lock. *Now.*"

"Okay, okay. Primed for a six-second burn, maximum setting. That should distract it if nothing else."

It didn't take much fluctuation to throw a Hammer laser off target when it was dependent on a beam from low orbit finding another one from a handheld gun bouncing along in a ship. This was precision stuff. Baird hit the control and watched the numbers cascade down his display. Then he spun around in his seat to look out the window. It was out of his hands now. The Hammer was locked on. He waited for the spectacular white-hot beams to light up the night sky.

And boy, was it impressive.

It was like a slow-motion moment in the middle of a thunderstorm. Unnaturally straight lines of lightning converged on a point beyond the walls.

Baird got up and took four strides to the window, dumb as that · was. But he had to *see*. Hoffman caught his arm. Maybe he had a better idea of what was going to happen; the old bastard had helped grill the whole planet with the Hammer, after all. The next thing Baird knew, Michaelson was yelling *"Brace, brace, brace!"* over the radio and a ball of light blinded him. He put his arms up instinctively to shield his eyes. The sound came a second later.

Baird didn't hear it; he *felt* it. It was off the scale. He felt like someone had split his head open with a hammer. Then the window shattered and his hands and scalp stung with cold needles.

For a few moments, he wasn't sure where he was. But he was alive. He knew that because he could taste the blood in his mouth.

Fuck. I think that worked.

"Mathieson? You okay, son?" That was Hoffman's voice, filtered through the cotton wool of Baird's numbed ears. "Shit, what a mess."

"Still got power to the system, sir. I'm fine. Better take a look at Baird—he was right in front of the window."

Baird focused on the light above him, but it wasn't the room's lighting. The bulbs had blown out along with the windowpanes. He was looking at the glow from a fire.

The radio net went crazy as damage reports flooded in.

"It's beached. Sir, it's *beached*. Landslide! Shit, *run!*"

"Polyps ashore! *Polyps!*"

Baird could hear rumbling like an avalanche gathering speed. Then the naval base alarm drowned it out. He hauled himself upright on the nearest desk, skidding on shards of glass and papers. Hoffman pushed him out the door.

By the time the fresh air hit him, his adrenaline was the only thing keeping him moving. Gears sprinted for the west wall of the base. He reached for the Gnasher shotgun slung on his back and went forward automatically toward the sound of Lancer fire.

"Where's the wall?" he asked. He was staring at open sea. Little clusters of wobbling white light scuttled from the horizon toward him. "There was a wall there."

"Shit," Hoffman said. "It took the cliff out. It took the goddamn *cliff* out, Corporal."

"Hey, don't dock my wages. I just killed a frigging whale-sized glowie. There's bound to be some cleanup."

At night, the scale of the damage didn't really sink in. Baird couldn't see enough to be shocked by the instant change in the landscape. He could see the polyps charging at him, though, and that was a lot more urgent. He aimed at the bioluminescence and found he could hit them better with the Gnasher, especially if he let them get dangerously close. They splattered his boots. He started to feel personal scores had been settled every time one of the ugly little assholes burst in front of him.

Most of the Ravens seemed to be airborne, playing their searchlights on the parts of the base where the fixed lighting had failed. Baird ran out of polyps and turned around to find Hoffman had gone.

"Hey, Colonel, you taking a break or something?"

He looked around. There was sporadic gunfire everywhere, but he couldn't see any more glowies. *Shit, where's Hoffman? And what's happened to* Falconer? Baird started backing away, reloading his Gnasher. He tried the radio.

"Baird to *Falconer*, tell me you didn't sink."

It took a while for Marcus to answer. "Nice. Destructive, but nice."

Baird fought down a dumb surge of pride. *Hey, I'm not after his approval, am I? Get a grip.* "Still got polyps."

"Baby, you need some ointment for that," Cole said.

"How many?" Marcus asked.

"Couple of hundred got ashore."

"And?"

"I think we got them all." Cole was okay, so Baird could get back to worrying about his own ass again without feeling bad about it. "Got to find Hoffman. I'm standing here on my own like everyone else knows where the party is except me."

Baird had been caught too close to too many explosions. He knew they were taking their toll. But as usual, he felt almost back to normal again all too fast, a weird kind of peacefulness that he knew was something connected to the shock. It was almost like having a local anesthetic and watching Doc Hayman slice you up; you could see the damage was being done, but it was all a long way away for the time being.

He moved forward past the barracks block, expecting to hear *Falconer* or even Mathieson on the radio saying that there was now a whole pod of pissed-off leviathans steaming toward the base. But all he could hear was the crackling of a fire. Yellow light flickered on a wall. One of the polyps must have detonated near something flammable.

Hey, I got the thing before it spewed even more of them. I didn't fail.

It wasn't until Baird turned the next corner that he felt the heat on his face and stopped in his tracks. He was used to stumbling into firefights and seeing some weird and desperate shit, but it took him a few moments to work out what was really going on here.

It looked like a camp bonfire. A moving carpet of embers sizzled, wheezed, and popped. From time to time something exploded like an aerosol can. Gears, Stranded, and Gorasni stood around it, most of them holding their weapons in the safety position or even slung over their shoulders. Three of them were hosing the pile with flamethrowers.

Hoffman held out his hand to one of the Gorasni and the guy passed him his flamethrower. The colonel stood in grim silence and laid down a stream of flame like it was some kind of ritual. Baird wanted to back away quietly and hope nobody had seen him.

The bonfire was actually a heap of dead and dying polyps. There hadn't been that many disgorged this time, but this response to them was the kind of overkill Baird had seen when Locust stragglers had caught up with the population escaping Jacinto. There hadn't been many grubs left, but every Gear and every unit charged in to slice them up, desperate to put the boot in one last time after so many years of taking shit from the things.

Baird had joined in then, too. A Stranded guy turned down his flamethrower's jet and stepped back to pass it to him.

"Be my guest," the man said. "You might not get the chance next time."

It was pointless, but Baird did it anyway, if only for the experience of opening up that jet and seeing how far he could shoot it. He wasn't sure if the ritual purged anything in him or not.

The naval base siren came to life moments later and sounded the all-clear. Hoffman walked up to Baird and slapped him on the back. He had that look that said his mind was on something even worse than a collapsing naval base and a whole new kind of enemy.

"You're a bastard, Baird," he said. "But you're *our* bastard."

It was one of the nicest compliments Baird could remember getting. He didn't get many.

"Somebody fetch the COG boys a broom," one of the Stranded guys yelled. "They're going to be sweeping this place clean for a year, if they live that long. So long, assholes."

They were all walking away. The Gorasni stood and watched them sullenly; maybe they thought the all-clear meant it was time to start the feuding again.

"You leaving?" Baird said. "And we had so much to talk about."

"Yeah, this is the last place we want to be." The guy had a handheld radio, the kind that civilian security guards used to use in the days before the world went to shit. "You're finished, COG. We're getting clear of you while we still can."

He walked away, talking to someone on the radio. Baird heard him say something about 1800, sunset tomorrow, and to get everyone together for the fleet.

They were leaving, then. That was something. Baird thought that was worth changing the map of the island to achieve.

He'd check what that actually looked like in the morning.

VECTES, SOUTHERN COAST: NEXT DAY.

One day, he'd be dead, and then all this crap would be over. That was something to look forward to, Hoffman decided.

He leaned out of the Raven's crew bay and surveyed the changed landscape as best a man could when he hadn't the slightest idea what he was looking at. The granite cliffs that formed the western limit of the naval base had fallen into the sea, exposing tunnels like a broken beehive and leaving walls trying to bridge thin air.

And the ancient cannons were gone. They lay somewhere below in the pounding waves. Hoffman thought of Anvegad for a moment and wondered if the Anvil Gate gun battery was still in one piece. He suspected it was.

But here, he'd lost a third of the base. At least most of the ships—were still afloat on the eastern side.

If we ever need to run again—can we?

One of the Raven's Nest carriers, *Dalyell*, looked as dead as the former Chairman she had been named for. She was listing to one side and down at the bows. Hoffman watched the activity on her decks as teams of Gears and seamen tried to repair her, an emergency pump at her stern spewing water over the side.

It was the hectares of tents and wooden huts that made him privately despair, though. Where there had been a growing city, temporary accommodation gradually turning into solid, permanent buildings a road at a time, the ground now looked like the aftermath of a Hammer strike.

I've seen this all before. I don't think I can stomach seeing this again. And again . . .

The road layout was still visible, a neat grid spreading out from the walls of the naval base into what had been open countryside and fields when they'd landed here. Nearly half the new homes had gone. Where there had been roofs, there were now piles of charred wood and ash.

But the people survived this time. This isn't Ephyra. You can always rebuild the bricks and mortar.

"Shit, sir." Mitchell stared down from the crew bay with him. "How much more of this can they take?"

Hoffman was trained to say uplifting things and crack down hard on the easily daunted. Morale mattered. It wasn't an illusion. Losing the will to go on was the difference between life and death in extreme crisis. But he just couldn't spout the required lines any longer because he didn't believe them himself.

Admiralty House was a wreck. It hadn't burned, but the roof and windows had been blown out. Paper was still drifting everywhere on the wind. And still people got on with the task at hand. It should have made Hoffman proud to see orderly lines of Gears and civilians moving equipment and supplies out of the main building to safe cover. Instead, it just broke his heart.

He reminded himself that he was entitled to just five minutes of negativity and despair per conflict, and then he had get back out there and do the job. He had to be seen to be holding it all together.

"Got to walk the course," he said. "Set me down there, Sorotki."

"What happened to the kid and his dad?" Mitchell asked. "You know. The bombers."

There was nothing like a brand-new monster to take your mind off the old ones. "Last time I checked," Hoffman said, "they were in the detention block."

"Only reason for asking, sir, is that the detention block's now forming a rather decorative breakwater down there."

Hoffman had another torn moment like so many; a burst of *serves you right, you bastards,* followed almost immediately by imagining what it was like to be locked in a cell and unable to escape as disaster struck. *Is that concern for those assholes?* He had his doubts. He suspected he was simply reliving his guilt and bewilderment that he had once left Marcus to the grubs as they overran the prison in Ephyra.

"Better check," Hoffman said. "But it's not a priority."

It was, of course. He wanted as many seeds of future guilt swept out of the way as he could. But it wasn't Mitchell's job to do that. He jumped down from the Raven and made his way from the main gate, through the barracks blocks, and out onto the parade ground. Deep fissures had opened up in the concrete. He expected the paving to subside under him at any moment.

New Jacinto had escaped the fate of the old city, though. It got an earthquake-sized shock, but it hadn't sunk.

Lucky. Or maybe fate's keeping us around to punish us.

No; *lucky,* definitely lucky. He *had* to think that. And thinking it made it so, because a man could choose to feel joy or misery by selecting the things he compared his plight with. It was all relative — pain, hunger, loneliness, joy. The trick was finding the comparator. By the time he got halfway across the open square, he was in a bullish mood again and ready to start over.

I survive. We all survive. And those who don't are out of it anyway, free, oblivious. Margaret, Samuel Byrne, every Gear I lost, every Kashkuri who died in Anvegad — and everyone on this planet who died when I turned that command key to launch the Hammer of Dawn.

Hoffman had never discussed that night with Prescott. It was the kind of soul-searching intimacy and admission of ghosts that you could manage only with the people you trusted, sometimes not even with the ones you loved. But at that moment he was in the right frame of mind to ask Prescott questions that had nothing to do with trusting the man.

The Chairman should have been back by now. Half the civilians had come back to New Jacinto even if their homes had gone. Hoffman was surprised by how easy they found it to move, but then they still had very few possessions that couldn't be bundled into a bag. It was the administration that was now weighed down by its attachment to material things.

"Is this damn building structurally sound, Lennard?"

Hoffman stood outside the main entrance to Admiralty House and looked up at the frontage. Staff Sergeant Parry was wearing a helmet, which was unusual for him.

"Can't guarantee it, Colonel," Parry said. "But I've been up to the top floor and I'm still in one piece, so if you need to go in, feel free. I shut off the power, though. The radio net's been transferred back to the emergency management response truck. I told the Chairman to mind where he steps."

"He's back, then?" *Asshole. Never told me.* "Up top?"

"Sifting through his office."

Fine. Let's lance that boil, shall we?

"I'll go up and see him." Hoffman found himself rehearsing his excuses for breaking into the desk, and despising himself at the same time for even feeling a need to. "Sitrep meeting at eighteen hundred today with Sharle and his team, in—hell, where's a safe, dry place to meet now?"

"I'll radio you when I find somewhere, sir. But we'll have a better picture of the habitability of the site by then. We've got water and generators, we've got food, the field latrines are intact, and the weather's good. All in all, it beats having grubs smashing through the sewers and water mains all the time."

Hoffman was going to make sure that Parry got a medal. Sappers had kept Old Jacinto running for all those impossible, terrible years, and now they were doing the same for the new city. Their never-ending job was slightly easier here. Parry had chosen to be a satisfied man, if not a happy one, living proof of Hoffman's theory.

But was Prescott going to be happy? It was time to find out. Hoffman climbed the stairs slowly, crunching on broken glass in the stairwell, partly out of caution and partly to give Prescott warning that he had company. When he got to the top floor, he could feel the breeze coming through the old sail loft. The roof had been ripped up.

Prescott was rolling charts and stacking them carefully in a cardboard box. His two close protection Gears, Rivera and Lowe, stood at the broken windows watching the cleanup. Hoffman wondered what Prescott felt he needed protection from at that moment, other than falling plasterboard.

"Victor." Prescott looked up, just a little too slowly to be natural. "So we lick our wounds and return to the fray. It could have been much worse."

"That's the spirit, sir." Anything less than a growl was sarcasm, and most people knew that about him by now. "Keep calm and carry on."

"Corporal, would you and Lowe excuse us for a few minutes?" Prescott knew Hoffman's tone only too well. "Take a meal break while things are quiet."

Hoffman waited for the two Gears' footsteps to fade on the stairs.

"That sounds as if you're expecting trouble," he said. "People are pretty shaken up, but they haven't started lynching COG officials yet."

Prescott was still a model of leisurely calm. "We stand at a difficult crossroads. There'll be many questioning my judgment and fitness to lead, for bringing them all this way to face more hardship."

"Is there something you want to share with me, Chairman?"

"Are you one of them, Victor?"

Okay, let's get down to it. "I'm the one who thought we'd be better off on an island in a more temperate climate. Not you."

"Ah, still taking sole responsibility for our joint decisions. Do you want to be a martyr, Colonel? Or a politician?"

"Cut the bullshit."

"I get a very strong feeling that you no longer have confidence in me."

Hoffman folded his arms. He had no idea why he made sure his hand was tucked loosely under his left elbow so that he could draw his sidearm instantly, but it was. Prescott had a pistol. Hoffman had never known him even to look as if he might use it under any circumstances. But now wasn't the time to test that impression.

"I wish it was an easy yes or no," Hoffman said. "There's not one major decision you've made that I would have done differently. I never saw you do anything dumb. I've never known you to even get drunk or screw a woman. But you're a liar, Chairman, and that makes my job too hard. There's no possible reason left for keeping information from your defense staff."

Prescott was still salvaging the contents of his office. He didn't even seem to be doing it as distraction. He walked around to his chair and rattled the desk drawer.

"This is really rather juvenile, Victor. You feel slighted because I didn't tell you every detail?"

"Like the existence of classified research facilities, like New Hope? That kind of shit isn't *detail.* It's what I *need to know.*"

"The army is the servant of the state. It's not the government, and that's who decides what needs to be known."

"True. But you're still a goddamn liar."

"So why did you do it, Victor?"

Prescott could have been fishing for information himself, of course. He had a talent for that. He homed in on faint guilt like a shark following a molecule of blood in the water. Hoffman didn't care what Prescott found out now, but he couldn't stomach the idea of being played again.

"Mistrust corrodes," Hoffman said. "Rots the whole working re-lationship. And this isn't any old job—it's about you and me keep-ing the human race from extinction." *What the hell. Say it. What can he do to you? What's left to break?* "I want to think that it's just some compromising pictures of you and a sheep. Just sleaze. Dumb, petty shit. I really do."

But Prescott wasn't sleazy or greedy or conventionally corrupt. Hoffman knew it, and for a moment that almost made him cave in. Prescott's motive was just salvation. It wasn't malice.

No. *This shit stops right here. His motive doesn't make any dif-ference to the consequences. I need to know. I need to know all the things he still won't tell me.*

Hidden things, buried things, encrypted things, things lurking under the surface waiting to drag him down—grubs, monsters, se-crets, it didn't matter which. Hoffman had had a gutful of them all. He wanted everything out in the open. He wanted to shine the light in its face and see it for what it really was.

Prescott's expression didn't change. Hoffman wanted a fight, an air-clearing showdown. He wasn't going to get one. He knew it. The Chairman tried the key in the lock, jiggled it around, and eventually got the drawer open. He looked inside but didn't actu-ally touch the data disk.

"You didn't really intend to cover your tracks," Prescott said. The wind whipped through the gap in the roof and scattered odd papers around. "That's far too sly for you. But seeing as you want to be told things—whatever information you have is also stored somewhere else."

"Very wise precaution."

"So what have you done with the disk?"

"Kiss my ass, Chairman. I'll tell you when you tell me."

"So you haven't managed to break the encryption."

You crafty asshole. I walked right into that. Shit, I must be get-ting senile.

Prescott could have done plenty to Hoffman right then. He would have been within his rights under the Fortification Act to draw his pistol and shoot Hoffman on the spot. Part of Hoffman thought he should have done just that, because he'd made that call himself in the past.

But maybe Prescott knew that calling in Gears to arrest the Chief of Staff—not just any old brass, a real Gear like them, one of their own—was going to unleash a shitload of trouble in its own right.

And maybe Prescott wasn't sure they wouldn't turn on him instead. He'd been prodding around that issue for weeks.

Hoffman now had no idea where to go next. He couldn't argue about what he couldn't decipher, he was pretty sure he couldn't beat it out of the man, and the animal reflex—to punch him right in that smug, fucking *patronizing* face—wasn't going to feel satisfying for more than a few seconds.

The only option left was to stop trying to guess what he was doing. It was letting him set the agenda. Hoffman simply had to ignore him. If that wasn't a bloodless military coup, he wasn't sure what was. The test would be which Gears followed him when the time came that his orders didn't match Prescott's.

Prescott just carried on gathering his stuff. Hoffman had to walk away and resist the temptation to pick up the ball left lying in his court.

He walked down the stairs, feeling like a complete asshole for not ripping the man a new one, but he knew that he didn't have anything concrete to object to except never knowing what resources Prescott had kept hidden.

But in a world of shortages, just hiding resources was a life-threatening crime.

Yes. It is. Look at me, what I did at Anvil Gate. I'd still do it again. You don't hold out on your neighbor when it's life or death.

Hoffman passed Lowe and Rivera on the way out. They'd put their helmets on a windowsill while they stood around in the lobby eating a snack, and they looked at Hoffman as if they were embarrassed. Fine; it was no secret that Hoffman and the Chairman didn't get on. It wouldn't even make the grade as gossip.

He forced himself to focus on the immediate problems—of settling the civvies into even more temporary accommodation and

making sure Michaelson had some kind of working fleet. He had
to catch up with Bernie, too. She was the only friend he had, the
only person who could and would hear him out. She'd put things
in perspective. She'd make him feel that he wasn't the most useless asshole in the world.

*So what do I do with this disk now? And how can I get through
two, three wars and still have to go running to Bernie to ask if I'm
right or not?*

He decided not to tell Michaelson about the disk yet, just in
case it dropped the man in the shit. Michaelson had enough on
his plate. He was also a political animal who actually enjoyed
playing these goddamn balls-aching spy games with Prescott. It
was going to be interesting to see if Prescott tried to recruit him.

Michaelson took Hoffman for an inspection tour of *Dalyell.*
The carrier was still taking on water, and the crew—a maintenance team, nothing remotely like a full ship's complement—
was struggling to locate all the leaks.

"Save her, or save her spare parts?" Michaelson said sadly,
splashing through knee-deep water. "Breaks my heart."

"She's worth saving as living quarters even if we can't fuel her."

"You look like you've had a fight, Victor."

"Stop changing the subject."

"I know you too well. It's the flushing around the neck."
Michaelson gave him a sly wink. "Let me guess. Prescott? Because it's not Trescu."

Hoffman struggled to find a response he could live with. If he
lied to Michaelson, then another relationship would be tainted.

"Very perceptive," he said. "But what you don't know can't hurt
you. Plausible deniability and all that bullshit. Let's just say I've
got some research to do first."

"Just remember he's a politician, Victor. They're not like us little people."

"Why do *you* hate his guts?"

Michaelson took a sudden interest in a run of pipework that
was sagging from the deckhead. "Can't pin it down, really. Not
sure I *hate* him so much as don't *trust* him. I just don't like the cut

of his jib." He shrugged. "I prefer the ones whose disastrous lack of judgment I can see and point at. It's his clinging to secrecy when there shouldn't be anything left to conceal."

Hoffman realized that Michaelson was right on just about every point, as he usually was. Hoffman didn't find Trescu's reticence anywhere near as threatening as Prescott's. Trescu was an Indie, and an Indie who'd seen his entire nation reduced to a few thousand people. He was bound to be wary of telling his old enemy everything. It wasn't the same as someone on your own team shutting you out of everything.

"I'm glad it's not just me," Hoffman said.

"But who's actually running the COG now, Victor? We are. Nothing can happen without En-COG or Gears. We don't have a confident, assertive civilian society—we haven't had one since E-Day, maybe even earlier. Now we have these dangerous, uppity, foreign ideas seeping in from Trescu and even the Stranded. Prescott knows that like he knows his own name."

"Your point?"

"He's probably afraid. Scared politicians usually get very punchy and posture a lot." Michaelson climbed the ladder to the next deck and tapped the heel of his hand against the bulkhead, listening as if he expected something to knock back. "Here's the question. Does he govern? Is he fit to govern? And if he isn't, who decides who is? Our only legal framework now is the Fortification Act. People are starting to talk about elections again."

"I just shoot bad bastards. Was that a question?"

"Only if you have an answer."

Hoffman had to think about that one. It was what Margaret would have called . . . *elegant.* "You love all this intrigue shit, don't you?"

Michaelson smiled. He could give as good as he got with Prescott. Hoffman couldn't. In that lonely desperation that usually tormented him when he was lumbered with a secret he didn't want to have, he almost took the encrypted disk out of his pocket to show him. Maybe Michaelson even had some encryption key that would open it.

But it felt like too much too soon. These were dangerous times. He'd talk to Bernie first.

"I don't love it," Michaelson said. "I just accept it's another warfighting skill I have to have."

"Yeah," Hoffman said. "Me, I prefer a chainsaw."

CHAPTER 19

I can't do anything else to help Anvil Gate until we clear the UIR out of Kashkur. The pass must stay closed, and I can't lose any more aircraft there. The UIR has offered to allow the evacuation of civilians from Anvegad if we withdraw from the garrison as well. They're quite elegant blackmailers, but I think the outcome is the same for the population either way.

(GENERAL KENNITH MARKHAM-AMORY, CHIEF OF GENERAL STAFF, TO COLONEL JAMES CHOI)

ANVEGAD, KASHKUR: THIRD MONTH OF THE SIEGE, 32 YEARS EARLIER.

"I think you must surrender, Lieutenant," Casani said. "We can't go on."

It was exceptionally hot in the council chamber that afternoon. The stench of the city was sometimes relegated to the background because hunger took priority, but at other times it was hard for Hoffman to ignore. The smell of smoke from burning garbage and bodies was almost a relief.

Hoffman had lost twenty kilos; he was one of the luckier ones. And while he sympathized with Casani and the thousand or so citizens who'd died of dysentery, starvation, or simply taken their chances and fled over the walls, he had less intention of surrendering now than he'd ever had.

Anvil Gate had gone past the point of compromise. They said that throwing good money after bad was the hallmark of a fool. Hoffman's defense of the fort had cost lives, but deciding now that it had all been a mistake simply pissed on their graves. If it had been worth *any* of their lives, then he'd die before he opened those gates to the UIR.

His orders were still to defend the fort. Nothing had changed. If he'd been told to hand it over, he suspected he would have stayed there alone, even though he now missed Margaret so much that he'd almost cried himself to sleep some nights. He could think of little else beyond ending—winning—the siege now.

"I never made you stay, Alderman," he said.

"But we have no guarantee of a safe evacuation without your forces withdrawing too. That's the offer on the table from the UIR. No compromise."

"I can't take that offer, and you know it." Hoffman felt the responsibility for the fate of the civilians sitting squarely in his lap, refusing to budge. Whatever decision he took would be wrong. "I won't be blackmailed by the UIR or anyone else."

Casani looked terribly haggard. It was partly hunger, but probably mostly the ordeal of watching helplessly as his city fell apart so fast despite its long and defiant history. Hoffman had switched off some weeks ago, and only allowed himself to feel whatever he needed to keep his Gears alive. He hardly dared think of home. It just made matters worse.

And the rations store had been raided again.

It was impossible to keep the garrison thief-proof now because so many of the internal walls of the fort had been smashed by mortars. There had always been a loose and uncertain boundary between city and garrison anyway, but now it had vanished, and the honesty and trust it relied on had vanished too.

We're all animals, deep down. And not so deep, either.

All the time that the ration packs had been disappearing in ones and twos, he was simply angry. But the Pesangs would go out and hunt some of the local wildlife to make up the shortfall. Now it had reached the stage where the thefts were compromising his Gears' ability to fight, and everybody knew that the penalty for stealing essential supplies in wartime was death. The Kashkuris here might have thought that nobody really meant that, because this war had been a permanent fixture for three generations, but this was an extreme situation—not stealing paper clips, but robbing fighting Gears of food during a siege.

Hoffman meant it. He had to. He was letting his Gears down if he didn't.

"Alderman, I'm not a diplomatic man," he said. "The food thefts will stop. One way or another, they *will* stop. My Gears found a man with a pantry full of COG rations. Geril Atar."

Casani had his chin resting on his fist, his mouth against his knuckles, looking halfway between prayer and trying to stay silent. Dust motes drifted in the shaft of sunlight that had managed to infiltrate the heavy drapes drawn against the heat of the sun. The place was airless. It felt as if the city was running out of oxygen as well as everything else.

"Atar has two children," Casani said at last. "He's a clerk. He's not a traitor. Desperate, yes. A threat? He's watching his family starve."

Hoffman found himself about to suck in a breath to rage at Casani about what Gears had to do, and why they deserved to eat what little was set aside for them, and how the civilians had equal allocations according to their levels of activity. He was about to let rip on why taking food from a Gear endangered not only them but a widening circle that rippled outward. But as soon as the first word formed in his mouth, he knew that was irrelevant. All that mattered was doing what was necessary to stop it from happening again.

Should have done it from the start. My fault.

Hoffman knew that if he'd been Atar, he'd probably have done the same, but he wasn't, and he had responsibilities to his men.

"We arrested him," Hoffman said. "He admits he did it. Hard to deny, anyway. You know what I'm going to say next."

"I'm not sure that I do, Lieutenant."

"You're the civil leader here. I expect you to carry out the lawful punishment."

"Are you serious? Execute a man who's starving to death anyway?"

"Your call, Alderman. If you won't do it, I will."

As soon as Hoffman said it, he knew he couldn't climb down. The trigger was as good as pulled. Casani wouldn't take any notice of him again, the thefts would continue, and things would spiral down even further. If anyone was going to come out this place alive, Hoffman had to keep control.

Casani sat back in his seat and started to argue, more to himself than to Hoffman. "What are we living for if we have no compassion? These are my neighbors. *Friends*. I can't kill one to save others, even if it would achieve that."

Hoffman cut him short. "You can take your people out of here. I'll get a message to the Indies to let you go." Hoffman watched the decision materialize in front of him. "If you head north, they'll have a lot of trouble shelling a scattered crowd anyway. Many of you will make it. But if you stay here, you stay under COG law. Do you understand?"

Hoffman had simply run out of time and energy. He could only see the objective. He got up and hauled Casani to his feet, gripping his biceps, and pushed him toward the door. Atar was in a small side room down the corridor, guarded by Bai Tak.

The Pesang didn't look at Hoffman as he pushed Casani in front of him to the door and opened it. Atar was sitting on a wooden chair with his head in his hands; thirtysomething, thinning dark hair, still looking tidy despite the privations. An ordinary guy—no more or less. He got up when Casani entered the room.

"I'm sorry," he said. "I had to do it."

"I know," Hoffman said, "I'm sorry as well. But you know what the stakes are."

It had to be done quickly. Dragging it out was unfair to the man, and this wasn't personal in any way. Maybe that made it worse. Hoffman put the pistol in Casani's hand.

"Do it," he said. "It's the law."

"I can't. Not even a hearing? Not even a—"

"You don't have a goddamn *choice*, Alderman."

"How can I blame him? How can I say I wouldn't do it myself? He's watching his family *die*."

Hoffman wondered if it was hunger that had cooled him down to this tick-over level. He saw the world very clearly, and it was like this; without minimum rations, his Gears wouldn't be able to fight. They would die one way or another, but they had followed the rules, written and unwritten. This man hadn't, however understandable his desperation.

Sam Byrne wouldn't even let me bend the rules to get him and his wife and his unborn kid to safety. That's a Gear. That's a man. His life counts.

It didn't really matter who pulled the trigger as long as the civilians understood that theft of food in this siege was a crime that had consequences. Hoffman took the sidearm back from Casani's hand—always unsettling, that, touching a hand that wasn't familiar—and checked the chamber again. He motioned Bai Tak to stand clear. Their eyes met for a moment, and Bai didn't look shocked at all. He understood. This was survival.

Hoffman held the muzzle to Atar's head. He wasn't certain of the exact wording of the charge, but he knew it well enough, and there would be no appeal on technicalities.

"Geril Atar." He felt an idiot intoning these legalities. What would a lawyer like Margaret think of his clumsy delivery? "You've admitted to an act of injurious theft as defined by the Military Emergency Measures Act, that by stealing rations intended for Coalition soldiers you endangered them and their ability to defend the COG. The penalty is death, and in the name of the Chairman of the Coalition of Ordered Governments, I shall now carry that out."

Atar said nothing. Hoffman met his eyes, looked aside, and pulled the trigger.

He'd killed at close quarters before because that was what infantry did, but he'd never been an executioner. It felt strangely anticlimactic. Maybe that was the heat and the hunger, too. He lowered his weapon and tried to take in what he'd done.

I must talk to Pad. The thought kept going through Hoffman's mind. *Pad understands this. He says snipers do it in the cold of the moment, full awareness of the consequences of* not *killing the target, not a reaction to threat. He'll explain it to me.*

Casani was staring at the body on the floor, sobbing. Hoffman just wanted the civilians to know that the sentence had been carried out. If Casani wanted to say who did it, that was fine. The rations would be left alone, and his Gears would stand a chance of finishing the job here. There were thousands of other Gears depending on them doing that.

Hoffman knew his conscience would gnaw at him one day, but not half as much as if he hadn't done it. He put the pistol back in his holster, beckoned to Bai, and called a medic to deal with the body.

"Tough, sah," Bai said, following him down the corridor and out into the hot, stinking street. "You did right. Right don't always feel good, though."

"Thanks, Bai." Hoffman had to blinker himself and simply look at the next objective. It surprised him that he could do that, but it was a *detached* kind of surprise, more a making of mental notes. "What have we got plenty of? What's the one thing we actually have supplies of and haven't used in this heat?"

Bai shrugged. There was almost nobody out on the street, and it was so quiet that Hoffman thought he could hear gunfire from across the mountains. The few Kashkuri sitting on their doorsteps or sweeping their paths just stared listlessly at the two Gears.

"Fuel?" Bai said.

"Got it in one. Get the platoon together, and round up the rest of the aldermen."

"Sah, you thinking strange things?" Bai looked alarmed. "What are you planning?"

"Surrender," Hoffman said. "Open the gates, and let the Indie bastards in."

*   *   *

MAIN GUN EMPLACEMENT, ANVIL GATE.

Lau En and Naru Fel came back from reconnoitering the Indie
lines at about two in the morning.

"Hoffman's waiting," Bai said. "Get a move on."

"Has he gone nuts this time?" Lau asked. "Seriously. He's not
really going to hand over the fort to them, is he? He's got *orders*."

"Just tell him how many there are down there. He knows what
he's doing."

Bai herded them into the small room that Hoffman used as a
planning office, the one with the dead captain's paintings still on
the wall. Hoffman, Byrne, Evan, Pad, and Carlile were huddled
around a desk poring over a street plan of the city.

"So?" Pad said. "How many for the fry-up? How many Indies?"

"About two hundred," Lau said. "Very young, most."

"Okay, we can probably get most of them inside the walls before we kick off." Byrne was marking lines on the street plan. "It's
pretty basic, Lau. Most of this city is wood, except the gun emplacement and the structural things we need, so we're going to
burn it with them in it. We've got plenty of auto fuel and dry
garbage loafing around. We soak everything with fuel, we rig a
few flamethrowers, a few concealed gun positions, snipers, and
then when they're in, we block them in and ignite the materials
simultaneously at multiple points. Rare, medium, or well-done."

Bai knew roughly what Hoffman had planned, but he couldn't
quite work out how the Gears and the handful of civvies were
going to escape being grilled along with the Indies.

Lau had obviously pondered this too. "How we get out?"

Carlile showed him on the street map.

"If we trap the bulk of them in this quarter, we won't have to,"
he said. "That's almost one hundred percent wood structures, but
the square here acts as a firebreak for the next block, and it's all
stone construction between this road and this one. We pull back
to there, and if it gets really shitty, we go down into the tunnels
and sit it out."

Lau didn't look convinced, but he wouldn't argue, and neither would Bai. They'd come this far and they were going to make this work. Bai made a conscious effort not to think of Harua, but he didn't manage it.

It's not going to happen to me. I'll survive this.

Hoffman hadn't said a word. Bai wondered if the execution was starting to sink in. The lieutenant was staring at the map in that defocused way that said he wasn't actually seeing it but rehearsing something in his head.

"I'd better do it now," Hoffman said at last. "We need to know if the Indie offer is still on the table. Got a comms channel for them, Sam?"

Byrne picked up the headset and listened while tuning the dial. "I know they use this one," he said. "Not encrypted, so I don't know how fast they respond to it. If this doesn't get their attention, we can just call Brigade on an open channel and let the Indies eavesdrop."

Bai sat back on the nearest desk. Hoffman was pulling an ambush on the Indies, probably the only chance they had of surviving but he still seemed thoroughly ashamed to use a surrender to do it. He really did take things like honor so seriously that lying over something this important was beyond his limit. He was an honest man. Rude, even insulting sometimes. But you knew where you stood with him, and Bai put all his faith in him because of that.

Hoffman took a deep breath, which made his cheeks look even more hollow, and put the mike handset to his mouth.

"This is COG garrison Anvil Gate, Lieutenant Hoffman commanding, to any UIR call sign in range. Please respond. Anvil Gate to any UIR call signs. Over."

Hoffman put his hand over his eyes and rested his elbow on the desk. It took a while for the response to come back, a polite and calm voice like someone who worked in a bank rather than an enemy who'd been shelling them for months.

"UIR Control Vasgar to Anvil Gate. This is Major Toly. Go ahead."

"I need to evacuate the civilian population of Anvegad." Hoffman sounded rough, and he wasn't acting. It seemed to hit the spot with the Indies. "Does your offer of safe passage for them still stand?"

"It does. But we demand the surrender of your garrison too."

Hoffman waited for a beat of five, now staring ahead at the captain's painting on the wall in front of him.

"I've got no other options left, Major," he said at last. "If you let the civilians leave, I'll open the gates and you can move in. But I won't open them until the civvies are clear of the fort. Is that understood?"

"You have my word," said the major.

Bai saw Hoffman wince. "Then I'll start moving them out now. If I see the slightest movement toward them, if I hear one cough that makes me think it's a rifle round, then the deal's off."

Hoffman put the radio mike back in its cradle. He turned to Byrne.

"You're driving," he said. "We can't get them all in vehicles, but we can move the priorities. You take your wife, you fill the rest of that truck, and you drive east, okay?"

Byrne looked at Hoffman for a long while, licking his lips nervously. "Can't do it," he said. "Sorry, sir. I'll put her on the truck. She can drive. But I'm not leaving the lads. Or you."

Hoffman shut his eyes for a second.

"I could give you the crazy-bastard speech," he said. "But I have to move fast. Last chance. Go. *Please* go, Sam. Go with your wife and kid. I want you to."

"Yeah," Pad said. "We all bloody do. Get going, mate. Now."

Byrne shook his head. "No, it's about me. I can't run from this. I'm the platoon sergeant. That's what I am. I'll catch up with her later."

Byrne didn't give anyone a chance to carry on the argument. Hoffman just rolled his head, exhausted, and gestured to the door.

"Okay, let's crack on with this. Lots of fuel to move. Clear the city street by street, remember. Any civvie who decides to stay — either they have a rifle or they take their chances."

Bai and the rest of the Pesang squad started going around the houses on the west side of the city, banging on the doors and ushering people out. Some still wanted to stay put and needed persuading, but a lot of the men were former Gears anyway and wanted to fight. Bai wasn't sure if they understood what would be left of Anvegad after the gates opened, but it was too late to have second thoughts about that now. He moved on, door-to-door.

Cities could always be rebuilt, especially small ones.

It took six hours for the Gears to assemble the population and start loading the trucks and carts. Bai saw Byrne cuddling his wife, patting her pregnant belly and telling her that he'd see her at New Temperance. He helped her clamber up the step into the driver's seat and hung on to her hand through the open window until the last minute. Did he tell her he had the chance to go with her? Maybe some things were better left unsaid.

"You come and find us, Samuel," she said. "We'll be waiting."

The truck pulled away down the road, turned right, and then its tail lights vanished around the bend. Byrne stood there for a while staring into the night, maybe waiting to make sure that the Indies didn't break their word and open fire, and then he scratched his head and walked back to the gates.

"Okay," he said. "Let's finish the job."

ANVEGAD CITY GATES; SUNRISE.

What was it—seventy, eighty days? A hundred?

Hoffman had lost track of the length of the siege in the time it took to walk from the garrison compound to the outer gates. Sam Byrne walked beside him. Hoffman didn't need to put on an act to look like the defeated commander whose tragic last stand backfired; he really did feel like shit.

But that was because he was willing to fake a surrender.

It was like crying rape for no reason. It meant that the next person who really, *really* meant it would find it harder to make anyone believe them. It would make surrenders more uncertain, the enemy less likely to put on the safety catch and move into the international laws of decency and treating prisoners humanely. He'd abused an ancient convention of war that was as near as damn it *sacred*, and for good reason, but that still didn't make it feel right.

"Here we go, Sam." He looked up at the iron gates and their archaic but perfectly operational locking system of ratchets and cogs. His Lancer was slung in the low port position, magazine housing visibly empty, safety catch on. "Sorry I dropped you in this shit."

"It's okay, Vic," Byrne said. "You're a bastard, but you're *our* bastard."

Hoffman managed a smile. "I'll remember that and use it one day."

"Two-Six RTI, the Unvanquished."

"That's us, Sam."

Hoffman turned the handwheel, and the gates swung slowly inward. The UIR captain standing a few meters away with a squad of troops was a young man who didn't look as if he wanted to dominate the world or slaughter refugees, and that made the whole damn thing ten times worse. Hoffman needed an enemy he could loathe with every fiber of his being, an enemy so monstrous that anything he did was justified and right, because he hated the gray areas that didn't give him clear answers and left him wondering where his enemy ended and he began. Just once in his life, he wanted that complete clarity.

The young captain looked stunned for a moment, staring right past Hoffman. Of course; he'd probably never seen a city in this state before. Bombed and broken was one thing, but piled with garbage, uncremated bodies, and excrement was another nightmare entirely. He must have been able to smell the place three klicks away.

"Captain Benoslau of the Fifteenth Furlin Cavalry." The Indie saluted. "Lieutenant Hoffman, the Union of Independent Republics thanks you for your honorable decision. I now require your formal surrender."

Hoffman handed Benoslau his Lancer two-handed. He'd run out of ammo anyway, and he clung to that fragile approximation of honesty like a kid crossing his fingers behind his back while lying shamelessly.

"Sir, I want to talk about the conditions of treatment for my men and some civilians who've refused to leave. Will you come to the city authority's office?"

"We'll need to secure the city. My company will move in and occupy the area now."

It was all very civilized, and for a second, Hoffman thought, *Fuck it, let them have the place, let's not die over this.* But it was gone in the next breath, like a pointless impulse to heave a brick through a window after one beer too many.

"Go ahead," Hoffman said. "We're all in the old quarter anyway. Might as well follow me."

At that moment, it turned from a surreal ritual to the beginning of the endgame. This was the real battle for Anvil Gate.

"Oh . . . *God*," Benoslau murmured.

"We tried to burn as much as we could," Byrne said. "That's what happens when you stop the water and food supply to five thousand people. We've got dysentery and some kind of respiratory epidemic, too, so that's why we're all huddled up here. You might want to do the same."

Now it was down to the Pesangs and Pad to monitor the movement into the city. When the bulk of the 15th Furlins were inside, the gates would be shut, and the fires lit to cut off the main routes.

We might all burn to death. I never thought I'd just be curious about what it finally feels like to die.

There were machine-gun positions on the walls, of course. But they'd been there throughout the siege. Now they were idle and without belts.

And we have ammo.

The twin guns were silent again. Benoslau paused to stare up at them.

You'd be amazed how much explosive you can extract from a few of those big, shiny shells.

And there were eighty men with rifles, bayonets, and even ma-

chetes that would take your goddamn head clean off—if the fires
didn't get you first.

Sorry, Captain.

Casani's old office seemed suddenly even bigger and more
empty. Benoslau sat down at the table with his lieutenant, and
Byrne left them to it. Hoffman tapped his ear.

"You don't mind me keeping my radio open, do you? My men
need to keep in touch. They're pretty wrung out."

Benoslau took a water bottle off his webbing and handed it to
Hoffman. He also laid his sidearm on the table in full view. "My
apologies. I didn't think."

That gesture almost poleaxed Hoffman. This enemy wasn't
supposed to be compassionate, *better* than him. It was *not* how he
saw this event panning out. Despite himself, he twisted the cap off
and drank. There was, and never would be, anything that tasted
better than that liter of fresh water, however warm it was.

"Thank you," Hoffman said.

"Do I have to sign anything?"

He could hear the whispered exchanges between Pad and the
others in his earpiece. He had seen the ambush happening fast, a
frenzy of confusion, but he'd underestimated how long it took two
hundred troops to get their asses in gear and move into a city—
even a tiny one—and imagine they were securing it. The longer
this took, the worse he felt. He didn't want to find any common
ground with these people now, because it changed nothing, and
he still couldn't let Anvil Gate go.

The dead are still dead. Do your job.

"Yes, there really is a document," Benoslau said. The lieutenant seemed to be looking for it in his pack. Hoffman handed
back the bottle and steeled himself to stop thinking, *right now.*
"We have medics, by the way, and if any of your personnel are in-
fected or wounded, we can transfer them to a military hospital
rather than a prisoner-of-war camp."

"They're in," Pad's voice said. "Or most of them. Ready to roll."

Hoffman shut his eyes. This response was just a whisper. "Yes,
do it for Sander."

"Sorry, I didn't hear you, Lieutenant," Benoslau said.

The first explosion blew out the windows in the office; it must have been a lot closer than Evan and Carlile had planned. The ceiling caved in but didn't collapse completely. Hoffman ducked under the table to dodge the beams that were creaking and sagging over his head and drew his sidearm.

It was pure chaos from that second onward. The dust was as thick as smoke. He had to get out of that room and regroup with the platoon.

"But we were *talking*—" Benoslau said, as if Hoffman's worst crime was breaking his word about that. The man was on the ground, head bleeding, feeling around the floor for something. It might have been his sidearm or he might have been reaching to check where his lieutenant was, but he wasn't going to find the pistol anyway.

He knows that. So do I.

Hoffman still fired twice because that was what he'd been drilled to do. It was muscle memory, hardwired and independent of the voice screaming, *How could you do that, how could you do that to him?* in his brain. He found himself scrambling through the broken door, looking for escape before he'd even started regretting what he did.

Out in the street, the fires were taking hold. The Silver Era architecture, the carved wooden frames and gargoyles and plaster made with horsehair, went up like a match. Evan—somewhere, unseen—triggered explosions in a long chain all the way down the street that ran north-south. It cut the city in half, igniting an almost instant blaze down a whole block. The fuel vapor that had wafted from soaked garbage and filled empty spaces started exploding almost at random. Automatic fire rattled from every direction.

Hoffman no longer knew what was going to blow next. This was the point to start pulling back to the walls and concentrating fire toward the center. He ran for the stone stairs that led to the first-level gantry and got his first elevated look at Anvegad burning. He could already see three Gears down and couldn't tell who they were. But there were a lot more Indie bodies sprawled in the roads.

"Hoffman to all call signs." The radios were still working, so the comms room was still in one piece. "All call signs, fall back to the perimeter. Fire teams—get to the wall positions."

He didn't know if they heard him. But he did hear the Stomper, the belt-fed grenade gun, and when he reached the end of the gantry, he saw Byrne manning it with Jarrold.

Jarrold spotted him and pointed at the target taking all the Stomper's rounds. "Sir, Indies in the warehouse over there—about twenty. Bai Tak's gone into the alleys with other Pesangs."

"I'll find him. I've got to grab a rifle."

Hoffman retrieved one from a dead Gear who turned out to be one of the engineers, Hollis. The fires were spreading through this half of the city, but there was nothing Hoffman could do right then to move bodies out of the flame path. He knew he wouldn't even remember where they were if he went back later. He just had to keep moving out of the fire, engaging anything that wasn't a Gear or a civilian. The wholesale arson had definitely flushed them out into the open; there was nowhere to find safe cover without crossing that square, and that was where Evan's crews had moved the light machine guns. They just sat there picking off anyone who tried to get out. Hoffman moved back road by road, heading for the oldest part of the city that was all narrow alleys and overhanging balconies that no vehicle could get through.

This quarter wasn't on fire. Either the charges hadn't gone off or it was somewhere no fuel had been spread. But the Pesangs had chased a squad of Indies in here, and Hoffman wanted them out so he could find the engineer with the flamethrower and clear the area the hard way. When he reached the center of ten or so winding passages, he found Bai, Cho, and Shim. He heard them before he saw them, and it was the stream of unintelligible Pesan punctuated by shrieks of sheer animal terror that told him he'd found them. They came out of a small shop with their Lancers still on their backs and their machetes drawn.

"Did you lose them?" he asked. For some reason he thought they'd given up and were trying another tack. Then he looked inside the shop front. There was a damn machine gun aimed out of the front window, and five dead Indies in there, all hacked about.

Bai wiped the sweat from his nose on the back of his hand, as if the rifles were an afterthought.

"No room to fire in there," Cho said. "We do close quarters *our* way."

The fires were now a complete wall of searing heat and the rattle of weapons was gradually becoming more intermittent. Hoffman couldn't raise anyone on the radio now. The best he could do was search the relatively undamaged side of the city road by road, and work out who he still had standing.

His watch told him it had been an hour since the first explosion kicked off the ambush. He'd have to take its word for that.

Gradually, he found more of the gunners and his own platoon, some of them searching the stone buildings, some just blurs of armor as they ran past at the end of a road and were gone. He went back to the Stomper position while looking for Byrne. He could have been anywhere, but the Gears all knew to muster at the gun emplacement when they lost comms and could move freely.

"Sam?" Hoffman still approached it carefully, alert for any lone Indie. "Sam? Come on, man. Where are you, Byrne?"

Byrne hadn't left his post. He was still half-sitting, half-squatting on a shallow ammo crate with one arm draped over the Stomper and his forehead resting on the optics. Hoffman's stomach knotted instantly. He knew what he was looking at, but he still wanted to believe that Byrne had paused for a moment, exhausted. But he didn't move even when Hoffman went right up to him.

"Shit, Sam." Hoffman felt for a throat pulse, but then he saw the big exit hole in the center of his back. "Shit. I'm sorry. Goddamn it, I'm *sorry*."

Byrne would still be there when Hoffman had finally got his shit together. He made himself move on, counting off bodies on his fingers, trying to recall who he'd seen alive and who he hadn't. He decided to go back to the muster point. Pad was already there with five of the Pesangs and a lot of the gunners. Carlile had bad burns to his hands, but he was alive.

"We did it, sir," Pad said. "I got a call in to Brigade. They know we've held it. Still the Unvanquished."

"Yeah," Hoffman said. He could hear automatic fire, just the occasional burst. "So we are."

His legs wouldn't support him much longer. He went into the office and tried to sit down, but the chairs were gone so he slumped against the wall and slid down to the floor, eyes shut. He couldn't get the taste of smoke out of his mouth no matter how much he spat. It was probably all for nothing in the end. But the bastards hadn't taken Anvil Gate.

That wasn't going to be much comfort to Sheraya Byrne.

"Sah? Hoffman sah!" Bai Tak was standing over him, shaking him. "You got radio? Listen!"

The Pesang put the headset to Hoffman's ear. It was a helicopter pilot, some cheery woman with a double-R call sign, one of the new Raven pilots.

"RR-One-Seven to Anvil Gate, are you still receiving?"

Hoffman couldn't manage an answer. Bai Tak did the talking. "Anvil gate to RR-One-Seven, this is Rifleman Tak. Lieutenant Hoffman, he injured but he says, where the fuck you been, lady?"

The Raven pilot still sounded sunny and charming. "RR-One-Seven to Anvil Gate—there's a lot of COG traffic heading your way from both sides, ETA one hour, but stand by for air casevac in ten minutes."

Hoffman wasn't elated. Hoffman didn't weep for joy, or give Bai Tak a manly hug, or even come out with an astoundingly apt or funny one-liner to draw a line under the nightmare, as the movies had convinced him he should. Real life was a disappointment. He was just angry. He couldn't even frame that anger in a stream of curses. The near-unbearable thing was that two kids would now never know their dads. Hoffman couldn't imagine anything worse than that.

Bai Tak reached above him and took something off the wall. It was one of Sander's many small watercolors of Anvegad. He

rolled it carefully like a scroll and put it in the empty holster on
Hoffman's webbing.

"There, sah," Bai said. "For your Missus Hoffman. So she know
what you did at Anvil Gate."

THE FENIX ESTATE, EAST BARRICADE, JACINTO: TWO WEEKS AFTER THE RELIEF OF ANVEGAD.

Adam Fenix struggled out of the cab, determined to stand upright
and look well for Marcus's sake.

It was hard to explain to a small child that limping on crutches
didn't mean that his dad was badly hurt. The first impression
counted. Adam wanted Marcus to see only that his father had
kept his promise and come home. It was probably a memory that
would stay with the boy, and it had to be a positive one.

Elain opened the door—no housekeeper, as usual—and just
stood there expressionless for a while. Homecomings were always
difficult. They had so much to say and get out of their systems,
and yet Adam never knew if he wanted to hold her, or cry on her
shoulder, or rush to see Marcus, or . . . damn, he wanted to do it
all at once, and his father had never shown him how it was meant
to be done, only that it wasn't. Paralyzed by the overwhelming
relief—yes, he really *was* home, he wasn't dreaming this, and he
would still be at home when he next woke—Adam just walked
carefully up the steps and buried his face in her hair.

"When the news said that Two-Six was at Anvil Gate," she said
at last, "I thought it was you. I thought you were there. I thought
there'd been a mistake and you weren't wounded."

"I'm okay," he said. "It was Connaught Platoon. Poor bastards."

"Daddy! *Daddy!*"

Marcus came running across the tiled hall. Adam crouched
and opened his arms, ready to scoop him up; this time, Adam
would damned well *not* be like his own father. He'd do all the
spoiling and indulgently emotional things, all the hugs and love
and promises never to go away again. But Marcus suddenly

slowed to a dignified walk as if he'd remembered that he had to behave and be the man of the house. He looked Adam in the eye, the same height at that moment, as if he expected the same decorum of him.

"I missed you, Marcus," Adam said, straightening up. He'd lost the moment completely now and settled for ruffling his son's hair. "I really did."

"What's wrong with your leg?" Marcus asked. "And did you save everyone?"

Adam had lost more than half the Gears in his original company. It was the most painful question he'd ever been asked.

"No, I didn't save them all," he said. "But I'm going to change things, and make sure I save everyone else in the future."

Marcus looked up at him, that I-don't-believe-you tilt of the head that was probably just bewilderment. Elain took his hand, and Adam's.

"We can do all this on the doorstep," she said, "or be like normal people and go sit down in the kitchen. Marcus, go get the drawing you did at school to show Daddy."

Marcus went upstairs, all sensible sobriety, and disappeared along the landing. Elain squeezed Adam's hand.

"He's okay, darling," she said. "He's all very grown-up since he started school. But he's got this thing about making sure he knows where I am and that I'm safe. It'll pass now that you're back." She had that look, the one that said she was about to ask something she'd promised not to raise. "I know this isn't the time to ask, but how long are you going to be home?"

Adam had made up his mind. He didn't want anyone to misunderstand his motives. He'd had enough of the fighting, but it was a different kind of disgust, one that would change things instead of just turning his back on them while other men and women couldn't.

I don't want anyone to think I'm a coward. I don't want Marcus to think that, most of all. This is for him, too, because I'm damned if I'll see him lined up and used as a Gear.

"I'm not going back," Adam said. He'd rehearsed how he

would justify his decision, in case Elain thought he was too scared to fight. "I'm going to take that post at the DRA. Weapons research. Because nobody in this day and age should fight wars by walking infantry into battle or firing damn hundred-year-old cannons or starving each other to death in sieges. *There will be deterrents.* There will be weapons that mean politicians stupid enough to carry on this war are going to face the same risk of dying as the men and women they send to fight it. I'm going to *create* those weapons. I'll make these ghastly little demagogues *think twice.*"

Adam meant that like he'd meant his marriage vows. It was absolute, an oath, and he would live it. He could feel his pulse pounding in his throat. Elain just looked at him, tears in her eyes, and smiled.

"You will," she said. "Damn right, you will, Doctor Fenix."

"Just *Major*," he said. "My promotion came through. But it won't change my mind." He took the torn page of newspaper from his pocket and held it up for her. All the promotions were published in the press. "See? Second paragraph."

Elain read it. "Good grief, so many Royal Tyrans. You have to leave some glory for the other poor regiments, Adam. Oh, look— Helena Stroud, *Captain.* She's going to make General. Count on it."

Adam took the page back and smiled. Helena was welcome to as much gold braid as she wanted.

He noted, too, that Lieutenant Victor Hoffman, 26 RTI, had been promoted to Captain and decorated with the Sovereign's Medal for his defense of the Anvil Gate garrison. Adam wondered just what that unlucky man had endured for so little reward, and if he'd ever meet him to ask that question.

CHAPTER 20

I did you a favor. I knew you would be torn. The COG took away your natural sense of justice and replaced it with a rule book to deal with people who respect no rules. What are two more executions to Gorasnaya? Retribution. What are two more to you? A dilemma you cannot handle.

(MIRAN TRESCU, EXPLAINING TO VICTOR HOFFMAN WHY HE TOOK THE UNAUTHORIZED DECISION TO EXECUTE MIKAIL AND NIAL ENADOR)

ROAD TO VECTES NAVAL BASE, PRESENT DAY: STORM, 15 A.E.

"He's probably just gone off somewhere," Anya said. "We'd have found the body if he'd been killed."

Bernie slowed the Packhorse to ten klicks because that was the speed limit through the camp, but there was nothing to run down anyway. The devastation shocked her. It looked like the Stranded camp on the coast after they'd torched every last hut to stop the COG getting so much as firewood from it.

"Sorry, ma'am." Bernie tried to concentrate on the mike in her hand. "He's not a running-away kind of dog, but you're right—polyps don't haul off prey and lay up with it. As far as we know."

"We'll keep looking. Soon as he shows, I'll call."

"Thanks, ma'am. Mataki out."

The world was going to hell again, and yet the thing that worried her most was a lost dog. She wasn't sure if that made her insane, insensitive, or smarter than most. But animals were easier to love than humans. The thought of the poor little bugger lying hurt somewhere or just hiding in terror upset her.

But he's an attack dog. He won't piss himself and run. He's been hurt. Killed. I let him down. He trusted me, and I wasn't there for him.

"That's what you get for not securing him yourself, you stupid cow," she said aloud. "Never trust anyone else to do the important things for you."

She parked the Packhorse in the compound and noticed that the rat bike was already there. Sam must have burned through the woods, because she hadn't overtaken Bernie on the way back. There was a sense of urgency everywhere. It was reassuring in some ways, because she'd been certain that another setback like this would kill morale in New Jacinto stone-dead. There were only so many times you could stand looking at ruins and vow to rebuild.

Whatever else the bastards say about us—the COG doesn't give up easy.

But there were no bastards left, not unless you counted the Stranded now scattered to the four winds. The world she lived in was now wholly COG. Even Gorasnaya had settled grudgingly into it like some argumentative but ultimately reliable ally.

To the west side of the base, there was a brand-new sea view and a lot less dry land. It was a big, vulnerable gap in the defenses.

Bernie worked her way across the parade ground, skirting the cordoned-off crevasses and subsidence, and tried to take in a new coastline. Bricks from one of the broken buildings clinging to the cliff were still toppling into the sea as she watched. The massive guns were gone. But it was nothing new. Ephyra had been ripped up and demolished on a daily basis too. She'd just started to think that it was all slowly improving.

Should have known better.

The barracks blocks were heaving with displaced civvies. Her quarters were taken but she couldn't work up enough energy to be pissed off about it. Everything she owned was in her backpack anyway, so she was suddenly plunged back into the nomadic state she'd existed in for years on her long journey back to Jacinto. There was a vague comfort to it, the knowledge that she could just get up and go if she really had to. She could even sail out of here.

But I can't do that to Vic. Not now.

Control had moved to the infirmary wing. She reported in and Mathieson gave her a meaningful jerk of the head to indicate a meeting was taking place in the next room.

"Don't wander away too far, Sergeant—the Colonel wants to see you."

"Is he going to be long?" She draped her arm on her slung Lancer. "I was planning on getting my hair done, you see."

Mathieson wasn't used to her. The look on his face told her he wasn't sure if she was joking or not. Her armor was filthy with polyp fluids, her arms were covered in scratches and bruises, and she was sure she stank of smoke, dog, and cordite. Mathieson broke into a smile a fraction at a time.

"He's in with Trescu and Michaelson."

"The triumvirate."

"Why do you say that?"

"Because there's three of them, sir."

"I mean—never mind. Where are you going to be?"

"Sergeants' mess. Unless you've got new tasking for me."

"No, go get yourself a coffee and clean up. I've lost track of who needs an extra pair of hands until Major Reid gets back."

The mess—a couple of basement rooms, one of which had been an ice store—was deserted, and there wasn't any coffee. She poured herself a glass of the rum that the locals made from sugar beets and settled at the bar, chin resting on her hand. Eventually she heard Hoffman's boots approaching at his usual fierce pace and wondered how to open the conversation this time.

He just stared at her for a moment.

"Shit, woman, you look like death warmed up."

"You always did know how to make a girl feel special, Vic."

He gave her a pat on the back, typically awkward, and then relented and put his arms around her. It went beyond affection. It felt more like he hadn't expected to see her alive again, a really desperate, crushing hug.

"Okay, what's wrong?"

He tried to force a laugh, very un-Hoffman. "What *isn't?*"

"Tell me you've not assassinated Prescott."

She was joking, or at least she thought she was.

"Look, there's something I've got to show you," Hoffman said. "There's nobody else I can talk to about this."

"You're scaring me now, Vic."

Hoffman perched onto the bar stool next to her and slid something out of his breastplate. It was a data disk. He held it up between his forefinger and middle finger for her inspection like it was a cigar he was about to light. "Tell me what this is."

"Not the payroll details, judging by your face."

"I don't know what the hell's on it. All I know is that it's encrypted, none of the COG Command keys can open it, and Prescott didn't want me to see it."

"Where did you get it?"

"I broke into his desk."

"Well, bugger me. Honest Vic joins the fallible human race."

"What's so secret now that he couldn't tell me when we were going down for the third time?"

"He's the kind of man who thinks the time of day is classified information. It could be anything."

Hoffman gazed at the disk as if it was going to combust if he stared at it long enough. "I really need to find out what's on here."

"Ask him. Go on, have it out with him, once and for all. I'll back you up. I'm bloody sure Marcus will, too."

"Had the chance." Hoffman drummed his fingers on the bar for a moment. "Failed."

Hoffman folded his arms on the bar and rested his forehead on them for a moment. It was a rare lapse for him, a naked moment of weary vulnerability. Bernie struggled to think what Prescott might be up to. There were no secrets left in the world worth keeping, unless the Chairman had discovered a secret stash of coffee he was hoarding for himself. All the things that governments fretted about were beyond irrelevance now.

"Give it to Blondie," she said. She hated to see him ground down like this. "He'll be into that in no time. But just ask yourself what you'll do when you find out what he's hiding. You might not want to know."

"Whatever else I screw up, I always know how to pick a sensible woman."

"I'll do now, will I?" It just slipped out. She wanted him to understand that he'd hurt her all those years ago and that while she might have forgiven, she hadn't completely forgotten. "Last game in town?"

"Look, I'm not proud of how I treated you. But I've grown up. I'm sorry."

"We're *sixty years old*, Vic—it's about bloody time." She regretted it as soon as she said it, and knew she'd made her point. "And talking of secrets, are you ever going to finish telling me about Anvil Gate, or do I have to wait for your memoirs?"

Bernie had tried patience and sympathy. She'd dragged the story out of him a line at a time, but been interrupted or thwarted so often in the last few weeks that she wondered if she was meant to know the truth. Her best chance now was to provoke him.

"No. No, you don't." Hoffman reached for her glass, and she thought he was going to drink what she'd left, but instead he pushed it away to the far end of the bar. "Let's finish that story right now. Every last damn word of it."

VECTES NAVAL BASE WORKSHOPS: NEXT DAY.

It was definitely a day for telling the truth.

Hoffman felt as if a few years and a ton or two had lifted from him as he walked through the workshops in search of Baird. He'd never been sure if Bernie would stare at him in disgust when he told her the full story of Anvegad. But she'd nodded, said she would have done the same to the Indie officer, and agreed that the Kashkuri guy had got what was coming. For some reason, she didn't seem to understand that it was the Indie officer who haunted him, not the Kashkuri.

She'd also asked him if Sam knew her father had turned down the chance to escape with her mother. Bernie cared about those things. She'd been the one who finally told Dom how his brother Carlos had died. She knew what a tough call it was to decide whether to burden someone with the truth about a loved one, good or bad.

No, I never told Sheraya. So Sam probably doesn't know, either. And Pad didn't tell her, because he told me so.

And where the hell did he go? *Is he still alive?*

Samuel Byrne's decision was one of those things that would either be too painful to bear knowing or a precious revelation, and Hoffman had never known which. It was time he found out. He was the last man around who knew the sacrifice Byrne had made. That was something to be remembered and honored, not some dirty secret to be taken to the grave.

There *were* dirty secrets, but he wasn't going to bury those, either. He held Prescott's data disk gripped tightly in his fist. The workshops were big, echoing spaces that smelled of old oil and burning rubber, and today they were busy, full of people trying to salvage or repair what they could from various ships and vehicles. The hammering and drilling of metal hurt his ears. He tried to avert his eyes from the searing white welding arcs.

"You'll go deaf if you keep doing that," he yelled.

Baird's blond head popped up from the engine compartment of a Packhorse. He wasn't wearing ear defenders. Cole was. He winked conspiratorially and took them off.

Baird straightened up and wiped his hands on a rag. "If it's about your limo, Colonel, it's going to take me some weeks to get around to emptying the ashtray."

"Goddamn it," Hoffman muttered. He liked Baird's acid side as long as he followed orders. "You'll just have to do something else to avert my wrath, then, Corporal."

"Okay, my staggering range of skills is all yours."

Hoffman debated whether to involve Cole in this. Knowledge put pressure on everyone. Baird would have to do a mucky job and keep it quiet from his best buddy, and Hoffman felt he owed Delta more than that. He couldn't bitch about Prescott's lack of candor if he didn't practice what he preached. But he was also compromising these men by even mentioning the disk to them.

"You can say no to this, Baird."

"If you're trying to psych me up to say yes . . ."

"I've got an encrypted disk that none of the COG codes can open. And I shouldn't have it."

Baird got a look in his eye just like that damn dog did when Bernie said "Seek!" He *loved* this shit. He didn't just enjoy solving puzzles; he needed to solve them before anyone else could. He took comfort and identity from being the smartest kid in the class.

"Well, *that* narrows it down," he said.

"Prescott knows I've got it." Hoffman dropped his voice as far as he could in the pounding, scraping, drilling cacophony around them. "That's why you can walk away from this without any stain on your technical manhood. You too, Cole. You don't have to get involved in this shit."

Baird laid down the wrench. "Nice psyops, Colonel. You've got my undivided attention. Hand it over."

"What's Prescott gonna do about it?" Cole picked up the discarded wrench and continued working where Baird had left off. "Bust you down to private?"

"Better wash my hands," Baird said. "Don't want to leave any fingerprints."

Hoffman shoved the disk into Baird's belt. "I don't know if it's urgent or not. Might just be embarrassing pictures from his wild youth, if he had one."

"I'll be in my executive suite," said Baird, and strode off.

Hoffman paused a moment to look for a reaction on Cole's face. Cole just raised an eyebrow and went on tinkering with the battered Packhorse.

"I'll let Marcus and Dom know what's going on," Hoffman assured him. "But I don't want everyone knowing that the Chief of

Staff's been reduced to stealing data from the Chairman. Not good for morale. We've got to at least look as if it's a united front."

"Understood." Cole frowned at the Packhorse as if he was changing the subject. "Baird makes this shit look easy. Damned if I know what's wrong with this thing."

"The man's gifted. Don't know what we'd do without him."

"You ever tell him that? He'd appreciate it, sir, even if he gives you a load of bullshit about how he don't care what anyone thinks."

That was typical Cole. Hoffman gave him a slap on the shoulder. "Yeah, just for you, Cole. I'll give him half an hour before I go find him. He'll have it cracked by then and I can tell him what a smart boy he is."

Walking around for a while was a good thing to do right now. People needed to see the top brass out and about, doing something useful or at least looking like they were. It also gave Hoffman quiet thinking time. By the time he'd covered the distance from the workshops to the edge of the Gorasni camp, he'd worked out that he was going to offer to tell Sam about her father, and give her the choice of whether to hear it. It was all too much like Dom's situation. There was no painless way to tell someone their dead loved one had done something heroic and sacrificial. It would always be bittersweet.

The Gorasni refugees paused in their cleanup operation to watch Hoffman for a few moments, more curious than suspicious now, as if Trescu had put out the word that the COG bastard wasn't wholly bad and didn't need to be shot on sight. It was progress of a kind. Yanik waved to him as he went by. It seemed churlish not to acknowledge the man.

"Has she found her dog?" Yanik called.

He could only mean Bernie. "Not yet," Hoffman called back.

"Is a lovely day, yes? The *garayazi* have gone. No more Stranded. I can save *many* bullets now."

Yanik walked on, grinning. He didn't fret about shooting anyone and he probably wouldn't have lost a second's sleep over stealing classified data, Hoffman knew.

We've all done things we're not proud of just to survive. Or because we think it serves a greater good. Maybe I don't have the right to judge Prescott.

But that was bullshit, and he knew it. If Prescott had a secret this late in the game, then it was big. And Hoffman's duty wasn't to a single politician but to use any means necessary to maximize the chances of humankind making it through the next few years.

.Hoffman carried on walking, checking his watch every few minutes. *Half an hour, I said. Baird's probably cracked the encryption and found a way to turn the data disk into a perpetual-motion machine by now.* He made his way back through the naval base, skirting around roped-off holes and working parties until he reached the disused lavatory block where Baird had set up a makeshift workshop of his own.

The corporal was sitting on one of the toilets in a cubicle whose door had long vanished. Its black plastic seat was folded down to make a chair, and in front of it was a bench made out of old ammo cases. An odd assortment of disembodied components was spread around the bench, linked by strips of ribbon cable and wires like a set of entrails in need of a body cavity. It wasn't until Hoffman recognized a computer terminal—just the flat part of the screen, nothing else—that he realized what he was looking at. Baird had wired together an array of scavenged computer components to make a working system. He looked up, his expression grim.

"Couldn't fit all this in a case," he said. "Even if we had a spare one, which we don't."

Hoffman watched him for a while. Baird was a different man when he was playing with his toys. Hoffman actually felt sorry for him. Maybe that was why Bernie did, too.

"Well?" Hoffman said.

Baird shook his head slowly as he hammered at the battered keyboard. "You think I can do anything, don't you?"

"Yes. Can't you?"

"Not this time." He stared at the monitor for a moment, but it was clear that he wasn't seeing what was on it. He was just searching for the right moment to look Hoffman in the eye. "I can't open it. I've never seen anything like it. Don't think I'm making excuses—but this isn't anything the COG's ever used."

Hoffman wasn't sure what surprised him most, Baird's defeat or the fact that he admitted it so openly. Disappointment gripped him. This wasn't the time to tell Baird as much.

"You want to talk me through that, Corporal?"

Baird straightened up. "None of the COG security codes work, but you know that already. In fact, it doesn't look as if it uses any of the encryption technology that the COG's ever had—military or industrial. I'd guess that it's something that Prescott had built for him specially."

"I won't ask how you actually know all the COG encryption codes," Hoffman said.

"But you're glad that I do."

"Damn right I am."

"I'm going to keep at it. Anything that's encrypted can be un-encrypted, and *nobody* locks *me* out forever."

"Even knowing what you *can't* do with it tells me something." He thought of Cole for a moment and took his advice. "We rely heavily on your talents, Baird. I don't take them for granted."

Baird looked awkward. Bernie was right; for all his cocky bull-shit, he really didn't know how to handle compliments. "I mean, how unknown can an encryption key be? It's not like Prescott has a whole bunch of scientists holed up somewhere working on cutting-edge tech just for him, is it? It's got to be based on some-thing we already know and use."

"No." Did Prescott think they had a chance of cracking it? He hadn't seemed panicked, but then he never did, not even when he was about to press the button and incinerate most of Sera with the Hammer of Dawn. "Do what you can, Corporal. Let me know if there's anything you need."

Baird took the disk out of the computer's disembodied guts.

"You trust me to hang on to this?" he asked, half-offering it back to Hoffman.

"You know damn well I do," Hoffman said. "Make sure you don't lose it."

He knew Baird would now guard it with his life. It was a matter of pride as well as obsession. Hoffman walked away, careful not to look back, and reflected on the fact that Baird didn't seem to feel at all diminished by having to use a goddamn lavatory for an office. *That* was confidence. He almost envied it.

The day wasn't resolving quite as Hoffman had hoped. He wanted boils lanced and all hidden things made plain in the space of twenty-six hours. He wasn't going to get far with Prescott's secrets by midnight, but that didn't absolve him from clearing up the unfinished business of more than thirty years with Sam, business he didn't really know needed completing until Bernie pointed it out to him. Now was as good a time as any.

He wandered into CIC and found Mathieson. The lieutenant was eating a sandwich one-handed while he scribbled notes on a sheet of paper that was gray from repeated erasure and re-use. He pushed his headset's mike away from his mouth with an unconscious flick of his finger every time he went to take a bite, then flicked it back again. It didn't slow down his conversation with the patrolling Ravens one bit. He'd been stuck at that comms desk far too long.

"How you doing, sir?" he said, looking up. "It's all quiet now the Stranded have run away. Can't get used to it."

"Make the most of it. Longest we were ever without some kind of trouble was six weeks, and that was between the wars. We didn't get used to that, either."

Hoffman was suddenly distracted by the rest of Mathieson's meal spread around the desk. A water canteen stood next to the phone. There was nothing remarkable about a bottle of water, except this one was a UIR type, not COG issue. He knew all too well what they looked like. He'd stepped over them in the churned mud of battlefields, riddled with Lancer rounds and scattered around with the sad contents of wallets, and he'd drunk from one when his life hung on a thread at Anvil Gate.

Indies make me look at what I am. Maybe that's why I don't like Trescu.

The most traumatic memory he had to live with was an act of unexpected and shaming kindness that he repaid with a bullet.

That was an indictment. He suddenly felt he could never stand alongside the Tollen vets in remembrance, because his nightmares were of his own making.

"Something wrong, sir?" Mathieson asked.

"Just admiring your canteen."

"That's from Yanik. Don't worry, I didn't have to trade anything for it. He was just being kind. He probably feels sorry for me."

Poor Mathieson; he had no idea how much worse that made Hoffman feel. It was time to do something positive, something done for its own sake rather than to relieve his guilt. *Benoslau.* That was the officer's name. Captain Benoslau. Hoffman wasn't sure what he was going to do with that fact, but remembering the man's name was the least he could do.

"They're not all monsters, Lieutenant," he said, and changed the subject. "Look, I need to find Byrne. Does she hang out in the main mess?"

"You after a tattoo, sir?"

"No," Hoffman said. "I need a scar removed."

Mathieson knew when to ask questions and when to keep his mouth shut. He didn't say a word.

In the world they'd both known and lost, he would have gone far.

KR-80, ROUTINE SECURITY PATROL OVER
CENTRAL VECTES: TEN DAYS AFTER THE LAST
POLYP ATTACK.

Barber hung out of the crew bay, snapping recon images of the terrain beneath the Raven like a crazed tourist running out of sightseeing time.

"We haven't even scratched the surface of this place," he said. "The map doesn't tell us a damn thing. For all we know, there could be imulsion reserves down there."

The center of the island was an extinct volcano, four kilometers across with steep walls smothered in ancient forest. Baird stared down at the dense, deep-green ocean of the tree canopy, trying to concentrate, but all he could think about was why Prescott's data disk wouldn't give up its secrets to him.

"Sure there are," Baird muttered, "and I'm going to devote my life to charitable work. If it's okay with the tooth fairy."

Shit, he hated this let's-all-be-resilient, stiff-upper-lipness that was sweeping the camp like a dose of dysentery. The sooner people accepted they were even more fucked now than they'd been a month ago, the sooner they could get on with dealing with the situation. He wasn't being negative. He was being *realistic*. He glanced around the crew bay at the faces of the squad and knew he wasn't the only one.

"Bernie, you want to take a look over the northern sector?" Barber asked. "Might as well while we're out here. The mutt's probably running loose in the woods."

"It's easier to look on foot." Bernie sounded as if she'd turned away a lot of helpful advice over the last few days. "But thanks, Nat. It's kind of you."

Mac the psychotic mutt had been missing since the night the polyps first came ashore at Pelruan. Baird was sure that the dog had been minced to hamburger by some exploding polyp, but he wasn't going to say as much to Bernie. She loved the flea-bitten thing.

"If there was imulsion under here, they'd have drilled for it a long time ago," Marcus said. He didn't seem to have an opinion on the dog.

Dom didn't join in. Even Cole's lack of noisy cheerleading today was noticeable.

"So what do we do?" Gettner asked. "Sharle says we've reached the point where we can't run the fleet *and* be sure we've got enough fuel to reach the mainland when the time comes."

Gettner usually listened in to the crew bay chatter; it was hard not to when everyone needed the radio just to talk over the noise. But she rarely joined in the real conversation. Baird had never thought of her as being scared or in need of buddies like any other Gear. It rattled him a little.

"We won't be going back for a long time," Dom said.

"Yeah, but someone needs to make a decision *now*. We're still burning fuel like there's no tomorrow."

"There's not enough information to make a decision."

"There never is, but it never stopped us doing pretty decisive shit before. Is Prescott up to this?"

"He's been up to it for fifteen years," Barber said quietly. "Compared to what we've been through, this isn't even close to rock-bottom."

"Looks like he can count on *one* vote, then," Cole murmured.

Gears always griped. It was an art form, part of the military culture like bawdy songs and black humor. Baird felt he'd written the book on griping, not that he didn't have plenty of reasons. But he hadn't seen it creep over the edge into the unsayable stuff about lack of faith in the government before. Nobody thought the government could do much more than it already had. Even if Prescott wasn't loved, nobody had illusions about omnipotence. He was in the same shit as everyone else.

Actually, the government *was* just Prescott. Unless Baird counted Pelruan's town council, which had been carrying on in its own sweet elected way since the Hammer strike days, there wasn't an assembly for New Jacinto. It was hard to think about that normal stuff when every day was fraught with real physical danger.

"Well, we said we missed the grubs," Baird said. "We got our wish."

Dom stirred. "No, *you* said that when we didn't have any more grubs around, we'd start fighting each other, so we'd have to find something else to kill. And we did."

"Let's do the job, people." Marcus stood up and hung on to the safety rail. If there was an argument brewing, he'd always make damn sure he cut it short. Baird took the hint. He didn't so much feel intimidated as scolded and made to feel like a dumb kid. "Lots of island out there."

The Raven banked and headed northwest, skimming over forest slopes that fell away into hills and then gentler plains—farm country. The signs that Vectes had once been a much busier island were still there in the just-visible boundaries of overgrown fields. Baird sat eavesdropping on the submarine net for a few minutes, bored shitless by a landscape that could only have been of interest to someone who liked spending their day knee-deep in cow pats. He could hear the voice traffic between the two boats as they tested *Clement's* damaged systems. It was all very chummy now, with *Zephyr's* crew fussing over *Clement's* repairs and trying to help. *Clement* had taken a pounding when she blew up the first leviathan. With *Dalyell* still struggling to stay afloat and *Fenmont* out of action, the fleet was shrinking fast.

And that was what they'd need if they were going to get back to the mainland one day; lots of ships, and plenty of fuel to run them.

Baird managed to forget Prescott's disk for a few moments to crunch some numbers. A Raven's Nest slurped through half a million liters of fuel a day at full speed. Unless somebody came up with an alternative fuel source fast, the carrier wasn't going to be sailing much further than the five-klick limit.

"Nice and peaceful since the Stranded banged out." Gettner went on chatting. Barber looked at Baird and raised his eyebrows theatrically. No, this sociability wasn't like the old harpy at all. "What's the world coming to when we have recruitment and re-tention problems with parasites?"

"The Gorasni are still our best buddies, though," Barber said. "Which beats the alternative."

"Not in Pelruan. . . . Hey, look at the forest cover down there. And the waterfall."

"Yeah, scenic." Baird squinted at the picture-postcard scene. Prescott's data disk superimposed itself on the image uninvited. "At least we'll always have lumber and power."

"You can build boilers for the ships," Bernie said. "They didn't always run on imulsion."

Yes, he'd definitely oversold his skills. "I'm not so good with the miracles these days."

"That's defeatist talk."

"Have I missed something?" Gettner asked. She had a finely tuned radar for the little things. "What miracles?"

Bernie, arms folded on her chest, looked tired and distracted. "Nothing, ma'am. Baird's trying to develop a human personality because he admires our species. Just like in the movies."

Baird didn't manage to bite straight back with a withering response. He needed to learn to play off Bernie's lines a little better to maintain the illusion that nothing weird was going on. He recovered a couple of seconds too late. "Did they *have* movies when you were a girl, Granny? Didn't you just daub paintings on cave walls and tell each other stories about them?"

"I dunno," Bernie muttered. "Maybe I ought to ask your girlfriend in Stores. The one you keep making eyes at. You obviously prefer *mature* women."

"Hey, I'm only nice to her because I need her supply of ten-millimeter bolts."

Barber laughed. Maybe that was enough to divert him and Gettner from paying too much attention in the future. Baird went back to fretting about Prescott's data, wondering if the man had ever been a straight-up guy before he got a dose of power.

That's how it starts. You keep a secret from your buddies, the people you rely on to save your ass. It's for a good reason. It isn't even about not trusting them. You don't want to drag them into it. Then it gets to be a habit. And the next thing you know, you're hiding the really big shit, and you turn into Prescott.

Was that how politicians started? Did little Richard Prescott lie once to his mom about who took the cookies, found that it worked, and then never stopped?

"Okay, let's take a look at Pelruan," Gettner said. "We're going to have to cut back on these patrols, you know."

As they passed over Pelruan, Baird could see some of Rossi's detachment walking the perimeter. One of them stopped to watch the Raven and raise his hand in acknowledgment before the chopper turned away and headed south again. They were just above the trees, about ten klicks along the path of a stream, when Dom reacted to something below.

"Dogs," he said. "Look."

Bernie twisted in her seat. It was the Pelruan pack. The towns-people let them run loose to keep the Stranded away, but even now that the bums were gone, the dogs still had their routine.

"See Mac down there?" Dom asked.

Bernie shook her head. "If he was still with the pack, Lewis would know by now."

Gettner turned the Raven and headed down the next valley, where the stream flowed into the river. "Damn it, Mataki, we're going to find that dog."

"Doesn't he come when called?" Baird asked. "I mean, don't you have some kind of whistle?"

Bernie leaned back in the seat. "No need to humor me, Blondie. He's gone, poor little sod. He'd have shown up by now."

Gettner didn't take any notice. She followed the river, dip-ping over every patch of open grassland. It was a waste of fuel. Baird didn't want to be the one to say so, not in front of Bernie anyway.

"Bernie's right—he could be anywhere," Dom said. "That's five thousand square kilometers to search."

"You know how many hours I spend looking down on this ter-rain?" Gettner snapped. "I see the dogs and I know most of the places they go. Come on, an experienced recon team, and you can't spot a dog the size of a damn pony?"

Humor her. Baird looked whenever the Raven banked far enough for him to see out of the door, but his mind was else-where. *How many red cars can you see, Damon? Shut up in the back there. Yeah, like a goddamn day out with the folks . . .*

"Hey, I see it," Cole said. "Well, damn—you got that mutt trained, Boomer Lady! Look at him!"

"What?" Gettner snapped.

"It's the dog," Cole said. "He's down there, tryin' to keep up with us!"

Marcus hung on to the safety rail and leaned out. Baird couldn't see what he was looking at until the Raven descended to hover and he suddenly got a good view of the meadow below. Yes, it *was*

Mac: he was trotting around in a circle now, head lowered against the downdraft as if he was a Gear waiting for extraction.

"Thank God for that," Bernie said. "He's a fast learner. Raven noises mean the food lady as far as he's concerned."

"He should run for office," Baird said. "Even if he does lick his own ass, he's still a more impressive candidate than Prescott."

Gettner brought the Raven down slowly. "Okay, I'm setting down. Nat, keep an eye on the pooch in case he gets too close. Mataki? Stand by to grab him."

It was a small scrap of good news but sometimes that was all it took to lift everyone's mood for a short while. Bernie jumped out and ran at a crouch to grab Mac by his collar to haul him back inside. By the time he landed on the deck with a thud, claws scrabbling for purchase, it was obvious that he hadn't had much fun in the last few days. He looked pathetic, in fact, with patches of matted fur.

"That better not be catching," Baird said.

Bernie checked him over as the Raven lifted. Baird grabbed a safety line to hitch to his collar just in case Gettner did some fancy flying as the chopper headed west to resume the coastline recon.

"What are you trying to do, lynch him?" Dom said. "If he falls out, he'll just strangle himself."

"Okay, so I'll make him a proper harness. You want to hold him?"

"Hey, cool it." Bernie tried to examine Mac in a forest of boots. There was very little deck space in the crew bay with six personnel embarked. "We've got him now. Thanks, everybody."

Cole frowned. "Looks like he's been *welding*. He's covered in burns."

"Polyps." Baird risked parting Mac's fur to check the injuries. The matted patches revealed raw skin. "I bet he's been hit by an exploding polyp."

Bernie cuddled the dog. "Awww, brave boy! You took on the polyps? Good Mac! We'll get the nice doctor to take a look at you."

"Yeah, Doc Hayman's going to love veterinary practice," Baird said. The burns were starting to worry him. They looked new. "How long does it take a burn to heal? Just checking."

"Depends." Marcus turned his head. "Why?"

"These burns are *fresh*. As in not a week old, which was when we last saw a frigging polyp land ashore."

Marcus shut his eyes for a second. "Then we've still got polyps on the loose."

"Better find them fast."

The deck tilted as Gettner swung the Raven around again. "No way of telling how far a dog's traveled, is there, Mataki?"

"No," Bernie said. "He could cover half the island in a day or two."

"Okay, then we head back to his last position and center a search on that." Gettner took a breath and her radio clicked as she opened a channel to CIC. "Control, this is KR-Eight-Zero— possible Lambent contact, north of the island. No visual yet but signs of a recent attack. We might have more polyps on the loose."

Mathieson's voice snapped back instantly. "Roger that, Eight-Zero. I'll alert all call signs."

"Make sure you pass it on to the civvies too. No telling where those things might be."

The Raven skimmed low over the trees, following a square search pattern from the point where they'd found the dog. Barber peered down the sights of the door gun, looking for scuttling movement beneath the branches.

"Do they breed?" Baird asked. "Polyps, I mean."

"You want the pick of the litter?" Dom said.

"Ha, very funny. Just wondering how much we have to worry about glowies being on the loose—just hyperventilate a little, or totally shit our pants."

There was still nothing out of the ordinary to be seen, but then polyps were small targets to spot from the air even without trees and vegetation obscuring the view. A herd of cattle suddenly scattered and ran across the field below the Raven.

"Hey, Major," Dom said. "You're spooking the cows."

Gettner sounded puzzled rather than indignant at being warned for low flying. "They don't normally bolt like that."

Baird craned his neck to see when the cattle ran out of steam and stopped. But they didn't. They kept running. One actually cleared a low hedge like a horse jumping a fence.

"Shit! Did you see that?"

"What?"

"Show-jumping cow. Wow, I'm waiting for the complaints from the farmers to start flooding in, Gettner."

And then Baird saw what had scared the herd.

The trees shook violently. For a moment he thought it was a sudden gust of wind, but then the green pasture below split open like an earthquake had hit it, exposing dark soil and roots.

"Hang on!" Gettner yelled. "Whoa!"

The Raven banked sharply. Baird was on the opposite side of the chopper and saw only blue sky for a few seconds. Then the horizon leveled again and he was looking at a vastly changed skyline.

A charcoal-gray twisted column towered above the trees, its trunk covered with glowing red blisters. The last time Baird had seen anything like that, it was punching its way into the Emerald Spar imulsion platform. The trees were still shaking violently. Then another stalk punched through the soil, and another.

"Oh, fuck." Bernie gripped Mac's collar tightly. "They're here."

"Control, this is KR-Eight-Zero, contact in grid Echo Five." Gettner always sounded irritably bored on the radio, but not today. Her tone was even but Baird could hear her voice shaking a little. "We've got a major stalk incursion, grid Echo Five—three stalks so far. We need some firepower up here fast, Mathieson."

Baird had seen all kinds of depressing, terrifying, and incomprehensible shit over the last fifteen years. But this was the moment when he started to think that the end was really coming. Vectes was the last place on Sera where humanity thought it was safe. But it wasn't safe any longer. The stalks had reached the island. They were growing in its heart. There was no escaping them now.

Baird aimed his Lancer, futile effort or not. He couldn't see if they were disgorging polyps yet. And as much as he liked the taste of adrenaline, this wasn't quite what he had in mind.

"We're *so* fucked," he said.

Marcus didn't turn a hair. He never did. He just scowled at the instant forest of grotesque, glowing stalks and took up the door gun position opposite Barber.

"Get us as close as you can, Major," he said. "This is going to take some time."

Baird squinted down his sights and wondered what the hell those blisterlike things on the stalk's trunk were for.

He knew he was about to find out the hard way.

ABOUT THE AUTHOR

Novelist, screenwriter, and comics writer KAREN TRAVISS is the author of five *Star Wars:* Republic Commando novels, *Hard Contact, Triple Zero, True Colors, Order 66,* and *Imperial Commando: 501st;* three *Star Wars:* Legacy of the Force novels, *Bloodlines, Revelation,* and *Sacrifice;* two *Star Wars:* The Clone Wars novels, *The Clone Wars* and *No Prisoners;* two Gears of War novels, *Aspho Fields* and *Jacinto's Remnant;* her award-nominated Wess'har Wars series, *City of Pearl, Crossing the Line, The World Before, Matriarch, Ally,* and *Judge;* and a Halo novella, *Human Weakness.* She's also the lead writer on the third Gears of War game. A former defense correspondent and TV and newspaper journalist, Traviss lives in Wiltshire, England.